**Praise for the
Trickster Novels**

Trick of the Light

"Rob Thurman's new series has all the great elements I've come to expect from this writer: an engaging protagonist, fast-paced adventure, a touch of sensuality, and a surprise twist that'll make you blink."
　　　—*New York Times* bestselling author Charlaine Harris

"A beautiful, wild ride, a story with tremendous heart. A must read." —*New York Times* bestselling author Marjorie M. Liu

"A terrific premise. It's got Vegas, angels, demons, and a hunt for a mysterious artifact that by comparison makes Indiana Jones look like he was grubbing in the dirt for Precious Moments kitsch. If I had only three words to describe this book, they'd be: Best. Twist. Ever."
　　　—*New York Times* bestselling author Lynn Viehl

"Thurman weaves an amazingly suspenseful tale that will have readers so thoroughly enthralled from the first page that they'll be unwilling to set it down. *Trick of the Light* is meticulously plotted, completely fresh, and one of the best books I've had the pleasure of reading. Readers are in for a wonderful treat!" —Darque Reviews

"[An] inventive new series. . . . Trixa comes off as a strong-willed heroine with a long-standing ax to grind, yet that is only one facet of her character. The plot is suitably complex with enough clue dropping along the way to point attentive readers toward Trixa's true nature while still packing plenty of surprises." —Monsters and Critics

"Another strong offering from the author of the Cal Leandros books. Thurman is adept at creating fresh characters, and snarky heroine Trixa's first-person exploits in Vegas have distinctive details that leave a lasting impression. Fans and new readers will be clamoring for more." —*Romantic Times*

continued . . .

"Thurman has created an enjoyable extension of her world in *Trick of the Light*, with a heroine who (like Cal and Niko) has an unconventional family, an antiauthoritarian attitude, and a cheerfully vengeful nature. . . . Thurman has an easygoing manner with her dialogue and description. . . . The outcome of this story opens many new possibilities for this novelist, whose work compares well with Jim Butcher and Laurell K. Hamilton. This novel heralds the launch of a strong second series, and readers of urban fantasy will have much to anticipate with Trixa's future adventures."
—SFRevu

Praise for the
Cal Leandros Novels

Madhouse

"Thurman continues to deliver strong tales of dark urban fantasy. . . . Fans of street-level urban fantasy will enjoy this new novel greatly."
—SFRevu

"I think if you love the Winchester boys of *Supernatural*, there's a good chance you will love the Leandros brothers of Thurman's books. . . . One of *Madhouse*'s strengths is Cal's narrative voice, which is never anything less than sardonic. Another strength is the dialogue, which is just as sharp and, depending on your sense of humor, hysterical."
—DearAuthor . . .

"A fast-paced and exciting novel. . . . Fans of urban fantasy will love this series."
—*Affaire de Coeur*

"If you enjoyed the first two wisecracking urban adventures, you won't be disappointed with this one; it has just enough action, angst, sarcasm, mystery, mayhem, and murder to keep you turning the pages to the very end."
—BookSpot Central

Moonshine

"[Cal and Niko] are back and better than ever . . . a fast-paced story full of action. . . . The plot is complex enough to please mystery fans, with supernatural elements that put this in the company of Jim Butcher and Charlaine Harris."
—SFRevu

ALSO BY ROB THURMAN

THE GRIMROSE PATH

PATH

A TRICKSTER NOVEL

ROB THURMAN

A ROC BOOK

ROC
Published by New American Library, a division of
Penguin Group (USA) Inc., 375 Hudson Street,
New York, New York 10014, USA
Penguin Group (Canada), 90 Eglinton Avenue East, Suite 700, Toronto,
Ontario M4P 2Y3, Canada (a division of Pearson Penguin Canada Inc.)
Penguin Books Ltd., 80 Strand, London WC2R 0RL, England
Penguin Ireland, 25 St. Stephen's Green, Dublin 2,
Ireland (a division of Penguin Books Ltd.)
Penguin Group (Australia), 250 Camberwell Road, Camberwell, Victoria 3124,
Australia (a division of Pearson Australia Group Pty. Ltd.)
Penguin Books India Pvt. Ltd., 11 Community Centre, Panchsheel Park,
New Delhi - 110 017, India
Penguin Group (NZ), 67 Apollo Drive, Rosedale, North Shore 0632,
New Zealand (a division of Pearson New Zealand Ltd.)
Penguin Books (South Africa) (Pty.) Ltd., 24 Sturdee Avenue,
Rosebank, Johannesburg 2196, South Africa

Penguin Books Ltd., Registered Offices:
80 Strand, London WC2R 0RL, England

First published by Roc, an imprint of New American Library,
a division of Penguin Group (USA) Inc.

First Printing, September 2010
10   9   8   7   6   5   4   3   2   1

ROC REGISTERED TRADEMARK—MARCA REGISTRADA

Printed in the United States of America

To Michael and Sara
(who take me to lunch when I'm out of mac 'n' cheese).

Acknowledgments

To my mom, who suggested why didn't I give my old dream of writing a go. If I become a victim of artistic Darwinism, I blame her; Shannon—best friend, designated driver for SDCC, and *undesignated* sherpa for various other events; my patient editor, Anne Sowards; the infallible Kat Sherbo; Brian McKay (ninja of the dark craft of copywriting); Agent Jeff Thurman of the FBI for the usual weapons advice; the incomparable art and design team of Chris McGrath (an art GOD) and Ray Lundgren; Lucienne Diver, who still astounds me in the best possible way at every turn; great and lasting friends Michael and Sara; Linda and Richard, and to fellow author Lisa Shearin, who has shown me the Light and the Way—in the church of promotional bargains—and assisted in a time of need. Plus she adopts dogs. What's not to love? And to Dakota, my original literate dog, my werewolf superhero—life without you is a poor imitation at best.

Prologue

Spilt milk.

My mama had a saying for every occasion under the sun, but even she didn't lay claim to that one. I didn't know who did, but everyone had heard it. It had been around forever. Don't cry over spilt milk. There's no point to it. You can't change it, can't put it back, can't make it better. You simply cleaned it up and went on.

Because that was life. Life wasn't always fair. And some things in life couldn't be undone. They could be avenged—damn straight, they could—but not undone.

They could teach a lesson . . . if anyone was around to learn from it—or smart enough to get the point.

Yet the bottom line was always the same—spilt milk was spilt milk. An inconvenience or a pain, an annoyance or sometimes even a tragedy. But whichever it was, it didn't matter. You might want to, but you couldn't turn back time. You couldn't close your eyes and pretend it was a bad dream. You couldn't avoid the truth and that was a cold hard fact.

You couldn't unspill that milk.

You couldn't make it better. You couldn't make it right.

I stood and looked at the shattered glass, jagged

tears glinting in the sun. I looked at the metal coated with blood—so very much blood—the same color as the darkest crimson rose, and I decided the hell with old sayings.

I was *undoing this.*

I was *making this right.*

And I'd like to see the son of a bitch who thought he could stop me.

Chapter 1

Life was a trick.

That was what it boiled down to in the end; life was one big trick, one huge April Fools'. You might think that could be a bad thing . . . depending on whether you were on the giving or receiving end. But that didn't matter as much as you'd think it would. It was what it was. At the very end of it, we all ended up on both sides. The universe was fair that way, because everyone, without exception, had something to learn. We were all naughty in one way or another.

And tricks were lessons in disguise. They taught you right from wrong, safe from dangerous, bad seafood salad from good seafood salad. Have you ever had bad seafood salad? That's the worst eighteen hours of your life and a lesson you'll never forget. Have you ever put an old lady in the hospital after mugging her for her Social Security check? The lesson regarding that, you might not live long enough to remember or forget.

Life was a trick, a trick was a lesson, and I was a teacher—the majority of the time. I didn't teach in a school. The world was my school, and I had a zero-tolerance policy. I taught the teachable. And the others? Those who couldn't or wouldn't learn? What's a woman to do in that situation?

Apply a "Darwin's rules" attitude and let the pieces fall where they may.

My name is Trixa, and I'm not a woman. I'm female, most definitely that, but I'm not precisely a woman. Trixa was one of the names I'd had in my lifetime, one of many—we con artists had quite a few. This one though ... This one was one of my favorites, because I *was* a trickster, born and bred of one of many trickster races. It was why I enjoyed the name so much. I'd rubbed who I was in the face of my enemies for the past ten years and not once had they seen past a simple name. Demons, some were stupid and some were bright, but all were arrogant, which made them blind. The same went for angels. As they were flip sides to the same coin, it wasn't surprising. And humans ... Please, don't even get me started on humans. They were the entire reason we tricksters existed. Or since we had predated them, I guess we chose them as a reason to exist. Those of the supernatural world never were quite as much fun to fool, to put in their place, and life could become fairly pointless without a purpose. Everyone needed a purpose.

Without a purpose, why get up in the morning? Why eat? Why not just meld with the earth that made you and wait to turn into fertilizer? Someone could grow some nice marigolds in you. I liked marigolds, but they weren't much of a career choice.

Taking humans down a notch or ten, that was a purpose all right, and damn entertaining too. Not that I ever received a shiny red apple for educating the masses, but taking pride—and more than occasional excessive glee—in my work, that was enough. Although jewelry would've been nice too. I liked jewelry better than marigolds.

A variety of tricksters were loose in the world—pucks,

also known as Pan, Robin Goodfellow, Hob, and so on. They were one race of identical brown-haired, green-eyed cocky immortals. All male—in appearance anyway. A person would need several PhDs in biology to get a handle on their actual reproduction, but you didn't need a GED to get a handle on anything else regarding them, physically speaking. Sexually speaking . . . not speaking at all because it was rude to with your mouth full. They not only cowrote the Kama Sutra, but they posed for it as well. That's all I'm saying.

There was my partner at the bar, Leo, better known as Loki, who was a god first and foremost, and only a trickster because he excelled at it and enjoyed it, but not because he'd been born one. His was a calling, not a birthright. There were also those among us who were just spirit . . . energy, gossamer molecules strung together like a kite string, no more solid than the wind, and even I had trouble understanding them. And kicking back to have a margarita with them to talk work, that was completely out of the question.

Then there was my kind—shape-shifters. We were hundreds, thousands of legends—Coyote, Kitsune, Kokopelli, Nasreddin, Raven, Maui, Veles—too many to name. Most people had long forgotten those names, but we were still only a Wiki away. We weren't immortal, but we didn't have to worry about watching our cholesterol either. I'd been around to see the sky darken half a world away when Pompeii had died. My brother and I had watched it and for a moment we were put in our place. We had held hands and felt an unfamiliar feeling of mortality sharp and cold cut through us as the sky turned from blue to black. We could trick all we wanted, but nature itself would always have the last laugh.

But now? Now I was still a trickster, but a shape-shifter no more. I was a thirty-one-year-old human—I was actually all human races on Earth. I had done that always. Genes speak to genes on a level people can't begin to detect, and if I were all people, then I went into every situation with the tiniest of edges, my foot in the door. It had been more helpful back in the day ... when family, clan, tribe, had mattered to a constantly warring people. They were still constantly warring, but the genes mattered a lot less now. And that was a good development for humanity in general, but I still tried to keep that edge.

While I was all races, two did rise to the top. That's what people saw. Eyes I'd admired the last time I'd been on the Japanese Islands, the mouth that was a fond memory of the years I'd spent in Africa, and wildly corkscrewed black curls and skin that were a mixture of both places. I'd spent a lot of time rethinking that hair every morning when I fought the good fight with it and usually had my ass kicked and my brush broken. Ah, well, who the hell was I to say what it should do anyway?

Did all of that make me a romance heroine who had men flinging themselves at my feet to protect my dainty foot from a puddle? Carrying all my groceries like I was a fairy princess with a wet manicure? Hell, no. It had them tilting their heads trying to figure me out. People liked to label things. I puzzled them, which was good. People needed to be puzzled, curious, unsure. That's what kept you alive in this world. It was what made life interesting.

No, I wasn't beautiful. I chose this body. I *made* it. Why would I want to be beautiful? Fields of wildflowers were beautiful. Waterfalls were beautiful. Secluded beaches were beautiful. Size-zero vacant-eyed and vacant-stomached runway models were beautiful ... at least that's what society told us, but society had a vacant brain to match those vacant eyes. Not one of those things, vacant or otherwise, could put a pointed heel of a boot through a demon's stomach and a bullet in his scaly forehead. I could. I was unique.

I could not . . . *would* not be tagged, identified, labeled, or stamped.

Unless it was by the fashion industry. I scowled at the sweatpants and T-shirt I was wearing as I came down the stairs that led to my apartment over my bar, Trixsta. The sign in the window was red neon to match everything else red in my life. Did that mean I wore a lot of red clothing? Maybe. But more than that, it meant I signed my work with the color—names changed; colors never did. I applied that signature to all my work, and I still did my work, my true work—human or not.

And Las Vegas was the perfect place to do it—a city of deceit and sin. It was a wonderland for both tricksters *and* demons. We did have demons aplenty, but as far as I knew, there were only two tricksters here currently: me and the one fiddling with the television.

Leo turned the TV on and wiped a film of beer off the screen. My bar was small; the brains of my clientele even smaller. It was the only excuse to waste good beer—or mediocre beer with good beer prices. If you couldn't tell the difference, that was your lesson for the day. A trick a day kept boredom away, but the thought of making money off the drunken or idiotic couldn't cheer me now, not with what I had to do.

"Exercise," I muttered, and then repeated it because it was simply that horrifying. *"Exercise."* I glared at Leo as if it were his fault. It wasn't, but he was the only one around to blame, so I took the opportunity. "I have to go run, lift weights, and do other things banned by the Ge-

neva Convention. If your Internet steroids arrive, don't
go wild and take them all at once."

With his long black hair pulled into a tight braid, copper skin, and eyes as dark as his hair, he looked pure
American Indian, and he would look that way for four
or five more years—but for one exception. That exception showed itself right then. Leo disappeared in front
of me and where he had stood flapped a raven who
croaked, "Must be jelly. Jam don't shake like that." I
thought about swinging at him, but I settled for retying
the knot on my sweatpants. Lenny or, as we called him in
raven form, Lenore—Poe, you couldn't avoid it—landed
on the bar. "Want fries with that shake?" he added as he
preened a feather.

"You'll be the one who's fried and served up with
mashed potatoes and cornbread stuffing when I get
back," I promised, enjoying the vengeful mental image.
"I'll make you the early-Thanksgiving special."

If birds could snort, Lenny would have. At one time,
three months ago, Leo might've been able to give me
something to think about. After all, he'd been a god; I
wasn't. But both of us were human, more or less, now, at
least for the next four or five years, thanks to my showing off and an artifact who thought the experience might
do Leo some good. For me, there were no shape-shifting
powers, no powers of any kind except a natural biologi-
cal defense against telepathy and empathy and the ability to tell my own *païen* kind when I saw them no matter
what shape they wore. Leo was one up on me. He was
stuck in human *or* bird form, and it was my fault. I'd
drained my batteries by overusing my powers to take
down the killer of my brother in an extremely showy and
vengeful way. I wasn't sorry. The bastard had deserved it.
He'd killed my family, my only sibling. For what I did to

him, things dismemberment-loving demons themselves
would've applauded . . . no, I wasn't sorry. I would never
be sorry for that. I'd only regret I couldn't do it a few
more times.

Oddly enough, even after that show, a sentient artifact that I'd been using as a bargaining chip against
Heaven and Hell had thought at the time that I was a
good influence on Leo/Loki. The Light of Life, the artifact, had decided he should stick around with me for
those four years it would take me to recover my shape-
shifting abilities. As it was more powerful than Leo and
I combined, it didn't ask us for permission either. It neutered him—on the god part at least. The rest of him, I
assumed, was in working condition. Although as I had to
exercise, it would've been nice for Leo to have suffered
a slight bit more. We'd see how many funny quips about
my weight he'd make while buying Internet steroids *and*
Viagra.

Not that my humiliation stopped there. My mama
had laughed herself sick when I told her anyone or anything thought I was a good influence. Then again, Leo
had been a very bad boy in his day. He had once wanted
to end the world—Ragnarok, the Norse end of days—
and that had just been for kicks and a way to waste a
boring afternoon. But that had been when he was Loki,
a long time and a lot of raging darkness ago. He was
different now. So many say they want to change; he was
one of the few I'd seen do it. He was one of the few with
a will stronger than the shadows that had filled him up,
shadows that were there still but leashed. Is it nobler to
be born good or to be born on the farthest end of the
bloody spectrum and have chosen to be good? When I
looked at Leo, it was an easy question to answer.

Ancient artifact or not, he would've stayed with me, to

help if worse came to worst. He was that way. I would've done it for him if the situation were reversed. Friends ... You didn't take them for granted. But that didn't mean I had to listen to his jokes about my ass. That was the great thing about being a shape-shifter. Calories? Fat grams? Whatever. Turn them into extra hair or an extra inch in height or shed them as pounds of water. Or in the other direction, if you wanted to be a two-hundred-pound coyote with the voice of an avalanche, take the extra you needed from the dirt, rock, or the moisture-soaked air around you.

But now I was human, and had discovered living off diner food. ... It was less than a block away; what could I do? I packed on five pounds in two weeks. She Who Would Not Be Labeled had become She Who Must Find the Nearest Gym. Leo, with his damn male metabolism, was still sucking down all that was fried with no signs of a potbelly as of yet.

Men. I hated men sometimes.

But I hated demons more. And as I ran down the sidewalk toward the grubby gym seven or eight blocks away, I got to prove it.

I kept a slow and steady pace. It was February now and still not too bad. When it came to summer, I'd drive to the gym, seven blocks or not. If you ran in the Vegas summer heat, you were either insane, suicidal, or a fire elemental out for a stroll. I ran past porn stores, liquor stores, more porn stores, a tiny car lot ... and that's where I stopped. I saw the blinding flash of a grin and puppy dog brown eyes, man's best friend, as a perfectly tanned hand patted the cloth top of a black convertible as the mouth moved a mile a minute, pouring like the best caramel syrup over a pudgy tourist. A car salesman. A used-car salesman. If you're after someone's soul, you should be a little more imaginative with your disguises than that.

Not that this guy was after someone's soul. I usually didn't interfere there. That was between Heaven and Hell and that tug-of-war known as humanity that lay between them. They had some reasonable enough rules set up. First, you had to be of age—mature mentally; no trading your soul for a Tonka Toy or a pony. These days that tended to mean you were old enough to drink, vote, and die. Second, you couldn't trade your soul for a righteous and selfless act. You couldn't trade it to save the polar bears or stop world poverty or even save your child. Hell and demons either weren't allowed or simply couldn't do good, no matter how many souls they received in exchange. Which made sense—evil did not beget good. Bad luck for the polar bears.

No, Heaven and Hell could play all the games they wanted. As one puck had first said a long time ago, caveat emptor. Buyer beware. Grown-up boys and girls should know better and if they didn't, well, Darwin had something to say about that too.

But this sleazy guy—demons and pucks both loved the used-car-salesman front—wasn't after a soul. I could tell by the especially bright glint in his gaze. He was after some old-fashioned fun. Ripping, shredding, tearing a man to pieces and if his soul whizzed upward like a sky-rocket, I doubt the demon much cared. Maybe he wasn't hungry. Demons ate souls. God no longer sustained them with his light and love and Lucifer was fallen himself. He couldn't. Demons had to feed themselves and Hell was nothing but one big pantry. But demons enjoyed other things than a light snack. They had hobbies the same as anyone else. Theirs simply happened to be killing. To a one, killing was their one true passion. Trading for souls was entertaining and good nutrition, but killing someone . . .

Souls were a McDonald's hamburger, but killing for sheer butchery alone was an all-day ride at the amusement park. This demon was going for the loop-to-loop roller coaster all the way. It was Sunday and the lot was closed, but he had lured some dumb-ass tourist lost from the main strip into the lot. The road to Hell is paved with a lot of things . . . some of them Hyundais. I sighed and hopped the rope that acted as an imaginary barrier between sidewalk and lot to follow the two men inside the tiny two-cubicle office. The shades were down. In Vegas, winter or summer, the shades were always down or that purple couch you bought six months ago would now be lavender, and a pale lavender at that.

Rather the same shade as the face of the tourist who was panicked and struggling to escape the one hand that held him by the neck. He was bent backward over a desk, his flailing arms knocking papers and salesman of the year awards onto the floor, and sometimes . . . just once in a while, you did get annoyed with the gullible. But you were more annoyed with one damn stupid demon who had set up shop literally six blocks from your territory. A human had been running this place three days ago, a potbellied pig–shaped man with a comb-over and enough nose hair to trim into bonsai trees. That alone marked him as nondemon, but he was gone now and a demon had moved into his place.

Demons were so easy to spot it wasn't even close to a challenge. This one had shiny blond hair, soulful brown eyes, not one but two dimples, and he threw off sex appeal by the bucketfuls—plus a manly I-could-be-your-best-bro, bro. He would appeal to men, women, and little old ladies. His charisma covered the spectrum. As

I had made this body, so did demons make theirs. And they always liked theirs bright and shiny as a new penny. It was bait after all, part of the lure.

"Six blocks." I pulled my gun, a Smith & Wesson 500, from the holster in the small of my back. That's why I kept my T-shirt loose. To cover the toys. "You set up your perch here"—I waved my other hand at the room around us—"sniffing for the innocent, the unwary, and the idiotic like this poor schmuck, and you do it six blocks from my place. My home. *My* territory." He gaped at me. While I hadn't bothered to find out about him before now, neither had he bothered to do the same regarding me—a little sloppy on my part, a little fatal on his. The sloppiness stopped now. I blew his head off before he had time to blink his eyes or blink back to Hell.

He shimmered for a second into a man-sized brownish-green lizard with dragon wings, dirty glass teeth, a once-narrow but now-shattered reptilian head, and oozing eye sockets. The Smith had taken care of that. I doubt his eyes had been that same soft and soulful brown anyway. Then he was a pool of black goo on the worn carpet of the office, and while I felt for the cleaning lady, I had security tapes to wipe, a tourist to toss out on the street, and a gym to get to before all the elliptical trainers were taken. The tourist rolled to the floor, gurgled, and passed out either from lack of oxygen or lack of intestinal fortitude (balls for the more succinct of us). I wasn't disappointed. A little judgmental, but not disappointed. It would actually make things easier on me.

"Good old what's-his-name. I'm surprised he lived to this millennium." The voice came from behind me. A familiar one, not in a good way either. I looked over my shoulder to see Eligos—"Call-me-Eli," he would always say with a grin that would suck the oxygen out of a room and half the brain cells out of your head. If you were human. Truly human, not just temporarily human. But that didn't mean I couldn't tell he was something to see all the same. Damned and damn hot, what a combo. He was also very probably the smartest demon I'd come across—what Hollywood likes to call a triple threat. Demons themselves were afraid of Hollywood, the only place where humans were more frightening than any Hell-spawn.

"You can't even remember his name?" I kept the gun loose and easy in my grip and blew a curl that had escaped my ponytail holder out of my eyes. "Some brotherly love there."

"Would you have me sing 'Danny Boy'?" He was sitting on the other desk, one knee up, chin propped in his hand, his hazel eyes cheerful—if bright copper and green could be called hazel. "I have an amazing singing voice. I could've been Elvis. But I did eat him, so six of one, half a dozen of the other. You always have to be specific with the trades. Famous singer . . . good. Famous singer who doesn't swell to the size of Shamu on fried peanut butter and banana sandwiches . . . better. But humans aren't very detail oriented. Short attention span. They're 'Tomorrow is another day.' Yadda yadda yadda." He switched from leaning forward to leaning back and locked his hands across his stomach. "But all beside the point. I want to talk to you, Trixa."

"Your attention span isn't all that great either, Eli, or do you remember what happened to the last demon I 'talked' to?" I wasn't talking about the one I'd just blown away. He'd barely been worth breaking stride for. I was talking about Solomon, my brother's murderer.

He smiled, so flawless and white that an orthodontist would've fallen to the floor and genuflected before him and then no doubt offered him a blow job. Male or female, it wouldn't matter. Humans are slaves to their hormones and no one manipulated hormones like demons. "Oh, I remember. I'll remember that for all eternity. A: You made me piss a pair of Armani jeans that I was quite fond of. And B: You gave me the challenge that will occupy me to the end of time. Or the end of you, whichever comes first. It was worth losing the Light to you *païen* for that. Do you know how long it's been since I've been challenged? Not since the Fall." He shrugged and waffled a hand. "And even then, eh, we knew it was coming. Truthfully, I didn't care if we ruled in Heaven or not. I just wanted to mix it up. Make a little trouble." The smile was even brighter. "Because, Trixa, sweetheart, trouble is the only thing that makes existence bearable."

I'd promised the Light, an artifact from even before *païen* time, to Eli if he verified that the demon I'd suspected killed my brother was the real deal. He delivered. I didn't. I lied. Sue me. I'm a *trickster*. I lie, cheat, steal. . . . It all comes with the name. Although I did it typically to show a few humans the error of their wicked ways, make them a little better, and hopefully a whole lot smarter. But Eli hadn't known that at the time. The same as everyone else, he'd thought me human. But when it all went down—the taking of the Light, an unbreakable shield that would protect *païen* from Heaven and Hell, neither of which much cared for us, and the passing of Solomon—Eli had seen little Trixa in a brand-new way. When I'd finished with Solomon, before he melted to the black of liquid sin, he'd been in so many pieces, it looked like it had been raining demon parts. I'd shape-changed my heart out on that one—not that I had a heart in regard to Kimano's killer. But I had been something to see *and* be. Bear. Wolf. Fox. Spider. Crow. Dragon. Shark. All in one. And as I'd told Solomon then, when ranked, it went something like this: gods, then tricksters, and then a damn sight lower . . . demons. I'd told him and I'd proved it.

And Eli had been part of the audience.

As far as he knew, I was still trickster, shape-shifter, all that had made Solomon look as if he'd fallen into a wood chipper. I had my shielding against empathic and telepathic probes to keep Eli thinking I remained all that I'd been. I might be semihuman, but I'd die before I lost that last defense. I'd lost my offensive abilities for a while, but nature makes sure every creature keeps their defensive ones until there's nothing left to defend. It was a fortunate thing too. While angels had telepathy, and a host of other annoying habits, demons had empathy. It made it so much easier to trade for a soul when you could *feel* exactly what a person desired.

I needed to keep Eli believing I was a trickster at the top of her form, because while the ranking went gods, tricksters, demons . . . humans were far enough below a high-level demon like Eli that you'd need binoculars to see them. I still had my trickster mind, but I had a vulnerable ninety-nine percent human body and that made things more difficult.

"Fine. If you want trouble"—I checked my watch—"I can spare five minutes. That should give me time to kill you, wipe the tapes, and maybe browse for a new car while I'm at it." I smiled. I doubted I was too impressive a sight right then. I was an explosion of messy waves and curls anchored at the crown of my head with a ponytail holder. No makeup. The shirt that snarky Leo had had made for me that said SLAYER NOT LAYER on the front in the same bright red as my sweatpants, and a pair of beat-up sneakers. But Eli wasn't seeing me now; he was seeing me *then*, and I had that going for me for a few months at least.

"Oh, I want trouble." His eyes darkened and it wasn't with anger. Some serial killers had horrific childhoods that had tangled sexual and homicidal urges into one black, strangling noose. Demons had only needed that one spat with Daddy to get them there. "But it'll have to be another time. I want to talk to you about some demons." He straightened, turning serious . . . as serious as Eli came anyway. "Dead demons. Quite a few dead demons."

I tapped the barrel of my gun against my leg. "Really?" Now there was the best news I'd heard all day. "You want to throw a party at my place? I'll even throw in an open bar for the occasion, because, sugar, I am *that* excited about it. How many demons are we talking about? Fifty? Because I can do a theme party. El Día de la Muerte de los Demonios. Death of Demons Day. Like Cinco de Mayo only with piñatas that have little horns and forked tails."

"Cute. You're so adorable when you're tearing apart my rivals and blathering on about something to which you have no utter fucking clue." He smiled again. This time the white teeth had turned to the mouthful of smoky quartz fangs. "But that's fine. I'm happy to have this conversation later. Maybe I'll go out and occupy the time by burning down a church. Barbecuing the faithful. I always enjoy that. A big side of coleslaw and I'll be in hog you-know-where." At the last word, he pointed a finger skyward and mock fired it.

Technically, that was Heaven's problem, not mine, but despite the lying, cheating, and stealing part, I did have a conscience. Most tricksters did, as much as we'd

deny it. That, combined with Eli not being in the mood
for a little verbal sparring, was unusual enough to pique
my interest.

I sat on the other desk and rested my feet on the large
belly of the still-unconscious tourist. "Okay, grumpy
hooves. I'll give you those five minutes. Better yet, I'll
actually listen to you instead of killing you during them,
because I'm sweet as cotton candy that way." I checked
my watch again and snapped my own fingers. "Go."

And go he did. It wasn't fifty demons who had died.
It wasn't even a hundred. That wouldn't be that unusual.
Demons killed *païen* for sport and tricksters killed demons because of it. All *païen* weren't tricksters. There
were vampires, wolves (werewolves to the fictionally
inclined), nymphs, sprites, boggles, revenants, trolls, chu-
bacabra, pukas, and thousands more. Some could take a
demon and some couldn't. So, if a hundred demons died
in the past few years, that would be normal.

Nine hundred and fifty-six in six months was not
normal.

I tapped my feet on the unconscious man's belly and
watched it ripple for a second while I processed the
information. "All right. I see your point. Someone has
been eating their Wheaties, taking their vitamins, and
chugging a whole lot of Red Bull on top of that." Inside
I had more of a "holy shit, the sky is falling—don't let
the demon see you sweat" attitude going on. Something
that could do that . . . "Maybe Upstairs has decided to do
some old-fashioned smiting of the wicked and wanton.
Let's face it, you are both."

His teeth became human again as the smile became
smug. "True. Wicked and wanton and I stand by my rec-
ord placing in the top ten in my particular region of Hell.
But, no. Not even in the War—or the Sacred Scuffle, Po-

lice Action, Hallowed Hoedown, take your pick—we didn't lose a third so many. Who do you think was most likely to rebel? The holiest of the holy? The Precious Moments Angels? The simpering weaklings who were no better than fluffy baby ducks with halos?" He snorted. "No. We were the warriors. God's Righteous Fury. The Smiters, sweetheart, not the Smitees. Granted, we did pick up a slew of messenger angels, watcher angels— the minimum-wage pigeons who just did what they were told to do. And at that moment Lucifer was talking the loudest and God was letting the angels make their own choice. So we ended up with some weak-minded fluffy ducks after all. Like him." He jerked his head at the stain on the floor. "But even Daffy there, to lose more than nine hundred of him in six months? That is . . ." He shook his head and slid on a pair of sunglasses. "I don't know what that is. No one seems to."

I still kept my gun out as he slid down from the desk and headed for the door. Demons, higher-level demons like Eligos, moved faster than humans did. While I'd given myself an Olympic-conditioned human body when creating it, Olympic or not, it was still human . . . and five pounds heavier. "It's odd, impressive, and, all right, a little more than freaky, but why should I care? Whatever this is could kill every demon in Hell and it's not going to get my ovaries in a twist. There's a huge amount of 'I don't care' in this general area." I waved my free hand around me. "You kill my kind. I kill yours. This seems like a good thing for me and mine." I wasn't that stupid. If someone or something out there could do what Eli said, it was bad, bad news, because who knew when your kind might be . . .

"Next," Eli finished for me as he opened the door, a few blond hairs glittering in the dark brown of his hair, and looked back over his shoulder. Posed rather. Demons did like the hot rides they'd created to be admired. "I don't need to be an angel. I don't need telepathy to read that thought. I only have to know how smart you are. And that's almost as smart as you think." He grinned. "Nice T-shirt, by the way. Can't wait to prove it wrong."

The door closed and I slowly holstered my gun. Almost a thousand demons in six months.

Not in my best year ever. While I didn't care about the dead demons—no crying over spilt sociopaths—I did wonder what this thing might do if demons started to bore it. I made a mental list of anything and everything I knew of throughout history, mine and the world's, that could do something like this.

It was a very short list.

I went on to my workout. Dead demons didn't make exercise and conditioning unnecessary. An unknown creature making those dead demons made it only more necessary. Afterward I ran home to take a shower. I'd come to find out that some humans had the capacity to tolerate more annoyance and flat-out brutal torture than I'd ever given them credit for. . . . Having to genuinely earn your muscle—that was probably one of the most annoying things that I'd come across.

Give them credit? I *was* one of them now as much as I dragged my feet admitting it, trying to deny it with that minuscule one percent that wasn't human. The second I forgot that I was now exactly what I appeared to be would be the second a demon would do to me what I'd done to so many of them.

Either way, human, trickster or both, I saluted

Homo sapiens, respected them more than I ever had, but the gym shower? Even I had to draw the line somewhere. I kicked ass either with claws, paws, or one helluva fashionable boot, but you couldn't convince me that mold didn't have its own gods and demons, its own tricksters and unspeakable monsters. I know one clump bristled at me the first and last time I'd checked out the utilities. I recognized evil when I saw it. I saw it that day on seventies-era avocado green tile and some evil you simply had to walk away from. My bathroom was minutes away. I'd wait. And I'd gotten ridiculously fond of soap that smelled of oranges and felt like silk against my skin. I'd been human so many times throughout my life, but this one . . . this one . . . It had really taken. I wasn't scared of much, but that came close to doing it.

Four more years. Who would I be then?

Me. I'd still be me. Tricking and laughing my way through life as always. Nothing was going to change that. I'd said that the past ten years. I could keep telling myself the same thing as long as I had to.

When I made it home, the closed sign was still on the door. I grumbled as I unlocked the door. Maybe Leo in his god days could make gold coins fly out his ass, but I knew the value of a hard-earned or stolen buck. It was two in the afternoon now and he hadn't opened the place when I'd left? What was he thinking? I was surprised we didn't have a few of our regulars going into DTs right there on the sidewalk.

Opening the door loudly, I made sure to close it more so behind me. There's no point in being pissed off if there's no way to share it. But before I had the chance, besides the door slamming, someone said, "You look like you were kicked out of a wet T-shirt contest." There was a pause. "I didn't know you could get kicked out of those."

Zeke. Straightforward tell-me-the-truth-and-I'll-tell-you-no-lies Zeke. Because lying was too much of a bother for him and if you lied *to* him, well, he'd probably just shoot you. He was sitting at one of the tables eating a pizza. Double cheese, pepperoni, sausage, mushroom, peppers, olives, and a cardiologist on call. Eating it in front of me. And there were bags . . . bags and bags in front of the table, full of garlic bread and cheese sticks from the smell of it. The exquisite smell that put the plumeria-soaked breezes of Hawaii to shame. That was worse than the wet T-shirt remark. I narrowed my eyes at him and dripped on the floor as he chewed and swallowed a bite. "You're . . . puddle-y." He looked at his Eden House partner across the table from him. "Is puddle-y a word?"

Griffin quirked his lips. "I think fewer moisture-related comments and more eating might be a good idea."

Red eyebrows pulled into a scowl. "You are not the boss of me." Slightly lighter red hair was pulled into a short ponytail . . . dry, not cascading buckets like mine. Zeke's shirt was a plain gray long-sleeve T-shirt and his jeans were faded. What he wore didn't make much difference to him. As long as he had a jacket to cover his gun, he was good to go. Fashion didn't appear on his top-ten list of priorities.

"In fact, I am the boss of you," Griffin said, reaching for his own piece of the pie, only with more napkins. "And you're the boss of me tomorrow. Remember?"

"Oh, yeah." Zeke gave a grin. He didn't smile often, so he didn't have much of a repertoire to choose from.

Pissed and predatory. You-are-dead predatory. You-are-*beyond*-dead predatory. And this was the newest version that had cropped up since last November. Behind-the-bedroom-door predatory. It was also happy and since Zeke had spent most of his mortal life barely comprehending the word, I forgave the pizza. It was good to see him this way. More free and open than he'd ever been when he'd thought he was human. When he thought he and Griffin were human.

I know. Vegas, right? Is *anyone* human?

Griffin and Zeke had been demon-killing partners at Eden House Las Vegas. There was also an Eden House Miami, an Eden House Los Angeles, Eden House London . . . Eden Houses all over the world. They'd been around for thousands of years, a secret organization created by man to bring Eden back to Earth. The key word being man. Heaven had nothing to do with its creation, but once the angels saw a source of free labor, they took advantage now and again. And they certainly didn't have a problem with Eden House trying to eradicate every demon it came across. It did a good job . . . on the slow, lower-level demons anyway.

The angels and the demons had both been after the Light for a long time. I'd just managed to get there first . . . by a few seconds. Having narrowed down the location, both sides had planted sleeper agents in Vegas's Eden House. An angel, because even loyal humans couldn't be trusted with the Light, and a demon in case Eden House got to the Light before Hell did. They'd been given the same human bodies demons and angels formed when walking on Earth, only they had been children. Eight and ten years old. For a demon, that's a doable situation. Hang around with no memory of who you are, grow up, and then get activated by your Hell handler at the right moment. Because Eden House will recruit you as it tries to recruit all humans with empathy or telepathy. Nature was a marvelous thing. If angels had telepathy and demons had empathy, then so would the rest of what roamed the earth. Not everyone by any means, but it was out there . . . in humans and *païen*.

Hell had planned well. Griffin fit in fine. He was a demon. He had empathy, but more importantly he had free will. All demons did. All angels had. But after the Fall, God had taken the free will of the angels still in Heaven. Some had gotten it back. Relearned it. If they spent enough time on Earth with humans, they would slowly regain it. It was like riding a bicycle, only the lag time was usually much longer. Maybe God figured if they took it in baby steps, they'd get it right this time. No more pride goeth before the big trip down South. I wasn't sure that was true. I'd met a few real asshole angels in my day. But that wasn't my call.

Not all angels spent enough time on Earth to get their will back. Zeke had been one of those. When the angel in charge of seeking the Light had assigned an agent, he'd put Zeke . . . Zerachiel . . . in place. Zeke who'd had to learn free will about a hundred times faster than your average angel. Things hadn't gone well. To this day he struggled. He saw things in black and white. Not only in justice, but in all aspects of his life. That tended to make his decisions permanent ones. Once he chose a course of action, he almost literally couldn't stop and reconsider. *I need to catch the demon in the Jaguar ahead of me. Red light? Demon trumps red light*, and so a busload of German tourists was inconvenienced when his car smashed into them. It was just the way things were with Zeke. Sometimes people were inconvenienced; sometimes they were punished with good Old Testament eye for an eye.

And then sometimes they died.

I wrung the sweat out of my hair. "I guess you two are the reason my bar isn't open and making money. Is the demon under the table your excuse?"

Griffin, ex-demon, and Zeke, ex-angel, defectors of Heaven and Hell, looked at each other. "I told you she would know," Griffin snorted, and used the one hand not involved in eating pizza to pull a demon up into sight. Zeke helped by pushing the reptilian head up and back using the muzzle of a sawed-off shotgun.

"You're no fun," Zeke griped.

"It's not like hiding him behind bags of cheesy bread is some kind of master plan, guys," I pointed out, pushing aside those bags and pulling a chair over to the table to sit opposite the demon. And I had a piece of pizza. After today, I deserved it. And what was five more pounds? Just more force behind the ass kicking. I'd exercise, but if I couldn't eat pizza, cheesy bread, or my own weight in chocolate-caramel ice cream once in a while, I might as well let a demon take me down. What's the point in living without those things?

I looked over the demon as I chewed one fabulously cheese-laden mouthful. Swallowing, I said, "Tell me you didn't pull his wing off and bring him here like a cat with a present for my pillow. Killing them is one thing. Torturing them is something else." Even if they'd done more torture than we'd ever know. I swatted Zeke's free hand that was making for the last piece of pizza. "Bad kitty." I closed the lid on the box, saving it for myself.

"No," Griffin said, sounding defensive. And that was my fault. I tried to be careful about saying things like that these days. Griffin had been a demon, even if he hadn't known it until last November when the whole mess with the Light went down. He still didn't remember it. When he'd chosen Zeke and Leo and me over doing Hell's bidding, the Light had wiped his and Zeke's slate clean. He had only his human memories and a human body now . . . with bronze dragon wings that came and went when he wanted them to . . . but even if he couldn't remember, he knew. Every demon was a killer, a torturer, and a devourer of souls. And he'd been a high-level demon—not as high as Eli, but high enough that he would've outkilled your average demon, like the one he was holding, six ways to Sunday. Griffin had been one bad demon, very bad, which made it such a miracle he made one of the best humans I'd met.

"We found him this way," he went on grimly. "We were out hunting." They still hunted demons, although Eden House Vegas had been burned to the ground by Solomon and nearly all the members killed during the whole Light affair. What else would they do but hunt? That's what they'd been trained for, it was worth doing, and after being a demon killer for most of what you remembered to be your adult life, you were going to give that up and work at the Gap? Besides, Eden House did pay well and since they were now without a House here, Griffin and Zeke were all the organization had left to take care of the city until they rebuilt.

Eden House obviously didn't have a clue about Griffin's and Zeke's unusual status. Only one angel had known about Zeke being a sleeper agent and all the demons and angels at the battle for the Light had died . . . except Eli. As for Hell, they didn't give a shit about ex-demons and ex-angels. You had to give them that. Betrayal wasn't a bad word in their book. It was more like a compliment. It was pretty much every demon for himself . . . except when it looked like someone was out to take every single one of them down. Someone who seemed to have a good shot at it. Griffin and Zeke were good. I was good. But even the three of us couldn't come close to doing what Eli said was being done.

"And you found him where?" I finished the slice of pizza and went for the hoarded last one, ignoring Zeke's scowl of deprivation.

"Behind that new club five blocks over." There was always a new club in Vegas. Usually no point in remembering the names, they came and went so frequently. And they never closed. Gambling and booze and vomiting tourists twenty-four/seven. And no state income tax. Who said there was no Eden anymore? "We'd already checked the inside. No demons. We went out back to see if there were any in the murdering instead of dealing mood and this one comes falling out of the sky. Literally. Almost landed right on top of Zeke. He crapped his pants."

"I did not." Zeke's scowl deepened.

"Screamed like a drunk sorority girl in a haunted house?" Griffin's short bad mood had passed quickly—they always did—and his blue eyes were bright with humor. That with his blond hair made him seem more like the ex-angel than Zeke with his red hair and green eyes.

"*No*. And you're an ass."

Griffin grinned at him. "Learned from the best."

I looked past their fun at the demon. It was quiet, not struggling, not cursing us up one side and down the other. Demons came in different colors and levels, but well behaved wasn't included in the options package. This one hung limp in Griffin's and Zeke's grip. It was conscious. I could see its muddy eyes rolling

from right to left, but randomly. They weren't focusing on my guys' back-and-forth. They weren't focusing
on anything. Black drool dripped from its open mouth
and the one remaining wing twitched, but not in a co-
ordinated movement.

You had to hold on to demons to keep them from
flashing back to Hell. And you couldn't pop one in a
crate with a doggy chew and a pat on its cute little head,
and expect it to still be there when you came back. It
wasn't as much the physical that kept them from escaping; it was will. A cage didn't have will. Your hand on
a sword through its guts, that had will. Messy for your
brand-new rug, but it did get the job done. This demon
though . . .

I leaned closer across the table, touching my bottom
lip in contemplation with a short painted nail. Those
eyes . . . no, nobody home. "Either one of you getting
anything off him? Because I think you could put a
candle in his head and put him on the porch if it were
Halloween."

Both Griffin and Zeke frowned together. Empath
and telepath, and both shook their heads. "White noise,"
Griffin said.

"Veggie platter." Zeke shrugged.

Something had ripped off the demon's wing, but it
had done something else I'd never seen. It had driven
a demon catatonic. Now that would be a nifty trick. I'd
love to know how that worked. More dark drool dripped
from its narrow jaw. Maybe not. It was a murderous killing machine, but this . . . This was sick.

"Can you try a little harder, Kit?" I asked Zeke. He
lifted the fox-colored eyebrows—that color had me calling him Kit for a baby fox since he was fifteen. Not that
he was a baby anymore . . . but the nickname had stuck.

"Dig a little deeper? See if you can get even a glimpse of what did this to it?"

"If you'll puddle less, I'll do anything," he retorted.

"A pizza grudge is a nasty thing." I swatted his shoulder. He snorted and turned back to stare at the demon again. He focused unblinking for several seconds.

I was beginning to think nothing was going to happen when the demon screamed. And screamed and screamed and screamed. I'd heard demons scream in pain. I'd made them scream in pain, but I'd never heard anything like this. Ever.

Zeke's head jerked, his eyes rolled back, and he collapsed to the floor, out cold. Griffin grunted as if someone had kicked him hard in the gut and went in the other direction, facedown on the table. But he wasn't unconscious. His hands clenched into fists against his temples. I dived immediately for the shotgun that had fallen from Zeke's hands. My Smith was a nice gun, but shotgun slugs were even more of a sure thing. I put two of them through the demon's skull. I'd put away my fair share of demons, but this was the first time it was a mercy killing.

With most of his head gone, the demon melted to blackness as they all did, and the screaming stopped. In the room and in Griffin's head as well, because he was back up. There was a trickle of blood at one nostril from where he'd banged his nose on the table. "What the hell was . . . ," he started hoarsely, then forgot about the demon as he moved to Zeke's side. "Shit."

I was right beside him as Griff rested his hand on Zeke's forehead. It was my suggestion that had Zeke walking through the demon's brain to read his thoughts and it had been a stupid one. I tried not to make stupid mistakes, but sending Zeke for a look at what had driven a demon insane was one of the worst I could remember making in a long time.

I didn't have the talent for empathy or telepathy, only a natural defense against them. All tricksters did or we wouldn't be very good at hiding who we were from those who did have the gift, not to mention angels and demons. I could read someone's expression and body language though as if I had a map in one hand and a GPS in the other. But I couldn't do much with an unconscious face. "Is he all right?" He had to be all right. He and Griffin were my boys. I'd taken them in when they were teenagers. I'd thought I was keeping an eye on my competition. And it was just for a while. Everyone who takes in a ragged, dirty-nosed puppy tells themselves that, but those puppies worm their way into your heart even when they piddle in the corner. There's nothing you can do to stop it.

Griffin frowned. "He's not in pain." You don't have to be conscious to feel pain. Sad to say all three of us knew that.

Zeke wasn't in pain, which was good, but was he *there*? Was it still Zeke in there or was he like the demon had been? Alive but gone?

Griffin closed his eyes, concentrating hard, before exhaling in relief. He opened his eyes and smiled. "He's hungry. He feels hungry."

Good. That was good. Hunger and catatonia rarely went together. I shifted from my knees to an abrupt flop onto my ass. "Our Zeke. He's always hungry." I pushed aside hair that had plastered and glued itself to my forehead with sweat. "Do you want to punch me one for asking Zeke to do that?"

"You're a girl," he said immediately, then amended as I raised my eyebrows. "I mean, a woman."

"I am and one who can kick your butt, but you didn't answer my question." I leaned against his shoulder and ruffled his hair.

"A little bit," he admitted. "Must be the leftover demon in me."

"No. Just the overprotective demon-slaying partner in you." I smoothed the hair I'd mussed. "And next time I'll clear anything I ask Zeke to do through you first. You know him best."

"I do." After the rebuke that was milder than I deserved, he reached over and slapped Zeke lightly on the cheek. "Definitely enough to know when he's faking. He woke up a few seconds ago. Up or no cheesy bread for you."

Eyes opened combined with an irritable expression. "I was waiting to see if one of you cried. On TV they always cry at the deathbed."

Equally irritated, Griffin flicked his partner's chin with a stinging finger before helping him sit up. "You weren't on your deathbed, and what if I had cried? What would you have said?"

Zeke snorted. "That you were a pussy."

"That's what I thought." He stood and pulled Zeke up with him.

I stood too. "Are you feeling okay, Kit? You went down like a rock."

"I did?" he asked without too much curiosity, more interested in investigating the bags of bread. He unloaded one batch on the table and looked down at the black puddle on the floor. "Hey, the demon. What happened to the demon?" He turned back to me. "And when did you get here?" He looked me up and down. "You look like you were kicked out of a wet T-shirt contest. I didn't know you could—"

I cut him off before he repeated the whole insult. I let it go the first time. Twice was asking a bit much. "You don't remember me coming in?" I felt the back of his head for a bump or contusion.

He swatted at my hand. "You're being a mom. Quit it."

"I'm thirty-one," I retorted ominously. "I am not a *mom*. I'm definitely not your mom."

"You're six thousand and the last thing I remember is eating pizza and waiting for you to get here to see the demon." He forgot about the bread for the moment and searched the tabletop and then under it. "Where's the pizza?"

"I'm *thirty-one*," I said this time around, "the pizza is gone, the demon is dead, and you were trying to take a peek in his brain to see why he had all the mental capacity of a potted plant when you keeled over like a drunken Baptist minister."

"Huh," he commented before moving on to more important things. "Griffin, your nose is busted. If the demon did that, it's a good thing he's dead. So who ate the pizza?"

One thing about Zeke, he never let the little things in life get to him, and other than Griffin and food, they were all little things. At times it was annoying as hell, and at other times it was almost inspirational. To live in the now . . . no worries about the future or monsters that could turn demons' brains to oatmeal.

Right now it was vexing enough I nearly smacked him with the piece of garlic bread he was considering eating. Sighing, I tried Griffin instead. "You took a hit too when the demon went nuts. I saw it." I handed him a napkin from the table. "And your face felt it." He grimaced and held the napkin to the small drop of blood from his nose. "What did you pick up from it?"

"Terror." He wiped the blood away. "More than I've ever felt from anyone, even from people torn apart by demons before we could stop them. More terror than I thought a demon could feel. More than I thought even existed."

More terror than could possibly exist, and something so horrifying that Zeke's brain had shut down to prevent him from seeing it.

Well, wasn't that just peachy?

Chapter 2

I'd given the guys the update on demons dying right and left, a powerful creature running about—mission unknown and headed up to my apartment. By the time I took my shower, changed, and came back downstairs, the place was empty. No Griffin, no Zeke, no cheesy bread. There still was a large black puddle of demon goo on my floor though. Although I'd shot it, the guys had brought it, so technically it was their mess. But . . . I sighed as I went for the mop. Zeke had been knocked flat, had been unconscious, and Griffin was concerned about him. He'd seemed himself—and it was very easy to see when Zeke was not himself—but better safe than sorry.

Griffin probably had him at their house, feet up, TV on, and watching like a hawk for anything unexpected such as twitches, seizures, or the desire to not swap old porn magazines to the Jehovah's Witnesses for the *Watchtower*. After all, Griffin was making him get rid of them and in Zeke's mind this was a valid recycling program. Zeke might be an ex-angel, but he'd never had any sexual hang-ups, which rather made you wonder why people did.

Either way, they were gone. Leo wasn't back from wherever he'd disappeared to. I knew Leo. What was between us was something only the two of us could understand, but that didn't mean I could begin to guess where he went when he wandered off. I'd been born to hit the ground running, whelped to wander as all tricksters were, but Leo could make me look like a very mossy, very nonrolling stone. And when he was dating one of his bimbos . . . and they were all bimbos . . . I'd have to take him to the vet and get him chipped if I wanted a clue as to where he was roaming.

After mopping the floor, I flipped the sign to OPEN and settled down to business. I had three kinds of business in my life: serving alcohol, selling information, and tricking those who deserved it. Killing demons wasn't business. It was Griffin and Zeke's business, but for me . . . it was just my favorite hobby. My way of giving back to the community, by keeping a few more members of that community alive and undamned.

My first client didn't come for the first kind of business, but I gave her one anyway. I looked her up and down and gave her a whiskey on the rocks. She was more of a wine cooler girl. Fruity drinks, light beer, not a serious drinker, but she needed a real drink now.

She sat down at the table across from me after introducing herself and touched a finger to the glass. She gave me her name, a nervous half smile, and said, "Normally I don't . . . I mean, I'm more of a sangria, Fuzzy Navel person. Silly girl drinks, you know." Her smile faded. "For a silly girl."

But she wasn't a girl. She was a woman, just barely . . . twenty-two, twenty-three. Almost a girl, but unlike horseshoes and hand grenades, "almost" didn't count in this case. She took a swallow of the whiskey, made a face, but took a second swallow. "Better?" I asked sympathetically.

She nodded and pushed the glass aside. "Thank

you." She opened the purse in her lap—more of a bag really. It was big enough to carry around a sketch pad, pencils, a computer, any number of things. She had that artsy look. Homemade jewelry of silver wire with lots of polished stones and silver rings to match. Probably a vegan. She looked sweet and earnest and generally concerned for every living being. Probably had a bumper sticker for every endangered species on the planet. She certainly wasn't my usual clientele. She wasn't the kind looking for trouble or the kind looking to get herself out of trouble . . . unless she was caught breaking animals out of a testing lab. If that were the case, I'd give her my help for free. Turn the bunnies loose and stick a few death row inmates in those cages. Cute and fluffy versus killers with misspelled tattoos. It seemed like a fair trade to me.

It turned out I was wrong though. She was looking to get herself out of trouble—the very worst kind of trouble.

She took some photos out of the bag and was turning them over in her hands. "Somebody told me about you. What you do. That you know things that people shouldn't be able to know. And that you believe in"— she flushed—"things people say don't exist. That maybe you're psychic."

Now this was interesting. "No, sweetie, I'm not a psychic and don't pay any money to anyone who says they are." She flushed an even brighter red, revealing she already had. She was helpless and clueless, as out of place as a guppy in a shark tank. Poor little fish.

"That's a pretty necklace," she said, shuffling the photos faster.

I touched it. It was a pretty necklace, one Leo had

given me . . . a gold sun with a red garnet. Red for me, and the sun to banish the cloudy days of my past, the days of finding revenge for my brother, for Kimano. And that was all beside the point. She was postponing the difficult, the painful. We all do.

I dropped my hand. "Show me the pictures, Anna. It's like taking off a Band-Aid. The quicker the better. Let's fix you up, guppy. Let you sleep again."

"Guppy?" She rubbed self-consciously at the dark smudges under her eyes and curled her lips in a sad smile. "Little fish in a big scary ocean. Are you sure you're not psychic?" Not waiting for an answer, she laid out the first photo as if it were a card in a tarot deck . . . as if she were laying out her life. Past, present, and future.

She was.

The first photograph rested on the table and I turned it with my finger to make it right side up for me. It was a girl, about ten. She wasn't beautiful. She wasn't necessarily pretty either. But she had a sweet smile, freckles scattered over her nose and her dark brown hair drifting in a long-gone breeze. She clutched a kitten next to her cheek. It didn't look happy, nose scrunched, tail poofed, but it put up with the hug. It was your typical little-kid picture. Cute, but nothing out of the ordinary. "What was the cat's name?"

She blinked and smiled again. "Pickles. Actually Sir Pickles the Perilous. We both had delusions of grandeur."

Then she laid out the next one and the smile vanished so thoroughly I couldn't imagine she knew how to smile, much less just had been. This one was of a girl in a hospital bed. Half of her face was more or less gone, burned away. The eye was gone too, the hair a memory.

They'd tried skin grafts and they covered the skull and muscle, but I don't think anyone counted the operations a success.

She kept dealing out the photos. Eleven years old, twelve . . . "That's when they gave me my first wig" . . . thirteen, fourteen . . . "This is when I had my second prosthetic eye. The first never fit right." . . . fifteen, sixteen, seventeen . . . "This is me with my friends." They were pictures of her alone. On the couch watching TV. In her room on her bed reading a book. In a backyard with Sir Pickles the Perilous in her lap. Alone again. Always alone. "This is me prom night." It was another picture of her in a hospital bed. This time her wrists were bandaged. "And this is me"—the last picture—"on my twenty-first birthday."

She looked as she did now. Smooth skin, freckles, dark brown hair to her shoulders, clear brown eyes. There wasn't a single scar, much less the massive disfigurement of before, and in this picture she was smiling as she hadn't since she was ten. She was happy, so happy that she could've powered all the neon in Vegas with the sheer joy in her face.

"Oh, sweetie." I gathered up the pictures and turned them facedown. "I'm sorry. I am, but there's no help for you." I wished there were a way to soften it, but in this case there wasn't. There was only truth, ugly and inescapable.

This time when she blinked it was to clear the tears clinging to her eyelashes. Then she used the back of her hand to wipe them away. "He was our neighbor's gardener. He was new. He'd only been there for a few days, but he talked to me . . . over the fence. No one ever talked to me much except my parents. He just . . . talked. He didn't try to make me fall in love with him or anything like that. He didn't have to. He only had to be my friend. For a week I had a friend. And he was funny. I laughed for the first time since the accident. I spent the whole week laughing and actually not minding living, and then at the end of the week he asked me a question." She took the pictures back and tucked them carefully away. "I didn't believe in God. I didn't believe in the devil. I definitely didn't believe in demons."

"But they believed in you."

She nodded and ran fingers along her jaw. It was probably a habit—making sure it was real. "I didn't ask to be beautiful. I didn't ask to be famous or powerful or rich. I just asked to be who I would've been if the car accident hadn't happened. I'm not pretty. I'm average and that's fine. I never take average for granted now. I work at Starbucks to put myself through art school. I have a tiny apartment I can barely afford. There's a guy who lives down the hall who smiles at me at the mailboxes. I think he might ask me out. I didn't ask for anything extra. I only asked for . . ." She stopped and tucked her hair behind her ears. "I only asked for my life back. And I got it and it was wonderful, but now it's three years later and I know. Trading eternity for twenty years, I made a mistake."

Yes, she had—a big one. And she wouldn't get eternity. I didn't know why they bothered with that lie. I guess it sounded better than *And sooner rather than later, I'll eat your soul*. Eternity gave them hope. God will forgive. God will set us free. With nonexistence, there was no hope.

"I only asked," she repeated, eyes dry now. "I only asked."

"No," I exhaled. "You didn't. He asked. The demon

asked for your soul and you gave it to him. And there's
no way out of it." A helpless guppy all right. On the very
day she was able to give her soul away, someone was already waiting to take it. A good girl, a nice girl, and there
wasn't anything I could do for her. Free will was free
will. She didn't deserve Hell, but Hell she would get. I
didn't know her demon, but even if I had and killed him,
then another would step up and then another. "No soul
left behind". . . All bureaucracies had their mottoes.

Someone would always come for Anna, one way or
the other.

You couldn't save them all, and I wasn't in the saving
business per se, but if I could've saved anyone I'd seen
sell their souls over the years, it would've been her. But
I couldn't, so I sent her away, her and her pictures with
Sir Pickles. She went quietly. She stopped after a few
steps, turned to thank me politely for my time, and then
walked out the bar door into Hell.

Whether you waited twenty years or twenty seconds,
it was all the same eventually.

Hell was Hell.

Leo finally showed his face the next morning. I was already up. I'd opened the bar early to make up for yesterday's lack of profit. And I'd called and texted everyone
and anyone I knew in the *païen* world to see if anyone
had heard about the demon slaughter. So far I'd gotten nothing but a bemused feeling at the thought of a
seven-tailed trickster fox trotting around Japan with a
BlackBerry in its jaws.

Leo, on the other hand, looked like he'd gotten something. He could wear that stoic expression all he wanted,
but I knew him. "Not a new one," I groaned.

"I'm a man with needs." He shrugged as he put on

one of the bar's black aprons, wrapping the tie twice around his waist.

"Which are oddly enough always met with silicone," I retorted.

He shrugged again, but this time quirked his lips, "It's Vegas. You get a free boob job every time you fill up your car. How is that my fault?"

Big breasts, small brains, and underwear tiny enough to have been knitted by Tinkerbell—he did it every time. I could've blamed it on him being worshipped as a Norse god, lots of buxom blondes frolicking in the snow, but I wasn't sure that was it. I thought there was more to it than that. He did it for the same reason I slept with a black raven's feather under my pillow. If we couldn't have what we actually wanted, we went without or went for the exact opposite. I wasn't exactly proud of some of my past dates.

"Spots." I sighed. Leo and I had ties . . . unbreakable ones . . . two leopards with the same spots. Too much the same in the past, too much the same for now, but maybe . . . maybe not always. I had the feather to remind me of that.

"Spots," the one who'd given me that feather agreed, the curve of his lips softer; then he continued with a wicked glint to his black eyes, "Her spots are called pasties, I believe. She's a dancer."

"Stripper." I threw a towel at him.

"Who has goals in the theater." He caught it and polished the bar with broad strokes.

"She wants to be a porn star." I looked for something else to throw, but there was nothing that wouldn't come out of this month's profit.

"And she does charity work." He tossed the towel across his shoulder and folded his arms.

"She does you for free?" I smiled with caustic cheer.

He frowned. "I do not pay for sex, little girl."

"You only get to call me that for four more years." And five foot five was not that short. Maybe in comparison to the six-foot-plus American Indian body he'd chosen, I was somewhat smaller, but I was not little, most especially not when it came to temper, where it counted most. "So did you offer her free drinks here for the duration of your sexcapades or fix her refrigerator?"

That got the towel thrown back at me. "No, thanks." I folded it and put it aside. "I don't have to stuff my bra. Unlike some, I don't feel the need to be a double D or wax myself as bare as a honeydew melon. Barbie dolls are for little girls to play with, not grown, perverted men. Now, about our demon trouble."

That distracted him. "What demon trouble?"

I told him. He grasped the implications as quickly as I had. "There aren't many out there who could do that," he said thoughtfully, before adding, "one less now that I'm grounded."

"Godzilla to the hundredth power is running around and you have to get your ego in the picture," I said fondly. "Just remember, your biggest and baddest power now is dropping bird shit on people's cars." He kept reminding me how vulnerable I was now. I didn't want him to forget he was as well.

He ignored the insult—to his manhood and birdhood. "And Eligos is back." He turned and served a beer to one of our regulars—a walking handlebar mustache roosting on a skinny guy it was using for life support. The man was a person; he had a name. I knew it . . . first, middle, last, and nickname. I knew where he'd been born. I knew where he lived, who he lived with, how much money he made in Social Security checks. I made it my business to know these things about all my regulars, but one look at him and the mustache never failed to jump into the foreground—an entity all its own. It was like seeing someone with a giant if not friendly spider on his face. . . . It was difficult to ignore.

"We knew he wasn't leaving Vegas," I said as the mustache shuffled off to its customary table in the corner. "I'm surprised he didn't single-handedly found the place. This city is tailor-made for him."

"And I imagine he thinks the same about you. You caught his interest, and right now, being mortal, that is not a good thing," he said disapprovingly, as if somehow it was my fault that I might be more entertaining to kill than whatever it was that Eli usually came across.

"Don't think it's all about me. You're as intriguing or at least he will think you still are." I pinched his cheek. "He might even think you're more 'purty' than I am, you never know. A hot babe like you who has to part lusting strippers like the Red Sea just to walk among the common people. He might want to take you out instead of killing you. Of course he's not a blonde with breasts the same size and shape as the *Hindenburg*, but he won't drop a pastie in your soup at dinner either."

"I think I'll bring Morocco by the bar," he contemplated. "Let you meet her. I think you two will bond."

"Playing hardball. Cranky, cranky. I would think you'd be in a better mood having your manly needs fulfilled and all." I took my apron off and stuffed it under the bar. "Morocco. That's beautiful," I said solemnly. "Is that where her people are from? Lots of blue-eyed blondes there."

"I think she saw it on the Travel Channel," he replied with equal gravity, "and thought it sounded exotic."

I thought about spearing his hand with a tiny paper drink umbrella, then gave it up as a lost cause and advised, "Hide all your singles when she's around. I'll be back in a few hours."

"And you're going where while I toil at *your* bar?" he demanded.

"Out to play hooky with demons. You ditched yesterday, so I get to ditch today. Remember, this place keeps a roof over *your* head. Unless you want to take up stripping yourself." I gave him a wave and went out through the back office to the alley entrance. That was one thing Leo didn't have that a born trickster did. We were very aware of money . . . how much we had, how much someone else had, and how we planned on conning them out of it. We were magpies, and money—even in the day when money was shells, salt, or measures of grain—money was the bright shiny thing we loved. Some of us loved it more than others. There were tricksters who had an enormous amount of wealth socked away and some, like me, who kept enough just to be comfortably off when human. Leo didn't have that same need, that drive. When he needed money, he would get it. But when you were born a trickster, you always needed it, whether you spent it or not.

I did like to spend mine.

In the alley, I opened the door to my car. It still had that wonderful new-car smell and like my last one, destroyed in November, it was red—my color and it had been since my very first trick.

It had started with an apple.

No, not *that* apple.

Just an ordinary ripe red apple and a greedy farmer who wouldn't share with a cute little girl with tangled black hair and dirty feet. He probably blamed it on not praying enough to the local fertility goddess when he woke up the next morning to find every branch of every tree bare of even a single piece of fruit, but it was just a baby trickster teaching her very first lesson. Don't be greedy, and don't take anything for granted, because something could take it all away from you.

More than nine hundred demons had apparently learned that lesson in the past six months, taking their lives for granted, or so Eli said. And I trusted Eli's word. Oh, I so did not. Not even in the womb would I have been that naïve. If all those demons had been killed, more than Eli would know about it—other demons would as well. I only had to track one down and ask him . . . or her. Unlike angels, demons would wear a male or female body—whatever it took to get the job done. Angels, on the other hand . . . I shook my head and backed out of the alley into traffic on Boulder Highway, ignored the enraged honking, and sped off. I wasn't going to ruin my good mood thinking about those chauvinistic pigeons.

I met Griffin and Zeke at Caesars Palace. Zeke had been banned from the Venetian for trying to drown in one of the canals a demon disguised as a singing, then gurgling, gondolier. He'd also been blacklisted at the Luxor for excessive buffet use in one sitting. Zeke was not precisely a Renaissance man. When it came to killing demons and loyalty, he was at the top of his game. When it came to everything else—that's why insurance existed. He either didn't get it and didn't want to get it. Or he wanted to get it and you'd better get your ass out of his way.

Twenty minutes later I was walking past centurions with much better teeth than the genuine ones had had, breathed in air touched with smoke, adrenaline, and despair, and tracked down Griffin and Zeke in one of the bars on the floor of the casino. They were in a small booth in a gloom-filled corner. That was Vegas—all blinding sun outside but always twilight inside—no matter what time of the day. Illusions were kept whole by those shadows and Vegas itself was one big illusion. Inside that illusion, Zeke was nursing a beer and his partner an untouched whiskey from the smell of it when I sat beside him. The alcohol was camouflage or at least it was supposed to be. "Someone having a bad day?" I nodded at the half-empty beer.

"We came by the pool and Zeke had to walk past the buffet." Griffin gave his partner a shoulder bump. "Like Romeo and Juliet. Star-crossed lovers destined to forever be apart." Zeke didn't respond beyond sliding down a few inches and having another swallow of beer.

"Don't worry, Romeo." I patted his hand resting on the table. "The Luxor can't have e-mailed your picture to every buffet in town and new ones are opening almost every day."

"I hate people," he grumbled. "'All you can eat' means all you can eat. Lying bastards."

I patted him again. "I know. They're very bad and I'll punish them for you, I promise." After all, it wasn't that different from the farmer and his apple, and my punishment wouldn't involve gunfire. I couldn't say the same about Zeke in action. "But let's concentrate on finding a demon to chat with right now."

"Chat." He perked up and moved his hand inside his jacket to rest on one of the guns he always carried in a shoulder holster. His Colt Anaconda wasn't one of those. I wasn't sure they made shoulder holsters big enough for a weapon of that size. "Chatting is good."

"Not that kind of chatting," Griffin corrected. "We don't kill demons. . . ."

"In front of people. We don't kill demons in front of cameras—video or digital," Zeke recited with a bored expression, before adding, "And we don't kill demons in front of puppies." He let go of his gun and used his hand to tilt the beer bottle at me. "I made up that rule myself. Apparently puppies are easily mentally scarred. Griffin brings them up in my tutoring often enough, so it's gotta be true."

Griffin had "tutored" Zeke in his decision-making skills for so long and with every scenario he could possibly bring to mind—be it saving kids versus killing demons to saving a politician versus killing demons, which was a tough one regardless of how slippery your grip on free will—that I wasn't surprised to see Zeke giving him a hard time about it. I enjoyed it, in fact. Zeke had come a long way on a very treacherous path. He deserved to dish out a little mockery.

"So I hear," I agreed solemnly. "Now, spread out and let's reel in a fish."

Griffin had his empathy to feel a demon's emotions; Zeke had his telepathy to hear their thoughts. I didn't envy either of them those abilities. The things that demons thought, the things they felt—none of it could be pleasant. As for me, I had the eyes my mama gave me, which was all I needed. I made my way through tourists who had money pouring through their fingers like sand, I studied blackjack dealers who might promise to turn Lady Luck around if given the proper incentive, but it turned out Zeke was the first to snare one. It trailed behind him like one of those puppies Griffin was so concerned about in his lesson plans. That it was

Zeke that the demon had honed in on told me something immediately. This wasn't one of the lower-level
demons. They liked the easy marks. Get in, get the IOU
on the soul, and get out. They didn't like the difficult
prey when Vegas was so full of ones they could hook in
two seconds. This demon obviously liked a challenge,
because no one put off "I don't care" and "Get the hell
away from me" like Zeke did. And while Griffin had
taught him the basics of hiding his emotions just as
Zeke had taught his partner the same about conceal-
ing thoughts, Zeke rarely could manage to completely
hide his hostility toward demons.

This one was definitely bored and thought Zeke was
his Mount Everest. That made him higher level, but
hopefully not as high as Eli was. We were in a public
place and there was only so much we could do there. But
that also meant there was only so much he could do as
well. Griffin and I made our way out of the wandering
gamblers and walked back into the bar as we saw Zeke
make his move. By the time we joined him, he was staring at the demon sitting beside him in the booth with the
same expression he would've used for regarding dog shit
on the bottom of his shoe. It didn't bother the demon,
obviously, as he continued to talk smoothly.

"Okay, I got one first," Zeke said as I, and then Griffin, sat to one side of the demon, boxing him between us
and fellow demon bait. "What do I win?"

The demon, a man with prematurely bright silver
hair, ferociously intelligent eyes, a killer tan, and an absolutely amazing accent that made you think you were
back on Fantasy Island, let his salesman smile flicker.
He knew something was up. He was a smart one all
right and that made him only more dangerous. "What
is happening? I was but speaking with my new friend.

Zeke, you said your name was, yes, my friend? I am Armand."

Zeke went back to his beer bottle with his left hand.... His right was ready and waiting for a go at his gun. "We always want the ones who don't want us. Don't take it personally," I told the demon, resting a faux friendly hand on his shoulder ... holding him here. No quick trip back to Hell for him.

"Eden House," he said flatly, the accent disappearing and the charisma going with it. The eyes went from fierce to carnivorous. He knew his potential deal had gone bad from that very moment. I was surprised that Eli let another demon almost as quick-witted as he operate in what he now considered his city. "You're supposed to all be dead."

"You shouldn't listen to gossip. Look what happened to Eve," I tsked. Eli hadn't told the other demons about my trickster status ... as he knew it anyway. That was pure demon and pure Eli. When it was nine hundred of his colleagues dead, he was concerned, but if I took out ten or twenty, that only cleared out the playing field for him a little—lessened the competition.

And if this particular competitor wanted to think I was Eden House, I didn't mind being their mascot for this conversation. "But speaking of gossip, your coworker Eligos mentioned that someone was taking you out, knoshing on you by the hundreds like marshmallow Peeps. Those are good, aren't they?" I mused. "Pink or yellow, I've never had a preference," I said with nostalgia for last year's Easter, giving a quick thank-you to the German fertility goddess, Ēostre, and her candy-loving hares. Credit where credit is due. Then I forgot about sticky sweetness and got down to business. "So, sugar, have you heard anything about that?"

"Eligos talked to you?" he said with disbelief. "An Eden House lackey, spitting feathers with every word. I sincerely doubt that."

"The last standing of our House and we talk to Eligos and walk away," Griffin said coldly. In anyone's eyes, Above or Below, that made us pretty damn tough. "We are not to be fucked with." That too.

"Something to think about, Peep," I said, my hand dropping to his leg and still anchoring him as I used my other hand to pull my Smith that I'd shoved down behind the leather cushion we were sitting on before we'd gone hunting. It was a good place to raise it, hidden in the shadows moving up behind his shoulder to bury its muzzle against the base of his spine. "And exactly what is he thinking, Zeke?" Demons didn't have to talk for us to hear. We only had to get close to one and bring up the subject.

Eli might want to have a conversation that was in our mutual . . . possibly . . . best interests, but no matter how bright another demon was, it wouldn't be Eligos. Intelligence had nothing to do with sharing information with a bitter enemy who might, in one wildly improbable circumstance, be able to help you. Intelligence could let you see that picture, but only guts or an enormous ego would let you draw it. All demons had ego, but not all of them had the spine to match. Our friend here could, but it didn't matter if he did or not. I wasn't relying on chance, not when I could rely on Zeke instead.

Zeke's focus on the demon went unblinking. Armand—what a name for a demon to appropriate— didn't care for that. He hissed and bared still-human teeth. We were in public and that mattered to him as much as it did to us. The last thing Hell wanted was for people to not only truly believe in it, but to believe that it wasn't waiting patiently, that it was actively knocking at your door to do everything it could to drag you down. Heaven wasn't the only one with recruiters. And if you were too pious and pure, then tearing you apart was a very viable second option. No, Hell didn't want that getting around any more than the late Colonel Sanders wanted his recipe for extra crispy hitting the Internet.

I put more pressure on the gun, feeling it grate against the bony processes of the demon's spine. "Keep it together, doll, and it'll be over soon enough. Then you can get back to filling up your lunch box. But in the future I'd ignore those who ignore you. They probably have a bigger bite than you do." I kept my gaze flickering from Armand to Zeke as I went on to say, "Getting anything, Kit?"

Zeke's mouth twisted. "I got it. Now let me kill him. I don't give a shit if it's in front of the whole damn casino. He needs to die. For what he's done . . . he has to die and it has to fucking hurt."

It was difficult to say what would've happened next if Armand hadn't made his move. Eden House had connections in every branch of the government, local and federal, but they preferred to use their power as subtly as possible. If an operative could make his way out of his own mess, that would be ideal. If not, Eden House would step in and pull some strings. But shooting a demon in front of hundreds of people and trying to pass it off as one of those magic tricks Vegas was so famous for when that perceived "victim" turned into a puddle, there wasn't much Eden House could or would do for you. Because in this situation you weren't ridding the world of an unholy predator, you were breaking the rules. And Eden House, much like those Upstairs, didn't care for having their rules broken.

If they had any idea what Griffin had been and what Zeke had abandoned, they would've done their level best to kill them both.

That was why I was reasonably satisfied with the way things turned out. I wasn't happy the demon escaped a no doubt well-deserved death, but to keep Zeke out of jail for whatever length of time it took to prove that no body equaled no prosecutable crime was worth it. The hissing turned to snarling and the demon slithered from between Zeke and me, went on to flip over the table in one continuous movement of sinuous speed, and was gone onto the casino floor and out into the crowd in a matter of seconds. The movement caught the bartender's attention in midswipe at the inside of a glass. Then he shrugged. Cirque du Soleil was always in town. It was a commentary on the city that demons were so easily explained away. Or perhaps it was a commentary on the peculiarities of Cirque du Soleil performers. I wasn't one to rush to judgment.

Flexibility though, that was something to think about. Maybe like Leo I should do some dating of my own. Catch a show and dinner. Killing demons was entertaining, but a girl had to eat.

I hid my gun out of sight, returned to its holster in the small of my back. "Kit?"

Zeke shook his head and finished his beer in several swallows before echoing the bartender's shrug. "Same as that son of a bitch Eligos told you about. Nine hundred some of the murdering bastards dead. Like any of us are crying over that."

Griffin shifted almost imperceptibly beside me. Zeke

frowned at him. "Don't do that. Don't think that. It's not true, okay? It's not fucking true."

"It is true. I don't remember it, but it's true." Griffin pushed away the whiskey because at that moment it had to be too much of a temptation for him.

Zeke kicked me under the table. He'd known Griffin all his human life, but Zeke had never been good with words, not the non-four-letter kind, and now he was wanting me to fix this. Although I'd give it my best, in the end it was only Griffin who could fix himself, but I gave it a shot. "You were born seventeen years ago," I told him sternly, swiveling to plant a finger in his chest. "You're a twenty-seven-year-old human being"—with wings, but no need to go into that—"who has never done anything in his entire life that wasn't for the greater good, and, even better, for the little good." When it came to the greater good, there were often civilian casualties. That's why greater was slapped on the description, so that when you cried over a dead neighbor, friend, or family member, you could remember it was for the *greater* good. Their sacrifice . . . your sacrifice . . . wasn't in vain. That's why I cherished the little good. With that, no one worthy of life died. No one was hurt. There was a happy ending and only evil fell.

With a bemused expression, Griffin looked down at my finger denting his chest. "But before that . . ."

"No, no, Griff. There was no before that. Whoever that demon was before, it doesn't matter. He died when you were born, and when you chose us over Hell, you put a headstone and wreath on his grave. You're Griffin, no one else, and if Zeke won't smack you for thinking differently, then I will. Clear?" I asked with one last poke of my finger to his expensive shirt. "Or should I go on?"

"Unless you plan on sticking your entire hand in my chest and pulling out my heart to show me how big and wholesome it is," he said, "I think I have it."

"Big, wholesome, and bright and shiny as a parade of Valentine's hearts. I promise you that. Want a peek at my emotions to know if I'm telling the truth?" I offered. I could drop the shield that protected me against psychic incursions. I rarely did, but for my guys, I made exceptions. And when it came to situations like this, I didn't think twice.

"No. The offer is enough. That you believe is enough." He pretended to smooth his shirt. Zeke growled. "And you too," Griffin added. "I think that would go without saying though."

"Like you listen to me." Zeke slid out of the booth. "Did you believe me when I said the house on the corner was a meth lab? No."

"I did too believe you. I just thought you should let them blow themselves up, not do the job for them." Griffin exited the other side. "It would've happened sooner or later. They didn't have kids . . . or puppies. There was no hurry."

"It smelled. It made my eyes water." Zeke waited for Griffin to pay the bill. He was of the opinion that he provided a public service like a policeman and like a policeman, he deserved food and drink for free. That he didn't have a badge to prove it was the only flaw in his plan.

Griffin passed over some bills, waved off the change, and walked out with us. "I guess I should be grateful you waited until they were out before you blew up their house."

Zeke didn't appear the least bit sheepish. "Coincidence is a . . ." He let the words trail off, at a loss.

I tried to help. "Wonderful thing? Convenient thing? Fated thing?"

He shifted his shoulders. "Eh, it's a thing." And that was good enough for him. By this time we'd hit the casino floor and were headed for an exit. Griffin was about to swat him hard on the back of his head. I saw his hand rising, when a centurion moved in front of us, blocking us from the nearest exit.

The costumed throwback to Colosseum days said with a dazzling smile, "Render unto Caesar that which is Caesar's. Render unto God that which is God's—your middle finger will do nicely. And render unto me any and all sexual favors. A good deal of Rome did and who can blame them." He spread his shield and sword to show off what the fake armor covered. "Not their souls, of course. Most of them belonged to Hades or Pluto or whoever you had running the Roman underworld then, slim pickings in those days, but everything else . . . a never-ending feast of orgies and death. And *damn* it was good! Can I get a hallelujah?" He frowned at us. "No? Not even one?" Then he shrugged and that smile was back again. "But now there's Vegas, which is almost as good as Rome, plus there's air-conditioning and deodorant, because, seriously, it did get a bit rank at times back then."

"Eli, how did your pet tattle so fast? No telepathy among you lizards." I folded my arms. I had nothing to fear from him here. This was far more public than the bar had been.

"My cell. I gave you my card, but you never call anymore." He sang lightly, "You don't bring me flowers, you don't sing me love songs. . . ." Once he stopped the singing, his face darkened. "Do not bother Amdusias." That would have to be Armand. "He is a duke, like me. If he were to kill you before I have my chance, I would be very disappointed."

"You are a duke, aren't you?" My smile was as bright as his had been earlier. "A mere duke with a measly sixty legions of demons to your name. Aw, I feel for you, sugar. Always the bridesmaid, never the bride. Always a duke, never emperor. Never Lucifer himself." I'd studied so much demonology in my day, I would've owned Aleister Crowley's ass in Satanic Trivial Pursuit and had time left over to kick it in Unholy Pictionary too.

Eli stepped closer, dropping the sword beside his well-muscled leg. I noticed it was a real sword, unlike the fakes provided to Caesars's usual centurions, and even sharper than the ones once used by gladiators. Most certainly not OSHA approved. "A duke in Hell, but a king everywhere else, sweetheart. And do not ever forget it." He leaned in and nuzzled my hair. "Amdusias is a duke as well, one who used to have thirty legions of his own. We both have fewer now, thanks to one of yours. And he does my scut work for the privilege of being in my mere presence. Eager to learn. And good lackeys are hard to find." He inhaled, then exhaled, the air rustling past my neck with an unnatural heat. "Oranges and honey. It's not only on you, but part of you. I could lay you down in an orange grove, Trixa, and cover you with that honey."

"Then you could eat me, and not in a way women usually care for." I gave him a push hard enough to move him back a few inches.

He grinned, unrepentant. "We all have our particular preferences, but we could have sex first and *then* I could eat you. I aim to please."

"You aim anywhere and everywhere and leave a trail

of blood wherever you go," I replied. Zeke was growling at my shoulder, but he knew better than to interfere. I knew demons and I knew how their brains worked . . . murderous mazes reflected in manic mirrors. They were twisted, but not insane. I'd faced worse than demons, far worse . . . and run away, but that's another story. "And why are you so sure this is one of my kind?"

"It's not Heaven; it's not Hell. There is no rhyme or reason to the levels of demons killed. No gain for an upper to take out a UPS-level demon. So that leaves only the *païen*. You and yours are always so full of surprises. It's why I like you, and I do so so like you." He saluted, his sword and fist banging his chest. "Hail, Trixa. To the end of our days. And they will end . . . for one of us." Cocky smile still in place, he melted back into the crowd until he was gone.

"Armand is his second in command, then," Griffin said, moving up beside me.

"Armand is a snack who's currently picking up Eligos's dry cleaning and having his car detailed," I corrected. "Useful for a while, but still a snack when all's said and done. Like Eli said, there's no point in a higher demon eating a lower one, but sucking the energy from one close to your level, that's worthwhile. And either Armand doesn't get it or he's hoping to turn the tables."

"He's stupid, then," Zeke offered as he rocked back and forth on his heels, already bored.

"Not stupid, Kit, but not quite as bright as his boss." He might be a duke in Hell, but he was no Eligos. The clock was ticking on him. My only regret was I wouldn't be there to see it hit midnight. Looking from left to right at my boys, I changed the subject. "Who wants lunch? My treat." Because when you didn't pay, it really was a treat. "But snap snap." I pulled out my phone and punched in a number. Why is it that the clairvoyant never call *you* first? I have a psychic to talk to." And, depending on what he told me, the clock was ticking on him too. Only much faster.

    Tick.

    Tock.

Chapter 3

The buffet owner did have it coming. First he tried to turn Zeke away at the door. Zeke was right: "All you can eat" means all you can eat—not all you can eat if you have a reasonably expandable stomach. If you mean all you can eat, excluding metabolism freaks who can eat their own weight in steak and crab legs before even beginning to eye the dessert bar, then you should note that on the sign.

Lesson one: Roaches in food? That's simply embarrassing. Fingertips? . . . That only gets credit if you chop off your own finger for a free meal. For that I have to hoist the flag of respect and salute. That is true commitment and hard to find in a human—such infants in their conning ways. In the old days, before I was stripped of my trickster powers, I would've put a goat in the salad bar, where it would have complacently grazed away. But in the here and now, I had to deal with what I had to work with . . . my brain and a few hundred in cash. It was amazing. You could go to the pet store, buy an on-the-smaller-size boa constrictor, smuggle it into a buffet in your shoulder bag, turn it loose in the pasta bar, eat up while screaming patrons ran in all directions, leave, return the snake—because, say, it didn't match your stripper wardrobe, get your money back, and the only downside was Griffin complaining there was a scale in his gelato.

He was awfully fastidious for an ex-demon, but as I'd told him and completely believed, he was human now. Or a peri if one wanted to be specific. Peris in mythology were half demon, half angel. In reality, they were expatriate angels who found Earth more to their liking than Heaven and obtained permission to "go native."

I'd met a few peris of the ex-angel persuasion, but Griffin was the first demon one—the only demon one in existence. But I know he preferred thinking of himself as human rather than peri because of all the "ex" that went with the label, which was fine by me. All humans, *any* human, should be as good as my boy Griff. We parted ways at the buffet parking lot. I headed back to the pet shop and then home.

The psychic I was meeting back at Trixsta wasn't half as fastidious or one-tenth as good as my boy. I'd told that poor little girl Anna to stay away from psychics and I'd told her that with good reason. There were three kinds of psychics in this world. First, there was the fake. . . . Everyone has to make a living and if you're that naïve, I could let a human do a trickster's work and not lose any sleep over it.

Second, there was the real thing. Usually human and connected to a plane of existence only they could see. To them, the world was one huge clock . . . every piece doing its part, every cog turning, and everything as it should be, no matter how horrible. They would never tell you ahead of time, but they'd smile sorrowfully as that bus finally ran your granny down and pat you on the back with a "There, there. What's meant to be is meant to be. But cheer up. She's one with the universe now."

Big comfort.

Big asses . . . but technically I couldn't punish them, but that didn't mean I didn't want to.

Third was also the real deal, but they didn't give a damn about philosophy or fate, Granny or the bus. They only wanted cold hard cash, and I understood that. You paid for something and they gave it to you. Trouble was, the second kind of psychics were right—as much as you might want to hate them for it. Things couldn't be changed. What will be . . . Well, everyone knows the rest of that saying. But these third kind of psychics *would* tell you. The second type wouldn't mention Granny and the bus. You'd find out in the fullness of time and they'd give you your money back with a smile of pity. They dealt in the light and the way, and that way, the best they'd discovered so far, happened to be blissful ignorance. Number three had no such compunction. Not only would he or she tell you about Granny but they'd even tell you the number of the bus that was going to run her muumuu-loving, orthopedic-shoe-wearing self down. Then they'd put your money away and shove you out the door to make room for the next client. The bastards wouldn't even bother to give you a Kleenex on your way out. And they definitely didn't leave you any money to soak up those tears either.

That's why I used only the third kind. They were sons of bitches, but they told you the truth, all of it. But I made absolutely sure that I wanted to know the truth before asking. Once it was out there, there was no taking it back, no matter how much you wanted to. That meant I didn't use psychics often. They weren't worth the pain or the money, and I usually could guess the future as clearly as they could see it. And the times that I couldn't, when people died . . . family died, it would be too bad for the psychic I was with when I lost control because I couldn't accept what they told me.

Fate. If you can't accept it, don't tempt it.

"You're late," came the complaint as soon as I walked into the bar.

"Galileo," I sighed, dumping my bag and taking him in as he finished off his—I counted the plates—seventh plate of potato skins and cheese sticks. "You're looking . . . your handsome usual self."

Four hundred and fifty pounds if he was an ounce, he beamed over four double chins and patted greasy fingers on his Hawaiian shirt that sported hula girls and rather obscene monkeys peering up the grass skirts. "You know what they say at the Vatican, the sun doesn't revolve around the earth. It revolves around me."

I sat down opposite him, wondering idly for a moment if I could actually feel the pull of a gravity well, then got down to the matter at hand, because, quite frankly, the less of Galileo I had to put up with, the better. He might come off cheerful as Santa on vacation, feeding the slots and catching a show, but he was a shark through and through for his forty-some years. Too bad for him that made him about six inches long with a teeny tiny dorsal fin and sitting across from Jaws. "I need to ask you a question. I'd ask how much, but I believe you've already eaten your fee and then some." I flicked a finger against one of the plates to make a ringing note hover in the air. "So I'm thinking we'll make this an even trade."

He laughed and smoothed a plump hand over what few black strands he had left for a seven-inch comb-over. "Sassy Trixa. Always joking, but you send me a client now and then, although this is your first time asking for yourself. Interesting. Interesting. So, I'm thinking, how's 'bout an even four grand? And maybe I get to see you in a hula skirt to match my shirt?"

I sent only the clients I thought tough enough to hear what they wanted to know to him. Not like little lost Anna. Her type I would never send to be gobbled up by Galileo Riogas. I smiled at him. "What a funny one you are. I like a man who makes me laugh." Four thousand dollars my gym-aching ass. Let's see how much of a shark he could be when he met the real thing. "And I do love to laugh." I put my elbows on the table, rested my chin in cupped hands, and asked him to do something I never had before—not in the days when I'd been undercover. "Why don't you see how I laugh, Galileo? In my eyes. Look. See how I laugh." My smile widened. "See *why* I laugh."

And he did look . . . because he had no idea what he was looking into.

Dark brown eyes widened to show the jaundiced yellow around them. His sausage fingers gripped the table hard. His voice struggled from a tight throat, and I think if he could've kept the words to himself he would have. But he wasn't strong enough. "I see . . . forests. Mountains. Deserts. Seas. I see animals with your eyes. I see . . . What is that?" He tried to close his eyes, but it didn't work out for him. "It floats. It floats like water come to life, with a thousand fireflies swimming in it, every color there is. It's heading for the sky, an iridescent phoenix." That was very poetic of him. Who knew he had that rattling around in his heartless lump of a body?

No human, no one that wasn't family, except for Leo, had ever seen me. The true me—as I'd been born. For tricksters it was our last line of defense—the ultimate truth beyond all our trickery. It was sacred, putting the face on all of our lies. Showing the man behind the curtain in the merry old land of Oz. I let this lump see mine because I wanted immediate and total cooperation . . . and because the image likely had fried that bit of his brain. He wouldn't remember for more than a minute at most.

He'd shut his eyes for a second time, succeeding for a moment, but they wouldn't stay closed. He didn't want to see, but at the same time he did. Curiosity, it didn't just take out the cats. People were far worse when it came to being nosy. Galileo, no cat and as nosy as they came, swallowed and leaned back. "The colors are gone." He swallowed again. "I see teeth and fangs and blood. I see . . . no . . . I hear you. I hear you laughing."

I tilted my head. "I told you I liked to laugh." I did laugh, once in a while, over flowing blood, but there had never been anyone who hadn't deserved to lose that blood. "Leo," I called. "Why don't you come here and visit for a second? Galileo has never looked deep into your gorgeous eyes either." I grabbed the man's arm as he started to get up. "Oh no. That's bad manners, Galileo. Don't be that way." My smile faded. "Like you shouldn't have been that way when I sent a Mr. Jake Stein to see you. I've told you before, I screen them, but some slip through and I don't know what you'll see in their future. I told you to let a fish go now and again if the truth might be too much for them to handle, but you didn't. You say you saw colors? I never hid my true colors from you, but you didn't listen. You told him the truth and whatever truth that was made him hang himself in his family's garage. Now"—I tightened my grip on his sweat-slick arm—"let's see what happens to you when you see Leo's truth."

"But . . . that can't be you." He was still trying to pull away as Leo approached from behind the bar, but con-

sidering the most weight he lifted in a day would be an
order of two double cheeseburgers to go, he didn't have
much success. "The blood. The fur and scales and your
smile. God, that *smile*." He was a psychic. He knew about
vampires and werewolves and things that go bump in the
night, but one little trickster, that he couldn't believe?

Then Leo was certainly going to be educational for
him.

Leo pulled up a chair beside me as I squeezed Galileo's arm. "A smile is just a frown turned upside down.
What do you think, Leo?"

Galileo's gaze moved to Leo's black eyes and he froze.
He stopped trying to pull away, he didn't blink, and I was
positive he gave up on breathing for a while. After almost
a minute he sucked in a breath, whistling and weak, and
moaned, "The end. You almost ended it. Ended us all.
You tore down mountains, boiled oceans, nearly pulled
down the sky. You were the Omega before there was an
Alpha, and you did it for no reason. For *no reason*."

"Boredom is a reason." Leo gave a shrug of accep-
tance. "And I'm in a program. I'm in recovery now. Ten
thousand years Ragnarok free."

Galileo crossed himself, several times, and was turning a rather pretty if unhealthy shade of lavender. I honestly didn't care. Fate was fate, after all. Maybe that man
I sent to him, Stein, would've killed himself regardless of
what Galileo told him, but if the son of a bitch had kept
to our referral agreement, I wouldn't have to be wondering about it now. I'd been meaning to take care of the
situation for a few weeks now and this was an opportunity to both clarify and conduct a business arrangement.
I've always been a great believer in time management.

"Galileo," I said patiently.

Nothing.

I sighed and snapped my fingers in front of his glazed eyes with a little less patience as he muttered the Lord's Prayer under his breath, getting a good deal of it wrong. A very lapsed Catholic with an equally poor memory. "Galileo, before you have a heart attack or stroke, whichever you seem racing toward right now, I need to know what's killing the demons? More than nine hundred in six months. What's doing that?" I pulled a piece of folded paper from my jeans pocket and pushed it across the table to him, pulling one of his hands out of a praying position and slapping the wet palm on top of it. Within that doubled-up simple yellow piece of paper, a Post-it Note actually—so mundane and ordinary—was a scrap of demon ichor left from last night when Griffin and Zeke had brought in the one-winged, mentally absent demon. That hadn't been mundane and ordinary at all.

"Come on, Galileo," I prodded. "It's right there. Right under your hand, right in front of your eyes. What do you see?"

I was hoping he wouldn't shut down as Zeke had. Zeke was a telepath, but Galileo was a psychic. Zeke saw some things; Galileo saw everything, and no matter how worthless a creature, he excelled at it. Elvis might have been the King of Rock and Roll, but Galileo was the King of Psychics . . . at least in Vegas, probably in the entire Western Hemisphere. He was disgusting, perverted, greedy, and an entire dictionary full of more slimy adjectives, but he did know his business. He didn't have talent. He had Talent with a capital T, and throw a little boldface on there while you're at it. Zeke was good, but no better than your average angel . . . ex or otherwise. Galileo was an Einstein, and one with an excellent sense of survival. He might be able to see from a safer mental distance with that talent of his.

If it didn't burn out like a flickering lightbulb. Zeke had gone down. If Galileo went down, considering his physical health, he might not get back up. As long as he did it after giving over the information . . . what will be, will be. The psychics said it often enough—now one of them would have to live with it.

Or not.

If Galileo had ever done a selfless thing in his life, I might have cared. But I knew his type. I'd known those like him for a long, long time. They were born without that ability to care for anyone but themselves. Despite psychology textbooks, loving yourself doesn't automatically mean others will love you. My hand might rest on the back of his, but I wasn't feeling any love. "The demon blood, Galileo. What took the demon? What destroyed his mind? And hurry up," I added, "because you're looking a mite peaked there, sugar."

The pale violet color of his round moon-pie face was only darkening. Leo exhaled and heaved out of the chair. "I'll call 911. If you get anything out of him before he hits the floor, dinner's on me."

"Galileo," I said sharply. "Now. *Now*. Tell me what you see."

His lips framed a word, but I didn't hear it. He tried again. "Sic . . . kle." He wheezed and repeated, "Sickle."

His forehead hit the table with a thunk, but he was still there . . . barely, but still there, eyes rolled back—the yellow a dull shine. "Am . . . I . . . dying?"

"Galileo, sweetie." I patted his hand that rested beneath mine. "You're the psychic. You tell me."

He'd live, the EMTs said, although their best guess was that he'd end up in open-heart surgery.

If so, the surgeons would probably pull Wilbur from

Charlotte's Web plus his five piggy cousins out of the
man's heart, and he'd live to destroy someone else's
hopes prematurely. Take away their few days of blissful
ignorance that they had left to them.

What will be will be.

Or maybe not. Maybe Galileo had learned his lesson when he was allowed a peek behind the curtain. He
hadn't seen the wizard, that was for sure. I didn't pass out
hearts, courage, and brains—I tested them. And Leo ...
Leo in the past would've taken them and kept them on
a shelf as souvenirs. So perhaps Galileo would behave.
As a matter of fact, he'd damn well better, I grumbled
internally as I cleaned the table he'd collapsed onto. Leo
had hauled away the dishes, but there was still an ample
amount of drool and crumbs to take care of. The psychic
wasn't a neat eater by any stretch of the imagination.
He ate like a fifteen-year-old toothless Saint Bernard,
spreading morsels of food up to six feet away.

Oh yes, he'd better behave. I would never forget
Jake Stein, a hopeful man with even more hopeful eyes
shortly followed by a noose. And I wouldn't forget this
outrageous mess either. Galileo didn't need a lobster
bib; he needed a tablecloth tied around what passed for
his neck.

"A sickle. That's all you were able to get?"

I looked over my shoulder with ill temper at Leo's
patronizing tone. "I could've gotten more if you'd held
back a bit. I wanted you to give him a glimpse of the
Loki trailer, not the whole movie, IMAX and all. You're
the one who all but stuffed a grenade into his heart and
pulled the pin."

"Sometimes an artist needs recognition of his work.
Past or not," he said complacently as his hand moved
in a brisk slapping motion toward my ass. The ill tem-

per on my face darkened into something that would've blown Galileo's heart to pieces just like that metaphorical hand grenade and destroyed everything else within a fifty-mile range.

Leo let his hand drop casually as if it had been a joke all along and he would never possibly ever consider slapping me on the ass no matter how frisky he was feeling. Men. Gods. Or a mixture of the two. All the same. "Remembering the bad old days get you a little worked up there?" I lifted my eyebrows. "Just don't forget why everyone who knows you or has heard of you or done a book report on you calls them the bad old days, all right?"

He grunted and fetched another towel to help me. "I won't forget. I won't go back. You know that."

"I do," I said, and smacked him on the butt instead. And I did know. I had more faith in Leo than anyone in the world except my mama. The two of them tied.

"And I didn't boil an ocean." He used the towel to return the favor, locker-room style, before finishing up the crumbs on the floor. "It was a lake. A very large lake, granted, but just a lake. And despite my past lake-boiling abilities, I don't know what we're supposed to glean from "sickle." Knowing Galileo, he most likely wanted a Popsicle to satisfy his sweet tooth before he shuffled off his mortal coil. Assuming there is anyone or anything large enough to shuffle that mass off anywhere."

"If he did mean death," I groaned, and sat down in Galileo's vacated chair. It was still warm. It was also still in one piece. Amazing. "That could be almost anyone or anything on my list. How many are on your list?"

"Mmm. About ten. The same as are on your list, only I was capable of putting mine in alphabetical order." He sat too as another of our regulars wandered in out of the afternoon light. Leo jerked his thumb at the bar. "Help yourself." That was also fairly regular around here. Our customers didn't cheat us, not our regulars. They didn't have to be psychic like Galileo to know better; they just knew . . . like a rabbit knows to hold still in the grass when the hawk soars overhead. Bunnies liked to fuck, but bunnies did not like to be fucked up. Our regulars were as smart as those rabbits . . . almost. They paid their tabs promptly and never eavesdropped. Everyone had an agenda. They were perfectly happy with theirs: alcoholic oblivion.

"Leave me alone," I said crossly. "I don't like A's." One time, the closest time that I was almost eaten, it was by an A. It was embarrassing. And not a little terrifying, as much as I hated to admit that anything could terrify me—me, Trixa, badass trickster. But if you don't admit to the truth, then you end up as something's lunch and that beat embarrassing every time.

There were things bigger and badder than me out there. Even some demons, despite how I spelled out the ranking. Regular demons no, but there were demons in Hell so horrific they couldn't come to Earth without destroying the ground beneath them and setting fire to the air they breathed. If Heaven had gotten one thing right, it was keeping them and Lucifer in Hell for eternity, because they were part of Hell itself. Embedded in it, one with their prison, there was no escape for their kind.

Technically that made me correct in my ranking . . . tricksters outranked demons; reading the fine print wasn't necessary. But there were creatures on Earth, *païen* creatures, creatures that began with an *A*, that could put an end to me, a very unpleasant end—to me and nine hundred demons. Unlike demons, however, they were completely mad, and while there weren't as many as there had been, it didn't matter. As long as there was one left and that one came for you, you ran until you couldn't run any farther. I wasn't saying I wouldn't go out without a fight, but some fights you can't win . . . and that's why you run and why you don't put your list in Leo's anal-retentive alphabetic order because *A*'s were a bad letter. They deserved to be on the bottom of the list or, better yet, on the back of the list where you didn't have to look at the name.

I wrapped my finger in the gold chain of my necklace. "In fact, let's just assume it's not the *A* one, because if it is, there's nothing we can do about it and if they want to eat demons, better demons than us."

Leo took my other hand, rubbed his thumb across the back of it, and said with absolute belief, "It's not them."

I nodded. "No, it's not." I clasped his hand hard. "So let's take a look at the other nasties."

"And none of them tried to eat you?" Leo asked with an affectionate humor that had me pinching the nerve in his hand instead of just holding it. "With your sparkling personality and gentle easygoing nature? You're sure?"

"I didn't say that. And one does have a scar in an area he might have been fond of at one time, but him I can handle. And I do sparkle. Shine like the sun, the moon, the stars, and every silver or gold coin I stole in the good old days." I smiled, good mood restored, because it still was the good old days for me. Leo had changed his ways, but mine didn't need changing.

We ended up laughing about long-past adventures as we made our way down that list. It made it easier. It balanced it out. Bad guy, good memory. Very bad guy, very good memory. Even worse guy, memories with huge gaping holes thanks to the massive amounts of wine we'd drunk that particular time.

Then suddenly closing time had come and the only progress we'd made was to have a good time reminiscing. But in my book, having a good time is the best progress you can make in almost any situation. Leo went home and I went upstairs to my apartment. I undressed, slipped into my favorite silk pajamas, brushed my teeth, and slept with all those memories swirling in bright colors. Wonderful dreams. Wonderful night.

All the better to make the morning even worse in comparison.

Chapter 4

Roses are red.

Sometimes.

The one was, and it was beautiful, starting at the bottom with the pure deep crimson that was almost black, the red of the setting sun disappearing into twilight. The petals then gradually lightened to a vivid deep red the exact color of freshly spilled blood. The flower wasn't full-blown, but a curve of a fresh bud not yet realizing its potential. Curves were good. I liked curves, whether on myself, because a woman should have curves, or in the impossible-to-follow swerves and convolutions of what passed for the thought processes of the male species. Males trying to wrap their minds around a concept that didn't involve a football or pulling a trigger. They were cute that way, like homicidal puppies. Curves of the body and curves of the mind.

As for color ...

Red was my favorite. Red like fire, a little arson warmed a girl's heart. But what was tied around the rose pulled away your attention too fast to dwell on the color.

I should've enjoyed the rose. Most women like flowers, right? I should've put it in a vase filled with water. After all, red was more than my favorite; it was my signature, how I signed my work as a trickster. What was wrapped around the rose was the same sort of thing . . . only a preemptive version.

Less of a "Gotcha" and more of a "Here I come, ready or not."

We were in no way ready for this.

So it was at eight, for once not sleeping in, that I stood and stared at the rose lying on the scarred and stained surface of my bar. Help me, Earth, Sun, and Sky. What were we going to do now?

I continued to stare at the rose, was utterly ignored by the Earth, Sun, and Sky, and finally decided to put it in a vase after all. I filled one from beneath the sink and carefully picked up the flower by its green stem. That same stem was wrapped in that black silk ribbon with an absolutely perfect bow. I made sure the material didn't touch the water. This was someone I did not want to insult, piss off, or even slightly annoy with the slightest hint of disrespect. One trailing black end of the glossy material was embossed with gold lettering. Only a few letters, a calling card if you will. It read KPONYΣ.

It almost looked as if it were English, if only with sharper angles than usual on the letters and the last symbol. It wasn't though. It was Greek. I read a lot of languages and spoke even more. You picked up quite a bit when you wandered about like I did. But your average sorority girl or frat boy could've read this too. And if they couldn't, they would've had to bong a beer for not memorizing the Greek alphabet, while standing on one foot, hopping up and down, and also, again, bonging a beer.

I'd taught some truly exceptionally entertaining lessons at colleges.

I studied the name with the same exquisite caution

that I would use in studying how to defuse a live bomb. Really, the two weren't that different. Cronus was either in town or was on his way. Neither was good. Considering the mutilated catatonic demon, I was guessing it was the first, which was far less than good. Leo and I had tried to figure out who could wipe out that many demons in so little time. Here was our answer.

The Greek legend, which for once was fairly close to the real thing, said Cronus was something other than a god. True enough. He was a Titan—he *birthed* gods, and was considered a creature of chaos and disorder. I, myself, rather approved of those two qualities, but he had taken it to an extreme. He was the only one in the world who could claim that he had reigned in Hell and ruled in Heaven—only Hell was Tartarus and Heaven was the Elysian Fields. One of the many pagan or *païen* versions of the final resting places of many religions, human and *païen*. Some human religions had one Heaven and Hell each and some religions had hundreds; we *païen* have thousands. Cronus had once dominated two of them. Two was enough.

Cronus was the seed to the Grim Reaper myth down to the sickle for harvesting souls instead of wheat and he'd been more than good at it.

Sickle. Galileo had been on the money, if not more articulate about it. Cronus and his sickle.

Then after years beyond the telling, Cronus left both Tartarus and the Fields and took to roaming the earth and it wasn't to spread justice or show off martial arts skills. No, far from it. Too bad he'd missed that *Kung Fu* show from the seventies. It might have mellowed him— doubtful though. Raging psychos rarely saw the silver lining, the rainbows, enjoyed the purr of a basketful of happy kittens.

Raging psycho would be a step up for Cronus. No, it was better to be accurate in situations like this. More than a step. It would be a whole staircase of them. Raging psychos were in preschool learning what Cronus had several doctorate degrees in. He didn't own the field, but it was safe to say he was MVP and then some.

"What's that?"

I looked over my shoulder to see Leo coming out of the back office. He was up and at work early too. After he saw this he might turn around and go home. I wouldn't blame him. Take that exotic dancer of his on a trip to Tahiti. Morocco in Tahiti, what could be more appropriate?

I nudged the vase with the rose down the bar toward him with one finger, my short nail eerily matching the petals above. "Bows don't necessarily go on presents."

"Cronus," he said. "Shit. Holy fucking shit."

While that was serious language for Leo, who had preferred ending worlds as opposed to cursing, it about summed it up. Cronus . . . he was all kinds of shit and then some.

"Yes. Cronus." I folded my arms, one wide gold cuff filigree bracelet glittering in the light. Wonder Woman had nothing on me. And we . . . we had nothing on Cronus. We hadn't even put him on our list, because it would've been ludicrous. Overkill. Like making a list of what could possibly ruin your camping trip. Rain. Cold. Bugs. Or an asteroid the size of the moon hitting your tent dead on. Cronus was the asteroid. It simply didn't pop to mind. Unfortunately, there were no coincidences in life. It was Cronus behind all this, simply because anything else that could take on that many demons would *still* shag ass as far from Cronus as it could get. Where the Titan stepped, all the *païen* world fled his shadow.

There was a new sheriff in town. And he was the kind that when he accomplished his business and left town, the town itself tended not to be there anymore.

Crumbling ruin.

Scorched earth.

Burned bones.

And one rose to leave on the grave.

"At least it's not the Auphe," Leo said as we both stared at the ribbon wrapped around the rose. The Auphe had been the *A* scribbled on the back of my list.

"Shhh," I hushed immediately. Just as back in the slightly older days when humans didn't say the devil's name for fear he would appear, we *païen* felt close to the same way about the Auphe. The less said about them, the better. The less thought about them, the better. The less everything about them, the better. Nature's first and best predator. Nature's first and best psychopathic murderers. Nature's first really big fuckup. I knew exactly where I was on the badass scale and I was varsity all the way when I was at full trickster status, but the Auphe? No one fucked with the Auphe.

Subject was over.

"Have you talked to him lately?" I asked. Lately for Leo, a benched god, could've been yesterday or five thousand years ago. I hadn't ever talked to him. I'd never seen him. I didn't want to. When I'd talked about that ranking of gods, tricksters, and demons, I'd left a few rungs out. Cronus was above gods and that would most likely make me nothing more than an annoying chirpy cricket in his eyes.

"Lately?" Leo grimaced. "Try never. He did send me the . . . ah . . . equivalent of a thumbs-up when I was toying with the world-destroying hobby. And don't ask what he sent. You don't want to know, but they—or what was left of them—did have a ribbon on them just like this one. I think"—he touched the ribbon with a careful finger—"it's his way of saying if we don't bother him, he won't bother us."

"You mean you," I pointed out. "He won't bother you. He might accidentally step on me and scrape me off the bottom of his shoe when he found the nearest curb."

"Not exactly eloquent, but not exactly wrong either." Leo decided eight thirty in the a.m. was fine by him to break out the liquor, opening a beer for me and then himself. "He spawned the great Greek horndog god Zeus, who would rape anything living and hump anything not. And with Zeus being a vast improvement over his father, I don't want to even guess what Cronus would do . . . to anyone, not now."

"Now that he's insane?" I prodded.

"He was always insane. Let's say, over time, probably exponentially more insane." Leo took a swallow of his beer.

"Well, we do know what he would do in one particular case. Demons." I tasted my own beer before getting my cell phone and making the call. Voice mail. I'd only called Eligos twice now since he'd hit Vegas last year and both times I'd gotten voice mail. How he made his quota, I had no idea. My Avon lady had five times his work ethic. If you can't reach a demon, you can't sign over your soul, now can you?

"Why?" Leo had already finished his beer and started on his second, which he tapped against the phone.

"Because he knows the what and we now know the who. Put it together and maybe we'll know the real why." I gave up on the beer and decided bad news of this sort called for something a little more efficient in perking up your mood. Godiva dark chocolate liqueur. I kept it for me and me only. It made one helluva martini and dessert mixed in one. That was the great thing about being human. Instant chocolate, instant endorphins.

"Again, why? Whatever it is that Cronus wants or is doing, there's nothing we can do but stay out of his way. And I'd have said the same thing last year before we were both temporarily demoted." He watched as I whipped up the world's fastest sugar-loaded orgasm, studying me intently before accusing, "But you're curious, aren't you?"

"Among other things." I told him those other things as I coated the martini glass in a slow slide of chocolate, then admitted, "But curiosity is one of them. That's why you'll always be an amateur trickster, studly, never a pro."

"Because I can suspend my curiosity and trickster-loving ways to not die a horrible death?" he said dryly.

"If you're careful enough, you don't have to die." The chocolate was all I'd hoped, the alcohol a little less. "And the curiosity isn't actually a choice. You're born with it."

"Like scaly sex appeal." The air shimmered across the bar and then Eli was sitting on a stool. He was wearing a brown bathrobe, expensive naturally, and his normally sleek pelt of straight hair was rumpled from sleep. Demons actually slept. There was an interesting fact. Or maybe they only slept while transformed into their human costumes. Regardless, I was glad he'd bothered with the robe, because I knew there was nothing beneath it. Eli in pj's—I just couldn't see it. He yawned and went on. "I'm assuming whatever you found out is earth shattering . . . as in a 'Kennedy killed Marilyn Monroe and her corpse rose from the grave to pull a zombie-revenge assassination' category of earth shattering. Because it is that early in the morning. That goddamn early." He cheered as he brushed a hand over his hair. "You want to know who really *did* kill them? If you're as curious as you say you are, maybe we could arrange a trade. I know you don't have a soul, not the kind I can take, but I have quite a few things I could think of that you could cough up that would make me a very happy demon."

"Happy? Really?" I smiled, put down the martini glass, lifted the rose from the vase, and tossed it to him. He caught it effortlessly and with an inhuman speed I'd unfortunately had to give up for a while. Turning it in his hand, he saw the ribbon . . . and read the name on it. "Happy now?" I asked. I didn't have to be curious about that, because I knew the answer.

One big fat no.

Since Eligos was in his human body, it had the same human reaction as any human body. He paled slightly. I was impressed. A lesser demon/human would've probably vomited on the bar. "This had best not be some pathetic version of a trickster joke," he said with a quiet as darkly malignant as a newborn cancer cell.

"Trust me, sugar, even I don't think this is funny." I returned to the martini. "We all liked it much better when Cronus was stuck in Tartarus or had that bipolar happy moment and skipped around the Elysian Fields keeping things in order. But those days are over. He's here in this world now. Has been for a few hundred years, but this is the first time he's decided to have fun. But for the life of me, I can't think why killing demons would be that entertaining for him. Like swatting a fly. A slow-moving, half-dead fly. Where's the sport?"

"There has to be a reason," Leo added. "Cronus is

mad as they come, but even if killing your kind were entertaining for him, he'd have still bored of it long before nine hundred."

Eli ignored the "reason" topic, which meant he knew the reason and had known it most likely when he'd had his chat with me at the car dealership. That made him more deceitful than I'd given him credit for and I'd given him very high credit in that department. It was too bad about him being a murdering sociopathic spawn of Hell. We tricksters did love deceit. If he were a peacock, his feathers would be brilliant, bright, and attracting every female in sight. But he wasn't a vain bird. He was a killer and right now a stronger and quicker one than I was. I kept that in mind as I regarded him over a surface of rippling chocolate. I also kept in mind that I was smarter. False modesty could kiss my ass.

"Where did you get this?" he asked, dropping it onto the bar.

"It was left on the doorstep. I found it when I got up this morning." I sipped.

"And why did he leave it here . . . for you?"

"Insane doesn't always have to mean impolite, but to be honest," I said, surprised the air didn't sizzle on my tongue when I uttered that word, "it's less for me than for Leo. Cronus was a . . . a fan, I guess you'd say . . . of his work. He has a certain respect for him, rather like you would for a precocious three-year-old who drew you an especially pretty picture for the refrigerator."

Leo growled at me but confirmed, "If we stay out of his way, he won't obliterate us. Maybe. But we know the same isn't true for you. Too bad." He gave a rumble of amusement. "Yes, too damn bad." Leo didn't out and out grin often, but he did now as he finished off his second beer.

"You wouldn't know why Cronus is into killing help-less little minnows like you, do you?" I gave Eli a second chance to tell us the why . . . although the why was only half of what I was interested in—the how I could use it to my benefit was something I was invariably interested in. "Don't want to share? Sharing's good for the . . . mmm . . . whoops. Not the soul obviously. Psychological well-be-ing?" I leaned over the bar and smelled the rose still in his hand. "Assuming you have a being to house that psyche in." I looked into eyes that were distant, the bits of copper bright in churning thought. "And, Eli? Sweetie, that's one assumption you can't be making for too long, you hear?"

He heard all right. Enough so that he was gone, bath-robe and all, but he left the rose behind on the stool. Off to Hell to tell his boss and up the food chain it would go . . . all the way to the top—or maybe bottom would be more appropriate. I walked around and replaced the flower in the vase before resting a hand on Leo's shoul-der to whisper in his ear, completing what I'd been tell-ing him while making the martini.

After nearly a minute, I stopped talking and went back to my chocolate elixir of the gods. You should never waste the good things in life. And where Eli had gone, there were no good things, not ever. "Flowers don't al-ways say, 'I love you,'" I murmured to the empty stool as I picked up the rose.

"You are a bad, bad girl," Leo said with a reluctant admiration. Coming from such a bad boy, that meant something.

"Yes, I am," I said with a satisfaction that tasted sweeter than the chocolate. "I most definitely am."

"What do you mean we can't kill demons?"

Zeke sounded as outraged as an eighty-year-old

meat-and-potatoes guy told he had to go vegan. "Relax, killer." I pulled up my hair and then tied my sneakers. I hated sneakers, but you couldn't run in boots. Or you could, but it wasn't cardio-effective. How many blocks did a chocolate martini equal? I *did* know who killed Marilyn Monroe, thank you, Eligos, spawn of Hell, and I even knew where Jimmy Hoffa was, or what was left of him, but blocks versus chocolate calories, that I didn't know. I only knew I had to run them off or outrunning demons was going to get more and more difficult. "It's just for a while—until Cronus is out of Vegas. You don't want to get between him and his nummy-num." Or whatever a demon was for him.

"Cronus . . . He was a Titan, right?"

I gave an approving pat to Griffin's knee as he leaned against the back of my car parked in its usual spot in the alley. "Someone studied at Eden House."

"I studied," Zeke complained as he gave the nearest tire a considering look and his foot twitched. I gave him a similar look and he rethought it, scuffing his shoe against the asphalt instead. Boys. Ex-angel, in reality probably older than I was, twenty-five human years genetically, but he was still a spoiled kid without his toys . . . dead demons. And that made him a strange spoiled boy, but weren't we all a little strange now and again?

Zeke would survive the vacation, I thought, although I was sympathetic. He could take up a new hobby. Golf. Tennis. Goddamn jogging, like me. Male metabolism—it was proof that God, the Christian one, was male. As I glanced at his flat stomach, my sympathy for Zeke decreased a tiny bit as Griffin spoke.

"You studied how to kill demons and weapons. I'm fairly sure you napped during mythology, history, scripture, and so on." Griffin folded his arms and looked up at a noontime blue sky, retrieving the memory from the sound of his semiexasperated exhalation . . . but only semi. It was Zeke. You rolled with the punches there. Zeke was Zeke. You had to love him or try to murder him in his sleep. There was no in-between. "Although the way you managed to sleep with your eyes open was impressive," Griffin went on to drawl.

It would've had to be. When it came to teaching I didn't think Eden House rapped a slacker's knuckles with a ruler. They were ridding the world of demons for the glory of Heaven after all, not putting together a bingo game and spaghetti dinner. There would be less rapping and more capping, one to the brain and bring in the new recruit. Bury the slacker in the rose garden. Good fertilizer wasn't to be wasted.

"I was not napping," Zeke emphasized. "I was in my happy place."

I finished with my sneakers and straightened. "And where would that be, Kit?"

"Someplace I can kill demons," he said as if it were perfectly obvious, and if I'd given it a fraction of a second of thought, it would've been. "There was no Cronus there."

"Believe me, that seems to be Cronus's happy place too right now. Griff's right. He's a Titan. He created gods. *Gods*, Zeke. I know you think you're badass, kicking demon tail right and left, and precious as a fluffy bunny while you do it." I bounced on my toes and began to stretch. I pretended I didn't hear a joint pop. I didn't ignore Zeke's irritation though. Why poke him with a verbal stick if I wasn't going to let myself enjoy it? I did love to tease my guys, but I also had to impress on them how serious this was or they would be squashed as quickly and easily as that fluffy bunny I'd compared

Zeke to. "But Cronus has killed more than nine hundred demons in six months. He's ruled one of our heavens. He was imprisoned in one of our hells but took it over. Think about it. He was thrown down into Tartarus and made everyone there the equivalent of his bitches in no time. The inmate became the warden. Makes you think, huh?"

Apparently not. "You're afraid of this guy?" Zeke asked skeptically. "You?"

"Hell, yes," I admitted freely. Damn, there went another joint. My once-conditioned body seemed to be falling to pieces fast. The maintenance on a human body was unbelievable. If you slept wrong, you were crippled for the day. How could a species manage to sleep *wrong*? How had they survived to swarm the earth? A bad mattress to them was like an asteroid to the dinosaurs.

Them.

Me.

Damn it.

"He can hop from dimensional realm to realm," I went on, "from place to place in this one, can kill nine hundred demons. . . . I hate to keep repeating myself, but, guys, seriously . . . *nine hundred* demons. Finds ruling a heaven and a hell not challenge enough, and when Leo almost destroyed the world, Cronus thought it was cute . . . like a puppy mauling your slipper. Or a kitten pouncing on a ball of yarn. You remember the Ark of the Covenant? Melting people's faces? Disintegrating their bones? He probably uses that as a retro lava lamp. He'll kill you and the worst thing is, he probably won't even notice that he did." I stopped stretching and checked that my T-shirt covered my gun. "And that's it. If that doesn't convince you, I give up."

"If he's so indestructible, how are you going to stop him?" Griffin asked.

"Stop him? How can we join up?" Zeke countered.

"We can't stop him, and you'll stay away from him or I'll paddle your behind, if he doesn't rip a cheek off like he did that demon's wing. So just go home, watch TV, get naughty, whatever, and be safe," I ordered.

Zeke looked disgruntled, but then again, he looked disgruntled ninety-nine percent of the time. If the demon-killing business ever lightened up, he could be a postal worker, no aptitude testing needed. Griffin, on the other hand, was the same sensible Griffin I'd always known him to be. He wore a more disappointed expression than I expected. . . . Griffin was a demon killer, but he didn't go into withdrawal like Zeke did. It wasn't the be-all and end-all of his existence. That was why I chalked up his glum look to there being less action lately, Eli having apparently warned his demons to steer clear of the four of us if they could.

I should've chalked it up to my stupidity instead. I might've been smarter than Eli, and might even be half as smart as I thought I was, but it wasn't smart enough to see what was coming. And I hated that. Screw my ego. I hated that one of my boys was in trouble, and I didn't see it. I let him down.

But that came later. For now, oblivious, I decided I'd rather run someplace more picturesque than the several blocks to the gym and drove to Sunset Park. Back to nature—at least as close as you could come in the midst of Vegas. There were ducks and geese and a pond. Unless you wanted your ankles pecked, you didn't run there. I had the respect . . . more accurately, the suspicious wariness . . . of a good deal of the *païen* world. On top of that, at times in my life I'd been worshipped, respected,

and feared by humans. And then there were demons . . .
ppffff. Let's just say that was the second bumper sticker
on my car. SLAYER NOT LAYER and I DON'T BRAKE FOR DE-
MONS. Next to Cronus, I might be a gnat, but compared
to everything else, I was content with my place in the
world.

Except for geese. Geese feared and respected no one.
No ankle, human or otherwise, was safe. It could be even
Titans like Cronus bowed to their pure, feathered evil. It
was worth thinking about. And I did as I thought about
other equally ridiculous things. I liked ridiculous things.
I avoided the pond and jogged to the mesquite flats for a
real run. Once there had been homeless people there, but
the police had run them off some time ago and I often
found the flats empty except for jackrabbits and ground
squirrels. It was quiet company, although at least once
during every run a chipmunk tried to commit suicide by
diving under my feet. They weren't bright, but they were
pretty to look at . . . much like Leo's dates, which made
me curse the rodents a bit more as I avoided squashing
their little furry heads as I ran. It was big of me to admit
that to myself, about Leo's women, and as a reward I
decided to cut fifteen minutes off the run.

There were also other animals on the flats, ones that
didn't throw themselves under me—cottontail, quail,
trails of ants, a hunkered-down spider here and there,
and tiny lizards darting along the cracked ground.

There were also the big lizards.

They appeared in a circle around me. I stopped in
midstride, kicking up a spray of dirt. There were eight
of them—demons in human form. Normally it would've
been like a convention of lawyers, the ambulance-chasing
kind. The ones with bright teeth and an even brighter
magnetism . . . an irresistible appeal that can convince

you to sue your own ninety-eight-year-old grandma
when you trip on a crack in her sidewalk. But all that
potential charisma, it was still a holstered weapon behind flat eyes. They stood motionless, arms at their sides.
Every one of them a prince made of pure poison. Flawless but empty of anything except hunger and hate.

And then there was Prince Charming himself—
Eligos. With a brown leather jacket, dark bronze finely
woven shirt and slacks, he forced me to say, "I'm way
underdressed for this party." I turned my head to take
the entire nine of them in. "All this for me, Eli? You do
know how to flatter a girl."

"I remember our last party. I wanted this one to end
differently." He smiled, but his nonexistent heart wasn't
in it. There was none of its usual carnivorously merry
gloating. "Think of my colleagues as doormen. They're
to keep you around while I make my Tupperware pitch.
I don't want to end up like Solomon before you've heard
me out."

"And you think they can do the job?" I asked scorn-
fully, not bothering to go for my gun. The disdain aimed
at Eli was pure bluff. I was good, but stuck in human
form, unless my Smith turned into a machine gun—
maybe a nice MAC-11—nine demons were too much
for me to handle. Eight lower-level demons maybe—I
was good with the Smith. But eight demons and Eli, no.
I knew my limitations. Just as Eli seemed to know his.

"Oh, they're all Daffys to be sure, expendable ducks
in a shooting gallery," he dismissed, not that the Daffys
protested. Better to be potentially expendable than to
have Eli promptly expend you then and there with no
hesitation. "But there *are* eight of them. And, yes, you
are extraordinarily good at the shape-shifting. It's a bear,
it's a wolf, it's a shark. Great magic show. But as long as

you don't pull Godzilla out of your hat, I think there are enough demons here to slow you down sufficiently for me to make my move. And it will be an exceptionally nasty move, I promise you."

Eight demons, and I would've made my own move. Eight demons and Eli, and I had to swallow my pride, be practical, and pretend I wasn't afraid, because everyone, unless you're suicidal or crazy, is afraid of dying. . . . Tricksters are no exception.

"Selling Tupperware, that is what you do, isn't it, Eli? Selling plastic for people's lives and souls. And you're good at it—I've seen you in action. Making a pitch to a trickster, though, ever done that? Someone whose very first word is a lie?" I sat down on the ground, fingers tapping on my knees, legs crossed. "Let's see your best, Eligos. Let's see your gorgeous ass in action."

"You doubt me?" He peeled off his jacket and sat on the ground opposite me, sprawled like a catalogue model. All that was missing was the price tag. I didn't know how many people found out Eli's price was more than they could pay, but I was willing to guess it was a whole damn lot.

"More like I don't doubt myself," I said, "but don't let that stop you. Here I sit, with bated breath, as the poets say. All the Daffys around us too, I'm sure." I knew Eli. He hadn't let them in on what he was going to say to me. They would know about Cronus, all demons did by now, but they didn't know about me. Daffys weren't worth Eli's time or secrets. I propped my chin on fisted hand and invited, "Sing your song, pretty canary. I'm listening . . . with every bit of my being. Think about that, sugar, every bit of a trickster's being, all aimed at hearing your story—true, false, or what falls in between."

"You're so positive you can tell the difference?" he

asked, partially offended, partially pretending. "You can tell my lies? With all my practice, which is a damn sight longer than yours, doll."

"Sweetie, you might embrace the lie, love it, spread it, wear it as a second skin, but *I'm* a living lie. I was born one and you can't compete with that." I reached over and tapped him on his nose with utterly false affection. "But go on, lizard boy. Give it your best. I'll still know the truth."

He did, and he was good, because it *was* the truth. Or the part of it that he told me. The rest he kept to himself. A sin of omission, the holy would say. Careful dancing and smart playing, I say. Some of the very best lies are the truth, only told for a sinister reason.

"Truth. That's so bizarre, so vanilla in the spectrum that it actually could turn a three sixty and become a kink. I'd marvel, but you're in a hurry. Fine then, changeling bitch," he said matter-of-factly. "Here's your truth. I want you to contact Cronus for us. I want you to negotiate on our behalf."

"Negotiate? I don't even know what he wants. Not yet." I would find out, however. As much as Leo wanted to stay out of this, I knew better. It wasn't going to happen that way, and that was my fault. But I didn't feel guilty. I did what I did. I was who I was. There was no sense in second-guessing myself at this late date in my life.

"No, you don't know what Cronus wants, but I do. That's enough. All you need to ask is what he'll accept instead. What will satisfy him in its place?" He raised his eyebrows. "Do you like how I told you that without telling you anything at all? Does that impress you? Rev your trickster engines?"

I took out my gun, slowly enough not to startle the

lower-level demons ringing me. I balanced it on my knee. "If I do talk to Cronus," I offered, "you don't think he'll reveal his big grand plan to a fellow *païen*?"

"As you said, he's mad. Who can say what the mad will do?" One of the flats' small lizards crawled onto Eli's hand and he lifted it to look into its tiny eyes. "Whatever the outcome, we'll deal with it then." The tiny lizard hissed at him. It seemed to strike a chord of brotherhood in him and he let it loose in the dirt.

More truth. I was actually getting tired of it. It wasn't challenging at all. "Why don't you tell me first, Eligos? If I face Cronus, and I don't see why I should, I want to be fully armed with all the information I need. Like precisely why he's killing so many of you." I swiveled and waggled the fingers of my free hand at the eight silent demons. "And doesn't that make you think? That if one was a *païen* Titan, crazy as a bedbug, who loved to kill masses of demons and was looking to get in some 'fishing' today, where would he look right now?" The mannequins continued to look blankly ahead, like soldiers. I sighed, trying again. "Maybe for a bunch of not-that-bright demons all in one place? Picking on a poor little trickster like me?" I tilted my head at the nearest nameless cannon fodder, my gold hoop earrings chiming cheerfully. "Shame on you."

This time six of them got the message, self-survival flaring in the formerly empty eyes as they disappeared. Two of them were more loyal . . . or more stupid. The first I shot before he had a chance to move. I wasn't as quick as Eli anymore, but I could still take a bottom-feeder demon. I could be in a ninety-year-old body and have done that, beaten it to death with my walker.

The second leaped at me, transforming to scales, bat wings, and a narrow, killing crocodile jaw. I rolled, shooting it in the eye right before it hit me. Without their brains and part of their heads, they both dissolved quickly to blackness and sank into the dirt. "Four *is* a crowd," Eli commented, unconcerned. Daffys come and Daffys go, and it didn't matter a damn to him . . . unless it was more than nine hundred.

I sat back up and returned the gun to my knee. "And where was that nasty move you were going to make?"

He curled his lips in a smug smile. "I made a different one." Hooking one finger, he tugged at empty air with it. "I caught you, Trixa. Whether Cronus is fishing or not, I caught my own fish. You're too curious for your own good. That's your flaw and a fatal one." The smile turned darker. "My favorite kind."

He was wrong and he was right, and I didn't call him on either one. I simply got down to business. "I'll talk to Cronus. Or I'll try. But you have to give me something to work with. He has to know that I know; otherwise he has no reason to meet. He's not a trickster. His curiosity doesn't rule him. Whatever he's truly after, what you know, I doubt it'll make much difference to me. I can't do what Cronus can do. Telling me the truth won't hurt your cause. It'll only help it."

That was how to tell a lie. The truth wouldn't hurt his cause, because if Cronus was involved, I was sure Eli's cause was lost anyway, but my cause? The truth would help that. "And," I had to ask because Eli would be highly suspicious if I didn't, "by the way, what exactly is in this for me, cutie? I don't remember that coming up as we play like kids in a sandbox." I let the dirt trickle through the fingers of my other hand, the one without the gun. "The bunnies and squirrels are sweet and all, the company entertaining, but . . ."

He had me pinned flat to the ground almost before

I saw him move. The difference between almost seeing and not seeing was the barrel of my gun jammed into his gut, just as something hard jammed my hip. Deceit and tricksters, violence and demons. Instant aphrodisiac for both. But neither of us was ruled by our hormones. We were both too smart, not to mention that I'd sooner shoot myself than ever do a demon.

"For six months. Do this for me and I won't kill your pet peris for that long," Eli said, his mouth a bare inch from mine and his hand around my throat, "and you know that I can. They're no more threat to me now than usual Eden House humans, which is to say not at fucking all."

My guys. My boys. He was threatening my boys. I pulled the trigger without hesitation. He was thrown off me with a gaping hole in his stomach, not that it did much good. To a demon like Eligos, that was the equivalent of a hangnail. He sat up as the wound closed. "A year," I countered. A skilled negotiator can experience emotion, but she can't let it affect how she makes the deal. The deal is all, especially when her family is depending on her.

He grinned, not taking it personally. That was another thing negotiators didn't do. "You would've made such a good demon, Trixa. You have that instinct—the go-for-the-heart-and-balls-all-in-one instinct. It is the waste of an eternity. All right. A year for your pets."

He stood. "Cronus needs a thousand demon wings. Together they will form a map of Hell. It's a map to Lucifer, part and parcel of Hell's whole. Lucifer *is* Hell— think of him as a tree, appropriately dark and terrifying, with a root system that travels almost forever. Lucifer is the tree and we demons and the souls inhabit the roots, which is actually more horrifying yet fashionable than it sounds. Black and twisted and souls screaming under a sky that never stops burning. Location. Location. Location. But I have no idea why Cronus wants to find Lucifer himself. As you said, Cronus already has had a hell and heaven, so why would he want another? We demons don't even want to know where Lucifer is. As we fell, we saw his true self. What he truly was—pure raving asshole. If I want to see that, I can look in the mirror." He felt his jawline. "A handsome one in my case, but all the same."

"You don't actually see Lucifer?" I said with a generous dose of skepticism—the only dose I carried.

"Nope. We can take his orders without having to see him. But while we don't have to see, we can't avoid listening. Great intercom system. And he's not happy now. Bitch, bitch, bitch. So find Cronus's price as promised." He lifted a black bloodied hand from his stomach to his lips, then leaned to leave that black kiss on my cheek as I sat up. Sealed with a kiss. So dramatic.

As if any seal could guarantee my word or promise.

"A thousand demon wings creates a map to Hell. Who came up with that? Wasn't MapQuest available? No Internet service Downstairs?" My skepticism was thicker as I wiped his blood away.

"God." He looked up at the sky and waggled a few fingers hello. "It was his last gift to the pigeons. If a second war comes and angels actually make it into Hell, it won't do them much good if they can't find the boss. If they can't find him, they can't destroy him, and if they can't destroy him, they can't destroy Hell. And, yes, we have the Internet, but it's dial-up. Wouldn't be Hell otherwise." He bent down and retrieved that expensive jacket.

"Do what you do, Trixa, and if Cronus doesn't rip

you apart and remove all traces of your existence from space and time, you have my number. Let me know how it goes." He put his hand, thumb, and finger in the universal "Call me" gesture, and he was gone.

I had his number all right. I only hoped he didn't have mine.

Standing, I started running again. My legs shook a little and I didn't holster my gun. The squirrels didn't give me any grief over it. Eli had shown me something from his past, something I didn't like, and I didn't have to accept.

Pride goeth before a fall. Great big smug pride goeth before one damn long, hard fall. That went for everyone. Angels, demons, humans . . .

But not tricksters. Not the careful ones.

The Holier Than Thou didn't always get it right.

Chapter 5

I'd told Eli that a trickster's first word was a lie. That, not so ironically, was a lie. I think mine was actually two words. Give me. Mama said she didn't know if I was hungry or wanted something shiny. She gave me something shiny and I ate it. Either way, she'd pointed out, she knew I'd be satisfied. I was a helluva trickster, but I knew I'd never be half the one my mama was. I also knew I couldn't fool her, not ever. Mamas are that way. I also knew there was one other person I couldn't fool . . . and with our history, wouldn't try to fool.

Although it might have been easier on my ears if I had.

"You are insane." It wasn't quite a shout, but it wasn't anything close to a normal tone of voice. "*Insane.* If you were ever sane to begin with, which I'm beginning to highly doubt. Or bright, because if there is any intelligence behind this, I can't fathom it. My last date was Einstein compared to what's running wild and free in that skull of yours. There certainly doesn't seem to be any gray matter slowing it down."

Leo was manning the bar per usual when I came back from my run with a request that he give Cronus a call. And while "call" was not quite the right term for getting the attention of a Titan, neither was "manning" for Leo if he kept up that kind of talk. "Let me get this straight," I said, before I acted on the "manning" issue, "I'm lacking sanity and fall below the minuscule IQ of your current bimbo du jour? Is that how you want to sum it up?" The one customer, another of our regulars, Bud, got up from his table and sidled hastily for the door. There was a man who knew his Darwin.

Leo opened his mouth as I picked up Bud's abandoned table . . . and not one joint snapped, crackled, or popped. It was amazing what adrenaline could do. It was also amazing how much adrenaline could be generated by being out and out pissed off. "Why don't you say that again for me, *Lenore*?" I lifted the table higher. "In case I didn't hear you right the first time, because, damn if I didn't think you little birdies were smarter than that. Maybe when I pop you in a cage and stuff a cracker in your beak, we'll get some blissful silence around here."

This time Leo closed his mouth and rammed both hands into his hair, completely destroying the black braid. He tossed the black cord that had held the plait together on the bar and tried again. "I apologize. You're completely sane and frighteningly intelligent and I know what you're trying to do. It's a good thing, but you don't actually have to talk to Cronus to pull it off. Lie. Manipulate. Do not throw yourself under the truck to make the blood on the bumper look more realistic. Use verbal red paint. Be a trickster. Be who we are."

He had a point, but . . .

"Aren't you just a little curious?" I asked, dropping the table.

"Odin, forgive all I have ever done." Leo folded his arms on the bar and rested his forehead on them, his spill of hair hiding nearly all of it from sight. "I realize it is much more than I could name in a day and a night, but forgive. I see from your side now."

"Actually looking to Daddy. I'm happy you and your family have made up. And, PS, Karma—isn't it great?" I said with far too much enjoyment at his gloom, my annoyance disappearing instantly. I shook my hand and wrist as the adrenaline faded and a mild ache settled in. "Besides, Eli isn't stupid. Somewhere nearby he'll have a demon or two watching. And whether they report back to him or disappear because Cronus kills them, he'll have his verification. He'll know I actually did talk to Cronus."

"Or Cronus will kill you as well and put me on a rhinestone leash like a poodle for the rest of eternity. Let us not ignore that possibility." He straightened and pulled his hair back in a strict, martial ponytail. "Which is the least of what he could do if he's irritated with our presumption."

"Yes, but while I was born curious, you were born presumptuous. Plus wicked and more than mildly immoral." In the bad days, Leo would've done this just for the hell of it, but I wouldn't point that out. I was comfortable manipulating the majority of the world, but never Leo. I would ask—but I wouldn't push. This was, like he'd said, our lives on the line, and while I was ready to risk mine for my calling, I wasn't ready to risk his for him. I walked to the bar, framed his face, and kissed his forehead. "I would be perfectly happy with you inviting him here and then leaving. Fly far away on those raven wings of yours. I'll talk to Cronus. I'll do it alone and I'll be fine." Before he could protest, I asked firmly, "When have I ever not been fine in the line of duty?"

He exhaled. "Only when you refuse to see how vul-

nerable you can be, even at your best, and, yes, I know
how very good your best can be." Pulling the sun necklace out from under my T-shirt, he arranged it in place to
the right of my heart. "I'll make some calls to those who
can do more than use only Verizon now. Being human
or a raven isn't much help in finding a Titan, but I'll see
if I can get some assistance from those who happen to
be getting a good laugh at my expense now. I hope you
appreciate that. Risking death and derision all in one."

For the former Loki, risking death was a walk in the
park; risking derision was a sacrifice for which there
wasn't enough gratitude in the world.

"And," he added, "we might be being presumptuous already. Just because Cronus has only gone after
demons, wants a map to Lucifer, doesn't mean this is
all necessarily only about Hell. With Cronus, you can't
assume. He's *païen*, but so am I. History knows what I
tried to do, and on a smaller scale that all *païen* aren't at
peace and love with one another."

It didn't get much truer than that. "Which is why we
really do need to talk to him. If it's only Hell and Lucifer he has a problem with, then I'll join his cheering
section. I'll wave pom-poms, do the splits. Rah-rah-sis-
boom-bah."

"And if he has a problem with some fellow *païen*, you
think he'll tell us?"

"Why wouldn't he? He would think there was nothing
we could do about it and he would probably be right."

"But that doesn't mean we couldn't try," Leo exhaled.
"Does being a born trickster make the suicidal behavior
more prevalent? Because as it's only my hobby, I don't
tend to want to happily rush into death quite as often or
quickly as you. I don't enjoy seeing you do it either, not
in our current mortal situation."

"It's what I do." I walked behind the bar and re-braided his hair from the ponytail for him, not as tightly or neatly as he would've done himself, but close. "It's what you do too, although you won't brag on it. You should. You deserve it. Don't be ashamed. Being righteous and being wicked aren't mutually exclusive." I grinned and headed for the stairs. "I'll shower and change and be right back. Maybe we'll close up early tonight. Have dinner with Griffin and Zeke. They'll be needing a distraction. Going demon-free cold turkey will be driving Zeke crazy."

"And dinner will fix that?" He was back to skeptical again.

"You think too big sometimes, Leo. The little things in life can be just as much fun."

After all, demons weren't the only ones who gave Vegas a bad name.

"I thought we were going to eat?" Zeke complained.

"And we will, but we're going to have some fun first." I reached back and patted his knee. He was wedged in the back, using the two tiny seats as one. As his knees were rammed up close to his chin, I counted myself lucky he didn't snap at my hand when I patted. Griffin, who had won the coin toss, was in the passenger seat, and Leo . . . Leo was currently driving out of the city in his own car with a rental U-Haul attached. That was for fun too, but a little later.

"This thing is so small it should run on triple-A batteries," Griffin commented, on the part of Zeke since the car was not small. It was perfect. It simply wasn't made for a full-sized man to be shoved into the back. But too bad for them both. It was new, I loved it, and I was going to drive it.

"It's a Shelby Cobra. Have some respect. Triple-A batteries can't get you to one hundred and eighty-five miles per hour and this baby can." I pulled on my gloves—hunting gloves, silk for easier trigger pulling.

"It can go that fast?" Zeke, as always, was skeptical.

"When I'm driving it, Kit, it can fucking fly. Speaking of flying, while we're on the way to the sports store, tell me if you guys have gone out to the desert to practice? If you whip out your wings in a battle, you need to be able to use them."

"Why the sports store?" Griffin asked.

I smiled. "We're going to try for a few homers. And I'm not telling you anything more, Griff. It's a surprise. It'll work off some energy for you two."

Griffin gave in to the inevitable of that easily enough. He'd known me for ten years. He knew how much I loved my surprises and went on to answer my question. "We have been practicing. We've been out a few times. The last time went flawlessly until a female eagle took a liking to Zeke. She either wanted to do him or eat him. He does look like an overgrown robin with those copper brown feathers of his."

"A falcon or a hawk," Zeke growled. "Not a *robin*."

"And you weren't attacked by any horny birds?" I asked Griffin, laughing.

"No," Zeke answered for him. "He's not a bird. He's a dragon. When the light hits his wings, it's like"—he paused—"like the sun falling out of the sky."

I would've patted his knee again. It sounded simple, was simple, but that was beyond poetry for someone like Zeke. It swelled your heart and broke it all in one. But although Griffin looked tired, his hand beat my own to Zeke, so I turned my full attention back to driving, my smile turning from cheerful to affection-

ate. I continued to smile to myself, smug as a cat with
his own personal sushi chef, as I drove to the nearest
sports store and with the guys' help, discovered that
you could fit fifteen baseball bats in the Cobra's trunk.
Louisville Sluggers, satiny smooth wooden works of
art. When you taught those who needed it a lesson, you
taught it with style.

Next I pointed the car toward Fifth Street. It was
where the homeless had congregated in Vegas once
they had been kicked out of the parks. Rows and rows of
them lining the sidewalks, some even with tents. There
they lived and there they sometimes died. I'd seen it
in the news the past few weeks. Three men, bored with
all the drinking, gambling, and strippers that Vegas had
to offer, decided that beating up people down on their
luck would be the next-best alternative. Monopoly . . .
Grand Theft Auto—that wasn't enough for these guys.
And the homeless were easy targets. Some were hiding
from things they'd done, things worse than beatings, but
most were only people who'd lost their jobs and homes
or those who were mentally ill. Then there were those
that just didn't understand life. Or maybe more accurately, life didn't understand them. That was a hard road
to walk and these people didn't need homicidal asses
making things any worse for them.

The police made an effort. They cruised Fifth Street,
but bullies in baseball hats and sweats weren't easy to
pick out from the homeless who surrounded them, and
there was plenty of crime elsewhere in Vegas to keep
them busy. Even when one of the lost was killed, beaten
to death by three baseball bats. The police came and
went more frequently then. I watched from one of the
stores in a strip mall that lined the street, but that lasted
only about a week, and it was business as usual . . . except

to the men and women who huddled on the sidewalk in the night. Waiting—for the next time, because, as they knew, there would be a next time.

They were right. There was going to be a next time, hopefully tonight. We tricksters had a sort of knack for choosing the right moment. A physicist had once tried to explain it to me . . . about how time wasn't linear, that it was happening all at once, from beginning to end, but there was no beginning or end. There was only now, a billion nows, and that maybe tricksters could sense those other nows. That at some level we knew even if we couldn't see, and that was our knack for showing up at just the right moment.

It was an interesting theory, especially as he told it to me as I dangled him over the edge of a volcano. It had been intriguing enough that I let him off with a warning about staying away from naïve virgins in the future instead of dropping him in lava like an ancient one himself.

Now though, the subject was still baseball and base-ball bats. But this time, it was going to be just like real baseball. All-American fun—hot dogs, apple pie with a big scoop of vanilla ice cream, blue skies, and hitting one out of the park. The lost would only be lost for now, not lost forever.

I parked at the mortuary not far down from the strip mall where I'd done my surveillance. I filled in my boys on what we were there for and why. "You said you trick the unwary. You make people smarter," Zeke said. "How's this make them smarter?"

"No, I said I trick the unwary to make them wiser and I punish the ones who are beyond learning. Killing the helpless and the lost for entertainment is beyond educa-tion." It was dark, almost eight, and the mortuary's parking lot deserted; the living who took care of the dead were gone for the night. "School was over for these particular assholes before it ever began. No pizza days. No skipping class. No homecoming. No games. Well . . ." I opened the trunk and ran one finger along the polished wood inside. "A game, but one they won't walk away from."

"How long has it been since you just tricked, didn't punish?" Griffin asked at my side. Always the ex-demon with the Boy Scout questions, he was good as gold and better by far than any angel. I'd never figure out where I'd gone wrong with him.

"Every day, sweetie. Every time I serve a watered-down drink or sell a tourist a map to an undiscovered gold mine." I tugged at his earlobe and started loading him up with baseball bats. Which was true, but tricksters were also at times judge, jury, and executioner. Or in this particular case . . . a facilitator. Sometimes justice doesn't feel right unless you snatch it with your own hand. Vigilante was only a bad word in my dictionary if you didn't have your information straight. Then it might be your turn to be served up on the bloody platter of the wicked or the failed fact-checker. And there were no unemployment benefits on that platter, so it paid to make sure you were right in the first place.

When I finished with Griffin, I turned Zeke into my second pack mule. He'd given up on the grumbling . . . for the moment. He knew I took my job as seriously as he did his and sharing it with him to take his mind off his current unwilling vacation was me doing what I could for him. I was giving him his daily dose of violence . . . all in the name of what was just and true, of course, but like kiddies needed cartoon-shaped vitamins, Zeke needed some ass to kick.

Kick it. Shoot it. Blow it up. He wasn't that particular. It was easy to please Zeke.

With the guys carrying the baseball bats, we walked down the sidewalk, cars on the street passing us. Not a one was a cop car and not a one slowed down at the sight of what was being carried. Someone had once said that all that was necessary for evil to triumph is for wise men to do nothing. These days wise men did nothing a hundred times faster than they had a few hundred years ago, but they were still as blind and useless as they'd ever been. That was why a trickster, an ex-angel, and an ex-demon were going to step up to the plate.

As we moved among the homeless, skirting carts, piles of clothes, and cardboard beds, I saw the sheen of cautious and confused eyes gleaming under the streetlights. I took a baseball bat from Griffin's pile and parked it on my shoulder. "So? Any ex–baseball players here? Anyone want to grab a bat and show three murdering sons of bitches how to really hit one out of the park?"

It was a long moment before someone spoke up, but someone did. It only takes one push to get the ball rolling . . . only one person to get the mob ready to run.

"Girly, you know what you're playing at?" a voice of gravel rolling in tobacco juice spoke at hip level. I looked down to see eyes neither cautious nor confused. They were hard, dark, and knew exactly how to play, if I could convince him that I could too. "They're big men, did what they did. Steroid-popping, raisin-balled bastards who never did an honest day's work, but they know how to hurt people. And they're good at it. They ain't had to dig for their last meal out of the Dumpster behind a 7-Eleven and been happy to have it. Not many of us can say the same." He was about sixty-five with one leg ended in a stump at his knee. It could've been from war or diabetes. He had a beard, iron gray streaked with snow and half the teeth he'd once had at eighteen. But for tonight, he was a baseball player through and through.

I handed him the bat and then pulled my Smith as I sat beside him. "Sergeant, this girly knows how to level the playing field."

"How'd you know I was a sergeant?" He looked at the gun with approval. "And why not just shoot the bastards dead if you're carrying that in your panties?"

My panties were not where I was carrying it, but I let it go. "Because you, unlike the ones who are hurting you and yours, do know the value of an honest day's work. As for shooting them dead, why should they get to go that easily? Your friend didn't."

"Jimmy Whitmore." That was the name of the man the news said had been beaten to death. "The Whit. Always cutting up about foolish shit. He weren't no friend." A big hand clenched tightly on the wood. "Full of himself and I've seen brighter, but you're right. He didn't go easy."

"And neither will the ones who did that to him." I waved my free hand at Griffin and Zeke. "Go on, guys. Pass them out. Then find a spot while I sit a spell with the Sarge and talk a little trash."

"You from the South, girly? Tennessee? Alabama?" The eyes softened a fraction. "You have a way about you."

I smiled as I rested the gun on my knee. "Sugar, I'm from everywhere. There's no place in this world big enough to hold me." No yard with enough toys. No playground with enough swings. No amusement park with enough rides. No place I hadn't been. No place I wouldn't go. But that was the past and the future, in-triguing physics theories aside. And right now the pres-ent was good enough for me.

An hour passed and I was telling the sarge about my favorite memory of Tennessee. "Honeysuckle," I said in dreamy remembrance, propping my chin in my hand. "On those humid summer nights where you can stand outside and there's no air, only honeysuckle. You can smell it; you can even taste it." The last time I'd been there, it had been so strong and thick everywhere that I was surprised even now people didn't smell it on my breath when I exhaled. No one could smell honeysuckle and not instantly become a kid again, tasting the nectar. There was nothing in the world that tasted quite like that. Not the best of wine or the sweetest fruit heavy on an orchard tree.

"That's home, through and through." He nodded. "Too damn cold in the winter and a tornado every day in the summer, but the honeysuckle nights I miss. I rightly do."

Zeke interrupted the nostalgia, calling from farther down the street, sitting to blend in as I was doing. Wait-ing for those three bastards to come play. Griffin had taken the other side of the street, buried in the homeless and street noise. "Trixa," Zeke snapped, "some guy is ex-posing himself to me. Only Griffin gets to do that."

Maybe we were lucky Griffin was on the other side of the street. He considered their personal life to be just that and not shouted down the street over people's heads. I choked back a laugh, because Zeke was try-ing to be good since this was my show. Most times he wouldn't mention the little annoyances of life and take care of them himself, which was rarely a pretty picture. "Did you tell him to stop?" I asked.

"Twice. Which are two more warnings than I normally give," came the exasperated reply.

I shrugged to myself. Sometimes the Zeke way was the right way—once again, not pretty, but still occasionally right. "Sounds like someone needs a lesson. You can be a trickster intern for the night."

After that I heard a grunt, a loud one to make it as far down as I was sitting. I didn't hear a silencer's muffled cough though, which was good, but better safe than sorry. . . . "You didn't shoot him, did you?"

"No, I hit it with the butt of my gun." Considering the size Zeke's guns tended toward, that was one unfortunate flasher. "He's curled up and I can't see his dick anymore, but I heard a crunch. A nice, loud crunch. Is that enough of a lesson or should I go ahead and shoot him?"

He didn't know, truly didn't, and I could see why Griffin still tutored him in walking the line between the stark black and white of decision making. Who knew how long it would be before Zeke could actually see the gray instead of only guessing at it?

"What do you think?" I called back.

"That I should shoot him," he said promptly.

"No," I said with a loud sigh, and he heard it.

"Just a little?" he wheedled.

"No . . . unless the crunch wasn't sufficient and he tries it again. Then maybe. Now quiet down, Kit. You're making people a little nervous."

Sarge looked at me, squinting his eyes as some of the homeless began to move their scant belongings and themselves farther up or down the sidewalk away from Zeke. "You think, girly? That boy's not quite right in the head, now is he?"

"He's right in every way there is to be right," I said

firmly. "And he's lived through battles and a war you couldn't imagine. You know the good men who do nothing and let evil thrive? He's a good man who does something and, trust me, evil will never thrive if he's in the area. He's better than I am and better than you. Understand?"

The man held up his hands. "Hold your horses. You sure don't look like brother and sister. He looking all Irish with that red hair and you looking, well, all kinds there is. Ain't meaning to step on any toes regarding family."

He was right. Zeke was my family, my brother, just as Griffin was. I'd lost my real brother, Kimano, years ago, and vengeance, while satisfying, couldn't bring him back. But life had given me two more. Not my guys, not my boys, but my brothers. For a loner trickster who usually led the most wandering of lives, who made the most temporary passing through or ending of your life, I was picking up strays like crazy. They were anchors to my kind, Mama would be the first to say. I looked down the street to see Zeke swiveling his red head back and forth with a "Hey, what?" puzzled expression as people moved away from him.

No, not anchors, Mama. They were wings. They had wings when they cared to show them and they were my wings. I'd thought I'd been blessed to have one brother. Now I was blessed to have two.

"If you're going to leave, then take the pervert with you," I heard Zeke demand. "His dick touched my gun. Now I'll have to take it to the free clinic to be tested. Do you know how hard that is to explain?"

Blessed was a strong word. Fortunate. I was fortunate to have two more.

"Especially when it's the third time?"

All right, family. It was everyone's burden to bear. And bear it I would . . . with the same grace and style with which I bore everything else.

"Does anyone have any goddamn hand sanitizer?"

My cell rang at just the moment I was considering taking the bat back from "Sarge" and using it on Zeke. Very good timing. Griffin was excellent at that. "What is Zeke doing?" he asked before I could say hello. "You're zapping me with waves of irritation like a leaky microwave. Zeke feels the same as always—his usual nice Zen level of vexation with the world in general, and since I normally can only read what you want me to, I have to guess he's also having a little fun with you." He didn't sound especially sympathetic. Amused was more like it. He dealt with Zeke's quirks every day and he did it with the grace and style I was beginning to shed like a winter coat.

"Zeke is being Zeke," I groaned. Since I was assuming his taking his gun to the free clinic was a joke, I added, "The more he develops a sense of humor, the more worried I get. It scares even my kind."

I heard the grin in Griffin's voice. "I wake up to it every morning. I'd think a big, bad trickster such as you could suck it up a little. Ouch. Fine. You want me to come over to that side and make Zeke play nice?" The "ouch" would be from my escalating annoyance.

The picture of Zeke playing nice made all the irritation instantly disappear. It was too ludicrous to imagine. Zeke being a good boy—I would've laughed, but in that moment I saw them . . . two men meandering down the sidewalk from Zeke's end. They wore baseball hats and knee-length jackets bulky enough to hide a baseball bat. "Have to go, Griffin. I have two over here. Look for one on your side. It's time to get off the bench and play for real." I hoped that Zeke remembered we were here to help, but vengeance wasn't ours this time. And it wasn't Heaven's. It belonged to these people.

I made a quick call, then put the cell phone away and waited. They kept coming, not trying to look inconspicuous by hunching their shoulders or keeping their heads down. They swaggered, predators on the prowl and proud as punch. Except they were more like poodles on the prowl, teacup ones, strolling into the open mouth of a lion. Pulling the hood of my raincoat over my hair, I did some hunching of my own. Hopeless, helpless, lost . . . victim. Put out what you want others to see and they'll see it. Whether you're a pretender to the throne or to the gutter, the ignorant rarely see the chameleon. And if the chameleon is actually less a tiny lizard and more of Godzilla waiting to swallow you whole . . . that truly was your bad luck. You should've looked closer. You should've paid attention.

They passed Zeke, still sitting with his gun now out of sight. They hesitated, but kept moving. Zeke would never a chameleon make. We all have different talents. Looking harmless wasn't one of Zeke's.

They might have swung a wide berth around Zeke, but the two of them came on, through shifting people, focusing . . . focusing. There . . . Look at that. There was a woman, hiding under her hood, so withdrawn from the world, so *afraid*, she'd balled herself up, hoping to disappear completely. Bullies loved fear. In seconds they stood in front of me, baseball bats now out and hanging by their legs, harsh grins showing as they gobbled up a fear that wasn't there and saw a woman who didn't exist.

"Hey, bitch." A foot nudged my leg hard. "Look at me. I wanna see if you're worth messing up or if you're ugly as shit already."

Ask and you shall receive.

I tilted my head back, hood falling, and gave them a flash of teeth far more predatory than anything Animal Planet had on it. "Boys, boys, boys. You wouldn't know a 'messing up' . . . well . . . until I showed you one." I put a bullet in the right kneecap of one of them. The other one I left to Zeke. Fair was fair. He put a round in the back of the second one's thigh, throwing him face forward onto the concrete. They were both down, screaming in pain, and the cars on the street—they just kept moving. Just as they kept moving as I heard a muffled pop from across the street. Barely audible over the sound of the cars, but I'd been listening for it. Griffin had gotten the third. I didn't expect that any mistaken Good Samaritan would stop driving and get out to investigate when justice stood up, and they did stand up, all around me— worn men and women with baseball bats and a chance to take back a bit of the peace that had been stolen from them.

"See you later, Sarge." I squeezed his shoulder as he got to his feet with the help of a crutch on one side and a bat on the other. "Hit one out of the park for me."

"I will, little missy. Damn straight I will," he said grimly. "Thanks for this. It ain't no honeysuckle nights, but it's real damn close."

By the time the bats were raised for a second time, Griffin, Zeke, and I were halfway to gone. Ghosts and shadows. In the distance I could hear the approaching sirens. By the time the cops arrived—thanks to my call to 911—justice would've already been served. Those men wouldn't be dead, although they more than deserved it, but I doubt they'd see the outside of the hospital for a year—then straight to a cell for the murder of Jimmy Whitmore. Hopefully they'd get the death penalty, but even if they didn't . . . no one lives forever, especially crippled murdering scum in a prison surrounded by predators who'd see in them what they had seen in the homeless. Then Hell could do the cleaning up. The demons had to get their groceries from somewhere. As God didn't feed them his love and spirit anymore and Lucifer didn't have it to give—at least not to hundreds of thousands of demons—they ate souls. Every soul in Hell was consumed sooner or later. For these bastards I hoped it was later. Let the demons play with their food first, as they usually did, only for much longer this time. It was the one time I did regret souls don't have that eternity to suffer.

That checked off the first lesson of the night. It was time to see how the second was going.

Leo, as it turned out, accomplished his trickery as quickly as we had and didn't need our help. It was too bad. I'd been looking forward to seeing that one in action. Some evolving serial killer or just plain psychopathic ass had been killing pets in a certain gated neighborhood that encompassed several streets. He would kill them, in horrible ways that were no pleasure to think about again, so I didn't, and then would hang them in trees or, if no desert-loving tree was available, on mailboxes, the antennae of cars, whatever he could find. The majority of his victims were cats. Dogs tended to bark when approached in the middle of the night, but cats were quiet.

So was he. No one had caught so much as a glimpse of who'd killed their pets, their companions, sometimes, to the very lonely, their only friends.

Tonight though . . . Tonight the timing was right. I'd felt it for this psycho the same as I'd felt it for the ones Griffin, Zeke, and I had been waiting for. Tonight what was good for the goose was good for the gander. Or, better, what was good for the kitty killer was what was good for the kitty.

Leo had rented a U-Haul trailer and headed out of town on U.S. 95 to the Sheep Range that sits outside of Vegas. It makes up the eastern boundary of the Nellis Bombing Range adjacent to the Nevada Test Site with a wildlife preserve at the base of the mountains. Do you know a common fact about mountains and sheep? They attract those who like to live in the mountains and eat the sheep. Like a mountain lion or a cougar, whichever name you preferred.

One big pussycat was good enough for me.

Even though we were in our human bodies and had lost our trickster powers, animals still knew us by the lingering telepathic-empathic defense. They knew what people, and sometimes gods, didn't know. To a wolf, a trickster would be an alpha. To a lone ranging mountain lion, we'd be its mommy, no matter how old it was. They knew us, and they obeyed us . . . most of the time. This time had turned out to be one of those times. Leo found a full-grown cougar who would've nursed on Leo's leg if Leo had let it. But it was happy to ride in the well-ventilated U-Haul too, and then wait in the lovingly watered large silver-green sage bush of one house while Leo turned into Lenny, who could croak one very convincing imitation of a pet cat's meow. And as the meows became more smug—because no one did smug as convincingly as Leo, someone decided to put another notch on the handle of his bloodstained knife.

Here's another common fact—cats? The thing I love

most about them . . . next to their curiosity? There is no such thing as a tame cat. You see the survival-challenged tourists in Africa at the rehabilitation preserves where young abandoned lions are being educated to be reintroduced into the wild. You see them sitting next to that "tame" lion to have their picture taken, all smiles, and the next thing they know they're wondering how their neck managed to get in that good-natured lion's mouth. How had that five-dollar souvenir photo gone so wrong?

As any granny knows, five-pound Marshmallow with the poofy white fur, the slightly crossed eyes, the adorable purr, and who loves you dearly would eat you within ten minutes if he suddenly grew to the size of a Great Dane. It doesn't mean Marshmallow doesn't wuv you; it just means Marshmallow loves eating creatures smaller than he is more than he wuvs you. That's what being a cat is all about.

When our pet killer crept through the yard, softly calling, "Kitty kitty," until he came to a particularly large bush that a raven perched atop, he probably thought he wasn't tame either, but a carnivore out to kill, torture, and maim, if not devour. That's when a brown and tan head with happy-to-see-you, come-in-for-dinner anticipation in its yellow eyes came out of that greenery and proved him wrong.

It's amazing how fast you can go from "I taut I taw a puddy tat" to choking on your own blood.

One more lesson learned.

Our friend the cougar ended up back in the mountains with a full belly and some leftovers courtesy of another ride in the U-Haul, and Leo had called to give me the story on his way back. That left time for Griffin, Zeke, and me to catch a very late dinner. I was sorry I had missed the fun, but there was always more to be had.

As I went to bed that night, I did some wondering of my own. What did someone . . . some*thing* like Cronus, who'd thought it hilarious to eat his own children, according to legend and truth—what did he do for fun?

Chapter 6

Checkers.

It was true and I never would've guessed, but the world is strange like that. Cronus liked checkers.

He was waiting for me when I came downstairs that morning. Actually, not really. I gifted myself with an ocean full of flattery there. He was waiting for Leo. Leo had reached out and touched someone, as the commercials used to say, and that someone had in turn touched someone who in turn . . . Bottom line, Cronus was waiting for Leo to show up at work. Because this is where Leo had probably called from and to beings like Cronus, occupation versus a personal life . . . work versus your home, it was all anthills to them. And as powerful as Cronus was, in a way, that was a weakness too. An anthill was an anthill and so much trouble to tell the difference between them.

Waiting here would do.

I knew it was Cronus the moment I opened the door to the stairs and saw him. I had one hand still rubbing lotion on one arm when I froze—froze except for continuing to automatically rub in the lotion. When I'd figured out I was going to have to work to keep my weight at demon-kicking prime, I'd then discovered living in the desert when you can't shape-shift for a while is unbelievably hard on the skin. At the rate I was going, I would need an entire staff of cosmetic, nutrition, and health professionals to keep me from disintegrating in the next brisk wind.

But I was here now and still relatively moist and mobile . . . when I wasn't facing a Titan. Not that Cronus looked like a Titan. I had no idea what a Titan did look like and I was happy to keep it that way. I was a trickster. I bowed to no one, not ever, but I knew that seeing a Titan . . . That couldn't be a good thing. They had given birth to gods, were a level above gods, and Leo, a god himself, was hard to look at in his natural form. Not because he was hideous—he wasn't. He was glorious and terrifying, an infinite darkness and a blinding light, good and evil, the earth and the sky, exuberant life and the unending stillness of death—all in one. He was inconceivable and when you looked at him, even a trickster like me knew . . . his existence defied the universe itself. And that was a god. What would seeing a Titan be like?

Most likely similar to seeing a nuclear explosion at ground zero. Oh, hey, there were some lights and it was really hot and then I was less than ashes—all in a microsecond of a microsecond. And best avoided if at all possible.

Today, Cronus looked like a nineteen-year-old kid. He sat at one of the tables, hands folded on the wood with a checkerboard in front of them. He wore a simple short-sleeved black T-shirt, inside out and backward with the tag showing. It was nice and flat, not curled as tags tended to be after a few washings. He also had on jeans, but this time right side out and with the zipper in the correct place.

"Cronus?" I asked, letting the door close and taking

several cautious—any more cautious and they would've been going backward—steps toward him.

He didn't look at me or act as if he'd heard me at all—only stared ahead, over the checkerboard and at the wall. His hair was brown and not dark brown or light brown or any human color of brown at all. There was no depth to the color, no shadings, no bounce of light. Every single hair was the same precise shade of brown, from the root to the end, and the same as the one next to it. Mud. It was the color of mud, not the kind you'd want to play in as a mud pie–loving kid either. It was the color of toxic mud found around chemical waste plants . . . where frogs are born with six legs, the fish with two heads, and nothing else is ever born at all. As I moved closer, I could see his skin was poreless. If it had been shiny, it could've passed for plastic and he could've passed for a giant doll. But it wasn't—it sucked in the light the same as the hair and when I set across from him and saw his eyes . . .

I was wrong. He was a doll, the most cheaply made imitation of a human being you could find on a thrift store shelf after some little girl's brother had popped the toy's eyes out to see if they would roll like marbles. Cronus had only oval-shaped holes that revealed the shadows inside his skull. Shadows of men strangling their wives over the grocery bill, the drift of darkness that was SIDS claiming an infant's life between one breath and no next, the midnight cloud of poisonous gas mixed with volcanic ash that buried cities and killed every living thing for miles and miles and miles.

This was Cronus. This was the thing that had put on its casual clothes, a human suit it couldn't be bothered to get correctly although it could *create* living human beings if it wanted, beautiful, intelligent, amazing human beings. When you could make gods, human beings were as easy as chocolate cake out of an Easy-Bake Oven. A lightbulb and some batter. What was difficult about that? But it . . . No, best think nice, the better to play nice. . . . He . . . He had put on the casual attire, because the real deal was too much of a boring chore, and was impassively waiting for Leo to show up and play checkers.

Gods, Titans, how they both got their rocks off, it was usually freaky. The kind of freaky that would have a cross-dressing Furry who put pickles where pickles weren't meant to go giving it all up and deciding *The Price Is Right* with a microwave dinner was as far away from vanilla as he planned to ever get again.

Checkers though . . . That was a new one. Not chess, the supposed game of Death—just simple, childlike checkers.

As I sat in the chair across from him . . . badass mother trickster—that's one for you, TV censors—badass mother trickster, badass mother*fucker*, I reminded myself one last time. I opened my mouth to repeat his name, when the front door opened and a "customer" walked in. It didn't matter who had unlocked the door, Cronus or the demon in a much better human and a familiar disguise; it was just one more thing to go wrong. I put it aside and went on as he took a seat across the room and pretended to read a shiny new copy of Dante's *The Divine Comedy*. Cute. I wondered which circle of Hell he was on. The silver hair and dark eyes—it was our friend Amdusias, better known as Armand from the casino. Eli had sent a minion he might actually miss. He truly did want the info

on Cronus to offer up his future version of a fine cut of
Kobe beef in the hopes of getting it.

Because, after all, I might lie to him.

Me? Never.

Or Cronus might erase me from reality as if I'd never
existed, which would make passing on that info to Eli
difficult. That Eli, so thoughtful, always thinking of
others. Always thinking . . . period. Mother Teresa and
Machiavelli had had nothing on him. But time to get
back to the matters at hand—staying alive being part of
that. For that I needed to be in top form, my attention
focused.

"Cronus," I tried again. I didn't bother to introduce
myself. I had a hundred names, not quite legion but more
than a few, and Cronus wouldn't give a damn about a
single one of them. "Leo . . . Loki asked to speak with
you on my behalf."

Nothing.

"It's about the demons you've been killing, their
wings, the map to Lucifer. I was curious . . . just a little . . . as to what's going on in that whole area. Anything
the rest of us *païen* should be concerned about? Lucifer going to take a peek out of Hell like a groundhog?
Checking for spring or Armageddon? Should we head
to the Hearth?" The Hearth was *païen* sanctuary. The
Light of Life shielded us there, from Heaven or Hell. It
was our bomb shelter should the Penthouse or the Base-
ment decide to take us or each other out. The Hearth
was, ironically, the Noah's Ark for pagankind. We were
here first and we would be here last. End of story.

My questions to Cronus were good questions, I
thought, *païen* pertinent definitely, and Titan or not, he
was one of us . . . *païen*. Yet it was the same. Nothing.

"Okay," I exhaled, pushing the shower-damp curls back. I'd tried playing nice. It hadn't worked. Instead, I'd try playing a different way—I'd try playing first. "How about this?" Red was on my side . . . I took that as a sign. My color, my signature, my move. I pushed one of the round plastic circles forward on the board.

The head tilted downward, not as much taking in my move—Cronus didn't need his empty eyes to be aware of that—as taking in my sheer audacity to make myself known to him. To stand up on my back legs, tiny ant that I was to him, and wave the others at him. Look at me! I exist! I exist right now, right here, the same as you!

Or he simply wanted to play the game. I was sincerely hoping it was the game, because ants who get noticed almost always get squashed. By a snotty little kindergartner's foot or by the whim of a Titan. It didn't matter which. Squashed was squashed, to ant or trickster.

A long pale finger extended and moved a black checker diagonally right.

I'd made it one second without being stomped flat. Good for me. I made my next move silently. We know how to talk, my kind, not as much as pucks—no one alive, dead, or in between could touch a puck for talking—but we know when to stay quiet as well, which is something no puck has ever known. I knew, very clearly, that if a Titan didn't want to talk, I couldn't make him. I would have to wait him out or wait until Leo showed up and see if it was a Boys' Club. Guys and guys. Titans and gods. Too good to talk to down-to-earth fun-in-the-sun Trixa. I gritted my back teeth, then smiled victoriously ten minutes into the game as I jumped him and took his checker. Such a simple kids' game and this is what he played. "So this is what you do for entertainment?" I asked more cheerfully as another customer, a tourist this time, came in and sat at yet another table to study the plastic laminate with four wide and wonderful choices of appetizers. Fried cheese. Fried chicken wings. Fried potatoes with ranch dressing. And all three combined on one plate and fried just a little bit more. "You play this for fun?" I went on.

The unnaturally smooth lips parted. "For keeps." In the next moment with his turn, he took one of my checkers and the tourist immediately went limp, his face colliding with the table, his eyes nothing but red, blood trickling from his nose, ears, mouth. Gone . . . just like that.

For keeps. Cronus said it: He didn't play for fun; he played for keeps.

I decided right then I liked it much better when he wasn't aware of me or who was in my bar. A man had died because of me . . . and what I'd wrongly thought were some stellar checker skills. He'd died because of a stupid game—me and a stupid game that I hadn't taken seriously. I took Cronus very seriously, so seriously that I thought he was beyond something as petty and throw-away spiteful as this. Killing more than nine hundred demons, yes, that I could see. Killing one polyester-clad tourist, who I sincerely hoped was right with whichever religion, philosophy, or lack thereof he nurtured in his soul, over a move in a game five-year-olds mastered— that was no better than pulling the wings off a butterfly. Who did that?

A Titan asshole apparently.

Armand shimmered. He might work for Eli and as- pire to someday get lucky enough to stab his boss in the back to take his place, but I didn't think he liked what he was seeing. I didn't think he *knew* what he was seeing. Demons thought they were killers and they were. They thought they were monsters and they were. They thought they were evil and, yes, they were. They thought they were the first evil.

They weren't.

They thought they'd invented evil. They hadn't. Thought they were the very epitome of evil—they were only a shadow. I wasn't proud of it, but the first evil had been *païen*. Cronus wasn't the first evil, but he wasn't a shadow of it either. He was the genuine article and Armand was only another ant, the same as me, and running for his ant-hill, which was better known as Hell, as fast as he could go. It wasn't fast enough.

Cronus was gone from his chair and holding Armand up off the ground before pinning him against the wall, a butterfly soon to lose its wings. Armand, physically bound to earth, did what he thought would be his best chance of escaping. He changed to his true form: the scales, the snapping alligator jaws, the thrashing tail, jagged talons. They didn't help him. Cronus didn't bother to move as claws passed through the fake flesh that instantly repaired itself behind them. The only thing that helped Armand/Amdusias escape was his wings. If he considered death an escape and if I'd been the one facing a Titan who did not care for me at all, I would've happily considered it so. A vacation. A party.

I didn't think Amdusias agreed with me. He screamed as one wing was torn off in Cronus's hand. And then he was gone, a black puddle. His wing stayed, which was apparently a Titan trick, as normally it would've melted along with Amdusias.

I'd gotten to my feet to run. Not to help the demon. That was way beyond my capabilities and Amdusias wasn't my problem. Locking the door and preventing someone else from walking in on a scene of dead tourist, demonic puddle, and Titan holding a demon's wing like a cheap Vegas souvenir, that was my immediate concern. Large black puddles were easy to explain. . . . If cleanliness was your thing, then this wasn't the bar for you. A bizarre eyeless fake human, a red and ebony dragon wing, and an expired tourist soaked in blood, that was more difficult than what looked like a very bad bathroom leak.

I was about to lock the door when Leo walked in. He took in Cronus, the wing, the dead man, and he shook his head. "I don't know why I ever listen to you," he said to me. I closed the door and gave the lock an annoyed twist shut. I didn't worry about the blinds. They were closed. This was Nevada and this was a bar; there was no reason for them to be open.

"I feel bad enough about the guy," I said, folding my arms. Did I look defensive? Probably. I sure as hell felt that way. I hadn't planned on any collateral damage during all this unless it was demons. "I didn't know Titans took checkers so seriously—that *anyone* took checkers that seriously."

"Titans take all games seriously. I'm more of a free spirit. Make up the rules as I go along and then smash them into tiny pieces—along with the rest of the world," Leo remarked as he leaned back against the door, as casual as they came. "Rules never were worth my respect, not even my own. What's the point of creating something if you don't destroy it? What goes up must always come down. What we make, well, damn, we have to break."

It was said with a dark acid humor I hadn't heard in a long time from him. From the bad old days when world destroying was as easy and as natural for him as reaching for the remote. He'd been a bad boy before the concept of bad boy had been spawned. That's what Cronus would remember about him and that's who Leo would be for the trick at hand. Who he'd be for me.

Pretend to be for me. Only pretend. No trick, no information was worth Leo going back to what he'd once been.

Loki. Lie-Smith, the Sly God, the Sky Traveler. And one of the few that Cronus might actually give a real answer to—dark and chaotic enough to be at least worth a pat on the head like a clever little doggy. I could feel it coming from Leo as I stood beside him, ripples in a midnight black lake—the darkness of space where the earth would have once been before he incited a war to blow it apart. Only a might-have-been, but a very close might-have-been.

And Cronus remembered it.

"Sly one." This time when he opened his mouth, I saw what I hadn't seen before; there was nothing behind his lips, the same as his eyes. Only shadows of things no one should have to see. "What game play you now?"

"None that would take a thousand wings to find that fallen pigeon Lucifer. What use would you have for a failed pretender to the throne in a hell literally of his own making? What could he give you who've had that and a heaven too?" The disdain was automatic for Loki or Leo. Lucifer might have the power of all the demons in Hell combined, but to us *païen*, he was and would always be another pigeon with scales. We were stubborn that way. Lucifer was one of them; whether lording it above or hiding below, he didn't count.

At least he didn't until Cronus gave Leo the answer he wouldn't give me. It was one word. It didn't need to be any more than that.

One word to tell us why a Titan would devour Lucifer and make that Hell his own.

Chapter 7

"Rose."

It's what I said as soon as Eli manifested in my bar. I'd called him since Armand wasn't going to be making any calls ever again. Cronus had left after giving us our answer, losing interest in his pet Loki quickly or on the way to bag more demon wings—it didn't matter. He had slowly spun out of existence, streamers of faux skin and the slickly spongy material beneath it disappearing like a dust devil settling slowly to die. He took the wings and the checkerboard with him. The dead man and puddle of Armand he left behind.

I'd told him the Titan was gone, but Eli was no fool. He waited a good two hours before he showed up. Two hours I'd spent mopping up Armand while Leo covered up the tourist with a sheet. We'd seemed to have lucked out and he was either alone, a regular Vegas gambler who made the pilgrimage several times a year, or he wasn't alone, but whoever he was with had no idea where he'd gone. It was sad to say that if he were a lonely gambling addict with no one in his life to miss him, it would be a good thing for us. Sometimes to do good, you take the risk of others being hurt. It shouldn't be that way, but there are a lot of things in life that shouldn't be as they are.

The physicist I'd once hung over a volcano hadn't explained that one. The nature of time was simple. Why
all things weren't fair and just—he hadn't had a clue on
that one. Mama would say it's all about balance. There
can be no good if there's no evil. No right if there's no
wrong. No light if there's no dark. Then again, there's
often no mac if there's no cheese.

The last perked me up and I had less of a desire to
impale Eli with the mop handle as he straightened his
tie, although the mop was a loss anyway. You couldn't
get demon out of anything, not even cleaning utensils.
I'd already leaned it against the doorway leading to the
alley for disposal.

"I suppose I don't have to watch my back against
Amdusias any longer, although you can feel free to
watch any part of me, front or back."

He was wearing all black. Black suit, black silk shirt,
black tie with a muted pattern in a different weave.
Even a black rose, ironically. "I'm in mourning for my
comrade killed in action." He spread his arms and did
a turn so we all could get a good look. "But I'll still be
sexy. It can't be avoided."

"I do believe it can." I did the shot of whiskey sitting
in front of me. I was sitting two tables over from the one
holding up the dead man. "In so many ways. I don't need
Leo's help either, not that he wouldn't enjoy it."

"Just like old times," Leo offered from behind the
bar, having his own whiskey. His mood was more positive than mine . . . because it was like old times for
him—a faint reflection of them anyway. He might not
be that way anymore, but memories were memories, and
whether the world judged them differently didn't matter. They were Leo's to do with as he pleased. If he felt
nostalgic versus guilty, as long as he didn't reenact those

days, it wasn't my business how he felt about his mental echoes.

Still, Leo's upbeat was Loki's upbeat and Eli saw that plain as day. He came in smooth as oil on water, wary with the one whom he still thought a god. "I was always a fan of Vikings. Brawny men. Brawny women. Hard-drinking and hard-killing. And when they die—Valhalla. More hard drinking and hard killing. Destruction all the way around. What's not to like?"

"The killing in Valhalla isn't permanent. The next day the dead come back and that's what's not to like." Leo swirled his whiskey. "I like my destruction very permanent, but that's me, and not some worthless lizard who imagines he can comment on my playground, much less survive in it." It might've been odd to someone else seeing an American Indian telling you the downside of Norse afterlife from personal experience. But Leo had made his body as I'd made mine. He could deal with the details of that confusion on his own.

But tiptoeing around a god versus his ego, Eli didn't have a chance when he made that choice. "Ah, such a mouthy and aggressive god. Your playground, eh? Perhaps one day we'll see . . . when I beat you to death with a large set of monkey bars." Eli shifted his attention back to me. "'Rose' is what you're telling me Cronus said. Rose and only rose. Nothing else. Pardon me if I find that both wildly mysterious and completely inadequate." The emphasis on "inadequate" was as black as the suit.

He sat at the table with me, suddenly holding a glass of wine, which he raised to toast the dripping black mop leaning against the door frame. "*Valeas*, Amdusias. You were an almost satisfactory minion. Now, Trixa, my one true love, shower me with roses and explanations and we won't have to find out who is the baddest and most toned of asses around." He took a sip of wine. "Although the last, I think we both know, is obvious." His lips curled with a smug satisfaction. Smugness and Eli almost always went hand in hand.

I didn't pay attention to the ass part since I did know the answer and I didn't like it. "Since the big badass demon was too afraid to show up for two hours, we had time to hit the trickster network and linked up the word 'rose' with Cronus." I waited and I made him ask. Any chance to stick it to the demon whose ass might be a little bit more toned than mine.

"And?" He tapped his fingers on the wood of the table. "I can't believe you're so petty. Wait, you're a trickster, so yes, I do."

"Yes, I am, and yes, I am." I took the glass from his hand and a swallow of the wine myself. It was excellent. "Cronus, the Titan, a creature I wouldn't believe could love, did fall in love with, of all imaginable things, a human. That's why I was in the dark regarding any motivation for his psychotic behavior—not that he needs motivation. The few tricksters who heard the story passed it off as the very worst concocted of rumors, and we love rumors, even more than the truth. But a Titan falling in love? With a human? That was too ridiculous to repeat or toss into our gossip network. Yet the ridiculous and unthinkable turns out to be true or Cronus wouldn't be waging war on Hell. He did fall in love ... with a woman. Rose, Rosemary, Rosita—no one knows her exact name, only that she was his Rose."

"Was," Eli exhaled. "I sense a pattern here. Was. She was his Rose." He let his head fall back to stare at the ceiling glumly. "Let me guess. His Rose was a naughty, naughty girl. Stupid, *stupid* human."

"Maybe not that naughty. But she wanted fame, fortune, what most humans want, and Cronus, to test her love, loved her as a human. In a human body I'm guessing he was a damn sight more convincing than the one he showed up in here today." I grimaced slightly. Bad work was bad work, whether it was lack of talent or just not giving a rat's ass. "Emotions too. For some reason, maybe boredom, he did become human, if only temporarily. He felt as a human feels, he loved as a human loves, and Rose thought he *was* human. She didn't know about *païen* or Titans. But she knew about demons when one came around and enlightened her, tempted her, and then she traded her soul for what Cronus could have given her for free."

"He wanted proof that she could love him without knowing what he was and what he could give her and she ended up in Hell because of it—well, that and her human nature. I like that story. With the greed, lust, and pride, and being damned to Hell, it would make a nice combination of Edgar Allan Poe and O. Henry." Eli looked back down, took the wineglass back from me, waved his hand over it, and refilled it. "Water to wine is easy. Air to wine is much more impressive. Now you're telling me that Cronus is going to walk through Hell and go mano a mano or Titano a Demonio with Lucifer because some random demon took the soul of his lovely if shallow Rose."

"Demons are a dime a dozen and for a Titan to bother with an underling when he can take out the boss isn't going to happen. A demon took his Rose, so Cronus will wipe all demons, their home, and their king from existence. That's the Chicago way and it's the Titan way as well." I smiled. "And, with my curiosity taken care of, still not my problem. Now, if you could take the dead

tourist with you when you go, I'll consider that payment
enough. That and, you know, the sheer enjoyment I get
from seeing how screwed you are." I crossed both feet
on the spare chair and studied my new red boots with
heels that could slash a throat. It was a brighter red than
I normally chose, the color of a stripe in a candy cane.
Red didn't always have to be the color of blood. No, not
always. It could be the color of a fast car, a sexy dress . . .
or a rose.

Eli dipped a finger into the wine and turned it to the
blood I'd just been thinking of. "There's a way to stop
him. There's always a way to stop anyone, a way to escape anywhere. We made it out of Disneyland, didn't
we? The most boring place in eternity. The singing, the
praising, the showing humans the path of love and Almighty Glory. If we could escape that, we can escape
destruction at the hands of one miserable *païen*."

I dropped my feet back to the floor and folded my
hands, resting my elbows on the table. "Here's the
church." I raised my index fingers to meet. "Here's the
steeple." Then I moved my thumbs apart and flipped my
hands over and waved my fingers. "Open the door and
see all the people. All the never-to-be-damned people
because you and yours will be gone. But I do wonder
where the evil souls will go then. Many won't be damned
with you gone, but it doesn't necessarily take your kind
to make some people step off the path of the righteous.
You're good at it, but you're not absolutely crucial to
the process. They can do it themselves. Maybe some
païen afterworlds will snap them up. They'll be punished, if they deserve it, but at least we won't eat them.
Well, most of us won't."

Eli drank the blood. I don't think he noticed he
hadn't changed it back to wine, or maybe he liked the

taste. Once you've eaten thousands of souls, you have to begin to wonder what the container tastes like. Demons had wondered that a long time ago. They murdered, they stole lives and souls, and occasionally they ate one or the other or both at the same time. "I'll have to ask the boss about this first, but I think I might have a way to satisfy Cronus." He drained the glass without any visible enjoyment. Giving in to a *païen*. For a demon, it was a big sacrifice and they didn't like to be on the wrong end of the sacrificing. "What if we were to let all the Roses go? Every single one of them. He can find his and pop her in a freshly made body of his own design. That's a gesture large enough for even a Titan to take notice, I'm confident."

"Digest your Bloody Mary and keep thinking that. This is a *païen* the rest of us don't begin to understand and one who, for a while, became human. A god times ten became *human* and did not enjoy the experience. What he might take notice of I won't guess at. But, hey, sugar, you give it your scaly best." I paused, then pointed out the potential flaw in his plan. "And you are assuming she hasn't been eaten yet."

"You have a better plan?" He scowled, his eyes going from green and copper to black and copper.

"You think I'd tell you if I did?" I waved a hand at the tourist. "Remember, take him when you go. And, as I said, now that my curiosity is satisfied, y'all don't come back, ya hear? *Ever.*"

"If you are satisfied, then you're not curious about the right things." His eyes shifted back to human.

"It's not especially alluring when you say that with blood on your breath," I said with a stone-still calm.

"As if you've never had it on yours." The copper flecks were brighter and his words . . .

Hell, they were true.

But mine were always with good reason. I was justice. Eli was only Hannibal Lecter crossed with a T. rex—a sociopathic carnivore. I killed the wicked, if necessary. He would kill anyone and anything. But he was gone before I could tell him so. Not that I would've bothered and not that he would've cared. No, I wouldn't have bothered and he wouldn't have cared, but I would've cared . . . a little.

I shouldn't have. I did what I was meant to, born to, raised to, and I loved my work. But there was the occasional moment I wondered what it would be to be like Leo, have tricking being only my hobby. That my existence wasn't my occupation—and I could broaden my horizons. Take a vacation and let the stupid do what the stupid did. Let evil do what evil did.

But everyone had a calling, and I could no more stand by and let the ignorant and the sinister bumble about than I could wear gold lamé. I dropped my head forward and rubbed my eyes with the heels of my hands. "I save one only to lose another. That's not good math even for a two-year-old."

"It's not one for one. It's one for thousands, maybe hundreds of thousands," Leo responded quietly. "Unfortunate for him, but he didn't die for nothing. He died for a reason, died a hero, despite not knowing it."

"He died because I suck at checkers." I sighed, keeping my eyes hidden. "Eligos didn't take the body, did he? The bastard."

"No." I heard Leo give a sigh of his own. "I'll take him out to the desert tonight and bury him. I'd pick him a nice spot, but wherever he is now, he doesn't care."

It was true enough. Wherever he was now, better or worse, where his dead body was wouldn't make a difference to him. "Thanks." I straightened and rubbed my forehead. "While you do that I'll try to figure out what to do when Eligos figures out I lied to him."

"That will be more tricky than checkers," Leo warned. "And while you're at it, also try to figure out what we're going to do about what Cronus really wants."

It was hard to have a smart-ass comeback to that, because I hadn't one damn clue. And the consequences to that were exponentially worse than lying to a demon, even when that demon was Eli. Catastrophic came to mind, then went off in search of a bigger and badder word to take its place. Plain and simple . . .

We were fucked.

"Griffin's lost." He said it just that way—Zeke, sounding exactly the same as that last word.

Lost.

My brother, Kimano, lost everything when we were kids. Tricksters didn't hold on to things much. That wasn't us, not our lifestyle. Born to roam, and roaming was easier when you weren't dragging baggage along . . . of either kind, physical or mental. And that meant I should've let Kimano go when I avenged him. Unpacked him. Left him on the side of the road. At peace and firmly in the past. But I couldn't. I knew it. I didn't even try. Kimano was Kimano. Unique. I'd carry him with me forever.

But it didn't change the fact he'd lost everything and probably would've lost his brain if he'd had one to begin with. That was my mama talking, not me, but that didn't mean she was wrong. In fact, it meant she was right. Mama always was. Whether it was a shiny shell, a silver necklace, a wooden ball, a camel . . . How do you lose a camel?

The same way you lost your partner. You looked away for a minute or he outthought you. Kimano and Zeke weren't anything alike, but the result was the same. Kimano's attention span had been that of your average happy surfer dude and his camel had no trouble sneaking off. Zeke's attention ranged wildly from one end to the other . . . from the "I don't care, so it doesn't exist in my world" to the "on you like glue for as long as it takes to obliterate your ass." He wasn't Inigo Montoya. No one had killed his father. But he was prepared to die, if that's what it took to get the task at hand done. It wasn't Zeke's attention span that had him here. No, it was trust. He had trusted his partner and Griffin had done the same as that damn camel. Walked away.

Zeke hadn't lost him. Griffin had lost himself.

"Griffin's gone," he said again. The word was slightly different, but the meaning was the same.

It had been a long day. I hadn't opened the bar . . . again. Blood, dead tourists, dead demons, Titans. If there were such things as bad vibes, they were filling up the place today—another shot in the pocketbook, although money was the least of my worries. Cronus was my only worry right now, and while I thought on that, I went out. I shopped for some purely illegal guns, though nothing special caught my attention, grabbed a real nonmicrowaveable meal—if you can call a salad a meal and you can't—and came home to clean. If I'm cleaning, I'm in a bad way. I like things neat, but I don't necessarily like to make them neat personally. I'll do it, but I will put it off and off and off some more. But with a Titan taking over Hell and Leo hauling a body out to the desert, there was no time like the present.

I was working on the black stain that had once been Armand. I was on my knees on the floor with a heavy-duty scrub brush and cursing the demon with every swipe when Zeke kicked down the front door. At first glance, I wasn't that concerned; Zeke had a key. Sometimes he remembered to use it; sometimes he didn't. Sometimes it was important . . . ten demons in the newest club reaping souls. Sometimes it wasn't . . . I'm hungry. Feed me. This time it wasn't either. It was vital—to Zeke the most crucial thing in the world.

"What do I do?" he asked numbly. "He's gone. What the fuck do I do?" The glass in the door was supposed to be shatterproof. The pool of it around his feet as he stood in the doorway said I deserved a refund, but considering I'd all but stolen the bar, I couldn't complain.

I could find out what was going on with Zeke though. I stood and peeled off my thick rubber gloves. "Lost, Kit? Gone? What do you mean?" He didn't mean dead. If Griffin were dead, Zeke would know it and he wouldn't be standing here talking about it. He'd go through as many demons as he had to to catch up to Griffin—on this side of life or the next, it was as simple as that. I would do my best to take care of the former angel if something did happen to Griffin, but Zeke wasn't Zeke without Griffin and he knew it. Zeke was a ship, but Griffin wasn't his anchor. Zeke's ship had a hole in the hull and Griffin was the one bailing the ocean back out. He was the one who kept Zeke from plummeting to the darkest depths. For all that I was willing, only Griffin had that power.

"He went out this morning. He said he wanted to get some food, bring back breakfast. He's been doing it a lot lately. Going out for food instead of cooking. He likes to cook." He frowned. "He likes to cook. Why has he been going out so much when he likes to cook?"

Why indeed? "Kit," I verbally prodded him. "Griffin went out to get breakfast, and then what?"

He looked around as if he'd forgotten where he was before shaking off his reverie. "He didn't come back." One piece of red hair hung loose from the yanked-back ponytail he wore for fighting. "I called him and his phone is turned off." He hoped. Turned off was better than destroyed. "I looked, all the places we go." "Go" meant where they hung around looking for demons and "looked" meant he'd stolen a car. The two of them had only one car. Zeke's decision-making skills weren't compatible with driving as a rule. Passing a driver's test for a license could conceivably end up with him at the California agriculture checkpoint declaring an intent to smuggle a case of silicone breast implants and an Elvis impersonator in the trunk, not to mention a panicked test instructor in the passenger seat screaming for help.

"And no one had seen him?" I moved over to him and pulled him into the bar. Zeke would've asked too and asked hard. I took his hand and he was far gone enough to actually wrap his fingers around mine and hang on. Lost, damn it, was the worst word I knew.

"No," he answered.

"You can't hear him?" Zeke's telepathy was usually limited to a few miles, but with Griffin, I didn't know how far it reached. Maybe the city, maybe the country.

"No." Each no was sounding more and more bleak.

"How far *can* you hear him?"

"The world." Stark and simple. "I can hear him anywhere in the world."

I didn't think they'd tested that principle, unless it had been a mission while Eden House was still around in Vegas, but I didn't question it. If Zeke said it was so, it was so. "Then he's unconscious, which means he's alive and that means we'll find him. Stay here. I need my shotgun." One of them. It wasn't as if I named them. First, I wasn't concerned about the size of my nonexistent penis. Second, guns were for killing . . . no matter what some amendment said. Guns were for killing, nothing more, nothing less. You appreciated what a great job a gun did performing its function, but that's it. If you named something like that, something manufactured for the sole purpose of ending life, you had problems. You were sick.

I chose my Browning Gold, a semiautomatic and autoloading shotgun and not called Goldy . . . as tempting as it might be. As I clattered back downstairs, Zeke's gaze was so raw and naked that I wanted to look away, but then it focused on what I was carrying. "Goldy."

All right. Not sick. Different. Never had a pet when he was young—human young. Didn't have action figures or toys. Nothing to name in those foster-kid days. Zeke could call my shotgun whatever he wanted.

"Goldy." I kissed his cheek. "Now, let's get Griffin. Did you try Bubba?"

"Beelzebub." There was enough of Zeke with me, barely, to wrinkle his lip at that. "What could he possibly know? Demon wannabe. Stupid shithead."

"Exactly," I said. "A wannabe follows the real things. He listens. He could know things precisely because they have the same opinion of him that we do. He's a nut job. They wouldn't pay attention to him."

"Beelzebub" was a rare exception in the demonic sense. He was just a guy. He'd played around with a lot of things in his time, I'm sure. Rocker who couldn't sing or play an instrument. Goth who didn't have the ennui down quite right. Emo when emo was so very last year,

A satanist who really wasn't a satanist. After all, *Those books are thick. Reading is hard.* The Necronomicon *isn't even real. Who knew?* Patterning yourself on a bad late-night TV movie is easier than doing actual research. And, to give credit where it was due, the real satanists, who are rare and far between . . . the genuine ones, the down-and-dirty ones—they get their desire sooner or later. Off to Hell they go. A Twinkie or bag of chips to be devoured whenever the torture becomes boring for the demons. I didn't think that's what they had planned when they were butchering Wilbur the pig or Foghorn Leghorn the rooster on their altar while trying to say the Lord's Prayer backward . . . which would be the satanic DUI test. Instead of ZYXWVU, while touching your nose with a fingertip, you had to pull off "Amen. Ever and ever for glory the and, power . . ." while chopping off a chicken's head. They could chant and chop all they wanted. They still ended up as a TV dinner.

Bubba didn't go that way though. He was such a thoroughly slobbering, pathetic, slimy wannabe that the demons did the absolute worst thing they could to him.

They ignored him.

When you ignore someone for so long you forget they're even there, whether you're a con artist demon or not. You say things you shouldn't, and Bubba, although he couldn't do jack shit with the information, heard it all. And now we would go find out if anything he'd picked up today had to do with Griffin. And while Zeke couldn't find Griffin, I knew precisely where to find Bubba. . . . I had his pamphlet. *Tours of Satanic Sin City . . . because when the sun goes down, it all goes down.* He should've given up the satanism and become a copywriter. There was slightly more money in it and a whole lot less demon-on-human mutilation.

"Fine. Let's get the satanic shithead and ask him some questions. Only you'd better ask them." He closed his eyes and ground the heel of his hand against his forehead—still trying to find Griffin, on the inside if not out. "Because right now, I want to hurt someone. I really, really want to hurt someone. Too much."

"Trust me, Kit. I won't be walking on any eggshells around him, but I'll leave enough of him to do some talking." If he knew anything. When you've pinned your first and last hope on a satanic school bus–driving demon wannabe, you knew it was going to be a bad night.

We caught up with him at Carluccio's Tivoli Gardens. It was a restaurant next to the Liberace Museum and whether Liberace was a tricked-up demon, an angel of blinding light, or only an entertainer who thought rhinestones were the greatest invention of God and Man and wanted to outshine the sun itself, I didn't know. I was always curious, yes, but at times it was best to let some things go. Keep a little mystery alive.

Keeping Bubba alive . . . Well, we'd see.

His old school bus, painted black, naturally, with wispy white ghosts and staring, bloody red eyes, was idling by the Gardens, hoping to pick up some tourist action. There were reputable ghost tours in Vegas. Fun in the absent sun pointing out the gangster Bugsy Siegel's hotel, the Flamingo, the "Motel of Death" where many celebrities had died—I'd never caught exactly who those celebrities were—a haunted park with a "demon" child, and the Gardens, where Liberace's ghost occasionally had a snit fit. A phantom rhinestone wedgie was nothing to mess with, I was sure.

Bubba's tour, on the other hand, was not reputable, not licensed, not legal, and not especially hygienic—all of which kept him on the move, trying to pick up tourists on the go. The Gardens were his second fishing stop of the night and we caught him there just as he was leaving. I didn't bother to look for a parking spot, pulling up on the sidewalk and ditching the Cobra. It would either be towed or stolen. I didn't give a damn either way. If we could find Griffin, a lucky thief could keep the car.

I caught the bus door as it was closing, pushed it back open, and went up the two steps to stand just behind and right at Bubba's ear. "You weren't trying to leave without us, were you, Beelzebub?"

Zeke sat in the first seat, forming the point to our triangle. "Bastard." He had one of his guns out, a sawed-off Remington, and a white-knuckled grip on it. He wasn't worried about any threat from Beelzebub . . . a hundred Beelzebubs would barely get a yawn out of him. He was worried for Griffin, which might be Beelzebub's fall after all, threat or no threat.

"Go on and drive, Bubba." I leaned an elbow on his shoulder and smiled at our shared reflection in the long rearview mirror. "You don't look happy to see me. You don't look happy at all. But that's all right. I have a theory about people. Happy people aren't made; they're born . . . like golden retrievers—bouncy and cheerful and full of love and play. And then, sugar"—I nipped his ear hard, enough to draw a single drop of blood—"there are the rest of us. We aren't happy. We aren't bouncy. But we do like to play. Only I'm not sure that you want to play the kind of games I do." I tossed my Browning to Zeke and had a knife at Beelzebub's neck in an instant.

Bubba—I could think of him as Beelzebub with a straight face for only so long—was a thin guy. He had the requisite long hair dyed so black that it looked like the world's worst Halloween wig. He had multiple piercings, some of which I was sure were hidden and I didn't want to see, and what he thought were satanic tattoos ringing his neck, but what I was almost positive said "I suck Cthulhu's dick" in Latin. The tattoo artist had seen him coming a mile away. Bubba wasn't solely a wannabe demon. He was a wannabe *anything*. He was almost worth feeling sorry for if I hadn't thought he tortured animals as a kid, pulled wings off flies, killed birds with a BB gun. He had that look, that smell, that taste to the air around him. A trickster should've made him a pet project a long time ago, but like some projects, he wasn't worth it. When a chemistry project went wrong, you poured it down the lab sink and started over. Bubba had "Do over" written all over him.

"Bubba," I said softly, "some people say the fastest way to a man's heart is a hollow point. One nice explosion and then a pile of mush that no one wants on a Valentine's Day card. But I honestly don't care about the fastest way myself. I like the fun way." I moved the knife and suddenly the point sank into the flesh over his heart . . . not much. Only a fraction of an inch, but enough that he understood the seriousness of my play. "When a woman like me breaks a man's heart, we like to do it slowly." I smiled again at him in the mirror, wider, and showed my teeth in a flash of white. His dark brown eyes went a little more glassy. "Thoroughly. And keep it whole enough so that it looks pretty in a jar on my bedroom dresser."

"What . . ." He swallowed and the *C* in Cthulhu jumped spasmodically, but the words were somewhat braver. "I ain't telling you anything, Iktomi. You're Heaven's whore, you bitch."

"Sugar, sugar." I let my smile widen. "You know my last name. Aren't I the privileged one? Haven't I made the big time? Did you hear that while scraping and crawling on the floor for any demonic crumbs? On your knees for a bunch of the Fallen? I think that makes you the whore, not me."

"They'll see I'm loyal. They'll see I'm worthy," he insisted. "They'll take me to Hell, to the Lord Who Rules All Others, and he'll make me like them. Divine."

I hadn't seen much of the divine, Above or Below, but deprogramming a self-brainwashed cluster of idiot cells that someone's toilet had coughed up would take more time than I was willing to spend and more sympathy than I had. Griffin needed us now. This asshole . . . He didn't need the truth about demons; he didn't need me to hold his pathetic little hand. What he needed was to give me some useful information before Zeke decided to rip off his head bare-handed.

"And I'll be sure to throw you a going-away party when that happens." This time when I moved the knife it was to slice him across his upper thigh; although the black jeans—satanists did love their black—didn't show the blood, it was safe to say Bubba felt the cut. He gave a low-pitched scream, the steering wheel wobbled under his hands, and the bus began to climb the curb.

The dangers of interrogation in a moving vehicle. Time to adapt.

"A challenge. That's even more entertaining." I grabbed his shirt and yanked all one hundred and twenty pounds of him backward. "Zeke, take the wheel, would you? And don't run over anything." As always with Zeke, I made the directions very clear. "No people, no dogs, no cars, no motorcycles, and stop when the light is red, pretty please."

He slid into the seat and maneuvered the bus back onto the street. "Rules. How does everyone remember all these stupid rules," he muttered.

I turned back to Bubba, trusting Zeke at least until it came to the moment that we would run over something the size of a Volkswagen. I had to. I trusted him far more with driving than with chatting up Bubba. Bubbas are considerably more fragile than Volkswagens. I'd pushed him on the aisle between the left and right rows of seats. Now I rested the heel of my boot, three inches easy, on his stomach. I'd grabbed them along with my shotgun. Every weapon helps. "Now, this is the part where you pay attention to me, every bit as much as you do the demons you follow around." I leaned and the heel sank into his stomach until I almost imagined I felt his spine beneath it. "Because, Bubba, some boots are made for walking and some for impromptu colonoscopies." I leaned harder. "You can turn over anytime. I charge so much less than your average proctologist."

His pale face, pitted with old acne scars, was starting to turn lavender in the neon light spilling into the bus. "Bubba, you need to start breathing," I reminded him. "I can't kill you if you kill yourself first. Suck it up, sweetie. If you can't be a man, you damn sure can't be a demon. *Breathe.*"

He did, exhaling one sour-smelling huge gasp of air and sucking another one in. Demons were monsters, filth, undeserving of existence, but I had to admit, when it came to Bubba, I was on their side. I wouldn't have eaten him either. He was wilted lettuce on chicken salad that had gone bad two weeks ago. Hopefully that would be the lizards' downfall. "You follow them, Bubba," I said, "from bar to bar, casino to casino. You watch as they buy souls. You probably even watch them kill innocents behind parked cars or in empty alleys. You're a worthless piece of shit and there's no getting around it, but if you tell me what I want to know, I won't kill you."

Then I told the lie . . . setting the hook. "And if I kill you now, you know where you'll end up—in Hell . . . with the damned . . . the tortured souls worth no more than maggots crushed under Lucifer's heel. But if you tell me the truth"—I eased up the pressure slightly on his stomach—"I'll let you live, give you time to prove to them you're worthy of being a prince in Hell. You know they don't believe that yet." I flipped the knife, caught it, and then jammed it into the rubber matting a hairbreadth away from his head. "Well, Bubba? Do you want that time or not?"

He did. The deluded ones, the idiots, they always did. The ones who imagined death was the worst thing that could happen to them. They were oh so wrong.

But he talked and that was all I cared about. "What . . . what the fuck do you want to know?" His voice quavered and I smelled the alcohol on his breath. Yep, no way he was getting through the Lord's Prayer backward.

"Griffin Reese, one of the last of Eden House. You know him, just like you know me. In the past few days while you were lurking, stalking, drooling over the local demons, did you hear anything about Griffin? My Griffin—which means you know I'll make it hurt if you lie." I jerked my head back toward Zeke. "*His* Griffin—and you know he'll kill you if you lie. Slowly. Painfully. Enough so that demons will give him a standing ovation. So, Bubba," I said, leaning down until we were face-to-face, a bare inch apart, "tell me about Griffin before we're tossing pieces of you out the windows like confetti at a parade."

Talk he did, which was a good thing for him. I might have lied about him becoming a prince in Hell, but I wasn't lying about what Zeke and I would do to him.

Beelzebub closed his eyes tightly. "Reese . . . one of

Eden House Vegas's last sycophants. One of their last canary lovers here. Wiping his ass with their feathers. Worthless fucking Boy Scout."

Boy Scout—the very thing I'd thought about Griffin and the thing only *I* was allowed to think about him. Not this worthless wannabe. I dug the heel in again and he yelped, "He's been hunting on his own for weeks, leaving his brain-dead partner home watching cartoons and acting as if he had something to prove. My side set up a way to prove something back." The sneer twisted his thin lips. "No man can take on Hell. No man can take on demons alone and win. If he's gone, and I guess he is or you wouldn't be here, it's because my kind took him. Set a trap and took him." His grin showed yellow teeth with a gap between the front two teeth. "They'll show the *man* what the *demon* can really do."

Man. Demon. Like he had something to prove. I'd thought Griffin had seemed tired lately, distracted, and he did have something to prove . . . or he thought he did. He was a peri, the first of the ex-demon kind, and while he didn't remember any of his demon days, he still knew. He had been a demon. He had done what demons did and worse than your average low-level demon. Griffin was intelligent and imaginative. He might not remember, but he could conjure up some likely scenarios in his mind's eye. I'd only known Griffin as a human and he was the best human I'd come across in my long life. He wasn't a Boy Scout. He was a Boy Scout to the power of a thousand. He protected the innocent; he helped Zeke and made him more than functional— he gave him a life. He'd saved more lives than he could keep count of, but it wasn't enough. Once it had all come out three months ago . . . Leo's and my trickster status, Zeke and Griffin being unknowing agents of Heaven and Hell. Angel and demon. Being an ex-angel annoyed Zeke, but he could deal with it precisely because he was Zeke. But Griffin finding out he was a demon, even if that status became ex-demon when he chose humanity over Hell . . . I should've known.

Griffin had been what he thought to be the worst of monsters, those he'd fought to the death after being recruited for Eden House. He had nothing to prove to any of us, but he had an enormous amount to prove to himself. Fighting demons with Zeke helped now that Eden House had fallen, but that wasn't enough. He had to kill more of what he'd once been, save more people that in the past he would've killed. But Griffin was too good. Held himself to an impossible standard. I wasn't sure he could save enough to save himself—to give him peace.

"Where?" I retrieved the knife, the rubber of the floor matting ripping. "I can put this in you anywhere you want. Pick one. Because if you don't tell me where Griffin is right this damn minute, *I'll* pick one and you won't like it. And the next spot you'll like even less."

He said he didn't know, that maybe there was this place they'd talked about, but he wasn't a hundred percent sure and I believed it. This useless brownnoser of all things demonic probably didn't know anything in this life that was a hundred percent. If he did, he wouldn't be kissing monster ass every minute he wasn't working or sleeping. A hundred percent sure or not, though, it was all we had.

The last thing he said before we threw him off the bus was suddenly pitiful after his boasting of Hell's might and how he'd be a part of it. "Don't tell them I told you. Don't tell them . . ." And then Zeke kicked him through the door, the last words swallowed up by the sound of his impact against the pavement, the scream as something in him snapped—an arm or leg. It didn't matter. He had known about Griffin for weeks.

Of course I was going to tell them. The wannabe would find out what it was like to get what he wanted ... to be noticed by demons. If we left any alive.

Chapter 8

A repossessed house isn't the same as a possessed house and shouldn't be frightening, especially in Vegas where it's all stucco, everything looks the same, and you could drive to five different houses before you ever recognized your own. There was no stereotypical haunted house "look." Besides, a repossessed house, scary qualities aside, didn't make a good spot to hide. Right now there were hundreds of them and if you threw a rock at two real estate agents, chances were fifty-fifty you'd hit a demon, but usually houses still were not a good place to hole up for a demon. Normally if they didn't want their bad behavior noticed, they'd take it out of town to the desert where only the burros and jackrabbits were there to see . . . or to hear.

Which made it odd that if they'd set a trap for Griffin, they would bring him to a house within yards of other houses . . . except the entire neighborhood was abandoned. Half built on the edge of town, those few who'd lived there at its conception had lost it all when the housing market crashed. Apparently the developer had too. Skeletons of houses were slowly falling apart, dead before they were even fully born. No one was left to hear the screaming . . . and demons did love to make their victims scream—and beg and plead, but mostly

scream. Sometimes for someone to save them . . . anyone . . . God, Jesus, Allah, Mommy. Usually no one did.

Life was like that. If there was a master plan in place,
fairness didn't seem to enter into it. And as much as my
kind and I tried to make up for that . . . vengeance is
never as good as remaining innocent and whole.

"I can't hear him. I can't hear him. I can't hear him."
Zeke was in the front seat, a .480 Ruger in his hand. He
was rocking slightly, back and forth. The chanting and
rocking made him look like a lost child. The gun and
murderous rage that made his face as blank as an executioner's hood made him look anything but.

I'd taken over the driving. I wanted Griffin safe almost as much as Zeke did, but I didn't want to plow over
the top of some granny's ecofriendly little hybrid to do
it. Cute, save-the-planet green, and made for getting
caught in the undercarriage of a bus driven by a hell-
bent-for-leather man with tunnel vision for saving his
partner. "If you don't hear him, then he's unconscious.
He's not in any pain. That's good, right?" I stopped the
bus on a road now covered with layers of dirt except for
one clear set of tire tracks. Demons could pop in and out
as they pleased, but they couldn't do it with people. Either they had to have permission, like the old completely
false myth of the vampire needing an invitation, or the
person wouldn't survive the trip. I didn't know which it
was and I didn't care right now. All I cared about was
Griffin and if they brought him here, they'd have to do
it the mundane way—in a car. About two blocks away
one house, a finished one that had once had landscap-
ing that had since died, hosted a light—one light that
flickered, in and out, like a campfire or like a tiny bit of
Hell itself.

"I *can't* hear him. How can that be good? How can

that be any fucking good?" Zeke bolted to his feet and was through the door into the night and running before I had a chance to snatch at his shirt, an arm, anything at all. Desperation—where human speed ended and more-than-human began.

"Shit." I was right behind him, or so I thought, as he began to pull away from me. Maybe Zeke always heard him, even when Griffin was asleep. There could be some internal hum all the time, ocean waves against a subconscious shore, a mental heartbeat. I'd thought Zeke would know if Griffin was alive or dead, but I might have been wrong. He could be running on nothing but hope or denial, and I couldn't know for sure, because I couldn't catch him to ask.

I pushed myself to go faster when I knew there was nothing left to give, but surprisingly I was wrong. Desperation worked for Zeke and it worked for me as well. I ran through the door of the house only seconds behind him to nearly crash into him. He was still, looking up, as stunned as someone watching the sky fall—the moon and stars, all coming down in an impossible crash and burn. The end of days. The end of life . . . the end of his life.

"Now, now, Tweetie. Don't look so sad. He's not dead. I keep my promises . . . well, almost never. But this time I made an exception."

I ignored Eli's voice as I followed Zeke's unwavering focus to Griffin hanging above us. His wrists were tied together and that rope wrapped several times to the wrought-iron rail of the second-floor loft. His feet hung just inches over our heads. In the low light, candlelight, I recognized without thought, I could see the purpling bruise that covered one side of his face, from temple to jaw. His shirt was ripped and bloody, but not saturated.

The slashes were superficial, but the head wound, that wasn't. Eligos was telling the truth though. Griffin was still breathing. He was alive, but unconscious. That's why Zeke couldn't hear him now, but would hear him again.

Absolutely goddamn would.

Zeke was growling now. It wasn't the sound a human would make, nor an angel or demon. It was the sound of fury incarnate and Eli was a trigger pull away from being a puddle incarnate dripping off the chair he was currently sitting in. I'd looked away from Griffin and there was my least favorite demon in all his glory through the arched doorway to the right . . . having takeout on the dining room table by candlelight, which I knew he thought brought out the highlights in his hair. I was not in the mood for that or any other of his vanities.

"It's Thai." He tilted the chair back and waved a fork spearing a piece of chicken. I could smell the coconut curry. "I didn't think you were ever going to figure it out and get here. I would've eaten my compadres instead of wasting them to grout cleaner if I'd known you'd be so long." That's when I saw the pools of black on the tile floor surrounding the table—enough to have been at least ten demons.

"So who told you?" he added as he leaned back farther and forked the chicken into his mouth. I put a hand on Zeke's wrist before he could raise his hand and pull that trigger.

"Get Griffin down, Kit," I murmured. "We need to get him to a hospital. He's the important thing now, not Eligos." Zeke often couldn't see reason or rather, he saw a reason that escaped the rest of us, but he saw the truth in what I said and was gone instantly up one side of two sets of stairs in the foyer that led up to the second floor.

"Come on, Trixa. I saved your peri from some flunkies who thought they had enough brain cells to actually have ideas and *plans* of their own." He snorted. "Plans . . . Can you believe that? I told you I wouldn't make a move on your pets for a year, and I went wildly above and beyond that promise to save this one from demons other than myself. I think a little reward . . ."

"Beelzebub," I said, cutting him off. "We left him on Tropicana Avenue. He was mostly in one piece if you're interested in changing that."

"Ah." He made a face. "You made that far too easy. You're no fun at all," he grumbled, dropping the fork into the Styrofoam container. "I was ready to use my wiles, the pure sex appeal that comes off me in waves. Hell, it comes off me like a damn tsunami and you go and ruin it by just giving up that piece of fucking worthless shit."

I gave him a smile, but it wasn't for him or for me. . . . It was for Griffin. There was only one reason I hadn't killed Beelzebub myself . . . because having a demon do it would be the worst death Beelzebub could suffer. His blackly pathetic hopes would die before his body did. Death of spirit, death of body, and it still wouldn't be enough to pay for having a part, no matter how passive, in what had been done to Griffin.

"Think you're clever, don't you?" Eli said, waving a hand through the flame of the several candles surrounding his dinner. The flames spread over his hand before he extinguished them with a snap of his fingers. "But I know what you want, his death to be the slightest edge more horrifying because it comes from his most eager hope. Perhaps his last hope. I like the way you think, Trixa. But guess what? I'm no one's subcontractor and I've done you favor enough today. Hanging around aboveground where Cronus could take my wings, all to

save a former fellow rebel. I'd think you'd be grateful . . .
not trying to shovel more work onto me." He pushed
the container of Thai food away. "I remember him, you
know. There isn't a demon in Hell I don't know, but your
pet . . . Glasya-Labolas . . . he hung with the big boys.
Not as big or bad as me, naturally, but neither was he
a former Candygram pigeon. He had balls. He was on
the front lines in the Fall—one of the willing, not the
wandering. Justly damned, not drafted. A true soldier,
a warrior of God and Lucifer. And after we set up shop
Downstairs, he did things. . . ." He grinned, happy to be
spreading the news. "Let's just say he set the bar a little higher for those who someday might hope to be . . .
well . . . me."

"He's not Glasya-Labolas. He's not a demon. He's
something so different from you, you could never comprehend it." Before I could move to stab him with the
fork he'd discarded, Zeke called my name. I stepped
back out of the doorway and beneath Griffin's unconscious body.

"Catch him."

I looked up to see Zeke's face, pale and set, as he
began to saw through the rope with one of his many
knives. "I won't let him fall," I promised. No, no matter what Glasya-Labolas had done, Griffin would never
fall.

The rope snapped. Zeke caught it and fed it hand over
hand until I caught Griffin around the waist—a tumbling
mass of limp legs, arms, and flopping blond hair. Either
the hair or his soap smelled strongly of strawberries and
I had an instant flash of who'd last done the shopping.
Ninety-nine-cent shampoo. In the basket it goes. Pink?
So what if it's pink? It's ninety-nine cents. Zeke, so very
Zeke, and so very Griffin to have used it anyway, al-

though on the weeks he shopped I knew he'd drop fifty dollars on shampoo alone.

It was a warm moment that vanished quickly when I realized that holding up one hundred and seventy pounds of unconscious male when I now had a completely human body wasn't precisely easy. I'd have to start lifting weights along with the running.

With Cronus in my life? I should live so long.

I eased Griffin to the floor, made it look simple, and pulled my phone to call 911. It was a triumph over protesting muscles, the second part of it, but I did it . . . because Eli was watching. In the midst of it all . . . Cronus and Griffin . . . Eli was still watching and if I forgot that, I wouldn't be around to worry about living with a Titan on the warpath. A demon would take me out instead. "Do me a favor, Eli," I said as I put a thumb on Griffin's right eyelid and lifted it and then followed with the left. His pupils were equal and reactive to the light. That was good, very good.

"Do you a favor?" He sounded interested and, worse yet, sounded as if he were right at my shoulder . . . ghosting up without me hearing a single scuff of his shoe. "You would owe me a genuine debt? One you would actually pay this time instead of being the liar and thief you were last time?" He said liar and thief with an oddly possessive affection. He'd said it before—fooling and cheating him while killing Solomon was as intriguing as it got to a demon bored with eternity.

"One I would pay," I replied after I finished with the 911 operator. Zeke was beside us now, his hand cupping Griffin's jaw and then his forehead resting against the slowly rising and falling chest. Listening . . . and not for a heartbeat. As much as he hated Eligos and Eligos being that close to any of us, he could see only one thing now.

"And how could I possibly take your word on that?" came a rightfully skeptical question.

Like Zeke, I had eyes for only one person and that wasn't Eli. I had one aim, one goal, and I'd do anything to accomplish it. "In Kimano's name. In my brother's name, I'll return the favor. Now take the car the demons drove out here with Griffin or the bus and drive away. I want something I can build a story on for the cops."

"A small favor, then. Mine won't be." His hand was on my shoulder, but with a far different emotion than was passing from Zeke to Griffin. "You didn't ask about the Roses."

"Those Roses are your plan. Your scheme to stop Cronus. That is not my problem and has nothing to do with me, apologies to the Roses," I dismissed. It was the best way to sell a concept to a mark. Make them believe the idea was theirs and theirs alone and they'd do all they could to make it happen.

"My plan. Exactly. And the boss liked it." Eli's hand tapped a finger on my shoulder. "He did simultaneously explode a few of his top advisers and it sounded as if he'd destroyed a small chunk of Hell, but that is the best part of not knowing precisely where your boss is"—and why Cronus wanted to—"since you don't have to see the expression on his face when things aren't running as smoothly as he'd care for."

I could hear a siren in the distance. "That sounds wonderful for you, Eli. Your work ethic astounds me. Now take the car and go."

This time the clamp of his hand was painful, but I didn't let him see it. "We set the Roses free an hour ago. Find out if that satisfies Cronus. Find out soon." Then he was gone to drive off one of the vehicles to create more of an evidence mishmash for the cops. As for the freedom of the Roses satisfying Cronus, unfortunately for Eli and Hell, that wasn't going to happen.

But it certainly satisfied me.

The hospital was as most hospitals are or I was guessing. This was only my second time in one. But they were similar. Busy, sharp with the smell of alcohol, and staff who positively wouldn't consider letting nonfamily members stay with a patient . . . unless you were the patient's power of attorney—that would be me. Eden House demon slayers weren't the only ones with a library of fake IDs to hand out. When it came to kicking Zeke out . . . there was absolutely no admittance, and then there were the absolute exceptions. The doctor and the nurses each had a quick look at Zeke and that was the end of that. No calling security. No urging him out. Zeke, at the moment, was why people in the Bible feared to look upon angels.

They were scary sons of bitches, some of them. It hadn't been a demon or Lucifer who'd killed the first-born of Egypt. It had been an angel. The staff in the ER saw, unknowingly, in Zeke what people had cast their eyes away from in ancient times—the inexplicable or a reckoning. Trying to toss Zeke back out to the waiting room was a reckoning waiting to happen. Wisely, no one took him up on it.

The police had come and gone and I'd given them a story about being kidnapped by two men with guns—we sacrificed my favorite shotgun and Zeke's Ruger for verisimilitude—very pasty white men who beat up our friend, robbed us, and then left us—not to die, but probably because they were late for the latest World of Warcraft campaign or a slot machine appointment with their grandma. They were, after all, incredibly, unbelievably practically glow-in-the-dark white . . . with socks . . . and sandals.

About time that slice of the population had the blame dumped on them for some fake crime. I was happy to even the score a bit, although good luck narrowing down "two pasty white men" in Vegas where the tourists primarily came in two colors—alabaster and fake-tan orange.

Zeke went with Griffin for the CAT scan and I waited, pacing—no hard plastic chair for me, no standing still when my boys might need me. I called Leo and filled him in. "Goddamn kid." He sighed at Griffin's one-man quest to make up for a past that wasn't his anymore. I'd reminded him Griffin might be older than Leo was; you couldn't be sure. Correction, I couldn't be sure. Leo could. "Older than you, little girl, maybe, but he's not older than I am."

"Because you're forever, 'Grandpa,'" I mocked, an argument we'd long thrown back and forth between each other.

"Damn close." He sounded smug. He sounded less so when I told him Hell had set the Roses free. "That's nice for the Roses, escaping torture and being a demon's supper, but it doesn't help us with the Cronus situation or the Eligos situation when he finds out what you've done. You managed to kick Hell's ass and fuck up intentionally all in one. That is quite a trick."

"But it's a good one, isn't it?" I asked, an excitement no trickster could deny sparking through me . . . distant fireworks on a passing Fourth of July. What I'd done was more than good. It was, for one, nearly impossible to pull off. Second, it saved thousands of souls from horror, then nonexistence. Third, and best of all, it screwed Hell itself. You couldn't ask for a better hat trick than that.

but that would be an insult to what they had. The description fell so very short. Yet Griffin had walked out the door on that and disappeared. That hadn't been part of his plan, but it had happened.

Worse, though, he'd taken his bucket when he'd gone, leaving Zeke sinking fast. There was no Zeke without Griffin—the same as there would be no Griffin without Zeke. They both had a responsibility to each other that they thought they understood, but they didn't, not entirely. There was no one without the other and when they fought demons, it was something they had to remember. Saving your partner was pointless if you didn't save yourself too, because, in the end, it was one in the same.

"Griffin." I bent down and cupped his cheek before kissing the corner of his mouth. "I had no idea you were such an idiot."

He blinked a few more times as the thoughts swam in and out behind the blue and the puzzlement began to clear. "Oh. The demons."

"Yes. Oh. The demons." This side of his face was unbruised and pale, faint blond stubble beginning to show on his jaw. "If you keep trying to make up for something you never did, especially alone . . . If you keep trying to prove to us something we already know is true, then you won't be around very long. And if you're not, then Zeke won't be either. Did you think of that when you left this morning when you were lying to Zeke with your thoughts?"

He swallowed and slid his gaze toward Zeke, who was most meticulously not looking back at him. "No . . . wasn't. I'm sorry."

Zeke kept his head turned away. "Trixa, tell the asshole he's not half as sorry as he's going to be."

"Kit says not half as sorry as you're going to be," I parroted faithfully and somewhat gleefully—the relief was so great. "You screwed up, Griffin, and it's time to take your medicine. I'm not standing in the way of that. How would you learn if I did?"

"I'm not the teacher"—he coughed a dry cough, the same as you gave after a long sleep—"anymore?" His hand tightened on Zeke's again.

"Not for a while at least." I patted his chest now covered in a hospital gown. "It'll do you good. I think you might've forgotten we all have lessons to learn. We're all teachers and we're all students, and I'm thinking, sugar, you're due a little detention."

"Not a little. A lot. A *lot*." The glower was directed at me over a shoulder, and I obediently relayed the message, using my fingers to comb through Griffin's tangled hair, but the blood and dirt were there to stay until the next shampoo, the hospital version or strawberry scented.

"I almost feel sorry for you when he does speak to you." I gave up on his hair.

"He is speaking to me." He raised his free hand to rub unsteadily at his head. It had to hurt. Being pulled out of a coma wasn't going to change that. "Just because it's not with words or thoughts"—he closed his eyes—"doesn't mean anything. What he feels . . ." The hand fell back to the bed as Zeke's head bowed. No words, but they were communicating and it was heartbreaking to see, as necessary as it was. Now Griffin would have a whole different guilt to deal with. I hope he dealt with it better than the unnecessary ex-demon one.

"I'll go get the nurse. They'll give you something for the pain once they get over your practically supernatural recovery. Just don't tell them quite how supernatural." I patted him again, his shoulder this time, the same spot I gripped when I reached across the bed to touch Zeke. "I'll be back in the morning." I'd only be one in a crowd in the next few minutes. I'd let Zeke have what small amount of extra room there was going to be. Miracles tended to suck the oxygen and space out of a room, and now that I had Griffin back, both my boys safe and whole, there was a catastrophe heading my way—heading everyone's way. Mama said there was always a catastrophe coming. Someone's world was always coming to an end. It wasn't our worry to change every ending, only the endings we could. Know your limitations, girl, else you become one yourself.

This time though, Mama didn't know. One ending could be every ending this time. One fall could be everyone's fall.

"Thanks, Trixa, for saving me." Zeke gave a discontented grunt. "For helping Zeke save me," Griffin corrected himself.

"My not-so-great pleasure. Don't get yourself in trouble like that again, not the self-made kind anyway. Besides, I was only along for the ride, to make sure Zeke didn't tear Vegas down to the foundations to find you." I paused at the door to look back at both of them, but particularly Griffin. "Remember that. If I wasn't here, what Zeke would've done and I can't say I blame him. He's listened to you for all his life"—all the one he could remember—"so now I think it's time you listened to him for a while." I held up a finger. "Except on running over grandmas driving tiny ecofriendly hybrids with your big satanic bus. Listen and learn, but there are limits."

I raised three other fingers to join the first and give them a quick wave good-bye as I left. They needed the time, and I would only be a third wheel to that bicycle ...

or a second wheel to the unicycle. Codependency, it isn't ever a good thing in the human world, but in the supernatural world, sometimes it could be the very best thing—for some the only thing that kept them sane.

I notified the nurse, who ran for the doctor. I called Leo to tell him to skip the hospital and go home for the night. Then I followed my own advice, ducked under the frame that had once held glass, and walked through my door. Despite the gaping hole in it, I knew nothing would be missing. In this neighborhood, no one except desperate drug addicts tried to steal from me. And if a stranger tried, he wouldn't leave this neighborhood without an ass-kicking he wouldn't soon forget. My neighbors loved me. Free-alcohol Fridays made sure of that. As I stood on the shattered glass Zeke had left earlier—one more chore for the morning—all the lights came on simultaneously. The jukebox, which was decorative—it hadn't worked since about the time they'd stopped making records—came to life, and the sounds of "Hallelujah" by Leonard Cohen filled the room. It could've been worse. It could've been "Teen Angel."

Because that was who was waiting for me, minus the teen part. Shoulder-length blond hair, white wings barred with gold, and eyes the color of the water where the *Titanic* had sunk. Dark gray-blue. Oh, and he had a sword.

The angel quirked his lips very slightly. "You wouldn't believe what a bitch it was getting this through airport security."

I shot the jukebox with the gun hidden in the dead plant by the door, put the weapon back, and then dropped my face into my hands. I liked Ishiah. I trusted Ishiah to a certain point, which was big for a trickster. But I did not need this. I didn't want this. I didn't even want to *see* it. Not now. I was exhausted. I had too much on my plate and I just wanted to sleep.

"Trixa," the voice coaxed. "It won't be like last time, my word, not that you have anyone but yourself to blame for that." There was that attitude. That disapproving, condescending attitude. "I'm here to assist you. Only that. There will be no last time this time."

Last time. I didn't want to talk about the last time. I didn't want to think about the last time. I wished the last time could be erased from time itself altogether, because I would never live it down. Not until my dying day.

Last time. Why did he have to bring it up? I considered taking out the gun again and doing to myself what I'd done to the jukebox.

Hallelujah, my ass.

More like Hellelujah.

Chapter 9

I went downstairs in the morning, late . . . around eleven, but it was a long night and I'd called Zeke around eight a.m. to hear Griffin was doing well, but was still an asshole. Reassured about his physical health if not the lack of improvement in his assholery, I went back to sleep for another two and a half hours. When I did get up, I dressed for success after showering. No sweats or T-shirts for running or the occasional footy pajamas for comfort sleeping. I wanted this particular angel to know I was in business and meant it as well. With a thin long-sleeve sweater in psychedelic swirls of dark red, bronze, and black; black jeans and boots; and a flashy gold and garnet of earrings to match the tiny stud in my nose.

Leo was there . . . at the opposite end of the bar, staring unblinking at the angel who had taken a stool at the other end. He might have spent the night on that stool, or on the couch in Leo's office, gotten a hotel. . . . I didn't know. Last night I'd walked past him without a word and gone upstairs to sleep. Where he did the same didn't worry me. He more than could take care of himself, the scar on his jaw told you that. Now he was staring as unblinkingly back at Leo, giving just as good as he got until he heard me. Then he swiveled, took me in, and gave a grave nod. "The new look becomes you. And from Mica to Trixa Iktomi. That suits you as well, but a last name? How human of you."

Mica had been like Cher or Madonna. One name needed only, for the last time I'd seen Ishiah—who wasn't technically an angel anymore, although I'd known him when he had been one, making his list of who went into the Roman orgies and who walked righteously by. Stick up his ass the same as all of them. Not worth wasting your breath on with his "Thou shall not this; thou shall not that" sanctimonious attitude. But when he went native . . . retired and became a peri, he mellowed. Slowly, but he had. The last time I'd seen him, the infamous *last time*, he hadn't been bad at all, especially considering what we'd done to his bar. At the time, although he was retired, I hadn't considered him on our side by any means. It was one of the few times I'd been . . . not so much wrong, but not quite right either. When Ishiah had gone native, he'd thoroughly done that deal. He tried to stay neutral . . . like Switzerland, only without the corrupt banks.

No, Ishiah wasn't a bad guy.

"Swoop your feather-duster ass over here and give me a hug, sugar." I spread my arms and hugged him hard when he stepped up. The wings had been put away and I could feel the muscle of his back under his shirt. Leo snorted. He was either jealous or playing at being jealous. I did the same for him, both kinds. We were good for each other's ego that way. But, honestly, a peri and me? No. He might be an expatriate of Heaven, but I could still get a whiff of the holy off him and that wasn't the best of cologne for turning me on. But he wasn't bad for a peri and a friend to many *païen* kind, so I hugged him again before stepping back. "Do I look that different? I can't remember what I looked like during the Exodus."

So many looks, so many outsides; it was what was inside that made you. It was the inside you had to remember.

"Your hair was black and straight, your skin was a darker brown, and your eyes were pale blue-green. The color of glacier lakes, you told me." He continued while raising an eyebrow, "Shameful that it is, you were still vain then too. And don't call it the Exodus. It's disrespectful."

I was not vain. I never chose cookie-cutter beauty. I chose to be different, exotic, wild, and everything most people saw every day on separate people but combined into one unforgettable whole. Why have a boring vanilla wafer when you can have a chocolate chip–peanut butter–coconut-caramel cookie? Vain. Hardly. But disrespectful, that I was and claimed with pleasure. "Why not? That's what it was. Why let a perfectly good word go unused because your kind used it once and capitalized it first?"

An Exodus it had been too—seventy years ago in New York City. Eden House New York had still existed and angels and demons were everywhere. Angels had been ordering their Eden House human soldiers to wipe the demons clean from the city, but that wasn't going to happen—they didn't have the numbers and angels rarely fought these days when they had their humans to do it for them. The demons were determined to take out Eden House and have one helluva good time in the process. No one knew what made each side take a stand there. There were hundreds of cities worldwide and they had a presence in all of them. Why was each side determined to make New York theirs and theirs only? I doubt they knew themselves. Sometimes there doesn't need to be a reason, only egos and idiocy.

Seventy years ago those egos and idiocy blew up. It

became so blatant that people were starting to notice—even oblivious people living in their mundane, no-surprises-left-in-the-world existences. They began to question. They began to look—they saw miracles and horrors, and while it was written off to religious hysteria for a few weeks, someone else noticed too—noticed the danger.

We did. The *païen*.

There were plenty of us in New York. An aware human population was the last thing we needed. Our numbers were dropping as the years spooled out and if humans found out about angels and demons living among them, how long would it be until they found out about us? How long would we last if they did?

We hadn't waited to find out. I hooked an arm with Ishiah and led him over to Leo. "You damn sure missed out, Leo. They bussed in all the *païen* in the tristate area and some of us came from even farther to get in on the action. We steel-toed their asses out of the city like Adam and Eve out of paradise. Nearly every *païen* species alive came together. It was unprecedented." I smiled, warm and happy at the memory. "Every demon who dared poke his head aboveground to shake the sulfur off his scaly feet, we killed. We caught every Eden Houser alive, kept some of the badder of us from eating them, tied them up, and put them on those same buses we rode in on. Sent them out. And after they'd seen us, not a one came back." Only the head of each Eden House knew about the *païen* kind—vamps, weres, tricksters, revenants, on and on. The soldiers didn't know. Demons were enough for them to handle, their bosses thought, and thought right. They not only didn't return, but a few ended up seeking mental health care ... of the inpatient-hospital kind. Pretty white coats that tied in

the back. Demons they could take, but us? That drove
them over the edge. Please. Crybaby candyasses.

And since then, neither angel nor demon has shown a
molting feather or scaly ass in New York City.

"It was like Mardi Gras." I leaned against Ishiah's
shoulder. By his expression, he had memories less
fond of the experience. "Beads, bondage, and breasts.
Wolves Gone Wild. And when those girls flash eight of
those honeydews at the guys, they get a whole mess of
beads."

Leo did look regretful on missing that, but he focused
in on Ishiah instead of dwelling on what might have
been. "And how did your ex-pigeon son of a bitch with
allegiance to no one manage to stay in the city? Obviously he did or he'd be pissed off at you, not contemplating fornication. Isn't that what your type calls it?" Leo
grinned darkly. "Fornication."

"I'm not contemplating fornication with Trixa,"
Ishiah said evenly—a little too evenly, a little too sure.
I wasn't vain, but I wasn't dead either. Give a girl some
validation. "I fornicate elsewhere." He folded his arms,
already on the defense, and I was suddenly more curious
than insulted. "The same elsewhere, the same someone,
in fact, that convinced your kind to let me stay in New
York. I don't call it fornication anymore." He presented
the information as if it were a secret handshake or a
cop's badge, and it was. We were brothers, comrades, or,
damn, practically in-laws.

"You're sleeping with *Robin*?" I said in disbelief.

"*Goodfellow*? You're screwing a puck? Worse yet,
that one?" Leo was even less disbelieving and did a good
imitation of being disgusted—which would be solely
because he couldn't keep up with a puck. Few could,
verbally, criminally, or sexually, and no one in the world

could keep up with Robin Goodfellow. Ishiah called me the vain one; he had his nerve. Robin was vanity walking . . . granted walking practically on three legs, rather than two, but vanity was vanity—well deserved or not.

Leo wasn't done. "He's a walking, talking dick. . . ."

"Literally," I interjected on Goodfellow's behalf.

It was a good thing Leo's powers were temporarily on hiatus or I might have been nothing but a scorch mark on the floor. There was some history between Robin and me, but even I had my limits. That puck could talk the paint off the walls, the skirt off the waitress, and the pants off the doorman . . . and that had all been in less than thirty minutes. Shortest date of my life, but one that had put me off the mere thought of sex for months. The man had a mirrored ceiling in his pantry. His *pantry*. I didn't want to guess what he had in his bedroom. It was bad enough running for my millennia-gone virtue because I was nosing around the puck's pantry. It was a toss-up between chocolate and curiosity by the way—as to why I was nosing it to begin with.

It went without saying that Ishiah had reserves in him I'd never dreamed existed.

I put my hand across Leo's mouth so we could get this conversation over with and his butt cheeks unclenched. "Robin did talk the rest of us into leaving the peris be. You'd always left us alone once you retired. It seemed fair. I couldn't figure out why he did at the time, what with that hate-hate relationship you had going on." Now I knew.

Ishiah's eyes shifted sideways . . . a bare fraction, but I saw enough of it for confirmation. Not hate-hate after all, but love-hate. Oh, those two had their plates full now. "Anyway, for Leo's benefit, let's wrap this up. We won. Ish let some of us party at his bar to celebrate. I was drunk for three days, hungover for a week, and that's the last time I saw Ishiah. It was also the last time my brain tried to crawl out of my ears to escape alcohol poisoning. The last time I tried to pick up a werewolf only to find out it was actually a German shepherd. The last time I grew wings and flew naked over the heads of drunken *païen* saying that I was Tinkerbell and they needed to follow me to never-never land. The last time . . ." I uncovered Leo's mouth. "Never mind. It was more last times than I can or care to remember and we won't discuss it again. Right?" I pointed a finger at Leo's chest. *"Right?"*

He studied me impassively, then smirked. I hadn't ever, in our long, long years of knowing each other, seen Leo smirk. He didn't do it. It wasn't his new, improved, laid-back yet solemn and kick-ass self, and it definitely wasn't his big bad "a frown is just your body methodically broken to bits and turned upside down" former self. This could, in no way, be a good thing. "I'm going to the office. I have some calls to make. You two catch up."

"Don't you dare call my mama! Don't you even think about it, Leo!" I called to his back right before the door shut behind him. Although she had to already know. There was hardly a trickster alive who didn't, but she'd love the opportunity to verbally smack my ass over it. "Oh, goddamnit, I'm dead as they come."

Ishiah coughed behind a balled fist and said mildly, "Blasphemy. Some old habits die hard."

"You've been a peri forever now, so get over it," I grumped. "Do you want to go down to the diner and get some breakfast? I'm starving."

"More like lunch, but, yes, that would be acceptable if . . ."

I raised a hand as I answered my ringing cell. I recognized Zeke's number immediately when I pulled the phone from my jeans pocket and held it up. "Kit?" I answered. "Is everything all right? How's Griffin?"

"Fine, fine, everything's fucking fine," came the dismissal. "How do you say asshole in German?"

"*Arschloch*, and you'd better tell me you didn't call me just to ask that," I demanded, but it was too late. As I'd cut off Ishiah, so had the click of a disconnected cell phone done to me.

"Problems?" Ishiah raised his eyebrows. Ishiah was the peri who probably did know about Zeke, who'd become a peri by virtue of not retiring but by telling Heaven to kiss his ass, but he certainly didn't need to know about Griffin, the only peri with demon wings. He might be all right with it; he might not. It didn't matter. Tempting fate was something I did with my own life, not my friends'.

"Actually more of a daily routine." I grabbed my small leather backpack and jacket. I already had my gun on me. It was time for about three pounds of biscuits and gravy. Carbs were good for the brain. Bad for the ass, thighs, and heart, but good for thinking, and with Ishiah here, there was bound to be serious thinking ahead. "Let's go eat and you can tell me why you're in Vegas, how you got here. . . . I know it wasn't with those wings of yours. Was it by bus or plane? And how did you get that sword through security?"

He had flown . . . by plane. The wings did work, but flying across country would take a while, and he'd bought the sword once he arrived in Vegas. It didn't do for peris outside New York City to go unarmed. Demons liked killing them as much as they liked killing angels, only peris were more vulnerable. When they retired, they could keep the wings and transform to a human body, but that was it. No zipping up to Heaven, no flashing in and out of existence, no changing from flesh to a crystal statue that was the true form of an angel, one that looked like it belonged in an art gallery and not moving around in real life. Ishiah had been one of the very high and mighty in his day, so he had a difference of such to him. Give him a few weeks of storing up energy and he could give a light show like he'd given me last night. But that was it. A Vegas magician could do a hundred times better. I told him so. Leave the shows to the experts, I'd advised.

He'd have puffed up those feathers like an outraged rooster if we hadn't been in public. Keeping them invisible for the moment, he finished up with his food and told me why he was here. I was on my second helping and had a ways to go, but Ishiah was an efficient creature, always had been, and I listened to him as I kept scooping up some gravy with the softest of biscuits you could imagine—the cook had to be from the South. No Vegas cook could make biscuits worth a damn.

"Heaven sent me," Ishiah said. He paused—I didn't know if he expected me to fall to my knees at the privilege or if he was expecting a choir hidden in the diner's back kitchen to burst into song, but neither happened and he went on. "After what happened last year, they thought you'd be more willing to listen to me than an angel still in good standing." He frowned. "Though the higher-ups don't seem to know what exactly did happen three months ago. They know Oriphiel"—now there had been a snooty dick and a half—"never came home and a powerful demon named Solomon was killed. There were some rumors about an artifact of some sort, but Oriphiel didn't share much about that. He seemed to think that was his mission and his alone. Ah, and someone outed you and Leo as tricksters."

That would've been Eligos, the only one besides me and mine left standing at the final battle for the Light. "No, Ori wasn't a pigeon who played well with others, and that's saying something. Good at bossing, sniffing around where he shouldn't be, saying what he shouldn't say, but cooperation—there was a word that escaped him." I took a swallow of juice and raised it toward the waitress for a refill. "And Upstairs is right. I wouldn't listen to another of their kind after him. He was such an ass that I didn't mind watching Eligos play a few head games with him." I caught a last dab of gravy on my plate with my thumb and studied it. Humans in all their imperfections had created a food so perfect that if a heavenly choir was around, they should be singing about that.

"Eligos told me once Solomon couldn't play in his league. Neither could Oriphiel. If he hadn't wanted a certain something all to himself . . . power all to himself . . . maybe things would've turned out differently for him." I mirrored Ishiah's frown back at him, but mine was with an eye to a past longer than three months ago. "Your kind, Ishiah, your kind isn't nearly as careful as they ought be about that. The power. It's in all of you, that itch. That need. One-third of Heaven falling wasn't some fluke." I went on before he could deny it. I'd given him a truth. What he did with that truth was up to him. "So what's almighty Heaven want to pass on that needed sending you here? Think they could throw a little Aramaic message in some holy ice cubes in my fridge. A postcard from St. Peter at the pearly gates. Something I could sell on eBay at least."

He pretended to have not heard my warning or my

desire to make some cash on eBay—guns and boots aren't free, boys and girls—and went to the heart of the matter. "Eligos is here, then." The long scar on his jaw whitened. "Wonderful. I'm not surprised he'd be involved in anything that had to do with angels dying. And I came because we know about Cronus. Heaven isn't blind. When more than nine hundred demons die that quickly, Heaven keeps an ear open. Demons talk, so the fact that the wings were being taken wasn't a secret long. All angels know what can be done with those wings. Cronus wants Hell and Lucifer, but we don't know why. But nothing good can come of it. I'm here to find out what I can and to let you know that now, in this particular case . . . Heaven and *païen* can stand together on this—to stop Cronus."

"Cronus is *païen*. What makes you think the rest of us don't stand behind him?" I asked. "Would rather stand behind him any day than have anything to do with a bunch of cloud squatters, present company excluded."

"You bunch are crazy, but none of you is as crazy as Cronus," he answered. It was a valid enough point, except that I didn't think Heaven would be much help.

"Maybe." I held up my glass for the waitress. "It's a nice gesture and all, much obliged, sugar. I just don't see that your former place of business has anything to offer. I wish they did, but unless we get . . ." I stopped and let a thought somersault around my brain for a second. It might not work. Ninety-nine point nine percent it wouldn't. Talk about your real hate-hate relationship. No, no bookie in Vegas would take that bet, but it was worth thinking on a little more.

"Trixa?"

I waved the unvoiced question away. "Never mind." I didn't think Ishiah would betray me by spilling a

THE GRIMROSE PATH 181

seed of a plan—we were on the same side in this. But while that was true, you could plan all you want, but know at the end something will either go wrong or, worse yet, go right at the wrong moment. Angels, real nonretired angels, were mostly windup toys. If you burdened their brains with a plan and someone, theoretically speaking, blew up the bridge they were supposed to cross, they'd cross anyway. Splat splat splat. If I needed their help, I'd tell them what I needed precisely when I needed it. There was much less chance of their screwing things up.

Then there was the saying, an oldie but a goody, that loose lips sink ships. Ishiah said demons talked and Heaven had listened. That's how they'd found out about Cronus and his quest for the map to Hell. Demons weren't the only ones who talked. Ishiah was no gossip, but someone Upstairs had sent him here. He'd report to them and then there was no stopping it. Secrets by their very nature fought not to be kept. Put something in a cage and it wanted out . . . just like with Pandora's box. No, I'd feel better if I kept the key to the box that held my ghost of a plan to myself—ghost of half a plan. It was safer for everyone. Smarter as well, and I did so pride myself on being smart.

It could be Ishiah was right. I was vain, but how could you expect others to appreciate your brilliance if you didn't appreciate it yourself?

I sucked the bit of gravy off my thumb and slid the check to Ishiah's side of the table. "Oh, there is a tiny thing, you should know about. Very small." I held my thumb and forefinger barely a half inch apart and gave an encouraging, pep-rally smile to show how very tiny a thing it was. "I lied to Eli about what Cronus wanted and conned him into turning a hundred thousand or so souls loose from Hell. I'm not sure he knows yet, but when he does, you might not want to be around for that."

"You lied to Eligos?" The check in Ishiah's hand became a tightly wadded ball of paper as his fist clenched. "To *Eligos*?"

"I've done it before. He seems to find it entertaining." I pushed my chair back and stood. "But I have a feeling when his boss, the big boss, finds out he was cheated out of that many souls, Eli won't find me quite as amusing anymore."

"Tricksters." Ishiah grimly smoothed out the check and stood to go pay. "All of you. Pucks or shape-shifters. Whether you're the kind with a survival instinct or not, you'll throw it away instantly for the chance at one good trick."

"It wasn't good," I corrected, vexed. "It was unparalleled. I saved thousands, maybe a hundred thousand souls." I didn't invent the big fish story, but I was sure it was a trickster who had. "I'd think I'd get a sainthood at the very least."

"A hundred thousand souls saved, but did they all deserve to be saved?"

The voice of conscience. I was glad it lived in NYC and not here. It wasn't as if I hadn't thought some of the souls might not be rightfully damned. Abusers, murderers, but I knew, I'd *seen* that one Rose hadn't deserved anything close to damnation. Leo had promised to pass along the word via his family. Our afterlives weren't Heaven or Hell. There was more leeway, more flexibility between what was evil and what was only naughty. Most of the souls would find the home they were due. Justice would be served, and if some did escape to wander alone, unable to touch the real world or any world for the rest of eternity, that was a punishment all its own.

"Your rules aren't necessarily our rules. I saved an innocent girl. I tricked Hell—that's what I was born to do. Chirp away, Jiminy. It won't do you any good." He kept the chirping silent, but it was implicit in the way he held himself as we walked back to the bar. Stiff back, tight jaw, braced shoulders.

At Trixsta's door—Leo had the glass fixed . . . nice of him—I stopped. "You didn't ask what Cronus wanted. What he really wanted."

"After what you did by conning Eligos, truthfully, I'm afraid to ask. You put yourself in Hell's crosshairs. Made yourself the target of every demon alive. I don't think you could survive that, trickster or not. That makes me think you took a huge risk because you know what Cronus wants and it's something you aren't going to walk away from . . . that chances are good that no one is walking away from. Plus, if you were going to tell me, you would have by now, and I know how impossible it is to pin down an uncooperative trickster. Heaven won't like it, but I know better than to think I can do anything to change that. You'll tell me when you want to and no sooner."

He was right . . . about it all. I took his arm and turned him from the door after calling for Leo. "Leo will take you to the airport, Ish. Go back home to New York and sex up Goodfellow five ways to Sunday. Hold on to what you have now. There's no guarantee the world will keep turning. That's true of any day, but with Cronus here, it's even more true . . . so go home. Give Robin my best." As Leo stepped outside, I asked him if he would take Ish to the airport and he did his pissed-but-I-am-stoic-and-rise-above-it expression. I smiled, squeezed his arm, and urged the both of them toward the alley and Leo's car. I'd called the restaurant this morning too. My car was long gone—to the tow yard or Mexico. "But whatever you do," I called to Ishiah, "stay out of his pantry."

Puzzlement and annoyed jealousy crossed the peri's face before he shook his head in resignation. "Tricksters." He asked one last time, "Are you positive you don't want to tell me? Who knows? It might save your life." Against Cronus? I wished Heaven had that kind of power. I wished anyone did. I shook my head and made a shooing gesture as if he were a particularly stubborn rooster and I was all out of corn. "Damn tricksters," he embellished.

He was disappearing into the alley when I challenged after him. "So close to blasphemy. So close."

The only thing he left behind was his growl to call him when I needed the help—not if, but when. It was irritating that he knew that I would. I almost hoped Goodfellow didn't give him any.

A puck not give it up? That would never happen.

After they left in Leo's car and I waved to them, I went into the bar, five . . . ten steps. Eligos came up through the floor as if it was nothing more than a hallucinatory mist instead of hardwood—the shattered hole about the size of a well's mouth. His claws tangled in my shirt, and we kept going up. When we hit the ceiling, it was the same as the floor . . . to Eli. I was in a human body, however, not demon, and it hurt, even with Eli ahead of me—by a nose, like they said at the racetrack, by a nose.

By nearly a foot, a head, in his case. He was in full demon form—copper scales, thrashing wings, a narrow dragon's jaw, broken glass teeth, a fury-filled black gaze with swirling specks as brilliant as coins weighing down a dead man's eyes. I caught flashes of all that as wood splinters, paint chips, and plaster chunks and dust fell around us as we ended up in my bedroom. If Eli hadn't been leading the way clearing a path, I would've broken my neck on the ceiling or crushed my skull or, hell, both.

We hovered in the air in my bedroom as I all but swallowed my tongue to keep from coughing at the dust or make a sound at the tearing pain in my shoulders that had scraped through Eli's new "door." A fully functioning shape-shifting trickster wouldn't, so I couldn't. "Lying bitch." It was calmly said, but the movement that went with it was anything but restrained. I flew through the air and landed on the bed ... almost. I never appreciated the difference "almost" could make until I hit the floor on my back. I'd fallen there like an autumn leaf ... if an autumn leaf weighed a buck thirty.

Buck thirty-five.

Buck ... no one's goddamn business.

I had red and gold scarves on the ceiling, hanging like billowing sails or the canopy of the bed of a princess. I didn't feel much like a princess right then, but I did feel as if I were sailing. On a smooth glassy surface ... not a ripple—only me and the red-gold of a setting sun as I drifted silently. Then the falling sun was gone and the Fallen took its place—fallen leaves, fallen suns, fallen God's own.

Everything fell, sooner or later.

"Lying, lying bitch. Useless *païen* filth. Not worth one-fifth the soul of a common whore." The teeth touched the skin of my face. "Cronus is still taking wings. Giving up those souls accomplished *nothing*."

I had told him this might be the case. A convincing lie cannot be told without some shred of truth to it. I blinked at the plaster dust in my eyes and took a shallow breath, the best I could do after most of the air had been

forced from my lungs when I hit the floor. I gave Eligos the best imitation of a triumphant smile as I could,
considering the pain and lack of air that, thanks to the
reaction to my smile, didn't get any better.

Eli hissed and wrapped his hands around my throat.
They started out covered with scales and equipped with
talons but in a short second turned human—as did the
face inches from mine. "Thousands and thousands of
souls gone and Cronus didn't give one good goddamn.
Or two or three goddamns." The hands tightened. I didn't
struggle. If I did, he'd see I was still weak. I could go for
the gun in the small of my back, but I wouldn't make it
with his weight on top of me. There was nothing I could
successfully do to escape him. I was hurt, dazed, and I
was being choked to death, and there was only one thing
I could do that might save my life—use the weapon I'd
been born with that required no shape-shifting at all.

I kept smiling.

I didn't let my body buck against the lack of oxygen as
it was so desperate to do. I didn't rip at his hands. If I was
turning blue, I did my best to make it look like a good
color on me—this year's must-have—and I smiled up at
that impossibly handsome face. His impossible face, my
impossible smile, an impossible thing not to struggle for
air. But I was out of all choices except one. So I smiled as
my lungs burned as if they were torched from the inside
out. I even smiled as dark blotches began to slide across
my vision . . . from sunsets to storm clouds.

Then another impossible thing happened. The pressure around my neck eased. I could breathe. I did, in
slow and even breaths as if I hadn't missed a one, much
less many. They, mainly Buddhist monks, say you can
control your body in more ways than you can imagine—
slow your heart, your respiration, fly above the needs

of your physical self. That was nice for them, but I still would've liked to have seen the Buddhist monk who wouldn't have gasped for air and tried to claw Eli's face off right then. The first at least . . . They were better about not seeking vengeance than I was. You don't see many face-ripping Buddhist monks. Good men, very good, very patient men.

I sincerely wished I had the strength for some face ripping myself, but I wasn't necessarily very good. Patient? It depended on how you measured . . . by hours or years. I liked my karma immediate. Face ripping was very immediate.

"You drive me fucking insane!" He grabbed at the coverlet from my bed and tore it to pieces, silk raining down like dead butterflies. Glaring at me venomously, he spit, "You knew. You knew Cronus wouldn't stop if we set his Rose free. Or did someone already eat his goddamn Rose?"

I raised a balled-up fist to my mouth and coughed. I made it sound like the phoniest of coughs, as if I were playing at being human—playing very badly, as if barely trying. It was a cover for opening my swollen throat and pulling in more air. "Oh, so much better," I answered before smiling even wider.

"Cronus never had a Rose."

Chapter 10

It was true. Cronus never had a Rose; he hadn't left one at the door either. He had left that ribbon, but I was the one who had tied it around a stem. I'd driven to the nearest florist, paid a ridiculous price for that one perfect rose—signature red, wrapped the ribbon around it and voilà . . . which would be French for "I made Hell my bitch." With a flower, a simple flower. Did it get any better than that? True, surviving it would be nice, but between living and pulling the ultimate trick—"suicidal tendencies" isn't just the name of a band. We can't help ourselves. We don't *want* to help ourselves. It wasn't an addiction. It was a necessity. Tricking was as crucial as breathing to most of us.

We were hell-bent for leather, and let the devil take the hindmost. We were rarely the hindmost, but if we were? We kicked ass every second on our way out. We'd jump out of the plane without a parachute and shout, "Geronimo" all the way down.

Geronimo, Eligos, you son of a bitch. Watch me fall and watch me laugh right up until I hit the ground.

Eli's eyes went from hazel to black to hazel again. Black copper full of fury, hazel full of reluctant admiration. He was a monster, a killer a thousand times over, and a sociopath who'd consider torture a mandatory appetizer. Yet he was like me too. He tricked, for a much more sinister reason, yes, but he couldn't help admiring a brilliant con. "You . . . ? There never was a Rose?"

I did love fooling a demon, a true demon—high-level, Hell's flip side to a trickster. It was a rush you never tired of. And while I *was* laughing all the way, if I could survive it, that would be a bonus. Dying for a trick was part and parcel of the job, but living to gloat about it afterward—that was good too. I hoped his admiration of the Roses and the truth would keep me alive long enough to be the smuggest girl in town.

"No. There was a Rose, but she wasn't Cronus's." I didn't try to sit up. There was no way I was close to that. Breathing was still an effort and keeping the appearance of it, ironically, effortless was more demanding. Instead of sitting, I linked my fingers across my stomach as if I were on a psychiatrist's couch, spilling my deepest, darkest thoughts.

It was deep and dark, what I revealed. Failure always is.

"She came to me last week, but she called herself Anna, short for Rosanna. She was a sweet girl. Average. Normal. She wasn't beautiful or an MIT-level genius. She was in art school. I don't know if she was actually any good, but she had dreams and dreams are nice." And they were. People without dreams die the same as people without a heart to pump their blood. To live a life without dreams is to be digging your own grave every single day.

"When she was a little girl she was in an accident and had half her face burned off—her ordinary, kind of cute, freckled face eaten away by flames." I remembered those restored freckles with a clarity of a life brilliantly magnified by tears. "But when she turned twenty-one,

one of you was nice enough to give it back to her. You do so love your charity work, your kind." I tapped my thumbs together and let my smile fade. "I told her I couldn't help her. She made a deal of her own free will and, sorry, so sorry, little fishy, but swim off and live with the consequences. Or, I guess I actually meant, wait until you die and then suffer the consequences . . . not live with them. She didn't though . . . wait, that is. She walked out the door, stood for a few seconds on the curb with her bag and her pictures of Sir Pickles the Perilous, and then she stepped into the path of a bus. There was glass and blood and twisted metal. Part of her is still in the asphalt of the road. That darkened stain in front? You probably didn't notice. Just one more stain in a world of stained things and stained people, but that—that is what's left of Rosanna." I'd heard the crash. I'd run to the door, and seen what had been glorious and whole turned into something pitiable and broken. The pictures were scattered with puzzled feline eyes staring blankly at nothing.

Nothing was all there was to see now. Anna was gone.

"And you, you with your infinite ego, thought maybe you could do something about your little Anna's soul after all when Cronus showed up. What a damn lucky break for you. Well, rejoice, you did do something. Chances are your Rose is free and long gone from Hell." Eli leaned his elbow on my bed, head against the palm of his hand, bemused as he ran the plan back and forth through his brain, savoring it—an envious twist to the corner of his mouth, before he finally gave in. "Okay, darling, I have to say I raise a glass to balls the likes of which I've never seen, except on myself. But I am going to have to kill you for this, and you are not going to enjoy the process at all. You keep me on my toes, and I do like that, but the boss isn't happy. *The* boss and if it's you or me—fuck, sweetheart, you know that isn't even close."

"As if you could kill me," I scoffed, while thinking, oh, for the days when that was true. "I did tell you that Cronus rarely can be bothered to note humans exist. Why would he want to *become* one? Fall in love with one? You were so easy, sunshine; it's rather embarrassing for you." I gathered myself, made the effort, and managed to get part of me upright and resting on my elbows in a move I hoped looked easy and painless, although it was neither. "Besides," I said, tempting—and demons knew all about that, "if you did kill me, how would you find out what Cronus told me he wants? Truth this time. No Run for the Roses. Because he did tell me. I only told you what *I* wanted instead. Now that I have that, I have no problem telling you what Cronus wants with Hell and Lucifer."

"How very unlike you, telling the truth." He reached with his other hand and ran a finger through the white dust on my face. "An angel made of spun sugar. In other words, worthless and lacking in flavor. All right, Trixa, savior of Roses, tell me. What does Cronus want?" Eli didn't take back the death threat—death promise—and he knew very well I noticed that, but I told him anyway. Why not? There was nothing he could do with the information and it had a good chance of distracting him from me.

Armageddon ten thousand times over has a way of distracting nearly anyone.

I didn't think he could settle on me more heavily, but he did. "What," he asked, "does Cronus want?"

"All," I answered. No deception this time. It wasn't needed.

He narrowed his eyes as the dust he'd scattered from my face hung in the light around him, hundreds of microscopic snowflakes, because winter was coming. The end was coming and, like the obliviously playful grasshopper of the parable, we weren't ready for it. I don't know what happened to that grasshopper . . . if he died of hunger or the industrious ant who'd stored up food all summer took pity on him, but I did know Cronus, like winter, had no pity. We might not die, but there are so many worse things than dying, and if Cronus succeeded, death itself wouldn't be an escape from him. Nothing would.

"All?" Eli straightened, dropping his hand from tracing patterns on my cheek and leaning back slightly as if it gave him room to think. "You asked him what he wanted and the only thing he said was 'All'? Well? What does that mean? All. He's ripped off the wings of nearly a thousand demons, only one wing per demon if you were wondering, that's what it takes, and the most conversation the son of a bitch can muster up about his wholesale slaughter of my kind is 'all.' It's meaningless."

I gave him a look every teacher slips up at one time or another to bestow on her slowest student. "Eli, you can't mean that. You don't get it? You? I'm disappointed." I leaned toward him as he had leaned away. "Don't be Eli, wearing your fancy human suit. Be who you are. Be Eligos. You know of Cronus. He's a Titan. He gave birth to gods, but no one gave birth to him. He birthed himself out of the universe . . . out of the sky and the earth. They were said to be his father and mother; that's a myth. He created *himself*—the ultimate 'I think, therefore I am.' He was once locked in Tartarus, a *païen* hell, and he took it over. Then he took over the Elysian Fields, a *païen* heaven. And it wasn't enough. One hell and one heaven weren't enough to occupy him and he deserted them. He was bored. What do you think it would take to satisfy him? What could possibly do it?"

His jaw tightened. "All."

"Exactly." When I was sure that one hand would support me, I ran a hand through the mess of my hair to shake at least a pound of dust free. "Your Hell, your Heaven, every *païen* hell and heaven and all the thousands of ethereal worlds in between. And, last but not least, this world. The one we live in now. There will be nowhere to go to escape him. If he consumes Lucifer and Hell, one in the same that they are, and adds that energy to his, he'll have more power than anyone could possibly conceive. He will rule every place that there is a place. If you think your boss is tough now," I said, my voice hardening, "you wait until you see your new one in action. Lucifer might be fallen, you might be fallen, but you're sane. You do enormous evil, but you do it with logic and reason. You enjoy it. You need souls and you like to kill in your off-hours. It's disgusting, but there is a twisted motivation behind it. Cronus is nothing like you. Cronus is outside your frame of reference. He could move past you and nothing would happen, and then a second later he could look at you and drive you and everyone in the hemisphere instantly insane. Worse," I said with a sigh, "he very likely wouldn't know he'd done it. He's a giant and you're a 'tiny slow-moving caterpillar on the sidewalk' demon. Fuzzy and cute, but powerless. There's nothing you can do."

"What about that artifact you stole?" he said abruptly. "The one that made your sanctuary for *païen* against God and Lucifer?"

"Heaven and Hell it can stop. Cronus would crumple our shield like tissue paper and toss it over his shoulder. Do you think we'd all still be hanging around if that weren't the case?" I snorted. "We'd leave you all a nice sympathy card and be running for the hills."

"Then why free the Roses at all? If they're going to end up in places worse than Hell, places ruled by Cronus," he demanded, "what's the point?"

"In case I can stop him." I lay back down and covered a yawn with the back of my hand. Long nights, crashing through ceilings; it was taking its toll. And the pain. Humans were the most gossamer of snowflakes. Touch one and you damaged it without the slightest intent at all. "I said you couldn't do anything, gecko. I didn't say I couldn't." I being Leo and me and any others who might come up with an idea, but I didn't need to share glory when there was no glory to be had at the moment . . . and no glory sparkling anywhere in the distance. "It's time for a nap now. Explaining it all to your tediously slow iguana brain exhausts a girl. I'll bill you for the floor and ceiling. Oh, and the bedspread. That was my favorite."

I closed my eyes and hoped for the best and readied myself to go for my gun if the worst came instead. His weight shifted on me as he said, "You are such an utter bitch." Each word was a shadow given teeth and appetite.

"Say it with love, sugar. I'm your last hope after all." I gave another yawn, but kept one hand free to go for my gun or the knife in my boot.

"Actually, for me, sweetheart, that was as close as it comes." He laughed, almost startling me. "I do have to give it to you. I am going to kill you, sooner or later, and I don't like being a mark. You can take that to the Vegas bank and break it, but the Roses? You led me right down that primrose path there, and I'll never forget it. I'll never live it down either, but you know I'm a demon of my word when I say"—he placed his lips at my ear—"neither will you."

Then I was alone. His weight disappeared. The tingle of him in the air fizzled out, a lightbulb dying after one last spark and sputter. He had probably gone back to Hell to report or to find a few humans to eat to fortify him before giving that report. Me? What did I do? Exactly what I'd said.

I took a nap.

Chapter 11

I was surrounded by pissed-off people.

It was a feeling I was used to, and I didn't take it personally, although one-third of it was very personal. "Leo," I said for what I thought was the third time, but I could've been wrong, because he'd yet to take any of it to heart, "if you're going to kill me, kill me. If it's too much work for you, wait, and Eli will do it for you. Now stop glaring at me before you get eyestrain and the vein in your forehead explodes."

Leo had found me when he'd driven back from dropping off Ishiah at the airport. It was a toss-up which was more terrifying—finding holes blown through the floor and ceiling of the bar or getting through the drop-off lane at the airport without having a power-inflamed, overgrown crossing guard scream at you for idling your car one second too long. Soon enough you wouldn't be able to do more than pause as you booted your passenger face-first onto the curb and squealed off, damn the horses and to hell with the luggage.

He'd discovered me on the floor, covered in plaster dust and unmoving . . . an effigy at repose on an ancient British tomb. He shook me violently, lifted me up, and then wrapped his arms around me so tightly that I might have spit up a little down his back like a surprised, dyspeptic baby. Only might have—I didn't look because I didn't want to know for sure.

"I thought you were dead. Odin, hang me—I thought you were dead," he'd said fiercely. It was warm . . . warm and comforting to be held that close, to be that cherished, to know you would've been that missed, all while I was still on the edge of sleep. It was I think the most reassuring, safe, and yet anything *but* safe feeling all wrapped into one. Cradled on the edge of a precipice, knowing you couldn't fall alone, but you could fall together . . . a feeling that anyone would've sold their soul for.

Naturally Leo had gone on to promptly ruin the moment.

"I thought you were dead," he'd repeated or, more accurately, accused, pushing me back away far enough to get a good look at me.

"I was napping." I'd tried to make it sound perfectly normal, which, considering the situation, it had been. I'd been too tired and in too much pain to drag myself up to the bed.

"What the fuck are you doing lying on the floor taking a goddamn nap and making me think you're dead? Are you that idiotic? Are you? I am mostly human now. You could've stopped my heart in my chest, but I'm guessing you didn't once think of that."

You'd have thought that if there were a diva in the room it would be me. Wrong. Hair had come loose from his ponytail and it fell in my face as he was yelling at me. I'd batted it aside, took a breath that hurt every rib I had, and had replied with what I thought was a valid argument. "You were a killer. You *are* a killer." Not that I was saying the killing wasn't for the side of all that was right and just. It was. "I'd think you'd know dead when you saw it."

Valid, yes. Polite and conciliatory, perhaps no.

"And, honestly? A heart attack. In your shape? Even your last girlfriend's IQ wasn't low enough to believe that old urban legend."

That hadn't improved the situation any. In my defense, at the time I'd still been a little fuzzy, and had had my ass kicked by a demon—which had never happened before. Never. I'd been somewhat out of it with my ego off crying in a mental corner. I had pulled off the Roses. I had talked Eli, more or less, out of killing me . . . for a while, but a demon had still taken me down. That had been hard to swallow and harder to admit when Leo had demanded to know what had turned my bar and apartment into a Habitrail for the world's largest hamster, with holes and tunnels everywhere.

The termite explanation wasn't my best lie ever. It hadn't gone over well and while he'd stripped me down, followed suit, gotten in the claw-foot tub, and turned on the shower to wash me clean of dust, dirt, and the occasional streak of dried blood, I'd told him the truth. I always told Leo the truth eventually. This time it was more painful than the scrapes and bruises that covered my arms from shoulder to elbow and blotched my ribs. Damn it, it was worse than painful. It was mortifying and beyond, so much so that it wasn't until I was sitting on the edge of my bed while wrapped in a robe, that I realized I'd missed something.

"We were naked." I'd stopped finger-combing the sopping wet tangle of my hair. "We were naked in the shower . . . together. You and me."

"Yes, we were and you were so busy telling me how you are the best damn trickster on the planet despite Eligos beating you nearly unconscious that it escaped you until this second." Impatient hands had dumped a towel on my head and briskly dried my hair from soaked to just damp. "All hail the queen. You can trick, fool, and fleece anyone, but notice when we're both nude and slippery from soap, inches away from each other? Now *that* you miss." The towel had dropped into my lap as I'd been summarily informed, "We're going to the hospital, Your Majesty. Put some clothes on. Or walk around nude. It apparently makes no difference to you either way."

That was how I ended up surrounded by pissed-off people. After a less than quick visit to the ER—bumps and contusions, nothing broken, take some Tylenol and suck it up, said the good doctor—Leo and I had ended up in Griffin's room. He'd been upgraded during the night from an ER curtained cubicle to an actual room with a view. The view was of another wall of the hospital, but it was a private room, which was good. A roommate wouldn't have appreciated the show that was going on. If I thought Leo was irritated—massively, volcanically irritated, then Zeke was a nuclear bomb.

"I *said* I'll do it."

I leaned in the doorway, gratefully—Tylenol wasn't the miracle cure-all that the doctor had assured me it was—and watched as Zeke faced down a nurse's aide who held a plastic basin full of soapy water and wore a stubborn expression that said if anyone was going to see Griffin in his birthday suit, it was going to be her. Considering she no doubt had seen more than her share of shriveled eighty-year-old penises in this place, enough to last her a lifetime, I didn't blame her for standing her ground to get a peek at something more aesthetic.

"I'm a professional. This is my job," she said firmly.

"And this"—Zeke jerked his thumb at Griffin in the bed—"is mine. Period. If anyone gives him a bath, it's gonna be me."

Griffin groaned. "How about I do it myself? Will that simplify things?"

"Fine." The nurse's aide deposited the basin on the bedside table and slapped the towels against Zeke's chest. "He's all yours. Maybe I can actually take my break tonight."

Zeke didn't move except to hold the towels until she was gone. He was a good warrior. He waited until any possible threat was either out of range or disabled, his attention fixed, stance ready. I started to imagine how he would've disabled her if she hadn't given up without a fight, but that led to progressively worse and worse mental pictures, and I stopped at the one of Zeke trying to stuff the towel down the poor overworked woman's throat.

Giving up the door frame's support, I passed Zeke, patting him on the shoulder, and sat on the edge of the bed. "Griff, you look . . . worse."

He snorted. "Thanks. I thought you were supposed to be an excellent liar."

"When I want to be." I took his Jell-O. Cherry. Yum. It really is about the small pleasures in life. I ate a spoonful. He did look worse. The bruise had darkened and spread on his face. It looked painful. I hoped they'd given him better painkillers than they'd given me. There were several pieces of paper on the table and I flipped through them. They were covered front and back with curse words. I spotted the German *Arschloch* Zeke had called me about the day before. In addition to that one, there was a hugely impressive number of English ones written down. If there was one he'd forgotten or that wasn't applicable, I didn't see it. "He's still not talking to you?"

"Oh, he's speaking volumes in his own way," Griffin said wryly. "I'm lucky his pen ran out of ink. But I deserve it. He also took my car keys, not that I remember where my car is, and I heard him trying to talk a security guard out of his handcuffs in the hall at breakfast."

"Trying?" That didn't sound like the Zeke we knew.

Wriggling his foot out from under the sheet, Griffin lifted it to show where his ankle was cuffed to the rail at the foot of the bed. "Since they took the catheter out, bathroom breaks have been difficult."

I was about to grin—Zeke learned his lessons differently than the rest of us, but he did learn them—until Leo said, "Handcuffs. Now that is the best idea I've heard today." That was enough to have my momentary slice of happiness fading, but worse yet, it was enough to catch Zeke's attention.

He accepted that the aide was gone, moved his gaze to Leo, who still stood just inside the door, and then turned to give me the same searching look, that expression he wore when he read someone's thoughts. "You showered together? And you didn't have sex? Why would you shower together and not have sex?"

"Oh God." Griffin covered his eyes with one hand and pulled his foot back hard enough to rattle the cuffs, but there was no getting out of them . . . or the room, as much as he might want to. As loudly as Leo was growling, I knew he wanted to.

"Oh." Zeke's attention was back on Leo. "She didn't notice?" His eyebrows knit, perplexed as his scrutiny dropped about three feet down Leo's body in an attempt to puzzle out the situation. "Huh."

"Oh God." It was repetitive, but that was understand-able. Griffin couldn't get out of the bed, but he could turn on his side and shield his head with the pillow, which he did. I carefully put the spoon down on the table as he disappeared beneath white cotton.

"Spying, Kit? That's rude. That is very rude." But this was Zeke and while you did tell him when his behavior was not acceptable, you also made allowances for his differences . . . his uniqueness. That's when you went to who was truly accountable in the situation. Leo. "You were thinking it loudly enough, he could hear it through your shield?" I charged. Normally no demon, angel, or peri could penetrate our shields unless we weren't being careful or we were all but screaming in our heads. "Un-believable. Do you want demons knowing things like, 'Oh, I'm not quite a god anymore' along with 'And my penis is this big'? Do you want Eligos to kill you? Bag-ging Loki would make his eternity. Besides, it was al-most three hours ago. I said I was sorry." I hadn't, but I made it a principle to never apologize when a lie will do. "Let it go already."

Now suddenly instead of one set of male eyes on me, I felt the heat of three, a highly unhappy heat. Griffin had given up the protection of his pillow to join forces with his comrades, and Zeke said disap-provingly, "That was not appropriate, Trixa. I'm disap-pointed in you."

Zeke thought I was inappropriate. *Zeke*. And he was right. Insinuating that a man's penis was no big deal, acci-dentally or not, wasn't definable. The dictionaries held no words strong enough to label that mistake. Catastrophic fell miles short of covering that error. I hadn't lived as long as I had without learning the massively sensitive issue all males, human, *païen*, or gods, shared. This simply wasn't my day. I couldn't lie well and I couldn't avoid a mistake so basic a high school cheerleader could've taught me a course on it on this miserable day—who had a PhD compared to me when I couldn't figure out how to open the door to the damn school. No doubt because the handle was phallic shaped.

I apologized, throwing my principles out the window. I did it quickly and hurriedly buried my attention back in the Jell-O. That was the best thing to do when you inadvertently or carelessly . . . semantics . . . didn't show the mighty penis the respect it deserved. Get past the moment as expeditiously as possible so everyone could pretend it had never happened. Leo, of course, wouldn't let it go. He'd gone on and on. This day wasn't getting any better. When you've been beaten up by a demon in your own bedroom and that was the high point, it was one seriously bad day. Finally I'd told him to either kill me or wait for Eligos to do it; I couldn't stand the guilt trip anymore.

"I'm going down to the chapel," he said. It's difficult to speak without moving your lips or unclenching your teeth, but he managed.

"And who are you going to pray to, Loki?" I snapped back. I was sorry, but I was getting less sorry all the time.

"Myself, and you'd better hope I'm not listening." He slammed the door behind him.

I snorted. Men. Gods. Gods-on-hiatus. All the same.

"You're in trouble." Zeke was grinning.

Griffin looked amused as well until I threw him under the bus without a second thought when I asked Zeke with all innocence, "Aren't you pissed at Griffin right now?"

"Oh yeah." Zeke by now had supplanted me in my

position on the edge of the bed, and had been automatically wetting and wringing a washcloth in the basin to
pass back and forth to his partner. Griffin was working on getting all the dried blood out of the creases of
his hands and the raw patches of scraped skin over his
knuckles. It reminded me how fortunate we were he was
still around. Taking on demons without backup wasn't
conducive to that. Zeke was as aware of that as I was. He
had been momentarily distracted, but he was back on
the scent now. "You are never getting out of the house
again. Ever. *Ever*. If I can find a goddamn hamster ball
big enough to put you in, I will. You're an idiot. A self-
ish, clueless idiot. Eden House thought *you* could guide
me? Thought you were smart enough to partner up with
me? Hell, the demons probably didn't even set a trap.
I'll bet you tripped and fell into one's open fucking jaws.
Maybe it wasn't even demons. Maybe a pack of poodles
mauled you."

Tickling the bottom of his foot through the sheet, I
said to Griffin's betrayed expression, "He's speaking to
you again. That's something, isn't it? You can thank me
later."

That didn't happen.

I wasn't surprised. Those thrown under buses aren't
often grateful, but with those who jump under them of
their own accord, that's not always true. But I didn't find
that out until later—when Rosanna showed up.

We took Griffin and Zeke back to the bar with us.
AMA—against medical advice—but since medical advice hadn't cured him, and Zeke had, it hadn't been
much of a deterrent. While Griffin had finished cleaning
up, he'd also told us about his solo demon hunts, every
detail. He'd found new hunting grounds we hadn't
known about—some bars, some hotels . . . and one in

particular that hosted pageants for people who wanted to dress up their four-year-old like a ten-dollar hooker. The poor kids couldn't sell their souls to get a normal childhood, but their mom could sell hers to ensure her little Savannah won that crown. I hadn't thought of that one. Griffin had been clever, too clever, but now we'd know where to look for him if he did something this suicidal again. There had been five of them, the demon safaris . . . The sixth had been the trap. Five solo demon killings—he'd had every reason to look exhausted in the past week or so as it was catching up with him. He didn't have every reason to be alive, however. He was good, but fate is capricious. If he'd been trolling alone and come across Armand before Armand had been turned into a demon-flavored milk shake on my floor or had run into another higher-level demon like Armand, there was every chance Griffin wouldn't have been around long enough for the demons to bother with a trap. That Eli had saved Griffin might not classify as a miracle in the holy sense, but it was wholly unexpected and I didn't want to depend on it again. As for assuming most of the demons would wise up and stay in Hell and out of Cronus's reach . . . First, they couldn't stay there forever. Eventually they'd run out of souls to eat. Second, lower-level demons weren't that intelligent. They didn't know when they were profoundly outclassed or they didn't have the brain cells to believe it. They wouldn't hide long.

All of that made it an easy decision. Until Griffin was back in top fighting form, he and Zeke could stay with me. It wouldn't be the first time the bar was a makeshift recovery room for them. After the last time, I'd learned my lesson and added a spare bedroom downstairs. Granted, you could only fit a single-sized bed in there and had to crawl up that bed from the foot as there was no room to walk beside it, but it was, as I told Griff and Zeke, all theirs—a home away from home.

"You told the doctor you had the best accommodations possible for me. Luxurious, you said. And when he still wouldn't sign the discharge papers, you all but smuggled me out of the hospital, and for this?" Griffin asked, looking much more healthy, bright eyed and bushy tailed, than he had a right to, aside from the bruise on his face. Yes, they'd definitely given him the good pain pills.

"Considering you were hanging in a foyer like a side of beef in a butcher's freezer yesterday, I think this is a step up, so don't complain. It's the only guest room I have and I fixed it up months ago especially for you two. Be grateful," I ordered.

"Didn't this used to be the storage closet?" Zeke stuck his head in and looked around. "Didn't you keep the toilet paper and cleaning supplies for the customer bathrooms in here? And the vomit bucket and mop?"

Picky. Picky. Picky.

"It's this or sleep in those bathrooms. You choose. And as those look like the ones in a men's prison, I wouldn't pick that option myself."

"Speaking of prisons." Griffin lifted his wrist and jangled metal. The cuff was off his ankle and now around his wrist which, in turn, was cuffed to Zeke's. "I know I've been an idiot. I know I wasn't honest and that's the last thing I want to be with you . . . dishonest . . . but this feels like a kinky sex movie. Could you take them off now?"

"No." Zeke didn't bother to waste a second thinking about it as he made a face. "It smells like ammonia in here . . . and ass. Ammonia and sweaty ass."

"Sorry, princess. I think you'll survive." This was what it was like to have ungrateful, spoiled children. I'd have to remember that in the future.

Griffin, not interested in the discussion of the smell of ass, sweaty or otherwise, tried again. "Zeke, I promise I'll . . ."

"No." Zeke didn't wait for the rest of the promise. "Start crawling. I'm tired."

Griffin exhaled, the guilt back in his face. It wasn't the guilt of doing things he'd never done, being what he no longer was. This was a guilt he deserved and for behavior modification's sake, I didn't pat him sympathetically on the shoulder. There were no Lone Rangers in this bar and I wanted him to remember that. "I'll bet you are," he said. "I know you are." Along with the guilt, you could see him picking up Zeke's exhaustion like the empath he was and wearing it with his own emotions and sensations. "You didn't sleep last night. You didn't sleep this morning. You stole that scalpel from God knows where, keeping me safe, watching out for me."

"It's not easy to do," he replied stolidly. "I'm supposed to be the stupid one. Not you."

"Jesus Christ, you're anything but stupid. Don't say that. Don't think it either or the verbal ass-kicking you've given me since yesterday, I'll give you five times over," Griffin warned. "If there's a stupid one here, it's me. Now let's get some sleep." He put a knee on the foot of the bed and started to crawl, pulling Zeke's arm along with him. "But you'd better be ready with that cuff key if any demons do attack. I don't want to die because you have a weird bondage thing."

"It's not a weird bondage thing," Zeke protested, following after him in the crawl up the mattress. "It's a perfectly natural bondage thing. The porn magazine said so."

With that I closed the door on them and left them to their own devices, hopefully sleep, but guys will be guys and a porno magazine would never lie.

"Did you get around to telling them about Cronus and the impending Armageddon slash slavery of worlds or did that, like certain other things, escape your attention too?" Leo, beer already in hand, asked at the bar.

"I think they deserve one night relatively worry free and, again, I'm sorry about the shower thing. It was enormous, I swear to you. So large that I trembled in its shadow like a tiny mouse fearing it would be crushed. Attached to a body that defines perfection itself. Michelangelo would've taken a hammer to *David* and smashed it to pieces if he knew what he could've sculpted instead. Every poet living or dead couldn't find a single word worthy to describe the beauty and majesty that is you." I let the door support me and my aching ribs as I gave Leo my most contrite look. I was too . . . sincerely contrite. It was Leo. My Leo. "Forgive me?" I tucked my hair behind my ears, then touched one of his folded arms with a single fingertip. It rested next to a small mole he'd had since he had first become Leo. I saw it every day. There was a comfort in that, in an unchanging thing, although unchanging was a curse word among our kind. "You know I can't let certain things catch my attention. Not yet. You and I . . ." I traced my finger along warm skin and smiled, a little wistfully, but the best things are worth waiting for. Our day would come and on that day, the attention I would give him would etch every molecule of him in my memory for the rest of my life. "We're not there yet. We're still too much alike in the wrong ways and not quite enough in the right ones."

"You're right. We're both stubborn, both hold grudges. We both are staggering in our hotness," he said with the gravity it warranted.

"But luckily vanity will never stand in our way." I pinched his arm lightly, rubbed the pale red mark, and said, "Stay on the couch tonight? You'll have to be up early in the morning for another trip to the airport."

"Your bizarre leaping to other subjects is something we'll have to work on. That, I'll never match and the level of Tylenol I have to take to stop the headaches is beginning to become a danger to my liver," he said, unfolding his arms and pretending to fish in his jeans pocket for a capsule or two. "Why the airport? Did you come up with something for Cronus? If you have, that will top even your Roses."

"It would, wouldn't it?" I started toward the kitchen to get a broom and dustpan for upstairs. I moved stiffly, the snowflake touched by a careless finger. Damaged. "Didn't you say back in January that Thor was hanging out with the Swedish women's volleyball team?"

"Last I heard." A crease appeared in his forehead. Now he did actually have a headache. If anyone would give you a head-pounding one, it would be Thor. "In the past months I've been getting a lot of late-night drunken 'Ha, ha. You're not a god anymore, douche bag' calls. A few 'nyah-nyah-nyah mortal dickwad' ones to add variety. Why?"

"I was thinking about something I saw on TV last year. It reminded me of Thor's hammer."

"Mjöllnir? It's a serious weapon, but it wouldn't stop Cronus."

"No, but what made it might," I said. "That and a trip to hell." Little h, *païen* hell.

It all came down to what I'd quoted to Eligos before, "I think, therefore I am." They were good words, those five. Words to live by for some. For others . . . maybe . . .

Words to die by.

Chapter 12

Tricksters are thieves, every last one of us. That was half of the job if you broke it down to the basics. You were either taking something a person wanted or giving them something they didn't want at all. It was a simplistic look at what we did, but in your life, sooner or later, you were going to steal something—a possession . . . a life. But only the lazy tricksters went for the life off the bat. I was not lazy. Those I tricked had to truly deserve to lose their lives if I took them. I'd said my very first trick had been to steal an entire orchard to punish a greedy man. I'd stolen my bar too. That was more in the range of a good-deed trick. . . . An alcoholic who owns a bar is never going to stay sober, no matter how many meetings he goes to. Not that it was mere convenience that I happened to need an identity and occupation in Vegas at the time—no, that was good planning. Good deeds are nice, but when you can make them pay off doubly, what's not to love? It was like getting a great dress and matching demon-stabbing stiletto heels, both on sale, only a hundred times the rush.

And being a trickster and a thief meant that you always kept your eyes open. I wouldn't steal, say, from a museum, but there were those who would. You steal from a museum, you steal from the world. If you did

that, I would punish you, because that was naughty—
depriving the world. Unless you were a trickster and
you were stealing something to *save* the world.

I hadn't stolen from a museum yet, but I, bad girl that
I was, kept hoping a justifiable reason would come up.

It was while keeping my eyes open several months
ago that I saw a special on an exhibit at the Metropolitan
Museum in New York City. I'd been about to change the
channel to sports for the customers—I mean, *I* was a living history and while I did embrace the entire keeping-
an-eye-out philosophy, just hearing the words New York
City still gave me a twinge of a hangover. I'd had the
remote in hand when Zeke went to point like a hungry
hound on a package of hot dogs. WEAPONS OF THE WORLD
had been emblazoned across the screen. Zeke did love
his weapons to, what I'd been beginning to suspect was,
an unhealthy degree. I'd been relieved for more than
one reason when he got a sex life that didn't involve a
trip to the gun shop.

I'd ignored the phantom hangover pain, made popcorn, and we'd watched. An occupied Zeke was a non-
destructive Zeke. In the exhibit, along with a varying
degree of implements designed by man to kill man, was
a representation of a something not designed by man.
Or woman or any creature primate related at all. It was
Namaru. There had been two races long ago, *païen*, that
had never made it into human mythology or folklore,
spoken or written. They had tended to keep to themselves although one of them had ties to the Rom. These
races were the engineers of the *païen* population. They
had a technology that would seem like magic to humans, who wouldn't have had a hope of understanding
it. I didn't actually understand it myself. No one who
hadn't created it would. I'd seen the objects that they'd

built though, the Bassa and the Namaru. I'd seen them work and that was good enough for me. The Bassa, a cold-blooded reptile race, had worked with metal most often. The Namaru, who'd lived in active lava fields like grounded phoenixes, had used what looked like stone, but did what stone couldn't begin to do. They were gone now, extinct and remembered only by the *païen*, but they had left things behind.

I'd recognized in that museum the result of the only weapon mold the Namaru had ever made—or an homage to that result rather. Mjöllnir, Thor's hammer—a stone sculpture of it. It was ornate and there was something slightly odd about the short handle, the intricate carving. Whoever had crafted the replica long ago had seen the real thing. It was otherworldly, like the Namaru. They had lived in this world, but the way they thought, what they were, to a human would be alien, and, like Cronus, inexplicable.

The first human swords had been Bronze Age and made using clay molds. After that, methods had been refined and humans came up with many ways to make all different types of weapons to kill one another. The Namaru, in their genius and simplicity, had only ever needed the one. It could shift itself to the shape of any weapon you wanted to make. Leo had chosen a hammer. I'd never seen the mold myself, but Leo as Loki had since he'd given Mjöllnir as a gift to Thor—there was a legend regarding that involving dwarven blacksmiths, betting his head, and turning into a fly, but basically it was all bullshit. Humans loved to weave elaborate tales around something as simple as, hey, dude, happy birthday. Storytellers and liars, I did respect them for that, and I absolutely loved a good story, no matter how fictional.

But why, back in reality, had Loki, who at that time

was bad to the bone and then some, done something nice for a relative he didn't much care for? I had a feeling it was a softening-up move. Thor wasn't bright. Hell, Thor wasn't even dim. He'd need one of his own lightning bolts up his ass to get that kind of wattage going between his ears. It all ended up with Leo/Loki laughing while Thor wondered how he'd ended up in drag at a banquet. Wide shoulders, an Adam's apple, and a drunken deep bass voice—it all ended in a vale of tears and one drunkenly confused Thor fighting off a bunch of pissed-off giants.

Born dumb frat boy. Born victim of Loki.

That might explain the drunken rants in the middle of the night, but Leo had said much later when he was on the straight and narrow, he'd given the weapon mold to Thor in a manly "Sorry, I was a dick and tricked you into dressing like a girl" apology. The sculpture in the museum reminded me of it. Sometimes the universe does give you a freebie, and I was hoping Thor still had Leo's present. I was very much hoping. And since Thor made calls to Leo, but didn't take them, Leo would have to go ask him in person. Leo had made up, mostly, with his family, Odin, and the whole crew, but there were a few holdouts and Thor was one of them.

But if we could get the weapon mold, it would make a weapon of your choice out of anything you poured into it . . . literally any substance you could conceive of, and I could conceive of only one that might have a chance against Cronus. The weapon's shape itself didn't matter much in this—as long as it pierced, but what it was made of did, no matter how difficult it would be to obtain. That was where my plan started. Ishiah and the angels were where it ended. Although without that piece of Namaru technology, the angels would be as useful as parsley on prime rib.

That the Namaru tech wouldn't work without a trip to a hell, not Eli's Hell, but a hell hard to get in and out of all the same, was a challenge. But I already had an idea about that—who can get into any hell, *païen* or otherwise? The dead. It wasn't the best idea, but it was all I had. For now we had to drop Leo off at the airport—the Swedish volleyball team was playing in Colorado today, and planes flew faster than ravens.

I was buckling up in the passenger seat of Leo's extended cab truck, large enough that it barely fit into the alley beside the bar—again with those shower issues—when from the seat behind me, Griffin said, "Now both of us are missing cars. That doesn't bother you? You love your car and you've only had it for a month. You could let me at least call some of the towing yards and see if it ended up there." As if my car mattered at all compared to saving his life. Sky and Earth loved his fluffy little demon-killing heart.

"Sorry, sugar. I forgot to mention that Cronus wants to get to Hell, find Lucifer, devour him in an unspeakable fashion, and then using that power added to his, he'll take control of every world, every heaven and hell, and every reality that exists. After that I'm thinking he'll play games with all the inhabitants that we won't much like. If that doesn't put the car issue into perspective, then think of the old saying, 'If you love something . . . meant to be . . . comes back.' You know how it goes."

"If that's true," Leo said quietly, his hand moving from the key in the ignition to rest now on the steering wheel, "how much do you love Cronus?"

Because he was here in the alley, standing in front of the truck.

He looked the same as before, a creepy doll from an old black-and-white movie come to life to kill you in your sleep. A plastic hand to cover your nose and mouth. Shadowed eye sockets to suck your life from you, streamers of golden light flowing from your eyes to be swallowed up by the lack of his. You'd be left a dried husk, drained, destroyed, nothing but a desiccated imitation of a corpse.

We should be that lucky.

"Whatever you do, Zeke," I cautioned as quickly as I could get out the words, "don't try to read his thoughts. Your head could explode and I don't mean that figuratively." I reached for my gun. It was a useless instinct in this situation. Picking up the truck and swatting Cronus with it would've been just as useless.

Cronus didn't appear particularly interested. Sometimes that was worse than when the predators were extremely interested in you . . . because if they were interested, you mattered. They could want to kill you, but you did matter. If you mattered, you could communicate, in some way have a dialogue—and if you could have a dialogue either physically or mentally, you could fool, manipulate, and *lie* your ass off.

If you didn't matter, you had to fall back on your fighting skills. Normally that wasn't a problem. Cronus, however, did not fall anywhere in the category of normal. He was looking idly to the right and then to the left. He moved slowly, as a crazy, possessed doll would, until it decided you were what it wanted, and then you wouldn't see it move at all; it would be that unnaturally, unbelievably quick.

Possessed dolls. I was watching way too much late-night television.

This time when Cronus looked, it was upward, and

that's when an angel fell from the sky. It shattered into thousands of shards on the hood of Leo's truck like a dropped champagne flute disintegrating on a marble floor. Angels weren't that delicate, no matter that they appeared like glass in their original form, soldiers of sharp-edged crystal. The truck wasn't responsible; Cronus was.

"Looks like Heaven wasn't putting all its money on Ishiah playing on your nostalgia," Leo said. He turned on the windshield wipers as the truck idled and silver-veined, cloudy pieces of someone's guardian angel were tossed aside.

I could believe Cronus had killed it so easily. What I couldn't believe was that we hadn't known it was up there. One rare cloudy day in Vegas and an angel tagged us. Being human was getting harder, not easier. Practice wasn't making perfect and if there was ever a time we needed to get things perfect, this was it.

I lowered the window and leaned out. "If you scratched Leo's paint job, he's not going to be as cute and sweet to pet when you're bored." I'd assumed he wouldn't pay attention to me, that he wouldn't see me. I was wrong, and I wasn't sure if I was happy about that or not.

Cronus was seeing me and for the first time in my life, I had a huge chunk of doubt that I could trick my way out of something. "The demons are all hiding." His voice was as empty as it was last time. Checkers all over again, only a dead angel instead of a dead tourist this time. "They can't hide forever. They can't hide long." He was right. Demons could stay in Hell, hide there, and Cronus could go there and try to find them, but Hell . . . Lucifer . . . was vast, almost endless. Cronus wasn't that patient and he didn't have to be. The majority of demons weren't that bright, as I'd thought in the hospital. They'd be back on Earth, fairly soon too, but Cronus wasn't one who wanted to wait. How many wings did he need to make that map, how many were left? Twenty? Thirty? More or less?

"Demon." His attention was back to the right, toward the bar. "In this place. It has been everywhere in this place. I want it. Make it come here." He rested his hand on the hood of the truck. It sank instantly and a moment later he lifted it back up as metal poured in a liquid stream from the plastic fingers. The same plastic lips smiled. I'd never seen a Titan truly smile, not a genuine smile. I never wanted to see it again. A blank-faced Titan bent on control of everything in existence was one thing; an enthusiastic, happy Titan bent on the same was . . . shit. Just holy shit. There'd once been a god, or what people had thought had been a god. Moloch. They made huge metal statues of him, built furnaces in his grinning mouth, and fed live babies into the fire. Feeding their god. Supposedly. The rumor went. I hadn't been in that area at the time.

But if those statues had existed, I think their smiles would have been identical to this one. Full of a heat to suck the air from your lungs, fire to cook flesh, the screams of infants. The screams of parents losing their children, sisters losing their baby brothers. Screams that never stopped, fear and pain that never ended. On and on until you were nothing but a scream yourself. Not a person, only a sound of terror that ripped the air until the end of time itself. And you could hear yourself—hear the scream that was you, the tearing and clawing of it in your mind so loud, so *wrong* you couldn't imagine how it didn't kill you.

Wishing it would kill you just to escape it.

"Soon." Cronus vanished, taking a handful of Leo's engine with him. That was fine. He could have that engine, as long as he took that smile and the screaming with him.

"Trixa?"

I kept my eyes front and center as I put off Zeke for a second. "Hold on, Kit. I'm doing my best not to pee my panties right now."

He waited for nearly five entire seconds. "I just wanted to know," he started, sounding profoundly put upon, "are we there yet?"

Bending over, I rested my forehead against the dashboard and laughed. I couldn't do anything else. Here we sat in an alley, in a truck destroyed by one stroke of a Titan's hand, we could've been destroyed ourselves, and Zeke was making jokes. If that wasn't more frightening than a Titan, I didn't know what was.

Leo caught a cab to the airport, while I changed my panties. It was worth it, pantywise. When you can laugh that hard in the face of a horror like Cronus, it was more than worth it. It was beyond amazing, it was extraordinary, and, what the hell, that pair had been on sale at Victoria's Secret anyway.

From outside my closed bedroom door, I could hear Griffin and Zeke squabbling as they sat on the top step. It was nice, that touch of normality. I'd told them what was coming, and they'd seen Cronus for themselves, but if you weren't a born *païen*, you couldn't know. You couldn't truly comprehend what a Titan was, not if it stood right in front of you and nearly screamed the sky down. You simply couldn't grasp it. They say ignorance is bliss. About now I'd settle for a little plain stupid if ignorance was too much to ask for.

Unfortunately, my boys weren't as blissful in other areas as I wished they were. There was a polite knock at the door to get my attention before Griffin asked through the wood, "Was Cronus talking about Eligos? Is that what he meant by a demon being . . . what? . . . embedded in your bar? Tainting it?"

Eligos had been in Trixsta only a few times—not nearly long enough to put a mark on it, much less taint it. And it wasn't tainted. What Cronus sensed wasn't demon—not anymore. "Yes," I lied in word, thought, and emotion, all the while buttoning my new pair of jeans. I was talented that way. "It's bad enough that his I-wanna-be-a-big-boy-in-big-demon-diapers Armand stained my floor, but now Eli has funked up my bar with demon BO. I don't think they make a room deodorizer for that."

It was Griffin who had wormed his way to the very heart of the bar. He'd spent several years growing up here, had been in the bar working every day and sleeping every night along with Zeke in what was now Leo's office. And after Eden House had recruited him and Zeke, he'd still come by almost every day. That was what family did. Years of Griffin were in every nook and cranny of the building; Griffin when he'd thought he was human . . . and, in his mind and his heart, *had* been human. But it wasn't his mind and heart that Cronus had picked up on. It was the physical that had lain under the human at the time. Now all that was left of that were wings. Beautiful, glorious wings—Hell-changed to glittering scales and exactly what Cronus needed.

That, however, was something Griffin didn't need to know and overprotective Zeke definitely didn't need to know. I knew. Leo knew too, I had no doubt. That was enough. We were lucky Cronus hadn't bothered to look past me as he was making his demand and smashing an angel to pieces. Another ignorance-is-bliss situation and I was grateful for it. Cronus saw Leo and he saw me, the ant who dared play a game with him. If we could keep his focus there and only there, it would be good. Very good.

"So when Leo comes back from Colorado, he might have something that will kill Cronus? That's the plan?" Griffin didn't knock politely this time, and he sounded rather skeptical. I couldn't say I blamed him.

"Colorado? We were going to the airport? I thought we were going to Disneyland," Zeke grumped in turn. I heard a distinctly disappointed thump against the door. That would be him leaning and sulking.

"I'm just wishing ravens could fly faster than a Boeing 727," I said, sliding my shoes back on. "We'll hit Disneyland next time. Or a gun range." A gun range was Zeke's Disneyland times ten. "And, no, Griff, sugar, that's not the plan. That's one-third of the plan. I'm the trickster and you're the Boy Scout. Don't forget that. If you don't balance out my devious ways, who will?"

"We would be happy to fill that role or make it unnecessary altogether." The voice was musical and flat all in one. Impossible? I would've thought so, but I was wrong.

Another angel. Could this day get any more holy and, consequently, more crappy?

He stood by the window, forming out of thin air as demons did. The gray light streamed through gauzy gold and red curtains. You would've thought that would add some color to him. It didn't. "Where is Hadranyel?"

I continued to slip my second shoe on and then straightened while reaching for the shotgun on my dresser. I didn't bother to hurry or try to conceal the motion. Angels knew very well how tricksters felt about them. They also had a conceit that didn't allow the realization we could be any kind of threat. "I didn't get his name. But I think he's in the alley. I have a broom and dustpan if you want to carry his remains home."

The angel stepped away from the window and from his natural crystal essence he changed into a more or less human body with short black hair. His wings were black too with a faint purple-blue barring at the bottom. His eyes were the same purple sheen; it was the shade that dappled a crow's feather in a bright ray of summer sun. "That is unfortunate." His wings were pulled in smooth and tight to his back as a hawk would do to its wings before diving on its prey. "Unfortunate for you. Hadranyel was somewhat more tolerant of your kind than I am."

He had short, sleek black hair, the black wings already in fighting position. His clothes were black as well. It seemed as if Heaven had sent down its SWAT team. But why? Ishiah said they knew about Cronus. Heaven, in all its glorious angelic ego, knew better than to take on Cronus, if it could avoid doing so. "And you are?" I knew what he was, but not specifically which one he was. I started backing up to lock the door before the guys could come in. That would only complicate things unnecessarily and they were already complicated enough.

"Azrael." The smile, cold and tight, was no brighter than his wings. Both were a gravity suck of darkness that fitted his identity perfectly.

Azrael, the Angel of Death, was as without compassion as any demon—a soldier and nothing else. He never sang any hosannas above a manger. He was a warrior. He'd been created for killing and only that. Heaven, ego and all, was indeed taking this seriously. When Upstairs threw down their A-game, they didn't screw around. Azrael was one of the big boys, an archangel, and did that make him smarter, faster, stronger, better, and far more kick-ass than your average angel? Yes, in-frigging-deed it did.

"Ishiah has already delivered Heaven's message. I'm a smart girl. I can hold a thought longer than a day. Why are you bothering with the big guns now? Why not wait until I have something to tell you?" I was almost at the door—too late, damn it—which was when Griffin and Zeke came rushing in, their shotguns ready.

Azrael took in Zeke with a faint lift to his upper lip. He saw what Zeke was. A deserter in Heaven's eyes. Not fallen, but not right with all that is holy either ... far from it. Then he saw Griffin and the disdain turned to disgust. Repulsion. Hatred. Eden House, if they rebuilt in Vegas, would never take Griffin back—I should've known that sooner or later Heaven would find out. I'd thought Eligos would whisper it to them. I hadn't thought an angel would be the one to give him up. That an angel would recognize the difference in Griffin between his former undercover body and the one he had now hadn't seemed likely. They looked identical and the human in Griffin now wasn't fake as it had been before. But this wasn't your ordinary angel we were talking about. This was an archangel. Where a lesser angel might be blind, he could see. "What is this? This is not sanctioned by Heaven, never would it be. It's an *abomination*." A sword sprung to life in his hand, one of flames. A fiery sword—with an angel, that was a given.

Peris Heaven tolerated. But the first ex-demon peri? Fallen was fallen in their eyes and that would never change.

"Don't say that," I warned, my finger already on the

trigger. "Angels can die the same as demons, and if you call Griffin that again, you will."

"I don't think we should kill angels," Griffin protested beside me, his shotgun barrel lowering slightly. "I think in the grand scheme of things that could be construed as not so much wrong but as not especially right either." It should stop boggling me that I heard these things from Griffin, who had many reasons not to care for angels, but it didn't. I had to cure him of this saintlike quality, because as everyone knew . . . the quickest way to sainthood was martyrdom. And as martyrdom came from a painful agonizing death, that was best avoided.

"It's bad enough what Eligos says about you," I told him. "I won't hear it from someone who is supposed to be about forgiveness and redemption. If he says one more damn word . . ." But he didn't have to. Someone else had already made up their mind; somebody had already pulled the trigger.

"He started it." Zeke pumped another round in his Remington, still aimed at what was left of my window. "Asshole. I hate fast assholes. They're the worst." There was no denying that Azrael had been fast in disappearing before the slug reached him. I was swinging back and forth between whether that was a good thing or not. In Zeke's mind—hell, in my mind too, he *had* started it. Zeke and Azrael were former comrades. Zeke didn't remember it, but he knew it. He knew he'd been an angel, used by another angel because of his comparative lack of free will, a pawn, and that history wasn't winning him over to Heaven's side. What had actually pissed him off though was Azrael calling Griffin what he had—an abomination. For that, the pigeon did deserve to be shot. As the man said, the angel had started it. Not that it wouldn't, again, complicate things and, truthfully, I'd never killed an angel before. They hadn't given me quite enough reason.

Azrael reappeared, this time with some friends. Two more angels, but these had the traditional white wings that marked them as your average angel, no more arch-angels. That was a good thing, although neither of the new ones looked in the delivering-messages-of-love-and-guiding-us-to-the-Promised-Land mood. They were more of the cast-ye-into-eternal-hellfire frame of mind from the sword in hand and the rage in their faces.

It had never been quite enough reason before, for me to kill an angel . . . Then again, there was always a first time.

"You let Cronus kill Hadranyel. You fight side by side with that creature once a demon, now worse than any demon. One that wears the skin and flesh of a mortal. One who doesn't know its place in this world. Which is not in this world or any world. The demons are enough. Now there is this atrocity—we will not add more monsters to this world of our making. We leave that to you." Azrael pointed the flaming sword at me.

"Are you calling me a monster or saying I make them?" Sticks and stones were nothing to me and neither were words full of prejudice and hate, because I had the solution to those. I might not have used it on my behalf, but what Azrael had just said about Griffin, that was more than enough motivation. I shot the angel to Azrael's left—aiming for the head. This was the kill shot I used with demons. They were one in the same long ago after all, angels and demons. "Could you be more specific?"

The angel I'd shot at lowered his sword as a warning hole appeared in the wall just to the right and another to the left of his head. I gave Griffin a quick approving nod for his shot that paired mine. He was not an atrocity, and he wasn't taking this lying down—his face, much less forgivingly calm and reasonable than it had been seconds ago, said as much.

Zeke, however, had not gotten the memo and neither had the angel to the right of Azrael. Not as quick as his fellow angel and not as wary of our abilities, he lunged at us. Then there was the sound of a shotgun firing, followed by that of bells as glass cascaded, touched here and there with gold, downward to the floor. Church bells— those that rang mournfully for the dead. Attacked, Zeke took the head shot. It was justifiable to him; he had a clarity of vision in this area that Griffin and I lacked. He held angels accountable to the same standards as everyone else, and who was I to say he was wrong? You make the wrong move—attack, and if you end up as a heap of margarita salt, you have only yourself and your tiny angelic brain to blame.

"Thou shall not kill. He should've known that. I know that. Thou shall not kill—unless it's in self-defense, for protection of the innocent, exterminating demons, or someone taking the last donut. That's the rule." Zeke finished reloading with a speed that would make a drill sergeant dab his eyes joyfully with Kleenex and went on to accuse. "You order us around as if you matter. You expect us to eat up your heavenly commands like fucking candy. Now let one more of you sons of bitches call Griffin an atrocity. Just one goddamn more." Zeke grinned and it was a grin that never would fit on the face of an angel. He aimed at Azrael again. "Because if there's any here, it's you, and since you don't like them all that much, I'll be happy to blow the rest of them apart for you. Really fucking happy. An eye for an eye, a bullet for a bastard."

I didn't know if Azrael heard that. He was lost in the sight beside me. "An angel. You killed an angel," he said as he knelt to sift a perfect hand through flakes of crystal. I saw disbelief and outrage as his hand clenched into a fist, but mourning? That I didn't see anywhere. Brothers-in-arms, but there was no camaraderie, no affection, no personal loss. As with learning free will from humans, some angels learned how to care as well ... most often the ones who went on to retire as peris. Azrael had learned free will, but not how to care. That didn't make him the flip side of a demon at all—it made him worse.

"You might think because Zeke was only an angel, not a high and mighty archangel, that it doesn't make a difference that he was *used* as if he were nothing, ordered about like a slave by one of your kind." I extended my shotgun and tapped Azrael on the shoulder. "But guess what, doll? That don't fly, no matter how many wings you stick on it. It matters, Prince of Heaven. If you treat your own as expendable, they will treat you the same." I tapped harder. "As for trying to kill us, it's not only boring, but a waste of time. Cronus killed your other angel, and if you think I have any control over Cronus, you need to check out if they have a heavenly rehab, because delusional doesn't begin to cover it."

"Zeke's right. You are no better than demons and I should know," Griffin said, and suddenly his wings were there and as bright and blazing gold as Zeke had described. They were brighter than when he'd first become a peri. Of everything and anything that was in this room, they were the only truth and purity that there was. No matter what he said or believed, Griffin didn't have an ounce of demon in him.

Shit. But wings were still wings and whether they had been transmuted into something completely new or

not, Cronus could still sniff them out. "Put them away,"
I told him urgently. "Put the wings away. Cronus barely
cares enough to tell the difference between angels and
demons . . . between demons and peris, so let's not give
him the challenge."

The wings spread until they almost filled the room
before disappearing. "Sorry," Griffin apologized. "They
sort of . . . slipped." I hoped they didn't slip like that in
the future. It was the same as having his fly unzipped.
XYZ . . . your ex-Hell-spawn heritage is showing. Azrael had narrowed his eyes at the sight of them, but
then looked back at the glittering shards beside him.
Ex-angel-on-angel violence and being lectured about it
from a far more ex in the ex-angel field to top it all off.
Surprisingly enough, it did get through to him—enough
so that he didn't try to attack again. I didn't chalk it up to
logic or a shred of good sense. He was more likely biding
his time until Cronus was handled, and then he'd bide
his time until the perfect moment to take his vengeance
on Zeke and rid the world of the first ex-demon peri,
Griffin. Then there was that annoying mouthy trickster.
An upstart *païen* who didn't know my time had passed.
He very well might start there.

Now that was the thinking of an archangel . . . and a
demon.

"Tell us what you would not tell Ishiah." The sword in
his other hand sputtered to flickers of flame and disappeared. "Those who sent him are satisfied to stay in the
dark for a while longer, but others of us are not. Tell us
and we will go." His tone turned suspiciously mild. "For
now."

The angels were disagreeing over how to face the
Cronus crisis. That was interesting but not surprising.
God had withdrawn from them, present but silent, and

given them free rein to develop free will at their own pace and make whatever decisions they wished with that will. Some of those decisions had turned out to be not so different from the ones humans or demons themselves would make, and being an angel didn't mean you automatically agreed with your canary compadres. Heaven's history was full of strife. That free rein God had given the angels, sooner or later, would end up the rope by which to hang more than a few by.

"Fine. If it'll get you out of here. I didn't tell Ishiah because I didn't want to ruin what could be his last days. You, sugar, I don't have that problem with at all." I kept my shotgun pointed at him. He might come over mild as milk and smooth as syrup, but he wasn't called the Angel of Death for passing out lollipops. He killed; that was his sole purpose, and from his history, he was more than pleased to do it—a very righteous and enthusiastic work ethic. Didn't that just figure. "Cronus wants Lucifer's power."

"Obviously," said the other angel, not nearly as impressed by the two bullet holes beside his head as he should've been. I shot him in the leg to reinforce the point.

"Don't they teach you manners in Heaven?" I asked, dropping the shotgun and pulling the Smith from its holster. The angel, leg already healing, started to move toward us until Azrael dropped a hand on his shoulder.

"Go," he ordered. *"Now."* The angel didn't hesitate, vanishing. Some angels were disagreeing with Azrael, but the ones with him didn't have that kind of guts. "I apologize." He didn't bother to try for a hint of sincerity. "Continue."

It was the best and quickest way to get rid of him . . . besides shooting him, and while Zeke had nailed the one angel, Azrael was far quicker and more clever than his companion had been. "With Lucifer's and Hell's power, Cronus will start taking over every world that exists. He'll have Hell. Then there's Heaven, Earth, Tartarus, the Elysian Fields, Hades, Tumulus, thousands of worlds, dimensions, and afterlives. They'll all fall like dominoes. Who knows in what order? You might get lucky and be far down on the list. But as closely as you are related to demons?" I pretended to give it consideration. "I don't think so."

"He is *païen*. Why do your gods not stop him?" Azrael demanded, his wings reminding me more and more of a cemetery's weeping angels, the color their wings would turn when Cronus blotted the sun from the sky and ashes would fall instead of rain.

"Because they are gods, what there are left, and he is a Titan. If you don't know what that means, go home and ask someone who does. We're rungs on a ladder, you and me, but Cronus is standing on top of Everest." I used the barrel of the Smith to point to the glittering heap beside him. "If you don't know that, you're no more use to Heaven than your friend was."

Unhelpful to the end, Zeke added, "There's some superglue in Leo's office. You know, if you've got the time to put the asshole back together."

Either he didn't or gluing a shattered angel back together wasn't an option. "I'll take this news to my brothers." Azrael's human form began to fade to an ice sculpture. "Or I'll find a Titan and tell him where a demon's wings can be found. Gold as Solomon's crown, quite easy to see if one knows where to look." The ice melted away, leaving his last words behind. "I will return and in a much less forgiving mood."

Angels, fallen or not, did love to get in the last word.

"Eh, Schwarzenegger said it better and in only three words." I lowered the Smith after he was gone.

"You think he'll tell Cronus about Griffin?"

Zeke tried not to sound too concerned, but I would bet my new decorative pile of angel shards that he was thinking about breaking out the handcuffs again. "No, Kit. He's not putting Cronus one wing closer to Hell, and Griffin's wouldn't work anyway. He's not a demon." Not that Cronus would be able to tell the difference, but the logic was sound. Azrael was a dick, as Oriphiel before him had been, but he wouldn't endanger Heaven for vengeance. Anything else, yes, but not Heaven.

But on to business. The plan didn't stop because a heavenly asshole popped in to make a bad day worse. It only slowed it down slightly.

"All right. Someone grab the DustBuster from my closet and clean up what's left of Daffy here." I holstered my gun. It was time to act on what I'd thought earlier. Only a select few could get into Greek Hell now. Hades was dead as were all the Greek gods I knew of except Dionysus, and finding what table he was passed out under would be impossible. The only other free pass into Hell rested with one particular segment of the population—the deceased. "And then let's find ourselves a medium."

Chapter 13

The dead . . .

The thing about the dead—how best to put this? Annoying? Yes. Self-centered? Sure. A pain in the ass? Most definitely. But the worst thing about the dead?

They would not shut up.

If you could find yourself a genuine medium and that medium could cast a mental net and snare a human soul still hanging around life like a bad aftertaste—best to pack a lunch, because you were going to be there a long, *long* time. First they wanted to tell you why they hadn't gone to the light, and it was usually something so piddly and insignificant that you'd roll your eyes as you ate the tuna fish sandwich you'd made for the trip. It never, contrary to ghost lore, was anything evil. If you were a murderer, you didn't get to flit around the ether giggling insanely or something equally trite. If you were evil, hell scooped you up in a heartbeat. If your religion had a hell. If you were evil and atheist, too bad, a hell would still get you—it just wouldn't necessarily be the Christian hell.

After they told you their big sob story, then came the messages. *Tell my mother this. Tell my father that. Tell my girlfriend, boyfriend, wife, husband I love/hate them.* One even demanded I tell the post office he was dead, so they could stop his mail. If they were long dead, and everyone they knew was gone as well, then they just wanted to gossip. *Did they ever catch Jack the Ripper? The Beatles split up? JFK is dead? Rudolph Valentino? We won World War II? There* was *a World War II? Did Pet Rocks and leg warmers ever catch on?* War of the Worlds *was just a hoax? Damn it, I killed myself so the aliens wouldn't get me.*

It was an ordeal. The medium should have to pay a client to sit through it. It was good there were no such things as ghosts that you could see or hear or you'd be nagged by them day and night. Luckily you needed a medium and money to arrange for that irritation and eventually you could leave, slamming the door on their questions, *An actor was president? The Terminator is governor?* There were certain things impossible to explain to a dead soul, because you couldn't explain them to yourself.

We stole a car. Leo's was as dead as they came. Only an automotive medium could help that situation. Mine was lost and Griffin didn't remember where he'd left his. Head injuries will do that . . . an hour to even days before the smack to the cranium, was gone, maybe forever. When we found a suitable car and it came to the actual stealing part, Zeke unexpectedly balked.

"Stealing is wrong." He folded his arms in the strip club's parking lot. The club was three blocks down from the bar. They say don't piss where you live, but I was in a hurry. This was convenient and quick and I was all about both at the moment. "It's a rule. Another rule."

Great. When we could least afford it, Old Testament Zeke was back, somewhat recovered from Griffin's disappearance. "Didn't you steal a car to go look for Griffin?" I asked, bending down to take a closer look at the door. How you broke into a car depended on when it was made, if it had an alarm system, if getting in without the key remote meant it would lock up the steering column, and, last but not least—I reached over and opened the door—if it was locked. Yet another good deed on my part. This guy wouldn't forget to lock his car again. The keys were in the ignition too. I liked convenient, but this wasn't fun at all.

"Yeah, but rules don't apply if it's Griffin." That was Zeke reasoning for you and I didn't fault him for it. "When it's not for Griffin, stealing is wrong."

"Fair enough. But if the entire world is taken over by Cronus, there's no telling what will happen to Griffin, and that's why we're stealing a car." I would've gone for the good-intentions excuse, but that wasn't the path to Hell, as they said. It was an express train if you didn't know what you were doing. Get out your ice skates, because it was a slippery slope if ever there was one. Not to mention I'd seen Griffin literally bang his head against a tabletop at Trixsta trying to get the concept across. Zeke wasn't ready for good intentions versus future bad outcomes. He was still working on good intentions versus immediate bad outcomes. It was a complicated theory to grasp. I wasn't completely positive I had the hang of it yet, although it didn't stop me from a whole lot of practice to prove that theorem.

"So don't think of it as stealing to save the world. Think of it as stealing to save me." Griffin was already climbing into the back to lie flat with knees up to make sure all of him fit. It was pain-pill time from the looks of it. I was still stiff and sore, but Griffin didn't look like someone had taken just one baseball bat to his face and head, but rather two or three.

Zeke didn't seem completely convinced, but he got

into the passenger seat. "I'll have to think about it." He had a bottle of water with him, which was unusual for him. He preferred his drinks to jack him up on sugar and caffeine—as if he needed more jacking up. He held the bottle over his shoulder to Griffin. He'd need it to wash down his pills. I'd seen Zeke walk into the bar wearing two different shoes before, but his guns were always immaculately clean, and he always had what Griffin needed.

Leo was the same. He never forgot my birthday; he never let me down. My brother had never remembered my birthday and stood me up more times than he turned up, but he never let me down either—not when it truly mattered. Love was love. It came in too many forms to count. . . . Sometimes it was a bushel of apples celebrating that first trick and sometimes it was as simple as a bottle of water.

"Thinking about it, that's a good idea," I replied as I adjusted the seat, humming, tuning the radio, and checking the mirror to make sure my hair wasn't an advertisement for electroshock. "You should think about lying too. It's a good way to make sure Griffin can't ever fool you that way again."

Swiveling in the seat, Zeke glared into the back. "Lying is wrong."

I grinned at Griffin's plaintive. "Are you trying to kill me? Jesus, when I bought my car, he threatened to cut out the salesman's tongue for lying."

"Did he?" I asked, curious, as I zipped the car out of the parking lot. I didn't mean "Did he" as in did he actually say that. I meant "did he" as in did he go ahead and cut out the man's tongue. With Zeke, there really was no predicting how that had ended up.

"He settled for washing the guy's mouth out with a

urinal cake. It was not a pretty sight." I heard the rattle of a pill bottle and the slosh of water. "Zeke, you are not washing out my mouth with any kind of soap, you understand?"

"I understand." Zeke faced forward again, his voice placid. "I'm not putting anything in your mouth for a long time. Very long. Months. And vice versa." He whispered an aside to me. "Is that an appropriate punishment?" Zeke didn't often ask. He almost always knew exactly what punishment should be doled out . . . in his mind. Unfortunately, he hadn't reached the fifty-fifty mark on being correct yet, but Griffin was different. If ever he was tempted to let someone off with a warning, it would be Griffin, but, in this case, Griffin needed more than a warning, considerably more. He had to learn.

"Perfectly." I tossed a phone book onto his lap. "Stick by your guns on it too. If anything will teach Griffin or any man a lesson, no sex is it. Now look up mediums for me. There're enough of them in Vegas—one has to be the real deal."

We drove past address after address. I didn't have to stop the car and check them out face-to-face. I was human, but I had enough of a tiny speck of trickster left in me to detect the genuine article—they pinged on my shield the same as telepaths and empaths. I drove past their places of business. Hovels of business. Séance/meth labs of business. Sometimes three combined into one. As we moved from one to another, Zeke had turned the tables on Griffin. I'd told him in the hospital it was his time to be the student, and I wasn't wrong. Zeke was taking him to school and educating him old style.

"Okay, think another lie at me," he demanded as he kept thumbing through the yellow pages. "Hurry up. I have to get this right."

Griffin groaned. "We've been at this for almost an hour."

"And I haven't gotten it right yet. I have to be able to tell. I have to see through them. Lie to me again." Licking thumb, turning page. "Trixa, West Sahara. Griffin, go on. Lie."

"Isn't it enough to promise I'll never lie again?" Griffin sat up, the lines in his forehead now eased, his pain pills having kicked in. More than contrite, more than humbled, he affirmed, "Because I never will. Whether I think it's for your own good or to prove myself, no matter what the reason, I will never lie to you again."

Zeke's gaze slid toward the back. "You mean it?"

"I mean it. I won't do that again. If you want to punch me for doing it to begin with, I don't blame you, and I won't lift a hand to stop you." Griffin was sincere, almost heartbreakingly so—his hair, smelling of my shampoo today, hanging forward, his face set and solemn. He had seen the error of his ways, and he was man enough not only to admit it, but to never repeat that mistake. He wouldn't leave Zeke in the dark, accidentally or not, again. It was a moment of such truth that you could almost pluck it from the air like a lazily flying butterfly. Gloriously bright. Real enough to touch.

"Yeah, that's sweet. You're like a prom date, you're so sweet." Zeke was eyes forward again and back at the page turning. "Lie. Now."

And I thought I was skeptical. I swung the car onto West Sahara as Griffin gave in and snapped, "Fine. You can cook. You help me with the laundry. You love thy neighbor. I've had better sex than with you."

"You're not trying at all, are you?" Zeke said with disdain.

I cut the lesson short, my audience part of it—which

was too bad as it was distracting me from thinking about Cronus making Armageddon look like a toddler play-date. I pulled the car into one of three parking spots by a cracked-stucco one-story building with one profoundly dead dwarf palm planted by the door. "This is it. Only damn real medium in Vegas apparently." I could feel him or her, bouncing off my radar. "A black thumb and can talk to the dead. It makes sense. You two can stay in the car. You're having too much fun. I don't want to break that up."

At first Griffin looked as abandoned as a five-year-old his first day of school—not a good look for a grown man. Then he frowned darkly in a manner most certainly not prom-date sweet. He regretted what he'd done to Zeke and still did, but me? The regret was fading fast in the face of being the victim of the newly patented Zeke tutorial. I slammed the car door and tapped the back window just as you weren't supposed to do on fish tanks. "Live and learn, sugar. Lie and learn too." I heard the locks snick fast, trapping Griffin inside. Zeke's grin was as dark as his partner's frown. Ah, for the ability to be in two places at once.

I gave up on my voyeuristic wishes and walked to the glass door and opened it. There was no old-fashioned tinkle of bells but there was the smell of burning sage. Someone was cleaning out the bad mojo or thought they were. Burning sage was an old custom and who was I to say it didn't scrub out the invisible stain of foul intentions, but I did know it had never kept me out of a building or a village, and my intentions? That all depended on whom they were focused on.

I also smelled dog. Lots and lots of dog. A truly massive amount of doggy odor overpowering the sage.

The office was one small room but with very little furniture, making it seem roomier than it was. There were two chairs against one wall and a tiny round table in the middle. Opposite the wall the chairs were parked against was the Dog Wall. I wasn't terribly surprised. There were at least thirty pictures of dogs. If you studied them, you'd see they boiled down to about six dogs. There was a gray-muzzled hound, a mutt (I had a soft spot for mutts) with a small head and big fat belly, a cocker spaniel with about four teeth left and the inability to keep its tongue in its mouth, a three-legged Siberian husky, a Chihuahua with an underbite (if there were hellhounds, Chihuahuas would be fighting for the job), and a German shepherd. I hoped the last wasn't the one I'd tried to pick up while drunk in New York. Werewolves versus German shepherds—add a few gallons of alcohol and it was a mistake anyone could make—even another werewolf.

"I guess you see why they call me the dog lady."

I'd heard the flush from behind a door and was already facing her when she came out. Her hands were pink from the recent washing and she had enough dog hair on the sweater she was wearing to have knit a second one and had enough left over for matching mittens. "Someone has to be the dog lady on your block. Why not you?" I had no problem with it. I liked dogs. I'd been a dog once or twice. Dogs were good people. Furry, but good people.

Her eyes were sharp behind bifocals. "That's very true, young lady, if a bit slippery of tongue. Pull up a chair." With her tightly permed short gray hair, she could've counted as a seventh dog herself, an intelligent poodle who might or might not nip you if she thought you deserved it. Rolling her wheelchair up to the table, she reached into a flower-patterned bag that hung from the armrest. It looked as if it ought to hold yarn and knitting needles, but it wasn't a half-completed scarf she pulled out. No, it was a .357 Magnum to be laid on the table. "Nothing personal, dear. But I've been robbed once. I won't be robbed again."

"No problem, ma'am." I pulled the chair up to the table and sat down. "I can honestly say I feel right at home." Guns and dogs, so far she was fine by me.

"Good. Then everything is right as rain. I don't believe in dragging things out. . . ." She lifted her eyebrows in inquiry and I hastily provided my name. "Ms. Trixa. I had a schnauzer named Trixie once. Good girl. Lived to be sixteen. Became a little senile in her old age and started doing her business in the bathtub, which is an annoying chore. Scrubbing the bathtub every day with bleach, but that's neither here nor there. I'm Mrs. Smith. You may call me Mrs. Smith, and I'll go ahead and tell you up front that whoever you want to talk to might not be around—probably won't be around—but there are no refunds. If I call for them and they've already gone on to their heavenly reward, you're still out two hundred bucks, Trixie, and don't be whining to me about it. Think of me as a phone call. Whether that person you're calling is home or not, you still have to pay for that call." A plump pink palm presented itself. "And that was two hundred, Trixie."

I started to correct her on the name, a pooping-in-the-bathtub schnauzer not the role model I longed to be connected to, but realistically, I'd been labeled worse. I put four fifties into her hand. "Now, I'd like to—"

She stopped me in my verbal tracks. "And don't be asking me to talk to Elvis or any of that nonsense either. He's not there. And anyone else famous who is, well, they'll drive you to tears and medication with their sobbing all over the place with what they've lost and who wronged them and whom they wronged. It's nothing but ego masturbation, Trixie, and I don't have the patience for it."

I gave a wary nod, beginning to lean away from the warm feeling that the guns and dogs had engendered. I hoped Elvis had moved on and Eli had been lying when he said he'd eaten him, but more than that, I hoped the woman let me finish a sentence. I had a mouth on me, yes, I did, and not being able to get a word in . . . That didn't happen often. "No, no Elvis. I just want—"

"Don't be expecting some sort of light show either. You want some two-bit magic, you have the whole strip to choose from. I talk to the dead. I don't set off firecrackers and crank up the dry ice machine." She picked one hair off her sweater—one hair out of hundreds—and let it drift to the floor. "Well, Trixie, girl, let's get going. I don't have all day to waste on your dithering. Who is it you want to talk to?"

"Anybody," I said quickly before her lips, covered in a thick coating of bubblegum pink lipstick, could part again. "Anybody at all. Can you just send out a general notice? 'Dead person wanted. Big balls required.'" Back up went her eyebrows. "Or brave. Brave would get the point across. This is less of a chat and more of a job interview."

"A job interview. I have to say, missy, even my Trixie was smarter than that. The dead can't do anything but talk. They can't haunt your ex-boyfriends, of which I'm sure you have more than a few. Young people these days. We always said why buy the cow when you can get the milk for free, but nowadays, you're squirting your udder at every man who passes by. Girls calling boys. Women calling men. It's disgraceful. My neighbors are into that bisexual, couple-swapping, orgy thing. 'Try'-sexual if you ask me, 'cause they'll try anyone, do any type of perversion. They leave their blinds open a little and I see what goes on."

I bet she did. All night long, armed with binoculars and popcorn. I'm a patient person . . . when patience is called for. When it will actually benefit you. This was not one of those times. I snatched up her gun before her hand had more than a chance to twitch toward it. I emptied the cylinder—the bullets rolling on the table like dice in a game of craps—smacked it back down on the table, and snapped, "Dead person. Big balls. Now."

She swallowed, her head suddenly bobbing from palsy. "Oh Lord. Oh me. I'm doing the best I can, dear. There's no reason to get so snippy." And damn if she wasn't edging her hand back toward that flowered bag again. What did she have in there now? Pepper spray? A stun gun? A cattle prod? Who knew? Who didn't want to know? Me.

I grabbed both of her hands and placed them firmly on the table. I didn't hurt her. She was old, she was frail, and, more honestly, she was the only medium I'd found. I needed her. "Dead person. Go."

This time she gave in to the inevitable, although I heard the annoyed click of her dentures against each other, and closed her eyes while mumbling under her breath. Whether the mumbling was cursing at me or calling out to the spirit world, I didn't care. I just wanted my dead person. I couldn't talk to my brother. Human mediums can't reach the *païen* and there are no *païen* mediums. We don't linger like humans sometimes do. Kimano was gone, to one of our better heavens, I knew. He deserved no less. It didn't change the fact I would've given almost anything to talk to him again.

Someday. When my time was up and it was time to fall so another trickster could rise, then I would see him again . . . if I had to search every heaven in existence. And I would. I would feel his hand in mine again. Rough and warm. My family, and I wouldn't lose him, not for good.

"Trixa."

I exhaled, annoyed. "Mrs. Smith, I don't have the time or the patience for this. Don't make me teach you a lesson about peeping perverts and bad neighbors, because it's awfully tempting. Just do the job I hired you to do."

The eyes, magnified by the bifocals, blinked. "Trixa, it's me. Anna. Rosanna." The pink lips curved in a shy smile. "Remember? With Sir Pickles?" She blinked again. "One of the Roses." The Rose. The one for whom I'd pulled the rug out from under Hell itself. "We know what you did for us. I know what you did for me. Tell me what you need. I want to know how can I pay you back, how I can thank you. How can I save you like you saved me?"

Sweet, shy Anna. She'd hung around, not welcome in the biblical Heaven because of the deal she'd made and not ready to pick a *païen* heaven, because of me. She'd known what was going on once she was freed of Hell. She had known about Cronus. The dead knew a good deal more than demons or angels if you asked them the right questions. She'd waited in case I needed help. She wouldn't have been the first one I'd thought of when I thought balls, but she had them all the same. She had determination and she thought she had a duty—to thank me. In all my trickster days I think it might've been the first thank-you I'd ever received.

"Anna." I gripped the hands I held in mine. "Little Anna, I'm grateful, but I don't think this is something you will want to do. It's dangerous, even to the dead. And it's terrifying—especially to the dead."

The brightness in her eyes was twice what it had been when she'd first come to me. "I lost my face, my life, my soul, and I stepped in front of a bus." The smile was less shy now. It was confident, daring, adventurous, and what Anna should have always been if her life hadn't changed so quickly. "I think I have a résumé in dangerous and terrifying."

"So you're James Bond now, are you?" I asked fondly.

"Better," she said promptly. "I won't stop and have sex with every woman I see on the way."

"Annie-girl, you are so worth it. Screwing Hell. Freeing all the Roses. You were most certainly worth it all. You are my poster girl of the year."

Her hands—in reality the dog lady's hands, but Anna's for the moment—shook mine playfully. "Then tell me. How can I help you?"

I told her, and to her credit she didn't flinch, not once. Not when I told her where I needed her to go, how difficult it was to get in, and how far more difficult it was to get out. I hoped dropping my name and the reason behind what I needed should be enough to help her pass whoever remained there, but I told her truthfully that I couldn't guarantee it.

She tugged me across the table and kissed me on the cheek. "We'll see. I only wish I had Sir Pickles with me. There isn't anything alive or dead that's not afraid of a smack from him. And when I'm done, where will I go?"

"Anywhere you want. We have more heavens than stars in the sky. Tell them I sent you, and I think you'll find one you like. Ask for my brother, Kimano, when you knock at the doors. I know you'll like him. All the girls do."

The pink smile widened and then, the same as a rainbow-sheened soap bubble popping under your curious finger, she was gone. Anna was gone and I was left with the much less amiable dog lady. I didn't blame that schnauzer at all for making a toilet out of her bathtub. She was not the most pleasant or reasonable of people. If we lived someplace colder, she'd no doubt force the dogs into ridiculous little sweaters or raincoats. Looking at the pictures on the wall again, now every canine face seemed to be pleading, help us. She brushes our teeth four times a day. She wheels us out in the yard and tries to wipe our asses with toilet paper when we go.

She did feed them though. That was something, every one of them fat and sassy on the wall of fame. It was better than the pound and near-certain death. I couldn't swat her for embarrassing dogs. But for being rude and peeping at her neighbors, I'd put that on the back burner.

"Thank you, Mrs. Smith. Despite yourself, you were helpful. And, please, the dogs don't care if it's one ply or two. They'd prefer you didn't wipe their furry butts at all."

"You ungrateful, pushy little bitch. Crazy too—ought to be locked up in the nuthouse with your talk of rivers in Hell. No crazy is killing or robbing me—you'll see that right here and now." I'd let go of her hands, and she was scooping up the bullets on the table. Her fingers were as nimble as those of a blackjack dealer, which was why I took her gun with me.

"I'll leave it outside the door. Don't shoot your mailman." I was passing through the doorway when I felt something hit the back of my head hard. A bullet fell to my feet and rolled across the floor. The hell with the gun, she'd started *throwing* bullets at me. I rubbed the stinging on my scalp and closed the door behind me in time to hear another one clink against the glass. With that arm she should've been pitching in the World Series. I put the .357 down on the concrete. She took very good care of her dogs. If I killed her, who would feed and love them?

I massaged my head again. Leo liked dogs. Tempting, tempting, but no. If being a bitch merited death, I'd be notching my gun belt every day. If I had a gun belt. Damn it, that stung. Human pain, yet another thing I could do without in the whole being-human realm. Their nervous system was far too fine-tuned, ridiculously sensitive. In other forms I'd had my limbs broken, my abdomen clawed open, and, on one memorable occasion, had a lung ripped completely out of my body and none of it equaled one menstrual period of the new and human Trixa Iktomi. That might be a small exaggeration, but it wasn't that far from the truth.

I knocked on the window of the stolen car and the locks snicked open. Sliding into the driver's seat, I took in the scenario. Griffin had his arm around Zeke's neck from behind in a classic choke hold. "Did the lesson take a turn for the worse?"

Zeke was tuning the radio. "He won't go through with it," he said without the hoarseness or lack of consciousness the arm across his throat should've produced. "He couldn't choke out a Christmas elf with this hold."

"But I want to. I very much want to," Griffin countered. The hard line of his arm, the clenched teeth, the face flushed with aggravation; it all said it was true, but . . .

"Ha," his partner gloated, "now that's a lie. I can feel

it. I can *see* it. It's purple. When you lie, I see purple."
Closing his eyes to concentrate on the color, he then
opened them again and focused back to the radio.
"Okay. You can nap now. You won't ever be able to lie
to me again, not even for my own good." Griffin's jaw, if
anything, went tighter, but he let Zeke go, then lay back
down in the seat. Being Zeke's student would give anyone a headache, concussion or not.

In a way, it was too bad. Griffin had chosen the wrong
thing to lie to Zeke about, but at the end of the day you
sometimes needed someone to lie to you, because some
days the truth was too unpleasant, too depressing to
hear. A good example would be Eli, carrying the heat
of Hell with him, materializing beside the car, tearing
the door off to throw into the street, and snarling, "He
needs four more wings. Four, and then playing *Where's
Waldo* is goddamn over. He'll have an X marks the spot
to Lucifer. Your plan, if you have one, better be in fucking motion, because the world is about to come to an
end.

"All of them."

Chapter 14

Three months ago when I'd lost my shape-shifting ability, I knew there'd come a time, sooner or later, when I would encounter a situation where a fast gun wasn't going to be enough. It wouldn't be because of any low-level demon, but Eligos had taken over Vegas when I'd killed Solomon. He would've taken it if I hadn't killed Solomon. Eli had said Solomon wasn't in his league and I didn't doubt him. He also thought I was the best toy he'd been gifted with in ages. He thought he was playing with fire when he played with me, and I had to keep him thinking that. If he knew what I was now, he would do to me what I'd done to Solomon. I had no desire to be in so many pieces that I had to be cleaned up with a sponge and buried in a bucket.

That was why I'd asked Zeke and Griffin to do something no telepath or empath, no angel or demon, had done before. Instead of using their powers to pull in thoughts and emotions, I'd asked them to try pushing out those things instead. I knew Zeke couldn't make someone see something that wasn't real. He couldn't make Eli see me change into a giant bear with the mouth of a shark and the tail of a dragon. But if he tried, worked hard at it, after months of practice, he might be able to blur my edges—to make it seem as if my outline was wavering. Shifting. Not a giant bear, but the beginnings of a change, my edges running like a rainbow of oil sliding over water. And if Zeke could do that, then it was possible that Griffin could send out the emotion of fear. Not a powerful thrust, but only a sliver—it could be enough. If Eli saw me shimmer, felt a spike of fear, he'd see a fully functional shape-shifter, not a hobbled one. If he saw it and felt it, it was doubtful he would take time to examine where those things were coming from—he or someone else. It had no precedent to make him suspicious of it and if you had a fully functional shape-shifting trickster in front of you, all your thinking was going to be concentrated on keeping yourself alive.

The guys had given it their best shot, practiced daily, and considering how lazy Zeke was, that was pure devotion. After two months of self-devised training, they'd tried it on Leo, who'd let his shield relax for the attempt. It had worked—more or less. Leo wasn't a demon, however, and although it had worked on him, I couldn't be sure it would on Eli. Still, I'd bet my life on many things along the way. Why should I start changing now?

"Well, Trixa? Is your plan going to save us?" Eli put his hands under the car and flipped us over onto our side. I hadn't put on my seat belt yet. I didn't slam into Zeke as I'd grabbed the steering wheel, but I didn't land on him with the grace and airy lightness of a ballerina either. I heard the muffled grunt as air left his lungs, but that didn't stop him from already having his shotgun in hand. The same went for Griffin in the back. But Eli was enraged and he was faster and stronger than all of us. Normally, I would've tried to talk my way out of this . . . but this time I didn't believe Eli would be listening. He was asking questions, but he was too furious to listen to any answers—too furious to do anything but kill us.

It was time to see if the boys could do to him what they'd done to Leo. I only hoped they'd been keeping in practice. I gave them a fleeting hand signal. They agreed on a "We are screwed" sign; then I used the steering wheel to pull myself upright, standing on Zeke's rib cage and rising up into Eli's view with the happiest, *hungriest* smile I had in my repertoire. "Plan, sugar? Who needs a plan when I have lunch in my face bitching up a storm?"

Eli stared at me, his face not even a foot from mine. "What's your pleasure,?" I drawled. "What part of you would you like pulled off first? Your handsome head? Rip your legs apart like a wishbone? It's all tasty. It's all good, Eligos. All good to me. Let's see how good it is for you." I took the risk and reached for him. I thought I'd guessed wrong, that the training and the work had been for nothing. I thought we were dead when my fingertips were almost brushing the front of his shirt.

Until he took one step back.

Another moment of trickster triumph. If my legs weren't al dente and in danger of buckling under me, I would've been one happy-go-lucky mass of conceit and smugness. I didn't like being vulnerable. I didn't like it at all. I'd been positive that I could get through four or so years without my shape-shifting ability. Pie, cake, cougar soccer moms—all things that are easy. It was feeling less and less that way all the time. I'd tumbled far down the food chain and I didn't like strapping on a fake fin to blend in with the other sharks. I wasn't afraid to die. Tricksters can't be . . . not if they want to do what they do best. But I didn't want to die without pulling off the trick first. I'd done the Roses. I could do Cronus too. If death came as I took him down, I wouldn't mind. I didn't fear losing my life to save this world and all worlds while punishing Cronus ... obliterating a Titan. It was my purpose. I wasn't afraid.

I was not.

Oh holy hell, I was terrified.

A human body? I might as well fight Eli by throwing Ping-Pong balls at him. And Cronus? A can of Reddi-wip would be as useful. Yes, I had fought off Eli before as a shape-shifter in human form, but I'd had extra speed, extra strength to draw on anytime I needed it. I always had an out, of becoming my true self, although I'd never had to use it. Then again, I'd never faced an Eligos quite so furious.

Furious with me, who was doing everything I could to stop a creature I couldn't have before when I was still whole, a creature that gods couldn't hope to stop. I was doing that. Me. And Eli, whose only contribution this past week in helping with Cronus had been brownnosing his boss, hiding in Hell, and waxing his legs to play a centurion at Caesars Palace, wasn't doing a damn thing except pitching a hissy like a thirteen-year-old spoiled brat whose daddy hadn't gotten the Jonas Brothers to play at her bat mitzvah.

I started to climb out of the car. "Stay right there, you bastard. I have a nail file, and I plan on skinning you alive with it." I had a knife as well, but that would be too quick. I didn't want quick. I wanted slow . . . slow and agonizing. I didn't approve of snakeskin shoes, but demonskin ones would work great with my wardrobe.

He took another step back, smoothing his hair with one hand and straightening his black-on-black suit jacket with the other. "I have things to attend to.

When I return, you can tell me how the plan is going then." He disappeared precisely as I leaped. Or tried to leap as Zeke had wrapped his arms around my legs to keep me inside the half-flipped car. I briefly thought about using the nail file on him, but he was trying to do what was in my best interest, and, quid pro quo, I didn't kill him . . . although it would've been a huge stress relief.

"Damn it. Damn it. Damn it. *Damn* it." I kicked at his arms, trying to get free. "He's gone. Let go." I kicked harder, but not enough to damage him. Zeke and Griffin were my boys. I couldn't hurt my boys. "Or do you want me to aim my foot at something more specific and valuable?" I could threaten them, however.

Griffin had pushed open his door, banging my elbow, which did not improve my mood. It didn't worsen it either, but only because it couldn't get any worse. Human emotions were the same as *païen* emotions, but like their nervous system, they were a shade too much. Too intense. Too sharp. Too everything.

When his feet hit the asphalt, he scrutinized me. "It's all right, Zeke. You can let her go. I don't see the nail file and you need your specifically valuable parts." Turning, he addressed the ten or so gaping people who'd stopped their cars to watch the show and announced, "Appearing nightly at the MGM Grand. The amazing Eligos and his lovely assistant." He indicated me, but was careful to keep his hand out of biting range.

Zeke released me. "You need anger management," he said helpfully. "The people in our neighborhood tell me that. Sometimes they leave pamphlets in our mailbox."

"Is that so? Including the people whose house you blew up?" I climbed out of the car without giving in to the temptation to put a heel where it would inconvenience Zeke and Griffin the most, instead using Zeke's shoulder to launch out of the car.

"No. They don't talk to me anymore. They either run or throw up—sometimes both. It's not very interesting conversation. I haven't found a common interest yet, other than they liked their house and I liked blowing it up." He followed me out of the car. "They're sleeping in their car in their driveway. If it starts to smell like meth, I can call you to blow it up. Explosions are a good management technique for anger. I always feel better afterward, but I can give you a pamphlet too, if you want. I have plenty. Piles and piles."

"When the next ice age comes, we can burn them for heat for a hundred years or so," Griffin commented as he followed me down the sidewalk when I started moving. "Where are we going now?"

"Home. Nearly being killed by a gecko calls for alcohol, gallons and gallons of alcohol." If we stayed here any longer, Eli might come back or, by fate's funny little quirks, we might be shot dead by an old lady in a dog-hair sweater. I wasn't waiting to find out.

"Back to the bar?" he asked.

"No, not that home." That wouldn't be home for a while, not with Cronus showing up there on an uncomfortably frequent basis . . . which would be any number of occasions more than zero. "I hope you guys keep your guest room ready for visitors. Fresh flowers in a vase. Chocolate on the pillow. I'm a simple girl with simple tastes."

Forty minutes and one expensive cab ride later I was standing in the doorway of a small bedroom with approximately fifty handguns mounted on one wall, ten shotguns on another, and a third host to enough knives to supply all the sushi chefs in Vegas. "What?"

Zeke asked, aware that I found it somehow lacking but not knowing why. "At least it doesn't smell like ass and ammonia."

True. I had to give him that. It was a step up from the storage closet I'd given him and Griffin—or it would've been if there'd been a bed. There wasn't. There wasn't a couch, no futon, not a sign of a sleeping bag. There were only two chairs, a table, and enough gun oil and cleaning supplies to take care of the army and half of the marines. "This is your happy place, isn't it, Kit?" I asked.

Griffin answered for him, "This is Zeke porn. I time him when he comes in here. Too long and I have to break out the fire extinguisher and cool him down."

"That only happened once, and you weren't supposed to tell anyone." Zeke waited for a moment, then bumped his shoulder against mine. "That's a joke, Trixa. It's not as good as an explosion, but it's supposed to cheer you up."

With Eligos, Cronus, and the very probable enslavement of all worlds, I didn't know there was anything that could. But that was wrong. That was human thinking, not trickster thinking. To the last second of our lives, the fast-talking last breath we took, we always thought we'd pull it off—pull something out of our hat . . . or our ass. And if we couldn't? We'd laugh the whole way into the maw of death itself. That was the trickster way. That was *my* way and being human wasn't going to change that in me. Nothing ever could.

I pinched his ribs. "Actually, it did and gave me a mental picture to share with Leo against his will. That's almost worth being embarrassed by a demon. Now about that alcohol. Someone whip me up a margarita."

But this was boys' town, testosteroneville, and nary a

margarita in sight. I made myself at home on a stool at their breakfast bar. It was ironic. I'd left the bar and yet my butt was still parked on a stool as Zeke peered in the refrigerator. "We have beer and . . . um . . . beer."

I raised my eyebrows at Griffin. "Wine too." He added, "I picked it out, not Zeke, so it's in an actual bottle instead of a box."

I slapped the bar. "What a salesman. Fill me up, sugar." Contrary to what I'd said earlier, I didn't want masses of alcohol. Now was no time to be fuzzy headed. All I was looking for was a sense of routine—unwinding, climbing into a bubble bath at the end of a long day with a glass of that non–box wine and relaxing.

Routine.

It bore repeating. I had thought that word and not as a curse. My mama would never let me forget it, if I were stupid enough to tell her . . . and my mama hadn't raised an idiot. Embracing routine. Forced to exercise. Experiencing human pain, wildly erratic human emotion. I rested my forehead on the bar. It had taken a long time for me to get the news flash that I couldn't turn being human into a cakewalk, but I'd finally gotten it. Sky and Earth, if I survived this, I didn't have an inkling how I'd survive the next four years.

"Trixa?"

"I think I'm having a mid-trickster crisis," I replied to Griffin, without lifting my head. "Ignore the meltdown and pour the wine."

I didn't melt down, as cathartic as that would've been. I waited for the wine and when it came, like a good little trickster/human, I straightened and got right back on the horse that had thrown me. In this case, life was the horse, and it had kicked me when I was down. It could kick all it wanted. I could be both human and not. I was the fox guarding the henhouse. Watch for the feathers in my grin. Hadn't that always been true? Damn straight it had been. It didn't stop me from draining the glass in two quick swallows, but I did feel better. Things were much more difficult than I'd planned for, but that *was* life . . . for everyone. I would make it work.

"About the medium and talking to a dead person." Griffin held up the bottle after pouring his own glass. "Care to fill us in on how that's going to help the Cronus situation? It would be interesting—that's a good word—interesting if you were to give us some information about the plan, *this* time, before Zeke and I find out this time that instead of being an angel and a demon that we're actually Batman and Robin."

That cheered me up more than the wine. My boy, trying to play rough with his big sister, trying to give me a verbal wedgie. It was cute enough that I wanted to pat him on the head and let him play an extra half hour in the sandbox. As an alternative, I embraced who I was and threw him to the sharks . . . for what I thought was the third time this week. "I'm full of information, sunshine. Like how you're not supposed to mix alcohol and pain medication."

Zeke promptly snatched the glass from Griffin's hand and drank it himself. "You're welcome," he said pointedly as he put the glass in the sink.

"Yes, thank you so very much for throwing yourself on the grenade like that for me." Griffin switched his annoyance to where it belonged—on me. "About the medium . . ."

I held up a finger to stop him and swiveled the stool to face the living room. "Shhh. Incoming."

Païen could almost always recognize their own,

whether we currently looked human or not—and, I'd found out, if we *were* more human than not. Sometimes you had to be face-to-face, sometimes not. Sometimes it was a whisper in the back of your brain and sometimes it was a scream. Oddly, I couldn't feel Cronus at all. He could be standing inches away and I would feel nothing. I'd told Eligos that the Titan was outside a demon's frame of reference. Truthfully, he was outside that of most *païen* as well. But Leo, I knew, and had known for so long, that when I sensed him, it was as if he were standing right behind me, close enough that I could feel his warm breath on my neck, the heat radiate through his skin as he leaned close . . . and swatted me on the back of my head with a newspaper. Romantic it was not, but that's what it felt like. Leo was a god and the presence of a god packed a punch. They were brimming with power and although Leo's power was now gone, I recognized him the same as I always had. Only this time it was double the jolt to the brain.

Griffin and Zeke's house, while impeccably neat on the inside and full of toys like a huge plasma TV mounted on the wall, was a drab and cracked stucco on the outside and located in North Town. If you wanted to live in Vegas and not worry about your neighbors catching a glimpse of you loading up the car with guns, this was the place. The cops would go there, but when you have a house stashed with your own guns as well as drugs to worry about, who's going to call them? And as the neighbors were more than familiar with Zeke, my boys were able to keep their toys. Their house hadn't been robbed once—or blown up. The neighbors couldn't claim the same.

Besides the plasma TV in the living room, there was also a leather couch Scotchgarded against gun oil and demon blood. When Thor appeared, he was already sprawled on it, his feet on the coffee table and the remote in his hand. "Dude. Nice TV. Is a game on?" he slurred, before his chin hit his chest, the remote hit the floor, and he was out. A split second of semicoherence followed by deep alcohol-fueled unconsciousness, and this was what I was pinning all of reality's hopes on.

Leo, who had shown up in midair in raven form with wings flapping, changed back to human form. I hadn't decided yet if I was happy or disappointed that the Light had let him keep his clothes as part of his raven-shifting ability. "Hail the Mighty Thor," he snorted as Thor began a drunken snore that anyone who'd owned a bar before could recognize. It was thick, loud, and accompanied by just enough drool to make it intriguing. "This is our third attempt to make it here. Midair over the Grand Canyon was scenic." That would explain the bird shape. There was never a designated nondrinking god around when you needed one. "I thought you'd come here since Cronus has marked the bar as his territory."

He might have marked it, but he wasn't keeping it. "Does he have the weapon mold?" I asked. It wouldn't matter if Anna came through with what we needed from Hades—the place, not the dead god—if we didn't have a way to construct a weapon out of it.

"Do you think I would have him come along if he did? I would've taken it and had him send me back ... blessedly alone. Right now his company isn't that enthralling. Hell, neither is his hygiene, and considering I clean the bar's bathrooms, that's saying something." Leo studied his foster brother, which was as close an approximation I could come to how the Norse gods sketched out their family tree, although fostering had a much different connotation to the Norse gods and the Norse people. It built ties of loyalty among families where before there had been none. Leo lifted his upper lip with an emotion that appeared to be anything but familial or loyal, and brotherly love was completely out of the picture. "I try to destroy the world once and they give me holy hell about it forever, but golden boy spends his life staggering here and there, leaving vomit behind him like a trail of bread crumbs for Hansel and Gretel to follow out of the woods, and he's raised on high. Worshipped above all others. Vikings named everything including their dicks after him. Unbelievable."

"I thought Thor was a great warrior, per mythology anyway." Griffin left the kitchen and went in for a closer look at mythology come to life. "Not to mention somewhat of a compadre of yours until you caused too much trouble for him to overlook."

"We were 'compadres' until I outgrew the drinking, until I puked every day all day, which would've been a week after I started drinking. Every creature he killed, it was because he passed out on top of it and smothered the poor bastard. He was born with a horn of mead in one hand and a woman's breast in the other. The hammer I gave him? The weapon of myth and mystery? He cracks walnuts with it." Thor was bringing out the Loki in Leo in a big way.

At Leo's last words, Thor's snoring hitched. "Walnuts . . . good." He drooled a tad more copiously and the snoring began again. As muscle-bound as artists of old had depicted him, he was dressed in a tank top— all the rage for Colorado in February—and a pair of sweatpants. One foot was covered with a black sneaker and the other one was bare. He did have shoulder-length blond hair, but from the dark roots and artificially even color, it was dyed. Worse, not only dyed, but it was a genuine at-home, from-a-box job. If you drank, that was your problem. If you drank too much to find a good hair salon, that was my problem, visually and aesthetically.

Being a god didn't automatically mean you were a shape-shifter. It also could mean you were big, dumb, and just very, very difficult to kill. Thor fell into the latter category. In fact, he might have been the entire category, hogging it all to himself.

"That's it. I need hair of the dog." The drunken dog that was lying on the couch. Leo headed for the refrigerator.

"Since he is here, in all his glory." I ducked as Zeke tossed Griffin a can of room deodorizer that was applied in earnest to the pile of Norse muscles, from big feet to bad dye job. He was pungent, there was no doubt. "Does that mean he's going to help find the weapon mold, knows where it is, or is he here to laugh at you when Cronus squashes us like bugs on a windshield?" I asked. "Not that I can't understand the entertainment value if I weren't one of the bugs myself."

Leo already had a beer open and half of it down. "He's going to help. I humiliated myself and apologized ... several times as he kept nodding off and missing parts of it. It's all forgive and forget for now—unless he sobers up, but as I've not seen that happen since Leif the Lucky discovered America, pissed on a tree, and then left, I think we're safe." He drained the rest of the bottle. "We just need to get to LA. Hopefully by then our stand-in from a bad wrestling movie will be awake, but still not especially coherent. We can point, he can send one of us in, and we have the mold."

"Which is where?" I stood and whispered the word "car" to Zeke. His face lit up with an enthusiasm that did not bode well for anyone who wasn't us, in particular the neighbors who were such a good release valve for his anger management issues in the past.

Griffin watched him make for the back door. "What did you say to him? Car? Did . . . oh hell." He followed after Zeke, but I imagined he'd be too late. Those unlucky neighbors were about to lose their temporary house on wheels.

"Which is where?" I repeated as the door slammed shut.

"The Natural History Museum in Los Angeles. Thor gave it to a pretty archeologist who worked there years ago and they put it in the Latin America exhibit recently." He shrugged. "You know how Namaru tech works."

I did. A strangely shifting race who built strangely shifting things. People saw what they wanted to see in what the Namaru had created, which is why archeologists had never found proof of the Namaru. They saw what they wanted to see and as they were unaware that the Namaru had existed, they never saw that. And as most of their work had been done in a material that resembled volcanic rock or black glass, Latin America wasn't that far of a stretch. Mayans had used knives of volcanic glass, beautiful things for a less than beautiful purpose.

"The question is," he continued, "did you get what we need to put in it? It's pointless to have a weapon-making device if there's nothing to put in it."

"Ye of little faith. I would think hanging around demons and angels would change that. I have someone working on it." I moved over to Thor's feet. "You take the other end, the potentially vomit-spewing end. Let's get him on the floor at least."

"The things I do for you, not counting celibate showers," he grumbled, and took his time wedging an arm behind Thor, securing his upper body and moving it to the coffee table, which took less than a second to collapse under the weight. "Well, he's on the floor, more or less. So you have someone working on getting into Hades, finding the River Lethe, and getting back out, and they're perfectly fine with this supernatural *Mission: Impossible*?"

"I engender love and goodwill wherever I go. People, dead people included, jump at the chance to do me a favor." I bent down and secured a hold of Thor's feet. "Ready?"

"Ready, yes. Convinced, no." But he bent down and we carried Thor out to the scrap of rock and sand front yard. It was a little after two p.m. and the afternoon sun did nothing for the god's orange skin. The Norse gods were a pasty group, excluding shape-shifters who were also pale in their original form, and they didn't tan unless they sprayed it on. This looked like another DIY job. Thor needed to start embracing outsourcing.

I waved a hand at the still-snoring, now-sandy god. "You bring this to the table and you have problems with whom I send into Greek Hell? I know you must be joking."

"No, I have confidence in whomever you sent. You're on a job. You're a professional. It's the love and goodwill issue that I was doubting," he said, as dry as the sand beneath our feet. "You can't blame me, with Cronus and Eligos showing up routinely. I know neither has love of any sort for you."

"Neither does the Angel of Death. It's an epidemic

lack of taste around here." To the left of us, a car started as I saw a man and a woman running away from us and down the block, which would be the type of reaction that Zeke tended to engender. Love and goodwill? He had Griffin, he has his guns—what in the world could he possibly need with goodwill? It wasn't necessarily the worst attitude to have, not in his particular business or his life, for that matter. It made things much more simple and expedient, as in blowing up your neighbor's house for being drug dealers and then "borrowing" the car they were subsequently living in.

"Okay. We have a car." Zeke popped his head up through the moon roof. "I told them I'd bring it back. I said it'd be fine, more or less, and that neighbors share. They didn't have a problem with it." None at all, although they were pelting down the sidewalk as fast as they could run, which was fairly quick as meth-heads often weren't in the best of physical shape. Love, goodwill, and enough speed to put you in the hundred-yard dash; it all came via the Zeke welcome wagon. "How many guns do we need? Or grenades?" He grinned happily. "I still have some grenades I swiped from Eden House."

It took twenty minutes to clear the car out enough to fit us all in, and I didn't want to know what was causing that bizarrely biologically slippery sensation under my boots, but we made it. Leo was driving, I was in the passenger seat, and an unconscious Thor was sandwiched between Griffin and Zeke in the back. It wasn't the most pleasant experience for the two of them as Thor, room deodorizer aside, wasn't growing any less pungent as time passed. They would simply have to survive as best they could. Suck it up. Cronus had caught the scent of Griffin's wings back at the bar, and that meant that leaving him or Zeke behind wasn't safe or particularly prudent. I was rarely accused of being prudent, but taking care of my boys brought out the cautious side in me . . . if one didn't count the seven guns and four grenades in the trunk of the car. Although, considering our situation, that was cautious. Being prepared equaled firepower, since the only god in the car still with functioning god-like powers was in an alcoholic stupor.

"I miss shape-shifting like crazy, but right now, I miss your big badass self more," I said to Leo.

"I still couldn't do anything about Cronus, nothing entirely effective at any rate," he said as he backed the car out.

"No, but you could take Eligos and Azrael and twist them into a nice pretzel. All we would need is the mustard." I leaned back in the seat, the newspaper doubling as a liner rustling under and behind me. I didn't want to know what was under my boots and I absolutely didn't want to know what was under the paper. I had faith that the universe, infinite in its wisdom, had put it there for a reason and I left it at that.

"Heaven couldn't leave it alone with Ishiah, eh? They had to play good cop, bad cop. Or rather, retired cop, homicidal cop." Leo put the sun visor down and fished for sunglasses in his pocket. I thought again how lucky he was that the Light had let him keep complete shape-shifting ability in bird form, clothes included, or he would've been falling through the air naked over the Grand Canyon. That was a mental picture. I tucked it away for further contemplation. "If you want to let Ishiah know what you expect of Heaven, now might be a good time. You might want to reach out and touch Hell too."

"You have it figured out, do you? You're so clever." I normally hated it when someone saw through my plan before I revealed it in stunning, occasionally body-part-splattered wonder. Leo was my kind though, and it was difficult to out-trick a trickster of his caliber. It might be by choice instead of birthright, but he excelled at the art. I hadn't made a genuinely serious attempt to hide anything from him in a long time. I hadn't kept the Roses from him for a moment. If we were all going to die or worse at the hand of Cronus, I wanted Leo to have something to amuse him on the way out. And if Eli's reaction of trying to strangle me had left him less than entertained, I had to admit that was my fault. I pulled out my cell phone and started dialing.

"The big plan." Griffin leaned up. "I'm still waiting to hear about this Titan-conquering big plan, particularly as you say Titans are invincible. Fill me in."

Both Leo and I spared him quick and intentionally frustrating silent grins before returning to the tasks of driving and me telling Ishiah what I wanted of Heaven. It was enough that Griffin did get a taste of the plan or a small part of it. From the "Oh shit" that floated forward, he found it not particularly reassuring. I didn't blame him. My plans, cons, little tricks, they were all things diverting, but reassuring didn't often fall into that category—not the way anyone but a trickster would define it.

As for Hell, I left Eligos a voice mail. It was only a matter of time, but there weren't any towers that far yet, and Eli wasn't going to be risking his wings or life up here for any longer than it took to attempt to kill me. There was the chance that Lucifer had lost patience with him. The Roses were more than enough reason for that, but Eli as Eli and Eli as Eligos had a way about him and a mouth that never stopped spinning things to put him on top. If any demon could talk his way out of Lucifer's bad side, not a playground I would want to be in, it was Eli. Hopefully they'd both be in a cooperative mood. And like every fifth grader knew, "One if by land, and two if by sea, and I on the opposite shore will be"...

Waiting for Hell on Earth. It was our only chance now.

Chapter 15

It was past eight by the time we arrived at the museum. It was dark, the time of the more adventurous things in life—such as robbing that same museum we could see through the trees from where we were parked across the street in a lot off Menlo Avenue. "Let me get this again. Thor is going to poof one of us into the museum to grab the weapon mold and poof us back out. That's your plan. I was going to ask why you didn't have him simply go and get it himself, but I think I figured that out on my own," Griffin said as he put his head out the open car window for well over the hundredth time. Taking a few breaths of fresh air, he pulled back in and asked, "I'm assuming there's a backup plan? Although why not just poof the artifact itself?"

"First off, he doesn't know precisely where it is in the museum, although if he were sober, he probably would. He does know where we are or I'm hoping he will." Since we were right in the car with him, although in his shape, that was a big assumption. "Secondly, don't call it poofing. Kids' cartoon characters poof. Gods materialize in an awe-inspiring storm of fire, subtly form themselves out of the shadows, or inexplicably appear out of thin air. They don't poof," I said.

"Why is that?" Griffin gave in and leaned against

Thor's shoulder. With the Norse god's size, there wasn't room to do anything else.

"Because it sounds ridiculous," Leo said, jingling the car keys, "and we don't like it." He jingled again, the clank of metal in a dungeon lock as they came to drag you to the executioner's ax. "Not . . . at . . . all."

"Gods are many things, but they're not ridiculous." Thor, determined to be an embarrassing thorn in my side, blew a spit bubble and kept on snoring, as unconscious as he'd been since the beginning of our trip. "Okay. Rarely ridiculous. And, Griffin, you should know I have a backup plan. My backup plans have backup plans." I turned around completely in the seat and shot Thor in the chest with my Smith. I muffled the sound with a pillow that had been left with the sleeping bag the guys were sitting on in the back. The pillowcase, not immaculate to begin with, blackened from the gunpowder. When I lifted it away, the tank top below showed a bullet hole, but there was nothing else. The flesh had already healed, and there wasn't a single drop of blood, but Thor's rhythmic snore did skip. That was something. I shot him again in the same spot.

"I'm sorry I doubted you. Houdini is banging his head sitting up in his coffin in wonder at the elaborate nature of this spectacular magic trick. A gun and a pillow. That beats a rabbit out of a hat any day." Griffin wasn't impressed, but Zeke was shifting in a way that said he was seconds away from asking for his turn. A silver lining in every gunshot, that was my Kit.

I regarded the skeptical one of the pair patiently. "You've been strung up by demons this week, sugar. Do you really want to be strung up by me too?"

"Sorry," Griffin apologized. "I'm hungry, I haven't

lost my sense of smell as I'd hoped, and I was expecting some sort of complicated world-class jewel thief equipment. You know, with wires and complex laser-generating electronics."

Leo gave a laugh that was far too amused at my expense, but I didn't mind. It kept him occupied with thoughts other than gutting Griffin with a pair of car keys for the poofing disrespect. Not that he would have, but it had been a long, odoriferous ride. We could all use the distraction. "Trixa and electronics? She can't program her TiVo. She can't work her cell phone. It still chirps like a flock of birds when it rings. She's set two, no . . . *three* microwaves on fire. Most couldn't do it that many times on purpose."

"I'm not technically gifted." I shot Thor yet again. "I'm not ashamed. We all have our weaknesses. If you didn't have a weakness, how could you hone your skills to work around it? Shape-shifting and the powers of persuasion are my skills. Those and the ability to drive a fast car in three-inch demon-gutting boots. I don't need TiVo to trick, and I don't need a microwave to kill, although it might be nicely ironic in some cases. Now let me do my job." This time when I shot Thor, it worked. That was another thing that didn't require technical skill: pulling a trigger . . . a rather sad commentary on weapons of the day.

Thor's eyes were open and on me. The color wasn't clear in the parking lot lights, but I could guarantee massively bloodshot was descriptive enough. I didn't wait long enough for any emotion to register. I didn't want to deal with a pissed-off, cranky, heading hard into hangover god. I wanted an amiable, still drunk but conscious one. "Give him a beer, Zeke," I ordered before smiling at Thor. "Hey, doll, Loki said you'd give us a hand." The same one that automatically grabbed for the beer Zeke dangled. Guns weren't the only necessities we'd packed. When dealing with an alcoholic god, it was a good idea to not run out of what kept him happy.

By the time he drank four beers, asked to see my breasts—not that that was how he phrased it—I was inside the museum. It wasn't an easy ride, far and away the worst I'd been on. I couldn't poof . . . damn Griffin. I couldn't *appear* or disappear at will—that wasn't one of my skills I'd been talking up earlier. But I could compare Thor's shortcut to the ones that Leo had taken me on a time or two in the old days. Those had been smooth sailing on a calm sea. Thor's trip was a roller-coaster ride off the rails and into the screaming crowd below. That I fell only three feet to the floor was something I was grateful for. I could've ended up in a display case one-third my size or inside the floor instead of above it.

I landed on my bare feet—boots were great for fighting demons but not for robbing a museum—and caught my balance. Gym and yoga classes were paying off in some ways even if they were at the mercy of the diner's biscuits and gravy. Leo had looked up the contents of the museum via their Web site on Thor's computer, after fighting off all the porn-bots, and said there didn't appear to be anything valuable enough to elicit the need of motion detectors throughout the building or around any specific exhibits. Most of what was here wasn't half as valuable as what your average collector bought off eBay. This wasn't the British Museum, full of gold and irreplaceable pieces of history. This was a nice, educational museum with the funding that went with that. That meant all the doors and windows had alarms. There would also be an alarm if you shattered a display case and there would be at least one security guard.

Easy damn peasy for any thief, including a nontechnologically gifted one such as I.

I'd appeared in a room full of dead, stuffed birds. While it was a teaching tool and the birds had died of natural causes, I didn't like it. It was the *païen* in me. We were of nature. We were nature in a very real sense and everything born of nature should return to it, birds included—they shouldn't be frozen behind glass. But humans were human and had long lost the connection to what raised them up and took them down.

The Latin American exhibit was to the left of the bird mortuary, both on the second floor, which was where Thor had put me, miracle of miracles. I kept close to the walls and in the shadows. The lights were turned low but not completely off. If anyone was watching a bank of video screens in the security office, I wasn't going to make it that simple for them.

Many of the ancient discoveries were, like the birds, set in a recess in the wall and behind glass. The weapon mold wasn't. It was halfway through the exhibit in a display case in the middle of the floor. It was set atop a square black marble pillar. The mold itself was colored black as well, inaccurately described as Mayan, age indeterminate. It wasn't their fault. Even if carbon dating could be used for dating an obsidian artifact, instead of relying on the layers of earth it was found within, it would be worthless against a Namaru one. Their devices were immeasurable and inviolable. They would fool any modern technology into thinking they were brand-new, older than wrinkly-assed Methuselah, or didn't exist at all except for the fact you could see it with your own eyes. As I was seeing this one. I could see why it stood separate. The museum might not think it was worth any more than the other Mayan artifacts, but it drew the eye as nothing else around it did. It would catch a visitor's attention immediately and draw them into the room. It was a showstopper, a shout formed of stone. They might not know why or how, but people on a subconscious level would know it didn't belong. It hadn't come from a human hand and it wasn't meant for humans. People being people, of course they'd immediately want a look at that. The old saying was wrong. It wasn't a cat that curiosity killed.

I moved closer. It was almost as black as the pillar beneath it except for a shimmer of silver gray that floated just under the surface. It looked like a block of volcanic glass twelve inches by twelve inches. There was carving along all the edges, looping and swirling. It was intricately deceptive, that design. If you thought it was Mayan, then the design would appear Mayan. If you thought Egyptian, then you would get Egyptian. If you thought Namaru, it would squirm like a living thing until it gave you a headache. Thor's archeologist must have been an expert in all things Mayan, because that's what she'd seen, that's what it had been labeled, and to most of the world, that's what it would be.

To me it looked like a nuclear bomb, and if the Namaru were alive today, you'd be able to make one with one of their new weapon molds. Fortunately, they'd lived in a time when weapons didn't have moving parts and there were no new molds, but that didn't lessen what that block could do. A nuclear bomb wouldn't work on Cronus anyway—what I could hopefully pull out of this chunk of dark rock just might.

My cell phone vibrated in my jeans pocket. Knowing that couldn't be good, I slipped it out, opened it, and

held it to my ear. I couldn't answer, not with my knowl-
edge of the security system being based on guesses. I
could only listen and hope it was the diner wondering
where I was as I rarely missed turkey meat loaf night. It
wasn't. It was Leo's voice, quiet and brusque. As fond as
I was of Leo, I would much rather it had been that fetal-
aged nineteen-year-old cook from the diner, worried I'd
fallen and broken my hip.

"Thor's out cold again," Leo said. "Useless steroid-
popping frat boy. There's no waking him up and Zeke
ever so generously emptied a clip into him, ruining his
silencer in the attempt. We can't get you out of there.
We're going to cause a distraction, and you'll have to
run for it."

Run for it. I was going to have to run for it carrying a piece of Namaru tech that not only was close to
the size of a concrete block, but would weigh as much
if not more. The Namaru had been able to create seemingly miraculous things, but those miraculous things invariably weighed a ton. If you wanted miraculous, there
was always a price to be paid. Sometimes that price was
blood and sometimes it was a herniated disc. Considering how long this run was going to be, I would rather
have forked over a pint.

I disconnected the call on Leo's further happy news
of, "We'll give you two minutes." I was glad he had faith
I was already in position, but when you can't bitch back
about the sudden change of plans and vagaries of fate,
nearly everything annoys you . . . faith included. Scan-
ning the area quickly, I found what I needed and in precisely two minutes, I smashed the fire extinguisher into
the display case. However loud it might have been, it
was completely overshadowed by the explosions I heard
outside. They sounded like entertaining distractions. I

wished I were the one making them and not the one carrying an artifact that had surprised me by not weighing as much as a concrete block, but weighing as much as two or three concrete blocks.

I made it through the bird room, RIP, and came up against a closed door identifying that the Dino Lab lay behind it. Closed and locked. This was the moment when your average thief would've become more irritated, but I wasn't your average thief. To me, that's when it became interesting. Let's face it, if you're not challenged by your job, if it doesn't get your adrenaline pumping, your brain cycling into overdrive, then your job isn't worth doing.

The Roses? Stealing a potentially worlds-saving device? That ... *that* was worth doing.

And picking an ordinary lock, such as this one—a simple pin-and-tumbler design—wasn't technology. Getting through it would be more like solving a puzzle or falling down the stairs in precisely the right way. If it took me a minute, I'd kiss Eli's ass. Putting the Namaru mold on the floor, I lifted my shirt a few inches and retrieved the pick and torsion wrench from my back pocket. After giving the pins a subtle but nasty raking with the pick, I turned the small wrench. It was as easy as actually having the key, only more rewarding. Picking up the stone block again was less rewarding as my muscles complained and the scraped skin on my arms echoed that complaint before going straight to pain as the barely new skin tore in what felt like three or four spots. But all in all, I was maintaining a high level of job satisfaction and sheer fun as I passed through the lab, down the stairs, and burst out onto the first floor. From there it was past the insect zoo, which I cared for even less than the dead birds. Zoos are a prison and humanity the reason those prisons are necessary.

I ran past the admissions desk and out the main entrance, which was unlocked, the steel mesh lifted as the security guard or guards had gone out to see what was exploding. It was cars. Four of them. That made sense. Four grenades in our trunk. Four cars blow up. I'd thought I was having a good time before. This was absolutely amazing—a party if ever there was one.

The museum backed up to Exposition Boulevard, was cornered by Menlo, and was fronted by a green space with grass, several trees, and a narrow jogging path. Now added to all that greenery were several burning cars. It was a pity to scar a beautiful area, but exploding cars in the street could hurt someone who didn't deserve it. The grass would grow again, if not shut behind glass; that was nature's way.

I saw two security guards by two of the cars. The other two bonfires were past three trees. I had to admit it was a great distraction except for all the light it put off. But in LA as in Vegas, it's never dark anyway. And when you're by several streets, the Los Angeles Memorial Coliseum, and a museum, you can take the word "night" out of the dictionary altogether. I was good at sticking to the shadows when I had to, but in this situation the shadows were scarce. I heard the shout behind me as I kept running. "Stop!" I wonder if that had ever worked. Did anyone the world over start to steal from a museum, get spotted, and then stop? *Sorry, sorry. I don't know what I was thinking. Here's your priceless Star of the Infinite Morning diamond back. Wait, let me rub off that smudge. There you go. Sparkly as ever. I'll handcuff myself, no problem. Happy to help.*

I doubted it. They all most likely did what I did. Ran faster.

The grass was cool under my feet and the damn Namaru block was getting heavier with every step I took, but I kept running. I saw our borrowed car come screeching across Menlo Avenue from the parking lot, causing two other cars to slam on their brakes to avoid a collision. I was almost there, almost home free . . . as long as they didn't have guns. I snatched a glance over my shoulder.

Ah, shit.

I dived to the ground. I didn't bother to try and protect the mold as I hit grass and it hit asphalt. Like all Namaru devices, it was virtually indestructible. It could protect itself. I could protect myself too, but I couldn't make myself impervious to electricity. The wires from the Taser sailed over the top of me and the darts hit the street next to the weapon mold. It was almost exactly simultaneous to Zeke jumping out of the car with his gun pointed at the guards less than fifteen feet behind me—the innocent, if inconvenient, guards.

"Kit, don't," I said on the end of a ragged pant for air.

Griffin's voice followed mine. "Think, Zeke. *Think*." Think about what you're doing, whom you're facing, what the situation was and who we were in it. The guards were the good guys. Misguided, as we were trying to stop a danger they couldn't imagine, but they were good nonetheless.

"I've already thought," came the reply, somewhat exasperated, the gun not wavering. "You two," he said to the guards. "Go away. Now."

But good doesn't always mean intelligent. It can mean brave and stubborn to the point of stupidity. Weren't some of the greatest heroes in written history those who didn't have the sense to say, *What the hell was I thinking? Let's wait until we have more men, spears, swords, and brain cells. Why are we even here? I could be home plowing the field and enjoying the nice spring day.* The second guard wasn't a plow-the-field type though. She was a hero. Only unlike other past heroes, she was going to live to tell about it.

When Zeke fell beside me, his entire body rigid, he didn't pull the trigger. He'd told the truth. He had thought. We should've had more faith in him. Zeke always knew right from wrong—it was the punishment area he had difficulties in, and you didn't punish guards chasing a thief. Instead, he took the punishment himself, although he did manage to keep an irritated expression on his face as he went down, which is an achievement when you have that many volts passing through you.

I grabbed my own gun, rolled over, sat up, and put a bullet in the ground twelve inches or so from the feet of the nearest guard. Ms. Hero. I hoped it made her think twice in the future. Do the right thing in the smart way. We needed heroes in the world, but heroes who didn't look before leaping rarely lived long enough to pass on their heroic genes. Whether it would make her think in the future, I didn't know, but it did make her think now. "I don't think I can say it much better than my friend. Go away is good and now is perfect. So go." Neither looked like a former marine, a cop moonlighting, or someone with a badge fetish but a psych profile that would keep you from serving up slushies, much less working in a field where you're armed. They were two museum guards, plain and simple, and that let them back away from a no-win situation, because they were bright enough, the hero included, to know that a chunk of rock wasn't worth dying for. Saving a life was, saving the world was, but a thing? An artifact? That wasn't. Too bad I hadn't stolen one of the dead birds instead. That would've made their decision go down a little easier.

As they backed up, hands in the air, Leo and Griffin came out of the car. Leo took the artifact, Griffin took Zeke, and when everyone was back in the car, I followed. We were flying down Menlo before I could get the door shut. When I did, I checked the mirror to see the guards running after us, trying to get the license plate. Unfortunately for them they'd get nothing. Amateurs, which we weren't, would know enough to remove the license plate in the parking lot. It wasn't our car, but if they tracked down Zeke's neighbors through it, they had no reason to take the fall for him and every reason to gleefully see him dragged to jail. It would be excuse enough for a block party.

"Who stole the cars and drove them into the park?" I asked, using the cause of the entire uproar as a footstool as I reached back and took Zeke's slack hand.

"I did. I keep in practice—as a certain trickster taught me." Leo steered around one car and turned onto West Thirty-ninth, and proceeded to get us thoroughly buried in the city. "I blew them up as well. I did have to wrestle the grenades from Zeke, but it was worth it. Fireballs and stealing—it was very satisfying."

"I'm glad you're having a good time." If it weren't for Zeke getting a small taste of sticking a fork in an outlet, I would be high on the experience myself. "Griff, how is he doing?"

"He's blinking. That's something." Thor remained unconscious, and Griffin had shoved him into the corner of the backseat. He also had Zeke's gun in hand before placing it in his partner's holster. It was Zeke's favorite gun, a Colt Anaconda, and Griffin knew better than to leave it behind. Zeke cherished that phallic-boosting piece of metal beyond all measure. "Hey, partner, when you can move again, be glad we didn't wait and try to break you out of jail later." He hoisted him higher in the seat, and I felt a twitch of fingers captured by my hand. "I'd hate to see what you would've done if they'd tried a full–body cavity search on you. Or have to mess with Thor poofing out all the ill-tempered redheads. With our luck you know one who would've been a pervert clown arrested for twisting his penis into balloon animals."

We took a corner at a speed that had Leo chuckling under his breath. I don't think he'd had this much fun in years. A bit of Loki wasn't necessarily a bad thing for Leo. After yet another corner, squeal of brakes, and blare of horn, Zeke was able to move his lips. He sounded as if he were shot up with novocaine, but he was understandable. "Being . . . good . . . sucks."

"No argument with you there." I squeezed his hand and then let it rest on the seat beside him before patting his cheek. "But other than getting Tasered, it wasn't bad. You helped rob a museum. Now how many people can say that? You're practically a professional jewel thief."

"I don't . . . wear jewelry." He moved slowly and sat up straighter. If they didn't kill you, Tasers were great for recovery time. "And fragging demons is better."

"There's nothing wrong with killing demons, true," I admitted, "but you have to widen your horizons. There's more to life than demons."

"Things like this?" he asked dubiously, trying for a look behind us as the wail of a siren erupted. The police car had turned left off a cross street and slid right onto our bumper. The cops had either gotten notice of the museum incident over their radio and tracked us down in a matter of minutes—lucky but unlikely—or they had been waiting on that street with a looming ticket quota and had spotted Leo's creative driving. It was certainly creative enough to be instantly noticed by anyone with a single law enforcement gene.

"Things exactly like this." I faced forward again and buckled up. I bounced slightly in the seat in anticipation as well. I had no choice. It was a car chase. There had been decades of American cinema devoted to the genre, and here was an opportunity to experience it. You had to live every moment as if death rode your bumper instead of the police. It made every moment irreplaceable—every one a perfect, brilliant jewel strung along the glittering gold chain of your life. "You can outrun them, can't you, Leo? You being so much more technically adept than me."

"That's a given. The question is, do you want the escape casualty free as that may take a few minutes more." Leo jerked the steering wheel and we took another corner. This time he didn't stick to the street. He took out a newspaper box, clipping it with the front bumper.

"Without casualties would be nice, unless it's someone mugging an old lady. Then you're a free agent. Do what you have to do." I braced my hands on the dashboard. "We should've switched. I love driving fast."

"Right. Then the only casualties would be us." Leo drove the car between two rows of pumps at a gas station. I leaned out the window to flip off the cops. I had no problem with them personally, but I didn't mind giving Leo more of a challenge. "Oh yes, that's helpful," he said. "Maybe you could moon them too. That's a thought. That might actually scare them off."

"Ass." I punched him hard enough in his ribs to have him grunting as the car left the station, bounced over the curb, and hit yet another cross street. This part of LA was full of them. It made car chases more interesting. But despite that and despite riding the sidewalk and nearly taking out a gas pump, Leo's version of a shortcut, the cops stuck stubbornly to us.

"That's what I said. If you show them your ass . . ." I punched him again, turning the words into a pained hiss.

I pushed at his shoulder and put a hand on the wheel. "That's it. You had your chance. Switch places with me."

"My chance consisted of forty-five seconds? Hell, no." This time he drove over the concrete curb in front of a liquor store and we were on yet another street, this time going the wrong way.

"I find it disturbing that if we die in a fiery collision, Cronus will still make us his bitches," Griffin said, ducking as Leo dodged oncoming headlights.

"When Cronus does Armageddon, he likes to get it right." I took my hand off the wheel, trying not to be greedy as Leo continued to weave the car around two more approaching ones. "Damning absolutely everyone, living or dead. Good or bad. Human or *païen*, and that means Thor the Indestructible too. If he's ever sober enough to realize it." That last thought gave me an idea, and moments later Griffin and Zeke had tossed a deadweight Thor out of the car. He tumbled across the street behind us and was wedged under the front of the cruiser as it hit him dead on. That stopped them. Thor was a big guy. A truck or SUV might have made it over him, but not a low-slung cop car. Right before both the car, lights flashing and siren screaming, and Thor disappeared in the distance behind us, I saw the beer can that remained clutched in his hand. He had one true love, but he was wholly devoted to it. You had to admire the dedication.

"It's nice to know he's good for something besides stalking a women's volleyball team and single-handedly supporting the Internet porn industry," Leo said, seemingly without remorse for letting us turn his foster brother into a speed bump. It did solve two problems at once. It stopped the cop car, and we managed to get rid of Thor. If he were sober, he would choose self-destruction over helping Leo, and if he was passed out or drunk, he wouldn't be any use. We'd been beyond blessed he'd been helpful at the museum. It had been a long shot, but with the limited time we had left, our only shot. As Leo had once said, *Fortune rarely favors the fucked*, but there were exceptions.

"You're sure he's not dead?" Griffin asked. "I think one of the tires went over his head."

"Unfortunately I'm sure. That won't give him a headache, much less kill him." Leo had us on the I-10 in twenty minutes and heading home. Only then would he pull over and switch places with me. He had hogged the car chase, short though it was, but I didn't blame him. I wouldn't have given one of those up either. As I took over the driving, Leo took a much-deserved nap. Zeke was only minutes behind him. He had been Tasered, which was a good excuse, but he didn't require one. Zeke was a napping fool, one after my own heart.

"He didn't need me to tell him what to do."

It was an hour later when Griffin spoke those words. It didn't surprise me he was the only one other than I who was awake. When you'd been in a coma, that was nap enough for a while. "With the museum guards?"

I said as I lowered the radio volume. "No, he didn't. Zeke's come a long way in the past few months, if you don't count blowing up houses."

"He has. He knows why he is the way he is. Before he never knew whom to blame except himself. Now he knows better. Finding out what he was helps him deal with who he is." Griffin exhaled. "I find out what I was and I can't deal at all."

"If it had been the other way around, would you have held that against Zeke?" I asked, already knowing the answer.

"No, of course not, so I shouldn't hold it against myself. But it isn't that easy, is it?" He was slumped in the corner of the seat Thor had occupied before being unceremoniously rolled out. I couldn't see much of him in the rearview mirror. Shadows within shadows. At that moment, it would've been the same in broad daylight.

"Nothing worthwhile is easy, but remember, angels have only ever fallen. You're the single one who has ever risen up. That makes you damn special whether you want to see it or not. For one moment you had all the memories of who you once were and you still turned your back on Hell. You chose who you are now, a life that might be shorter, a life without all the power, a life of doing good instead of destroying it. I keep saying you aren't that demon and you're not, but I have to give him credit. That demon made that choice with you. To stay you and to never be what he was again. In a way, he gave his life to let you live. Maybe we both shouldn't think of ex-demon as an insult. Maybe we should see that only makes what he did that much more extraordinary."

The shadows moved and the tone lightened. "You think I'm extraordinary?"

"Sugar, ordinary you are not. If you were, do you think I'd have spent so many years babying you?"

"Is that what that was? I thought you were whipping me into shape Spartan style. . . . Shit! Watch out!"

I jerked my attention from the mirror to what was in front of me, easily visible in the car's headlights—too easily. It was the Apocalypse, wearing that same inside-out T-shirt, same new jeans, and with the same eyes that were abandoned wells littered with bones of the doomed and the damned. He was standing on the road fifty feet ahead of me. I had less than half a second to decide which would be worse: to swerve off the road and most likely flip the car or to hit him head-on. I chose head-on. That was the unknown. I might do some damage; I might not, but rolling the car was guaranteed injuries. This was an old car with no airbags and the seat belts were questionable at best. I had to make a choice, and I did.

I chose wrong.

Hitting Cronus was like hitting a brick wall. He didn't move, bend, or break, but we did. I heard the shattering of the windshield and the scream of metal as the front of the car folded in like an accordion—felt the rear of the car come up off the ground. We weren't going to roll over, but we were going to tip and land upside down. With the speed I was going and the lack of give when we hit, we were going to fall hard. I didn't think the roof would hold, and I didn't think any of us were going to end up as anything other than dead with crushed skulls and broken necks. I thought all of that in less time than it took to take a breath. The mind moves quickly when it sees an ugly death racing its way. If there was anything I was sure of in that one frozen moment, it was that our lives were over.

Then the car stopped up in the air at almost a ninety-degree angle before slamming back down on all four wheels, which all immediately blew. I could see Cronus, blurry now as warm liquid dripped into my eyes. He had one hand resting on the mangled remains of the hood, the glass of the windshield diamond pebbles across the metal. He had stopped us and I didn't think it was out of the kindness and goodness of the black hole that was a Titan heart. "I smell the demons on you. Bring me one more demon out of Hell. One more or I don't start with worlds. I start with you," he said before switching to a subject with such abrupt illogic I nearly couldn't understand the words. "You should go home." He swiveled his head in the direction of our home, then completely around to face us again, the neck a twisted piece of inhuman taffy. "But you can't." The smile was as creepy and soul sucking as it had been before. "You can't go home when there is no home. Bring me a demon." He lifted his hand from the car and turned the world inside out. Gods moved themselves through the world. Cronus decided to move the world around him. It was indescribable, the feeling—worse than the free fall of an airplane falling from the sky. A thousand times worse.

I sucked in a breath and held it. I didn't vomit. I wouldn't. I refused. Zeke and Griffin weren't so fortunate. What Cronus had done to reality was horrifying to me, unnatural, but not unknowable. I was *païen*. I'd seen similar things, not as perverse in its magnitude, but similar. But to Zeke and Griffin, what had been done was beyond obscene and so alien to their minds and bodies that it couldn't be tolerated. I heard them push the doors open, crawl out onto the asphalt, and retch. If they could move and throw up, then chances were they weren't dying, which was good. The Titan hadn't detected Griffin's wings either and taken him, even better. The fact that he needed only one more demon now fell into a classification of which good and better weren't a part.

Prying both hands off the steering wheel, I wiped at the blood running into my eyes. I'd either been cut from flying glass or smacked my head on the steering wheel. "You can't go home when there is no home," Leo said beside me. He undid his seat belt before pulling off his shirt, folding it, and handing it to me. The tribal raven tattoo on his chest showed in flashes from the one working headlight and the lights of cars moving up behind us. This interstate was never empty, no matter what time of day.

"Thanks, Matthew McConaughey. I've gotten to see your bare chest twice this week. You're a shirtless wonder. I'm swamped with happy horny hormones." Despite the wit or dark attempt at it, I leaned against his shoulder as I held the cloth to my forehead.

"You can't go home when there is no home." He wasn't giving up until I admitted it, was prepared for it. "You know what that means."

I did. I knew. I shouldn't have cared. It shouldn't have mattered, not to me—not to who and what I was. But it did, and it hurt. It hurt so damn much. "I know," I said, closing my eyes and letting him take more of my weight. "I do."

And it broke my heart.

Trixsta was gone.

My home, the first I'd ever had, was gone. A pile of rubble was in its place. The only picture I had of my brother and me, the piece of amber my mama had given me, the whimsically painted headboard of my bed, its

carved leopards and birds that greeted me every morning, the claw-foot tub I'd taken far too many bubble
baths in, Zeke's first headshot from the target range
stuck to the refrigerator—an accumulation of ten years
of Trixa Iktomi's life, and it was all gone. Cronus had
brought it down like the Tower of Babel.

We'd stolen another car—carjacked it from a less-
than-Good Samaritan who'd tried to drive around
our wreck and keep tooling it toward Vegas and the
nickel slots. He'd made it to Vegas, but riding in the
trunk of his own car. We'd dropped him off at Buf-
falo Bill's Casino on the California-Nevada border.
Nickel slots to his heart's desire. We'd also torched
our "borrowed" car before we left—couldn't have the
VIN number tracing it back to the neighbors, and it
made a good distraction for the police and emergency
response teams.

But that was a thought that came and went, because
my home was gone and now I knew. Me and mine
weren't wanderers thanks to it being written in our ge-
netic code. There was another reason we were nomads
by nature. Some long-past ancestor had discovered that
if you didn't love something, you couldn't lose it. If you
didn't take in strays, like I had Griffin and Zeke, you
wouldn't have to watch them die. If you refused to see
that someone was more like you in the good ways and
not the bad, you wouldn't have to watch them leave
someday. If you never had a home . . . but I had. I'd lost
it and my confidence that I didn't need it, all in one. I
felt the loss of both like an ache straight through to my
bones. Who I was and where I'd chosen to be that person had vanished in the remains of a squat and unique
building. Unique being another way of saying ugly, but
ugly with character and meaning. You didn't have to be

beautiful to have those things. Trixsta had had them in abundance.

I missed it. That son of a bitch Cronus might get by with tearing down Lucifer and Hell along with him, but he wasn't getting away with what he'd done to my home.

"I have a copy of the picture of you, me, and Kimano," Leo said quietly beside me.

My mama would say it was foolishness. That a picture of Kimano and me was a picture of empty Halloween costumes, because you couldn't see who we truly were anywhere in the shapes we chose. They were temporary and forgotten as easily as an old shirt or pair of shoes you hadn't worn in years. She was wrong. No matter what we looked like, I could always see my brother and he had always seen me. Leo always saw me, and he always knew me. He knew how much that old black-and-white photo meant. Memories faded, the most precious ones as well. Time washed everything out on the tide, every year taking it farther and farther from sight. I wanted that one memory sharp and bright. I needed it. I nodded, but said nothing as I felt the warmth of his hand wrap around mine.

Boulder Highway was blocked off as fire trucks and an investigative crew looked over the wreckage. It was four a.m., but Vegas never sleeps and the traffic pileup was enormous, which is where we sat—one in a long line of cars. But I could still see. The buildings on either side were completely undamaged. It was as if a minute yet hugely violent earthquake had hit Trixsta and only Trixsta. A natural disaster, that was Cronus . . . one massive natural disaster, without mercy or remorse.

Zeke and Griffin were both asleep this time in the back. Considering they were bruised and battered from the wreck, I didn't wake them up to see the bones of Trixsta laid bare. It would be painful for them too. It had been their home for several years, more than Eden House had ever been. They would mourn, the same as I did, but they didn't need to do it now. They'd been through enough this week, and with Griffin having the only thing close to demon wings on Earth at the moment, they had other things to worry about.

We spent what was left of the night at Leo's condo, two hours later, after finally passing through the backed-up traffic. His place was in Green Valley, older but neat and well kept up. This was actually the first time I'd been inside. He tended to bring his bimbo du jour here these days instead of the bar as I'd produced a doctor's note that I was horrifically allergic to silicone. The fact that I'd filled the car of one of the overly enhanced actress/singer wannabes with tarantulas during their mating season also might've had something to do with it as well. I say, if you're not an animal lover, you can't be trusted anyway . . . and horny spiders are fuzzy and cute. I was merely pointing out her character flaws to Leo as an act of charity on my part. He, unreasonable bastard that he was, didn't see it that way.

We roused the guys and headed them for the stairs. "What happened to Trixsta?" Zeke asked, yawning, then wincing as his bruised jaw cracked loudly.

"Nothing that can't be fixed," I replied lightly.

Leo, carrying the Namaru weapon mold, spared me a dubious glance. "Nothing that can't be fixed," this time stubbornly determined. He knew better than to argue with that mood.

"Better than before," he confirmed, in my corner whether he truly believed it or not.

When we reached the second floor, a long walk for

those who have been in a car wreck, Tasered, and re-cently comatose, we leaned on the mauve stucco wall beside the door as Leo unlocked it. Inside was cultural pride as far as one could see. "Did you buy out IKEA," I inquired, feeling the first sliver of humor in hours, "or do they have one or two futons left in their store?"

Griffin looked around, his eyes settling on a bookshelf divided into so many spaces that it could have held fifty knickknacks easily. It only held one. "Do you have to make a pilgrimage to their headquarters once a year? Do you face Sweden and pray every day?"

Leo growled, "Do you want to continue to mock my taste in reasonably priced furniture or sleep in the car? It's your choice."

Griffin held up his hands in surrender and fell onto the couch, followed by his partner. I had gone to that ridiculously arty yet functional bookshelf and taken the one object there—a framed picture of Kimano, Leo, and me. Kimano looked as he most often looked, with straight black hair, dark skin, a puka shell necklace, and white teeth flashing in a laugh. The tides weren't carrying away this memory. I held the frame to my chest, silently daring anyone to bring it up, and asked, "Where do I sleep?"

Leo had a spare bedroom, but he put me in his room and the guys in the extra. I cleaned the dried blood out of my hair and off my forehead. The cut was an inch back from my hairline and had stopped bleeding. It would be fine and I'd be better than fine as my hair would cover it up and Eli wouldn't wonder why a shape-shifter was walking around with an easily healed wound. Borrowing a T-shirt from Leo, I slid under the covers of his bed, putting the picture on the bedside table facing me. "You coming?" I asked.

He'd stripped off his dirty and bloody shirt, the one I'd given back when I'd stopped bleeding. He also skimmed off his jeans and replaced them with a pair of loose black thin cotton pajama pants. They looked like what a ninja would wear to bed—or a dark god. He considered my offer. "I guess that depends on you."

I eased down gently, careful of my head and my torn skin, and pulled the covers up to my chest. I was exhausted enough to almost have double vision. I hoped it was the exhaustion as opposed to a concussion. "Unless you're into sexing up unconscious women, I'm afraid you're out of luck."

"No, that's not quite my thing." He turned off the light and lifted the covers to slide in beside me. The spread over us was a silver gray, almost icelike in color, and although it was forty-five degrees outside, the heat couldn't have been on higher than fifty-five inside. The furniture, the colors, the cold—Leo was missing Valhalla.

He moved closer and wrapped his arm around me as I turned on my side to keep Kimano in sight even in the dark. It wasn't the first time we'd slept together platonically. Sometimes you just needed someone who cared about you, understood what no one else could, knew you like no one else could. I couldn't promise the next time or the time after could stay platonic or if the thoughts themselves had ever been platonic to begin with . . . but if we lived, there was time enough to worry about that. Exhaustion dragging me into sleep, I murmured, "You should go home. When this is all over, you should go home for a visit."

He tightened his grip on me, and I felt his breath

rustle my hair. "I might. Maybe you should go with me. Odin loves you. It might get me some brownie points, especially since Thor isn't going to be telling any great stories about me after this incident."

"Maybe I will." I closed my eyes. "While they're rebuilding Trixsta." While I figured out exactly who I was, which wasn't who I'd been raised to be. Maybe one trip would solve all that. I exhaled, long and slow. Maybes didn't get much bigger than that. I opened my eyes for one last look at Kimano, his Cheshire cat smile the only thing visible, and then I fell hard and fast into sleep. I dreamed of gold wings ripped from Griffin and of being in Trixsta when it crumbled and crushed me. I dreamed of Valhalla, talking to Odin over a mug of mead, his one good eye glittering in good cheer and laughing through a long white beard, right before Cronus appeared behind him and ripped his head from his broad shoulders.

Finally I dreamed of Anna, with her soft unassuming smile, her average and wonderfully whole face, her freckles. I dreamed she said, dimpling, "Easy as pie." And then . . .

"Good-bye, Trixa. Every Rose says thank you, me most of all."

Good-bye. . . .

Good . . .

There were no dreams after that.

It was eleven in the morning when I stumbled out of Leo's bedroom. It wasn't quite five hours of sleep, but close, and if only one-third of what I needed to function, I'd have to make do. The morning light was too bright, the smell of food nauseating, the furniture too Lovecraftian in its bizarrely geometric shapes unknowable to any but the Swedes and Cthulhu's fourth cousin. I kept moving to the kitchen where Zeke was cooking something in the skillet. It looked as if it had all the four basic food groups, but it smelled as if they'd all been gathered or caught in a swamp. "Someone left a present for you," he said, one elbow indicating a countertop as he continued to earnestly scramble whatever he was cooking down to their separate molecular parts.

There it was, resting on the black granite countertop—a glass pitcher filled to the brim with crystal clear water. The pitcher itself was frosted with condensation and a heart had been drawn on it. Inside the heart, the name *Anna* was written in loops and swirls with a flourish at the end. The dream had been real. She'd done it, what most Greek heroes couldn't pull off, Anna had done. I'd had faith in her with good reason.

I heard Zeke switch off the oven before he moved to stand shoulder to shoulder with me. "Not much of a present though. Water. You can't wrap it. Can't exchange it for ammunition. You can get your own out of a faucet. Pretty cheap gift." He began to reach out a hand toward it.

"No." I caught his hand. "Don't touch it and don't drink it. It's from the River Lethe in Hades, the Greek underworld. If you drink it or touch it and get a drop in your mouth, you'll forget."

"Forget what?"

"Everything." I picked up the pitcher with the greatest of care and took it into the living area where we had left the Namaru weapon mold. "What your name is, who you are, who you were. Every memory you have will be gone."

"Huh." He followed behind me. "This is for Cronus too? You're going to set up a lemonade stand and convince him to drink it? Then he'll forget all about taking over Hell and wander off? And I thought some of my plans were bad."

"If I had a spare hand, I'd swat you. No, I'm not going to convince him to drink it. I'm persuasive, but no one is persuasive enough to convince a Titan on the warpath to stop for a cold one and a Super Soaker isn't going to do the trick either." I stopped with the mold at my feet. With a thought, a shadowed slot about six inches by one inch appeared in the top of once-solid rock. Kneeling beside it, I tilted the pitcher and poured the water into the block with exquisite care, not a drop spilled.

"Hey, what happened? What'd you do? Turn it on? And you're going to make a weapon out of water? Hell, we could've just gone to the grocery store and bought some balloons. We didn't have to go all the way to a museum, get Tasered, get in a car wreck, waste my grenades because Leo wouldn't share, if the big plan is throwing water at Cronus." By the time he finished, curiosity on his part had turned to exasperation for both of us.

I straightened with the empty pitcher in hand. "Kit, remember when you worked at the bar and someone wouldn't flush or didn't tip you or told you the fried cheese sticks you served them weren't hot? Remember how you would bang their head against their table because Leo told you rudeness is one of the seven deadly sins?" He opened his mouth to comment, but I cut him off. "I'm looking for a table."

He scowled and retreated back to the kitchenette, split the contents of the skillet onto two plates, and disappeared down the hall to the bedrooms. Lucky Griffin, breakfast in bed. Unlucky Griffin, Zeke had cooked it. "Your friend came through, then? Walked into Hades, picked out a souvenir, and brought it back to you?" Leo, who had waited for Zeke to pass, stood in the hall now, his hair half in and half out of the ponytail he'd secured it in for bed.

"I told you. Love and goodwill wherever I go." Letting the pitcher drop onto the couch, I stretched my hand back down and pulled the sword from the stone. I held it high, a blade seemingly made of glass, but it was water. All of it. The blade, guard, grip, and pommel, the entire thing almost five feet long. The Namaru alone could make a weapon out of water, one you could hold firm in your hand and one that could cut absolutely anything.

Leo folded his arms. "All Hail the Once and Future Queen, but it has been done."

Affronted, I complained. "Arthur only had to pull the sword out of the stone. I had to *steal* the stone and then pull out the sword. I deserve extra credit for that." I'd also pulled a five-foot sword out of a one-foot-square block of stone, which, while impressive, I couldn't claim credit for. A long-gone Namaru was responsible for creating that technical miracle.

"We're sure it was all worthwhile, that this will work?" He leaned against the wall. I could see him through the sword itself, his image wavering through the rippled surface of the blade.

"No, we're not sure of anything, but I scraped the bottom of my bag of tricks for this. If it doesn't work, no one will bitch that we didn't give it our best shot. Cronus will be giving them plenty of other things to bitch about. Torture, death, the sun falling from the sky, being thrown into another world where sharks are people and humans are chum." I pointed the sword at Leo, admiring the crystal sheen of the blade—straight and true. "I think I want one more meal at the diner. One more helping of biscuits and gravy in case it's our last."

"I know you don't equate that with the Last Supper, you with your heathen existence."

If anyone had worse timing than a demon, it was an angel. "More of a Last Lunch." I let the point of the broadsword drop toward the wood floor as I swiveled to face Azrael. Griffin was right or rather I wished he were right. The sudden appearance and disappearance should be somewhat akin to poofing. I knew I would appreciate a sound effect to let me know when an angel or demon shimmered into existence behind me. Bell the cat. If they both weren't so fond of their own voice, and they were, you often wouldn't have any warning. "You're not invited."

The disdain in the purple-black eyes was the same as it had been before. "If a sword could fell a Titan, don't you think we would have tried it?"

"With one of those flaming swords? Did you ever wonder where they come from, the swords made of fire? Whatever angel is passing them out up in the Penthouse, did you think he made them? It's ironic that all the smiting you and yours does is with weapons made by dead *païen*." If you could make a sword out of water, you could out of fire as well, the Namaru's natural environment. I smiled. "Why, sugar, you don't look pleased to hear that. Your feathers are ruffled."

"He looks ready to drop a load on a statue's head, I think you mean," Leo added, pulling the ponytail holder from his hair and resecuring it tightly.

Azrael ignored the insult and the one who'd delivered it. "That is not so. Our weapons are of Heaven and always have been of Heaven."

I didn't try to change his mind. In my life and my occupation I'd learned that you can change behaviors, with the right kind of motivation, but you can rarely change minds.

Logic was useless. My natural optimism had taken a beating from reality more than enough to learn that while truth and facts were nice thoughts, they required a reasonable medium to take root. Angels weren't often reasonable. It would be easier to pry the six-pack out of a NASCAR fan's hand than to change an angel's mind. "Did you want something, Angel of Death? Was Ishiah wrong in thinking you could do what needs to be done? Killing is easy for you, but leading—is that out of your depth?"

"I can do both, easily. You should remember that." His wings, often an indicator of an angel's mood, stayed flat. They hadn't been disturbed, although I'd told a tiny white lie and said they were. Azrael was right. I should remember he had no problem with killing, certainly no emotion attached to the act. Which was worse? To kill out of cold arrogance or to kill out of a hunger for violence? Angels and demons, if you asked me, the only difference was location. "I came to see if it was worth it. If we had a genuine chance or if all of this has been trickster talk and trickster ego. Liars, thieves, you hold nothing to be sacred and true, including your word."

"I always keep my word. There are plenty who would tell you that. They'd have to crawl out of their unfortunately early graves to do it, but they could tell you." I hefted the sword again. "This is a win-win for everyone, Azrael. Try to keep that thought in your tiny parakeet brain. We all stand together or we all fall, and that fall will make Lucifer's seem like a trip to the ice cream store. Just do your part and we might make it. Think how Heaven will look at you"—I nudged—"with adoration and admiration. They'll love your ass, put it up on a pedestal." As Lucifer's followers had once done to him. "You'll be the hero of Heaven." It did sound better than hit man of Heaven, but Azrael was not interested in heroics. He wasn't made that way. He was interested in saving his own life though and that would have to do.

"If you fail us, I shall kill you before Cronus has a chance," he promised.

"If I fail, trust me, death will be the least of my worries," I said. This time the wings did spread, because he knew—he knew, at least, that was true. For everyone. Killing didn't cause an emotional flicker, but thinking of how Cronus would make the rest of existence an endless damnation that Hell could never begin to dream of or match—that ruffled Azrael and good.

"Then do not fail." He was gone before I could make sure Ishiah had given him the right time and place. It didn't matter. I knew he had. Ishiah was thoroughly dependable and one of the exceptions that proved the rule about changing minds. Ishiah wouldn't let me down. I didn't know how he had been made, but it was far from the template of Azrael. Ishiah could kill, most likely had killed, but he would feel it and I thought he would regret it, whether it was justified or not. That made him a better person than I was.

"One tentative RSVP from Heaven," Leo said. "Now what about Hell?"

"That's going to be a roll of the dice. Cronus needs only one more demon. I'm hoping that's not because he caught Eli peeking out of Hell and took his wings. Without Eli, we're pretty well screwed." I put the sword down on the couch. It magnified the weave of the material beneath it. "He's the only high-level demon I know. . . ."

"Since you killed the others," he interrupted.

That was unfair. How was I supposed to know I'd need one or two later on? You didn't keep around a rabid dog on the off chance that Hollywood would call you to make *Cujo 2, Wrath of the Motherpupper*. "He's the only one I know," I went on, "and of all the ones I have known, the only one silver-tongued enough to have a hope at getting us what we needed. Not many demons could deliver up Hell itself."

"Maybe not even Eligos."

"Maybe not." I shook my head. There was no point in worrying about it as there was nothing we could do about it. "We'll have to keep our fingers crossed."

"You don't think that no matter how this ends, Heaven and Hell are going to think we didn't do our share?" he asked, knocking once against the wall in punctuation.

"They have a trickster and a god playing on the team. What more could they want?" I knew what I wanted. *Païen* kind as far from Cronus as they could get. Cronus was the sole remaining Titan. The others, like him, couldn't be killed . . . except by their own hand. Only a Titan was powerful enough to kill a Titan and they'd all eventually done just that, but to themselves. All that unending power, it led nowhere but to insanity. The other Titans had turned that insanity inward and died of it. Cronus was the only one who had turned it outward, which was apparently the ticket to escaping suicide. Unfortunately, outward also equaled homicide. Two "cides" to every story, but with a Titan the story was always a horror. I didn't want our kind near that horror. We were too few as it was.

"I don't know. Perhaps a functional trickster and god?" Leo said with a wry lift of his eyebrows.

"Picky, picky, picky." I narrowed my eyes as the raven tattoo on his chest appeared to move when he shifted positions. "Why don't you put on a shirt, Captain Kirk? Or are you going to try distracting Cronus by having him put dollar bills in your pants?"

"Oh, now you notice. It's the end of the world and

suddenly you can see. It's good to know what it takes. Next time we shower together, I'll arrange an Armageddon." He turned and headed back to the bedroom. That was serious talk from someone who had at one point and could again in the future when his powers returned. You had to feel flattered when someone was ready to end the world for a romp in the shower. Or that might just be me.

Yes, it probably was just me. I didn't mind.

You took your fantasies where you could get them.

Chapter 16

We skipped lunch at the diner. While I would've liked to have my potential last meal there, it was too close to Trixsta, or what was left of it. I didn't want the boys to see it, and I didn't want to see it either. It was best to fight on an empty stomach anyway. When there's a possibility someone plans on stringing you up by your own intestines, it's much less messy. Or a more mundane penetrating wound to the abdomen . . . Did you honestly want someone looking at the ground at your feet and asking if that was biscuits and gravy pouring out of the gaping hole in your stomach? No, that sort of thing took you right off your game.

Before we got into yet another stolen car, I had to ask Griffin a question. It wasn't one I wanted to ask, but it was part of the plan, the most important part. If he said no, I wouldn't blame him, except I knew he wouldn't say that. I also knew who would, and I respected him all the more for doing it.

"No fucking way," Zeke said. I hadn't seen him angry with me before. That made this the first time and it was memorable. He was doing it up right. Green eyes were always among the most beautiful, I thought, and yet they could turn hard in an instant, the deepest and coldest of ice, merciless as a riptide. "No fucking way you are put-

ting a bull's-eye on Griffin's chest. You're not singling
him out to that goddamn freak. We can all face Cronus,
but you're not dangling Griffin like a piece of meat for
an alligator."

"Zeke, it's not like that," Griffin countered.

"Griffin, it *is* like that." I had put the sword in the car
and now stood, hip against the metallic blue of the SUV,
a four-wheel-drive felony. "Don't think it's no different
than Zeke playing demon bait when you're on the hunt,
because it is. If Cronus gets to you, you won't be able to
fight him off and we won't be able to pull you back. He's
not a demon. If he touches you, it's over." For Griffin
and for us all.

"But you won't let him, will you?" he said with a cer-
tainty in his voice that was the best gift anyone could've
given me, and few, because of what I was, did. Unwavering trust.

"No, I won't." I touched his face and the bruise that
hadn't had time to fade. "But don't agree to this because
you think you have something to make up for. If you do,
I'll know it, and we'll go right back upstairs and let the
Apocalypse come. I mean it."

He shook his head. "I've seen the error of my ways
there. Ex-demon is now politically correct in my book.
It might be why Azrael finds me so disgusting. If I can
rise up and change my ways, others could as well. I want
to do this because it's the right thing to do." He bumped
Zeke's shoulder with his own. "It is, Zeke. You know it,
and you would do it too."

"I don't care. You almost let demons kill you. Demons. That's goddamn *pathetic*." Zeke pushed him with
enough force to shove him back a step. "How can I look
after you if you won't look after yourself, huh? How? I
fucking can't, can I?"

"Trixa won't let Cronus kill me." Griffin didn't push back. Zeke had been pushed enough this week, emotionally. He would've tolerated physically better. "And if she can't stop him, then I will. I promise, Zeke, and I've never broken a promise to you. Hell, I couldn't. You know that."

"Damn it. *Damn* it." Zeke hung his head. "Just . . . shit. If you get yourself killed, I'm not speaking to you again, and this time I mean it." He got into the back of the car and slammed the door hard.

"It's not fair to him." I was wearing the same clothes I'd worn yesterday to rob the museum. All black, but the fall while running from the museum guards had taken its toll. I had washed them this morning. There was something ignoble about showing up to a battle wearing muddy streaks on your shirt and gum on your knee. "But then again I guess it's not fair to any of us."

"I think you and Leo have had it easy for too long." Griffin curled his lips. "Time to know what it is to fight with a baseball bat instead of an Uzi." He opened the same door Zeke had shut. "Move over, you cranky bastard. Don't make me PDA you in front of God and everybody."

As the door closed again. Leo cracked his knuckles in the palm of his other hand. "An Uzi. I think that boy vastly underestimates who we are."

"Who we were," I reminded him. "Are you ready to be human?" I'd learned over the past few days that playing human was easy, but being human was a bitch. I'd lost a home I'd never thought I'd want, and I was a person I never thought I'd be. Still, I hadn't once in my life let a lack of resources stop me from doing what had to be done. That wasn't going to change now. Being human would only make the victory that much sweeter, life itself that much sweeter.

"We're going to get our asses handed to us," Leo said with grim humor.

"Oh, without a doubt." I sighed as I started around the car. "Cronus will need a shopping cart to haul them around in."

Because life . . . It wasn't always sweet.

Arrow Canyon is about an hour northeast of Vegas. I'd hiked it before, on feet and paws. A narrow canyon that runs several miles long with petroglyphs painted on the walls and a dam at the end; it's a good place to commune with nature or end it. Cronus wouldn't care how picturesque the battlefield was, but during the week and work hours, the location would guarantee hopefully that no bystanders happened to wander into the middle of something they couldn't imagine no matter how much acid they'd taken in their misspent youth. The hikers tended to stick to weekends . . . whether they had a history of wild drug-induced hallucinations or not.

Brown rock rose high around us as we walked about a mile from where we left the SUV at the municipal well. Leaving it was necessary as I didn't want it thrown at us, and I was sure that if it was around, it would be. We ended up at the trailhead of the canyon. There were creosote bushes, Mojave yuccas with their green leaves like pointed daggers at their base, and a blue sky with tattered clouds so white they almost hurt your eyes. As you went on, the canyon would narrow considerably. In a tight spot and near the dam were not precisely where I would want to be facing Cronus. There was no reason to make things ridiculously easy for him. If he was going to kick our asses, at least I wanted him to work up a mild sweat over it.

I'd sacrificed my favorite shotgun to make Griffin's

"kidnapping" by demons look more convincing to the cops, but Leo had an early birthday present tucked away for me in his closet, a Benelli semiautomatic shotgun. It would blow the head off a demon easily, but against Cronus it would be less of the baseball bat Griffin had mentioned and more of a toothpick. I'd left it behind. The sword was what I carried. The great thing about a sword made of water, besides how it glittered brightly in the sun . . . very fancy . . . was that it was light. It weighed less than the pitcher of water had and much less than your conventional broadsword.

Griffin and Zeke both were carrying guns as well. They wouldn't do any more good than Leo's own shotgun, but it was hard to go into a fight without some sort of weapon—natural or manufactured. "This is it." I scuffed the dirt under the black sneakers we'd stopped and bought on the way. Neither boots or bare feet were going to make it a mile over the Nevada desert, and Leo hadn't happened to also purchase me footwear for that early birthday present. "Where we make our stand." It wasn't especially auspicious that the word "stand" was almost always accompanied by "last."

Zeke shrugged. "Here or at the am/pm. Doesn't matter, except at least I could get candy bars at the am/pm."

"I only wish someone were here to write down those poetic words for posterity," Leo said. "They are epic in breadth and scope. Homer would be green with jealousy."

Zeke pumped a round in his shotgun. "There's not a whole lot poetic about dying," he said matter-of-factly.

He was right. I took a deep breath, feeling my mortality acutely. I'd always been mortal, but I hadn't been so vulnerably mortal. I hadn't been human, hadn't given them credit for staring into the face of death with nothing more to keep them going than hope, optimism, or ruthlessly channeled resignation to their fate. If we survived, I'd be tempted to give them a little slack in the future. "Griffin?"

As Leo and Zeke flanked him, Griffin showed his wings and spread them wide. Zeke had been right. They were the wings of a dragon, flown out of the heart of the sun to land impossibly on Earth. They were the same beautiful gold I'd seen before, untarnished and wholly undemonlike. Hopefully, Cronus wouldn't know that. As I stepped in front of Griffin, my back to him and the sword down and behind my leg, the Titan proved he didn't. He appeared twenty feet in front of me. Subtly this time, with no moving of the world, only a small ripple in the shadow of it. It was all the worse for that.

The emptiness inside him, the dark clots of nothingness that swallowed everything and anything, was pouring out. From his eyes and his mouth, it ran down the unnaturally smooth face ... down the inside-out shirt and cardboard cutout of jeans, down the offensively careless costume of a human being, and began to eat away at the ground beneath his feet. The earth was being unmade beneath him, unraveling in tiny pockets as you could for the first time see what reality was formed from. It was glorious to see and then horrible to watch it die. Cronus took a step and the world cringed beneath it. His blackly bleeding eyes fixed on Griffin and the word passed out of his mouth through the shadows. "Finally."

"Finally is right," I said. "Finally your days are no more. You took my one home, you bastard, but you're not taking the other." He wasn't taking Griffin either. Griffin had risked his life for my plan and Zeke had risked that much more. I wasn't going to let Cronus pass through me to Griffin and his wings. Pure and simple. It wasn't going to happen.

Cronus thought differently, proving it as he took another step toward us. He was at the end, so close to the culmination of what he'd started nine hundred and ninety-nine demons ago. He was within reach of tipping that first domino that would bring all the others down. He needed only one more wing to get the map to find Lucifer, to navigate Hell. But he didn't have to worry about finding his way around Hell—Hell found him just fine.

Out of the canyon mouth came a flashflood of demons. They ran on all fours. They had no choice. Their wings had already been cut off. Eligos and Lucifer, they took no chances. Eligos himself hadn't risked that his might be taken. His demons were without a general, but that didn't mean they were any less determined to bring down Cronus. Between the devil they knew and the devil they didn't want to, they'd take the first. They had a home to save, the same as I did. I'd asked Eligos for Hell itself, and he had given it to me.

The demons swarmed the Titan more quickly than I could blink, Komodo dragons with bleeding backs. He didn't try to get away. What did he have to fear from these Fallen when he'd already killed a hair shy of a thousand of them? When he touched them, they screamed and unraveled the same as the ground had. Or he ripped them apart, pieces of them turning to a dark rain in the air.

Yet behind them came the angels.

Fighting with the brothers they'd long cast down, some were as they'd been created, glass with daggered wings, blinding under the sun, with swords of fire. Some were in human form with feathered wings. Azrael, all glass and the farthest thing from human you could be except for Cronus himself, led from behind. Far behind, hovering over the canyon. I wasn't surprised. It was easy to kill when it wasn't your own existence you were risking. When you could be cut out of reality like a paper doll, wadded up, and thrown away, it was amazing how quickly an asshole like him learned caution, restraint, and to shut his annoyingly arrogant mouth.

For every demon who fell, an angel took his place. When that angel exploded, a stained glass window burst that filled the air; yet another demon was there to attack again. Cronus had multiple jaws fastened around each arm and leg. He had fiery swords plunged into him again and again until I could swear I could smell the stench of burned plastic. When the smallest area opened up, a shotgun blast came from behind me to put a slug into it. I heard Leo and Zeke both cursing behind me as the shotguns turned out to be as useless as everything else. Demons, angels, and man-made death, but the fake man who would be GodKingfuckingEmperor of All didn't go down. He tossed more demons away, some with a mouthful of whatever cheap fabric of reality made him. Angels—archangels some—were broken like Christmas ornaments rather than the fiercely lethal fighters they were. I ducked as one demon was thrown over me and heard Zeke curse again as he was hit and fell under his weight.

"Don't kill him, Kit," I said without turning. "He's on our side for the moment."

As I watched, they kept coming, pouring out of the canyon with a single purpose. There was something almost glorious in that, two opposite sides in what should've been an unstoppable whole. Cronus, however, was stopping them left and right. How many angels could dance on the head of a pin? It didn't matter. There might not be any left in Heaven to do the dancing when this was over, and if wings didn't grow back, demons were going to be much less awe worthy in paintings and sculptures. It could make you wonder why Cronus was putting up with it. Why didn't he simply move the world again—until he was virtually on top of Griffin to take that wing?

I didn't wonder. He was having fun. Killing was boring to a Titan, but this wasn't simple killing. This was a non-*païen* Heaven and Hell at his fingertips to obliterate. Even to Cronus, that was a change of pace. What he'd planned for after consuming Lucifer and Hell, he had a taste of now, and he liked it. With every slow step he took toward me and the wings that were behind me, he was having a goddamn ball. With every step his attackers, soldiers through and through, died in droves.

Then one could've wondered, where was the reason behind it? If every angel and demon fell and it did nothing but give Cronus a jolt of Irish in his coffee, why do it at all? What was the point? Where was the reason? I didn't wonder. I knew.

I was the point.

This world was the reason.

Anna—the Rose—had been the means.

If you can save someone, do it. If you can save someone and in turn have them save everyone and everything, do that too.

I walked through puddles of demon ichor so thick the ground couldn't soak it up. Closing what space remained between the Titan and me, I held the sword in front of me now and put it through the shoulder of one demon and the chest of an angel. The blade of water pierced them as if they were less tangible than a thought. The two feet of blade left I buried in Cronus's abdomen. He knew I was coming. He was facing me, he saw me—although he didn't need to—and he didn't try to stop me. What was one more dead on top of all the others, now oil and glass, that littered the sand? Only more entertainment. I'd been counting on that.

I smiled into the eye sockets that ran black. I always smiled when I took down those who deserved it. "I think, therefore I am."

Cronus reached down to touch the blade. The demon had torn free to tumble away and the angel had shattered. "What is . . . I know this. Don't I know this?"

The Namaru had made the water solid, able to be held and able to cut, but that was the funny thing about water. It could be solid, but once it was inside you . . . it was inside you. Once the water of Lethe was inside you, swallowed or rammed into your gut, you were well and truly fucked.

"I know this," he repeated, but the statement sounded vacant . . . each word void of meaning.

He knew it all right. He'd once been prisoner in Tartarus, below Hades, and then had ruled Hades and its Fields of Elysium for a time. He knew the River Lethe, the River of Forgetfulness—rather, he had known it. "Had"—it was such a good word.

"You think, therefore you are. But you're a Titan. You created yourself from the Chaos, a single thought in the nothing. If you can't remember who you are, what you are, how can you be anything at all?" Without that thought, that one "I am," a Titan wasn't a Titan. When you were your own creator and you forgot it all, even that single thought, how could you hold yourself together? How could you paste yourself onto the fabric of the universe?

You couldn't.

The shadows began to roll backward from the ground up, back into his mouth and eyes. "I . . . I am. . . ." The words, thick and slow, were caught in the moving poisonous waste and washed away.

"No, you're not." With the demon and angel gone, I shoved the blade farther into him. It was for my own personal satisfaction. In him an inch or a mile, it didn't matter. Lethe was inside him and part of him now, and he couldn't remember enough to undo that. "You're not anything at all. You're nothing. Less than nothing. You don't even *exist*."

The eyes stretched wide, the fake lips gaped wider, the shadows a waterfall, filling him up until his face began to distort under the pressure. He threw back his head to stare blindly at a sky he couldn't recognize, a sun he didn't know. The scream that tried to escape became a whimper as it too was sucked back inside him. And then he was gone, an implosion of time and space that took a small slice of the world with him. I almost tumbled into that rip in reality. I'd stood so close that I felt the black-hole pull of what lay outside of everything there was. I couldn't see it. I didn't think anything but the dead Titans could see that, but I felt it and it was horrible. It wasn't hungry or greedy; it was a complete lack of . . . life and death and everything between, before, after, and beyond. If I fell into it, that was fine. If I didn't, that was all right as well. A lack doesn't care—which made it somehow worse.

Then an arm went around my waist and I was yanked away and up into the air. The tear ate more of the world, several handfuls' worth, and then sealed itself up. It too, like Cronus and the sword with them, was gone. I could do without the two and didn't need the third anymore. I heard the beating of wings and grinned over my shoulder. "Those flying lessons paid off, didn't they?"

Griffin grinned back, the wind from his wings blowing the hair in his eyes. He was a kid who'd gotten the best present ever . . . to fly like Superman. "I'll have to practice carrying people more. Twelve feet up is all I can manage."

"Or we can hopefully not be in this situation again." He dropped lower until he could ease me to the ground, on which I sat down the second he let go. It wasn't that my knees buckled or anything that trite; it was for the sheer need of touching what we had only just saved. Touching air was the same; reality was the whole damn kit and kaboodle—I had no idea what a kaboodle was, but it came to mind as I scooped up dirt in my hand and held it up for solemn contemplation. "Kaboodle," I announced to Leo, who nodded.

"Damn fine kaboodle it is too," he confirmed.

"That it is." Legs crossed, I let myself fall backward to stare up at the sky. It was well worth staring at, and I did so happily until I heard two voices in unison say, "It's you." I propped myself up on my elbows to see Azrael and Eligos standing shoulder to shoulder and regarding each other with mutual disdain. Azrael had some disgust mixed into the pudding, but Eli seemed more glum, which was hardly like him.

"I can't believe I was replaced by you," the demon said. "It's embarrassing. They couldn't have gotten a flamingo or a canary? Both would be less insulting. The Canary of Death. It has a much better ring to it."

"You were an Angel of Death? Why does that not surprise me?" I snorted, sitting up and brushing the rest of the kaboodle from my hands. Cronus was gone, but suddenly the wingless demons remaining were more of a threat than they had been. Here was hoping we had a standoff between what was left of the angels and the demons. The cold war was over on Earth, but it was still thriving Above and Below.

"Not an Angel of Death. *The* Angel of Death. If I'd been around for the Ten Plagues, darlin', well"—he grinned, the curve of a sickle carved in the shape of a smile—"why stop with Egypt when it comes to firstborn? Show a little initiative and enthusiasm for your work. Santa Claus can visit the world in one night. So can I."

"You have changed none with God's punishment, grown no wiser but only more arrogant. I am not surprised, but I am the Angel of Death now, fallen. We could take you and your pathetically neutered brethren at this very moment." Azrael's sword wasn't of heavenly origin as he'd stubbornly claimed, but it worked all the same as it flared to life between them.

Eli, dressed in that brown leather jacket he was so fond of and a new hat that was made for finding myth in the desert per movie legend, let his dark grin widen. He pointed at the other demons and then jerked his thumb downward. They vanished instantly. He ran a finger along the fedora, then tugged it low over his eyes. "All right then, Az. Here's your big chance to take on your ex-boss. Let's see what a pretender can do with the title."

Azrael hesitated, scanned the approximately twenty-five remaining angels, then flared his wings and silently took to the air before disappearing into it, leaving a fury so thick you could taste it. He thought he was hot shit and he was, but if Eligos had been the first Angel of Death, experience and seniority did tell. I knew it told me something as all the other angels followed their leader. Eli had once said that Hell had worse demons than he, demons who couldn't leave, who would burn the earth beneath them with every step if they did. I didn't want to meet one of those. More powerful than Eli?

I didn't want to see that.

True or not, I didn't let Eli see it. "Where's your whip? You can't rob a desert tomb without a whip."

The smile shaded into something almost affectionate, if death itself could be said to have that softer emotion. "You're right. There is so much you can't do properly without a whip, Trixa-of-my-heart, you couldn't begin to believe it." He laid a hand over my own heart as Zeke and Leo growled behind me, but stayed put. They knew if I needed help, I'd ask for it. "You took out a Titan. First Solomon and now this. You keep getting more and more entertaining. I haven't had this much damn fun in centuries. I take my hat off to you."

He did. He disappeared, but the hat stayed behind, falling to the dirt beneath. I picked it up and put it on, giving the brim my own flick of my finger. "Here's for staying entertaining." He was still going to try and kill me someday; that was a given. That day wasn't this day though. This day was good.

My optimism was renewed. Life wasn't always sweet or true, but it was now.

Sweeter than sugar.

Chapter 17

Spilt milk, it couldn't be undone. That's what they said. They were wrong. Anna was proof of that. No good deed went unpunished. They said that too. That could be one they managed to get right.

I was in Leo's guest room, with my brother's picture. Curled up in the covers, I watched the play of light on the wall. I had a lot to think about: arranging for Trixsta to be rebuilt, getting used to the fact I actually had a home, being human . . . a trickster, yes, but a human one for the time being. Those were big things, enormous in my life. Then there was Leo and my excuse that we were too much alike, but he was the same as a home— something I wasn't supposed to want. I was told not to want. Shape-shifters were raised to change more than our appearances. Ours was a culture of the ephemeral. We moved from shape to shape, place to place, person to person.

We were the wind. That's the way the story went as long as any of us could remember. Who was I to change it?

Me. I was me. When had I let anyone tell me what to do? Except for my mama. I groaned and yanked the covers higher. These, especially Mama, were all things I wasn't going to solve overnight. It was going to take time, a few days, maybe a trip to Valhalla. There was time.

Once I got something wrapped up. That good deed coming back to bite me in the ass. I'd known Azrael would hold a grudge against me, Zeke, and Griffin. I'd known it from our first meeting. He couldn't bear that we lived; he couldn't tolerate our existence. He couldn't tolerate Zeke for rejecting Heaven and Griffin and me for who we were. Griffin, an abomination. Me, a mouthy abomination who consorted with his former superior. I did think the mouthy part was what had gotten to him most. I knew he'd start with me. It was only a matter of time. I had thought he'd wait at least a few nights, but patience and pride often trip up each other. He'd only waited hours. I believed Eligos was a better Angel of Death, the finest predators had infinite patience. Azrael had none.

"I see you, Azrael," I said quietly, staying on my side with the covers pulled up beneath my chin. Every little boy and girl believed their sheets and blanket could be armor against the monsters in the dark. Wouldn't it be nice if that were true? "You think death has never come for me in the night before? That I wouldn't recognize it?"

He stepped out of the corner, although his wings and his hair stayed part of the darkness. His eyes I could see. They didn't look any different than a demon's. "Your kind did this, nearly destroyed us all. Who are you to think you can walk away from that? Who are you to think you do not deserve punishment?"

Cronus had been *païen*, but that didn't make him my kind. He hadn't been anyone's kind in the whole of reality. Azrael knew that, but it was a good excuse to do to me what the Angel of Death was meant to do. If Cronus hadn't been *païen*, Heaven's own would've found another justification for what curled dark within him. Demons killed with a hot passion and Azrael killed with a cold satisfaction. Hot or cold, they both enjoyed their work far too much not to let it spread. Work, hobby, life. They lived to kill. Azrael wasn't Eligos, but that didn't mean he wasn't good at what he did, only that he wasn't the best. Now that I was human, it didn't take the best to kill me. It didn't take much at all, I'd discovered.

"Are you going to hide under the covers like a child?" Azrael stepped closer. "It wouldn't make a difference if you were. I have pity for no one, least of all you."

No, he had pity for no one, certainly not for me. It made it easy to have no pity for him in return.

"Eligos was right. You can't begin to fill his shoes," I said with a dose of contempt Azrael would find difficult to swallow and impossible not to react to. Releasing my hold on the covers, I shifted onto my back. As Griffin had risen, I thought it was time for an angel to fall. "And you're not half as smart as you think you are. You're certainly not half as smart as I am."

He was on me then, without a word. It was the same when he impaled himself on the sword I pulled from beneath the sheets. Not the Lethe sword, as that was gone, but Leo had let me borrow a nice steel one. Heavy and brutal in battle, those Norse roots couldn't be denied. "Heaven must be so disappointed in you." I looked up into the cold, sculpted face that hung above me and found nothing worth saving. "I know I am, and I know they are too."

They were the other angels who appeared out of the corner. Four more archangels, and they'd brought Ishiah with them, the only one still right with Heaven that I trusted. I'd told him Azrael would be coming, and he'd told others. Azrael had helped to save Heaven, but he'd done it without risking his own life—only the lives of his brothers. It was his way, self-serving, which I didn't think had gone unnoticed in the past. I thought his was a reckoning that was a long time coming, the battle the final straw. It helped as well that Ishiah had dropped a word in the right ears, pointed out that while Azrael had helped to sacrifice others in the service of Heaven, in the end I was the one who had destroyed Cronus. Killing me, that lowered Azrael to *païen* behavior . . . or worse, the demonic kind. Azrael had rank, but he had no friends among his fellow archangels, ones with the most will on high. With that will, they could make decisions Azrael wasn't going to like.

"You don't deserve to live," he hissed. "Life is wasted on the filth that is you."

"Is that any way to be?" I tsked. "You deserve to live, Azrael, for all time, but I don't think you're going to like it."

The hands of the other archangels fastened onto his arms as he reached for my throat. They pulled him up and off the sword. I dropped the weapon to the floor; I waggled my fingers at him in a mocking good-bye. "Send me a postcard from Down Under, that is if Eligos doesn't eat you." It didn't take the best to kill me anymore, but you at least had to be good. Azrael didn't meet either definition of the word.

The angels left, taking Azrael with them . . . Ishiah too, although I assumed they'd drop him someplace nicer, such as home back in New York. Other angels, Ishiah had assured me when I'd told him what Azrael would do, had been watching over Zeke and Griffin, as little as they'd liked it. That was Heaven's problem, not mine. If I saved reality, including their feathered asses, they owed me one. Keeping my boys safe had been that one. At least it had turned out to be only one night under the crystal eyes of Heaven's guardians. Trying to sleep knowing they were hanging around . . . It was worse than sneaking in past curfew when you had a mama with a hand quick to swat trickster butt.

Long-gone days.

I hit the pillows to plump them up and watched as Leo came out of his closet, leaving his shotgun behind. I trusted Ishiah . . . some, but trust or not, it was always smart to have a backup plan.

"Exactly how many men in a bedroom does it take to satisfy you?" The raven tattoo on his chest flapped its wings, which actually meant Leo was flexing. Men and gods, the vanity never ended. Sometimes you had to love that about them.

"That's an odd question coming from a man who just came out of the closet," I pointed out as I pulled the covers back for him.

He slid under them and wrapped his arm around me as I turned on my side, facing him instead of the picture of my brother. "Did you notice this time?" His hair was loose and far longer than mine, but that wasn't what he was talking about.

Men and gods and one who was both.

"That you were going to take on Azrael nude?" I moved my hand under the pillow and pulled out the raven feather I kept with me always. I hadn't lost it with Trixsta. I didn't think I could've lost it if I wanted to, but I could give it back. "I noticed." I put the feather in his hand and folded his fingers around it. "I don't think I need this anymore."

He tightened his fingers and hand into a fist, then opened it. The feather was gone, home inside him. "We are the same, you know. In all the ways that are right. Our differences, they are what brought us together in the beginning. Our spots, faded or not, make us whole. They don't separate us."

"From one leopard to another?" I asked, skimming fingers through a fall of hair suddenly full of black feathers.

"From one leopard to another," he confirmed before kissing me.

It wasn't sun and warmth. It was dark and cool, shadows and tricks, the echo of the end of the world, and the potential for the same locked deep inside. Locks can be broken and trust was nearly a fairy tale to me, but I knew if Leo's lock ever did break, it wouldn't matter. My trust in him never would, whether I was trickster or human.

And I did like being human, vulnerabilities and all. It made seizing victory and grabbing that gold ring more difficult, but all the more satisfying for it. Yes, I definitely liked this human life. I might come to love it. Only time would tell there, but for today? For this moment, drowned in feathers, silver silk, and the faintest scent of honeysuckle from a Tennessee summer night?

Life was sweet all right.

Sweet as it came.

About the Author

Rob—short for Robyn (yes, he is really a she)—**Thurman** lives in Indiana, land of rolling hills and cows, deer, and wild turkeys. Many, many turkeys. She is also the author of the Cal Leandros series: *Nightlife*, *Moonshine*, *Madhouse*, *Deathwish*, and *Roadkill*; a stand-alone novel, *Chimera*; and a story in the anthology *Wolfsbane and Mistletoe*. She is also the author of *Trick of the Light*, the first book in the Trickster Novels series.

Besides wild, ravenous turkeys, the velociraptors of Indiana, she has a dog (if you don't have a dog, how do you live?)—one hundred pounds of Siberian husky. He looks like a wolf, has paws the size of a person's hand, ice blue eyes, teeth out of a Godzilla movie, and the ferocious habit of hiding under the kitchen table and peeing on himself when strangers come by. Fortunately, she has another dog that is a little more invested in keeping the food source alive. By the way, the dogs were adopted from shelters. They were fully grown, already housetrained, and grateful as hell. Think about it next time you're looking for a Rover or Fluffy.

For updates, teasers, deleted scenes, and various other extras, visit the author at www.robthurman.net and at her LiveJournal.

Read on for an exciting excerpt
from the next Cal Leandros novel

BLACKOUT

by Rob Thurman
Coming in March 2011 from Roc

I was a killer. I woke up knowing that before I knew anything else.

There was a moment between sleeping and waking where I swung lazily. The dark was my hammock, moving back and forth. One way was a deeper darkness, a longer sleep. But there was more than darkness there. There were trees past the black, hundreds and thousands of trees.

And an ocean, blue as a crayon fresh from a brand-new box. A ship rode on its waves with sails white as a seagull's wings, flying a flag as black as the seabird's eyes.

There were dark-eyed princesses named after lilies.

Waterfalls that fell forever.

Flying.

Tree houses.

It was a place where no one could find you. A safe place. Of it all, vibrant and amazing, the one thing I wanted to sink my fingers into and hang on to for my life was that last: a safe place.

Sanctuary.

But all that disappeared when I swung the other way, where there were sibilant whispers, an unpleasant clicking—insectile and ominous—and a cold, bone deep and embedded in every part of me. If I'd had a choice, I would've gone with sleep, safe in the trees. Who wouldn't? But I didn't have that warm and comforting option. Instead I was slapped in the face with icy water. That did the trick of swinging me hard in the wrong direction and keeping me there. I opened my eyes, blinked several times, and licked the taste of salt from my lips. It was still dark, but not nearly as dark as when my eyes had been shut. There was a scattering of stars overhead and a bright full moon. The white light reflected as shattered shards in the water washing over my legs and up to my chest. It looked like splinters of ice. It felt cold enough to be. There was the smell of seaweed and dead fish in the air. More seaweed was tangled around my hand when I lifted it, the same hand that held a gun. A big gun.

A priest, a rabbi, and a killer walk into a bar . . .

A killer woke up on that beach, and that killer was me. How did I know that? It wasn't difficult. I slowly propped myself up on my elbows, my hand refusing to drop the gun it held, and I took a look around me to see a stretch of water and sand littered with bodies, bodies with bullet holes in them. The gun in my hand was lighter than it should've been. That meant an empty clip. It didn't take an Einstein to work out that calculation. The fact that the bodies weren't my first concern—it was pissing and food actually, in that order—helped too. Killers have different priorities.

I could piss here. I wasn't a frigging Rodeo Drive princess. There were only the night, the ocean, and me. I could whip it out and let fly. But the food? Where would I get the food? Where was the nearest restaurant or take-out place? Where was I? Because this wasn't right. This wasn't home. I dragged my feet up through the wet sand, bent my knees, and pushed up to stagger to my feet to get my bearings. I might have been lost. I *felt* lost, but I only needed to look closer, to recognize some landmarks and I'd be fine. But I didn't. I didn't recognize shit. I had no idea where I was, and I was not fine.

I was the furthest from fine as those bodies on the sand were.

That's when the killer realized something: I knew *what* I was, all right, but I didn't have a goddamn idea who.

I reached for me and I wasn't there. I took a step into my own head and fell. There was nothing there to hold me up. There was no home and there was no me. Nothing to grab or ground me—no memories, only one big gaping hole filled with a cliché. And that—being a cliché? It bothered me more than the killer part. That part I took so much in stride that I'd automatically used my free hand to start dragging the bodies further out into the water, where they'd be carried away. Out of sight, out of mind. The killer in me needed no direction. It knew it wasn't Joe Average, law-abiding citizen. It knew it couldn't be caught with bodies and definitely not these bodies.

They weren't human.

There were monsters in the world, and that didn't surprise the killer or the cliché in me one damn bit either. They both knew why I carried that gun. Monsters weren't very fucking nice.

I looked down at the one I was currently dragging through the surf. It looked like an ape crossed with a spider, which isn't a good look for anyone. It weighed a ton, was hairy with several eyes on a flattened skull, and had even more legs sprouting below. The mouth was simian, but there were no teeth. Instead there were two sets of mandibles, upper and lower. Both were dripping with something other than water, something thicker. At the sight, the base of my neck began to throb, red spikes of pain that flared behind my eyelids every time I blinked. I released Harry—hairy, Harry, close enough—into the waist-deep water I'd pulled it into and swiped my hand at the nape of my neck. I felt two puncture marks about three inches apart, then held my hand up to the moon. There was blood, not much, and a clear viscous fluid on my palm. It looked like good old dead Harry had gotten one in me before I'd gotten one in him.

The venom couldn't be too poisonous. I was alive and aside from my neck hurting and a massive headache from hell, I wasn't too impaired. I went on to prove it by wiping my hand on my jeans and going back for Harry's friends. Larry, Barry, and Gary—monsters that I took in stride as much as I did the moon up in the sky. Just part of the world. I'd forgotten myself, but the world didn't go that easily. The world I did know, it seemed, so I kept doing what kept you alive in this particular world. I towed all the bodies out into the freezing water—Christ, it couldn't have been more than fifty degrees—and sent them on their way. So long, farewell, auf Wiedersehen . . .

Goodbye.

I didn't wave.

When it was done, I slogged back to the beach and stood, shivering hard from the cold. I watched as the last body disappeared past the distant moon-spangled waves—they were nice, those waves. Scenic, too much so for monsters. After they were gone, I spun around slowly, taking in every foot, every inch of the beach and the empty dunes behind me with suspicion. Seeing nothing moving besides me, I holstered the gun . . . in a shoulder holster my hand knew very well was there. As I did, my skin brushed more metal. I pulled my jacket open wide to see three knives strapped to the inside, right and left, six total. I felt an itch and weight around my ankle, but I didn't bother to check for what kind of death-dealing device it was.

A priest, a rabbi, and a killer walk into a bar . . . no.

Four monsters and a killer walk into a bar . . . that wasn't right either.

A killer wakes up on a beach . . . the monsters don't wake up at all.

I was wearing a leather jacket, sodden and ruined. Something was weighing down the right pocket of it more heavily than the left. I put my hand in and closed it around something oval shaped. I was vaguely hoping it was a wayward clam that had climbed in while I was snoozing in the tide. That hope choked and fell, dead as the floating monsters. In the moonlight I'd opened my fingers to see a grenade resting against my palm. There was a cheerful yellow smiley face on the side. The hand-painted, slightly sloppy circle smirked at me.

Have a nice day!

I looked up at the sky, the beaming moon, and said my first words, the first words I could remember anyway. Baby's first words in his brand-new life.

"What the *fuck*?"

A killer walked into a motel. Okay, that was getting old fast. *I* walked into the motel, still damp, but at least I wasn't sloshing with every step anymore. It had been a twenty-minute walk from that beach. There had been houses that were closer, but they weren't vacation houses abandoned in cold weather. People were living in them, which meant I couldn't break in, my first instinct, and squat long enough to get dry and—shit—get dry. I wasn't ready to think beyond that point right now. There were other things that needed to be done. Important things, and while they gnawed at me with tiny sharp teeth to do them, they weren't willing to say what exactly they were. Do. Go. Run. Hide. Tell. But there was no "what" for the do, no "where" for the go or the run, and no "who" for the tell.

It was a thousand itches that couldn't be scratched. Annoying didn't begin to cover a fraction of how it felt. It did cover the no-tell-motel clerk however. Annoying covered him hunky-frigging-dory. Wide nose, big ears, enough acne to say puberty was going to last through his nineties, and frizzy blond hair that wanted to be long but ended up being wide instead. He was reading a porn mag with a hand covering his mouth and a finger jammed halfway up one nostril. That wasn't where your hand should be when looking at porn, but whatever. How he got his rocks off was the least of my concerns.

"Room," I said, slapping down four ten-dollar bills on the countertop. Fresh from a wet wallet, which was equally fresh from my wet jeans, the money quickly made a puddle around itself.

The finger descended from its perch and idly poked at the bills. "They're wet."

True that and not requiring a comment. "Room," I repeated. "Now."

He looked past me at the door. "I didn't hear you come in. How come I didn't hear you come in? We got a bell."

Correction, they had a bell. Bells made noise, and noise wasn't good. Any cat sneaking around in the shadows would tell you that. It'd probably also tell you talking to a booger-picking brick wall was pointless. I reached past the clerk and grabbed a key hanging on the wall. Lucky number thirteen. I turned and walked back towards the door.

"ID," the guy called after me. "Hey, dude, I need some ID."

I gave him an extra ten. It was all the ID he needed. Zit cream is pretty cheap at any local drugstore, and he forgot about the ID. But it was the first thing on my mind when I opened the warped wooden door to room thirteen, walked through chips of peeling paint that had fallen on the cracked asphalt of the small parking lot, and went into my new home. Hell, the only home I'd known as of this moment as far as my brain cells were concerned. I pulled the blinds shut, flipped the light on the table beside the bed, and opened the wallet. The clerk might not need it, but ID would be helpful as shit to me right now. Let's see what we had.

No, not we. There was no we ... what I had. Because it was me, only me. And I didn't know my life was any different from that. The clerk hadn't considered me too social, and I didn't feel especially social, friendly, or full of love for my fellow fucking man. I had a sliver of feeling that it wasn't entirely due to my current situation. If you forgot who you were, were you still who you were? I didn't know, but I thought it might be safe to say that I usually didn't have an entourage of partying friends in tow.

Other than the monsters from the beach.

So ... time to see who exactly the nonexistent entourage wasn't swarming around.

I pulled out the driver's license from the worn black wallet and scanned it. New York City. 375 Hudson Street. I was ... well, shit—I didn't know what year it was exactly, so I didn't know how old I was, but the picture that I checked against my reflection in the cracked mirror on the bureau across the room looked right. Early twenties probably. Black hair, gray eyes, flatly opaque expression—it would've been a mug shot through and through if there hadn't been the tiniest curl to his ... my mouth. One that said "I have a boot, and I'm just looking for an ass to put it up." Okay, social was out the window. I focused on the important thing—my name, printed clear and bold beside the picture. My identity. Me.

"Calvin F. Krueger," I said aloud. "Fuck me."

Calvin? A monster killing, walking goddamn armory with an attitude so bad even the DMV captured it on film and my name was *Calvin*?

Maybe my middle initial led to something more acceptable. F. Frank, Fred, Ferdi-fucking-nand. Shit. I laid the license aside and went back to the wallet. There was nothing. Yeah, a big wad of soaking cash, but no credit card, no ATM card, no video card. Nothing. I had the minimum ID required by law and that was it. That smelled as fishy as I did. I was going to have to get out of these clothes soon and wash them in the bathtub or the reek of low tide would never come out of them. And right now they were the only clothes I had.

After spreading out the cash on the nightstand to dry, I tried to wring out the wallet. It was worn and cracked, on its last legs anyway, and I kicked those last legs out from under it. It split along the side seam and out spilled two more licenses. I picked them up from the frayed carpet to see the same picture, same address, and two different names: Calvert M. Myers and Calhoun J. Voorhees. That I had aliases didn't bother me—I killed monsters. What was a fake name?—but the aliases themselves. How much did I hate myself?

Calvin F. Krueger, Calvert M. Myers, Calhoun J. Voorhees. Seriously, *Calhoun*?

Then it hit me. F. Krueger, M. Myers, J. Voorhees. Freddy Krueger, Michael Myers, and Jason Voorhees. Three monster movie villains, and I—a monster killer—was carting around their names on my ID. Didn't I have one helluva sense of humor? I thought about the grenade I'd tossed into the ocean, that cheerful yellow smile on a potentially lethal explosion. A dark sense of humor, I amended to myself, but, hey, wasn't that better than none at all?

The rank smell hovering around me and my clothes was getting worse. The stink was incredible. Good sense of humor, good sense of smell, and neither one was doing anything productive for me right now. I left the ID and the money on the table and went to the bathroom. I toed off black leather boots that were scarred and worn, like the wallet. They'd been used hard. Well-worn, they would've been comfortable if they weren't wet and full of sand. How they'd gotten worn, what crap they'd stomped through, I didn't know. I dumped them in the tub that had once been white but was now a dull, aged yellow. It had been used hard, too. I related. I felt that way myself: used hard and put up wet. I threw in my jeans, T-shirt, underwear, and even the leather jacket once I removed the knives.

As I did, a small bubble of panic began to rise. I couldn't remember. I couldn't remember a goddamn thing about myself. I didn't remember putting those weapons in my jacket, although I knew exactly what they were for. Knives and guns and monsters, they were the things that I was certain of, but when it came to me, I was certain of absolutely fucking nothing.

Shit. *Shit.* Okay, I obviously knew how to stay alive; those monsters on the beach hadn't just killed themselves. People who knew how to stay alive also knew not to panic and I was *not* panicking. By God. I wasn't. I was sucking it up and moving on. I was surviving. With or without my memory, at least I seemed to be good at that. Calvin the survivor—watch me in action. I was alive to mock my fake names, and I planned on staying that way.

Turning on the shower, I waited until the water was lukewarm and stood on top of the clothes. There were two small bottles of shampoo and an equally small bar of soap. I used them all, letting the lather run off of me onto the cotton and leather around and under my feet.

I learned something about myself while scrubbing up. I killed monsters, and they tried to kill me back with a great deal of enthusiasm but not just them. I had a scar from a bullet on my chest, one from what was probably a knife on my abdomen, and a fist-sized doozy on the other side of my chest. It looked like something had taken a bite out of me and had been motivated when they'd done it. Man and monster, apparently they both disliked me or me them—could be a mutual feeling. It was just one more thing I didn't know. I moved on to something I did know. Besides the scars, I was a little pale, but that could have been from near hypothermia or I could have been anemic. Maybe iron supplements were the answer to all my questions. Iron and bigger and badder guns.

I had a tattoo around my upper arm, a band of black and red with something written in Latin woven in it. Funny how I knew it was Latin, but I didn't know what it said. Yeah, funny, I thought despite the lurch of loss in my stomach. There was my sense of humor again.

The rest of me was standard issue. I wasn't a porn star, too bad, but I had proof of a Y chromosome. That was all a guy needed. That and some memories. Were a dick and a mind too much to ask for? That was something every guy had to ask himself at some point, even if I couldn't remember the first time I'd asked it. This time the question bounced back and forth inside my skull, hitting nothing on its way. I guessed that proved it was too much . . . at least for now.

My head still hurt and trying to remember made it worse. I gave up, closed my eyes, and scrubbed at my hair. I shook from the lingering cold of the ocean, but the warm water helped. It didn't do the same for my damned hair though. It had been in a ponytail, shoulder length. I'd pulled the tie free, but there was something in it . . . sticky and stubborn as gum or tar. It could have been blood from one of those supernatural spider-monkeys from hell. It could actually be gum. Maybe I fought bubble-gum-smacking preteens from hell too. I didn't know, and it didn't matter. You didn't have to know the question to be the solution.

The answer ended up being one of those knives I'd taken out of the jacket. The shit wouldn't come out of my hair for love or money, and I finally stood naked in front of the cloudy bathroom mirror, took a handful of my hair and sawed through it. I let the clump, matted together with green-gray crap, fall into the sink. The remaining wet hair fell raggedly about two inches past my jaw. I didn't try to even it up with the blade, slender and sharp as it was. I could have, some at least, but . . .

I turned away from the mirror.

Looking at my picture was okay, not recognizing myself less okay, studying myself in the mirror, not okay at all. I didn't like it. I didn't know why, but I didn't. A quick glance was fine; a long look was a trip someplace and, from the acid sloshing around my stomach, it wasn't Wonderland. I had guns and knives, scars and dead things; maybe I wasn't a nice guy. If I didn't like looking in the mirror, it could have been I didn't like what I saw. Pictures were only echoes. The guy in the mirror was real.

But it didn't matter why I didn't like it, because I didn't have to look. Problem solved. I spent the next fifteen minutes drying off and doing my best to hand-wash the funk out of my clothes before draping them over the shower rod to dry. By then I was weaving, and I had the next best thing to double vision, and a wet towel in my hand, which I used to cover up the bureau mirror. I didn't ask myself why. I was only half conscious and barely made it to the bed anyway. So to hell with whys. I pulled the stale, musty-smelling covers over me with one hand and slapped the lamp off the table to crash to the floor. I was too clumsy with exhaustion to switch it off. This worked the same. The bulb shattered with a pop, and it was lights-out.

I didn't think about it then, but the next day I did, when I had more than pain and drowsiness rolling around in my head. I'd woken up with monsters. I was alone, and I was lost. I didn't know where I was; I didn't know who I was. It doesn't get more lost than that. Wouldn't you have left a light on? Knowing what I knew and not knowing anything else at all, why would I want the darkness where monsters hide?

Because killers hide there too.

TRICK OF
THE LIGHT
A Trickster Novel

by

ROB THURMAN

Las Vegas bar owner Trixa Iktomi deals in information. And in a city where unholy creatures roam the neon night, information can mean life or death. Not that she has anything personal against demons. They can be sexy as hell, and they're great for getting the latest gossip—but they also steal human souls and thrive on chaos. So occasionally Trixa has to teach them some manners.

When Trixa learns of a powerful artifact known as the Light of Life, she knows she's hit the jackpot. Both sides—angel and demon—would give anything for it. But first she has to find it. And as Heaven and Hell ready for an apocalyptic throwdown, Trixa must decide where her true loyalty lies—and what she's ready to fight for.

MADHOUSE
by
ROB THURMAN

Half-human Cal Leandros and his brother Niko aren't exactly prospering with their preternatural detective agency. Who could have guessed that business could dry up in New York City, where vampires, trolls, and other creepy crawlies are all over the place?

But now there's a new arrival in the Big Apple. A malevolent evil with ancient powers is picking off humans like sheep, dead-set on making history with an orgy of blood and murder. And for Cal and Niko, this is one paycheck they're going to have to earn.

"Stunningly original."
—Green Man Review

ALSO AVAILABLE IN THE SERIES
Moonshine
Nightlife

Available wherever books are sold or at penguin.com

R0011

MOONSHINE

by

ROB THURMAN

After saving the world from his fiendish father's side
of the family, Cal Leandros and his stalwart half-brother Niko
have settled down with new digs and a new gig—bodyguard
and detective work. And in New York City, where preternatural
beings stalk the streets just like normal folk, business is good.
Their latest case has them going undercover for the Kin—the
werewolf Mafia. A low-level Kin boss thinks a rival is setting
him up for a fall, and wants proof. The place to start is the back
room of Moonshine—a gambling club for non-humans. Cal
thinks it's a simple in-and-out job.

But Cal is very, very wrong...

Cal and Niko are being set up themselves—and the
people behind it have a bite much worse than their bark...

Available wherever books are sold or at
penguin.com

NIGHTLIFE

by

ROB THURMAN

When the sun goes down,
it all goes down...

Welcome to the Big Apple. There's a troll under the Brooklyn Bridge, a boggle in Central Park, and a beautiful vampire in a penthouse on the Upper East Side—and that's only the beginning. Of course, most humans are oblivious to the preternatural nightlife around them, but Cal Leandros is only half-human.

"A roaring rollercoaster of a read...
[it'll] take your breath away."
—*New York Times* bestselling author Simon R. Green

Available wherever books are sold or at
penguin.com

R0010